ONCE UPON A TIME IN THE NORTH WEST

Garbhán Downey

GARBHAN DOWNEY

GUILDHALL PRESS

ISBN: 978 1 911053 04 0
Copyright © Garbhan Downey/Guildhall Press 2015

The author asserts his moral rights in this work in accordance with the Copyright, Designs and Patents Act 1998.

First published November 2015.

Guildhall Press
Ráth Mór Business Park
Bligh's Lane, Derry
Ireland
BT48 0LZ
00 44 28 7136 4413
info@ghpress.com
www.ghpress.com

A catalogue record for this title is available from the British Library.

Guildhall Press gratefully acknowledges the financial support of the Arts Council of Northern Ireland under the National Lottery Programme.

LOTTERY FUNDED

About the author

Garbhan Downey has spent twenty-five years in the publishing industry in northwest Ireland as a journalist, writer and editor. He has also worked for the BBC as a producer and presenter. A graduate of University College Galway, he lives in Derry with his wife Úna and two children. *Once Upon a Time in the North West* is his eighth novel.

Acknowledgements

It has always been a privilege to work with an institution of the calibre of Guildhall Press, but I am particularly appreciative of all their support for this book in this *bliain uafásach* (horrible year) for the Northern Irish publishing industry. Particular thanks to GP Managing Editor Paul Hippsley, who has yet again delayed his retirement to the sun until I produce the New York Times best-seller I promised him when I started writing many, many moons ago. This time next year, Paul…

The GP team of Kevin Hippsley, Joe McAllister, Declan Carlin, Peter McCartney and Jenni Doherty are the equal of any publishing house you would find in the world. I thank you for adopting me to your stable and managing my work with such craft and care. Not forgetting, of course, honorary GP staffer, Conal McFeely, whose foresight in developing the Ráth Mór Enterprise Park in Creggan (where we all work) has been such a force for good in our lives.

Thanks also to my friend and journalism mentor Pat McArt for reading the manuscript and to Sean Quinn of the Hive Studio, a star editor of the future, for his insights on the draft.

The support and advice from my parents, Áine Downey and Gerry Downey, for this book, and throughout my writing career, has been crucial. My heartfelt thanks to both of you for this, for all your great stories and for my lifelong love of storytelling.

My own children, Fiachra and Brónagh, though they might not have been aware of it at the time, were directly responsible for me writing this particular book. You challenged and confounded me with your astute questions about what life was like in northwest Ireland over the past century, so I hope I have gone some small way to answering you. I would remind you, though, that this book is a work of fiction, not an authoritative history, and not to be quoting directly from it in any exams. (Though, in fairness, the same warning could just as easily be stamped on some of the 'factual' accounts of the past century.)

There are many others – journalists, fellow writers, friends and colleagues at Ráth Mór and elsewhere – who encouraged and, in some cases, badgered me to get back to writing after my sabbatical. I greatly appreciate your confidence in me and genuinely regret that I did not write down every single name. But to all of you, my sincerest thanks. You gave me a much-needed shot in the arm or slap on the ear.

And finally, to the love of my life, Úna McNally, in this the year of our twentieth wedding anniversary, from proofreading to cheerleading, there is not, and has never been, any better. None of this would have happened without you.

To my friends in the newsroom

CHAPTER 1

The Derry publisher Seán Madden took his second stroke, aged eighty-nine, on 27 June 2012, just minutes after watching the RTÉ news report on the former IRA commander Martin McGuinness shaking hands with Queen Elizabeth II of Great Britain.

According to his granddaughter, Maeve, Big Seán's final words were: 'Hell's gotta be frozen over – I can die happy now.'

And while it's possible that his heiress at the *North West Chronicle* embellished the story, to set up a hook for the obituary, the old man would have appreciated the poetry.

CHAPTER 2

Special Agent-in-Charge Ally McCloud couldn't see the point of it. He was a good soldier, had just made SAC at thirty-one and knew there was no money in complaining. But he didn't need this.

As head of the FBI's Ireland Desk in Washington, he was already punching in sixty hours a week. He spent forty hours, minimum, at his Penn Avenue office, fighting fires for the Deputy Director – everything from transatlantic drug smuggling to corporate tax evasion. And loads of politics in between. He then got to spend the other twenty travelling in and out to Quantico to lecture increasingly baffled recruits on the Glorious Mystery that was the Irish Peace Process – and how the Yanks had delivered it. God Bless Uncle/Auntie Sam.

Finally, just to make sure he would never score another woman – ever – two weekends a month McCloud got to visit his field agents in Chicago, Philly, New York or Beantown. To make sure they were hitting their quotas. Though at least there, he got to enjoy a couple of lousy Jameson outside the confines of his Georgetown condo without it going direct to the DD.

But now, to cap it all, he had to drop everything and head off for six weeks to Ireland. All because some ninety-year-old buddy of the Secretary had been shot eighteen years ago and had died of 'possible complications'.

Complications? According to the briefing on McCloud's iPad, this 'victim' had recovered from his leg wound enough to be running half-marathons at eighty-three – and had still been playing three rounds of golf a week up until a year ago. This man had died fitter than the entire US Senate and all but a handful of thirty-year-old congressmen. Indeed, if he'd been any fitter they'd have had to shoot him. Again.

Yet there it was in bold print. The phrase that would wreck his life and his last shot at Susie Morrigan: 'Seán Madden: d. 27-06-2012, possible complications due to 1994 GSW.'

'Not playing this game anymore, McCloud,' Susie told him. 'You're a good-looking boy. Just how I like them. Tall and dark, and baby blues that could burn a hole through a bedroom door. But like I said from the start, if I don't get your full attention, you don't get mine. And if I don't get three consecutive dates on three consecutive weeks, you don't get to enjoy my Welcome-to-Susie party piece. And just to remind you, that involves three consecutive treats, too. Your own private hat-trick. So you think hard about that on your holiday to the Isle of the Fairies. Real, real hard.'

He briefly thought about resigning on the spot and applying for a job as a busboy at The Setanta Grill where Susie managed bar. But his training kicked in, and he started thinking of the last jumper they'd pulled out of the Potomac – bloated and blackened and heaving with maggots – and the blood began flowing back to his brain.

Susie wasn't the answer anyway. She'd never get past his parents. Sure, she had a smile like a halogen bulb and was pretty as a summer day, but she was just a little too sharp and about a year past settling down. Fun for a couple of months, sure, and a little dangerous, but he couldn't see her sitting beside him in a minivan, laughing at his singing while he tried to entertain the four kids strapped in the back behind him. Like his folks had done. They tuck you up, your mum and dad – and you never forgive them for it.

CHAPTER 3

Maeve Madden was delighted when she heard which real-life American VIPs were coming from Washington for her grandfather's funeral. David Cunningham from the *Londonderry Leader* only got the US Consul down from Belfast when the drink finally caught up with his mother. But the president himself was sending a special envoy to pay respects to Big Seán. A couple of senators, a Congress chair and a clatter of Kennedy cousins had already confirmed they would be flying in, too. It was the least they could do.

Mo O'Sullivan, who'd spent too many of her seventy years as General Manager at the *North West Chronicle* – and reputedly as Big Seán's mistress as well – was less impressed. She was convinced it merited a visit from the Veep, and she was determined to stand protesting at the door of the tiny, cluttered editor's office until Maeve looked up from the proofs of their Special Edition and agreed with her.

'Joe Biden is where he is by convincing the Philly Irish that he's a Derryman, born and bred; 'course, we all know he's really from Carlingford. But even so, would it have killed him to come over? He owes us. You'd have thought it'd have been like picking up free money. Five months to the US elections and all those expat American voters just looking for something to hang their hat on – plus some of the best golf courses in the world. Jesus, you'd think the man had a real job.'

Maeve laughed and affected a schoolgirl's voice: 'Whenever *my* boyfriend dies, he's going to have the Vice President *and* the President at his funeral. And the Taoiseach and the British Prime Minister.'

'You watch your mouth, Red. Seán wasn't my boyfriend: he was my friend and my employer. You of all people know that. And besides, whenever your boyfriend dies, there'll be so many pigs in the sky that there'll be no room for anyone else to fly in for the funeral. You know, because he's so imaginary and all.'

'Kinda tortured that metaphor a little, Mo, didn't you? You should really leave the clever stuff to us creative types.'

'I'm creating a mental picture right now, of me slapping you in the mouth.'

The two women glared at one another for a full five seconds and then, on cue, started to laugh. Mo had reared Maeve as her own daughter, after Maeve's journalist mother died suddenly when the child was just twelve. There had never been a father.

Maeve was almost thirty now, and Mo considered her reasonably well adjusted, given all the circumstances. But she was starting to worry that her charge was going to miss out on some of the joys of life, the fun. Maeve was very agreeable looking in a copper-headed, Amy Adams sort of way, but underneath the sweet façade, she had a shell of steel and a mouth on her like a wounded cage-fighter.

The psychologist had blamed 'abandonment issues' and prescribed trust exercises. But Maeve, then sixteen, didn't trust him enough to do them – she reckoned he was just trying to get into her head. And after he was convicted of trying it on with another pretty young patient, Maeve worked out that her own judgment was, in fact, as good as it gets. And this cynicism – or 'solipsism', as Seán labelled it – made her one of the best journalists in the business. He told her once that the only reason she ever dressed like a girl was to throw her opponents off balance. Everyone, living or dead, was an opponent; at best a fellow competitor, at worst an outright enemy. Except for Seán and Mo, and maybe Tommy Bowtie. And now Seán was dead, which worried Mo greatly.

'What are you going to wear to the funeral?' she asked Maeve.

'Jeans and T-shirt, same ones I've on me now,' said the editor, without looking up. 'Might see if I can find a bra, though. Have you any of the cute little sporty ones you used to squeeze into before you started shopping at Big Fat Ladies?'

Mo still did five miles on the treadmill every morning and was slimmer than Maeve. But she knew better than to swing at every ball; now was not the time.

'What about your great-grandmother's pearl necklace? Would you like me to get it out of the safe?'

Maeve put down her trademark silver Parker pen and looked up at her guardian. She wasn't going to go away until she heard what she needed. And Mo had waited out some tough people.

'I'm all right, Mo. Honestly, I am. And yes, I know what you're fishing at. I'm sad that Seán is gone, but I'm going to be okay. I'm happy to have had him for so long. Blessed, even, to use your word. He had a great life – an epic life – and I'm so proud to be his granddaughter and that he trusted me to take over the *Chronicle*. And yes, I'll wear the black Dior dress, the one you've already got hanging out on the back of my bedroom door. And the Jimmy Choo ankle boots to remind people I'm under thirty. And Connie's pearls, of course: there couldn't be a more appropriate place to wear them. I'm not wearing a hat, though. Seán was proud that I'd inherited his colouring, so I'm not going to let him down now by hiding it. I've an appointment to get the rattails weeded out at eight thirty tomorrow morning; it'll give me plenty of time …'

'Have you the eulogy done?'

'No. But only because I have to write it for the damn bishop's rhythms and not my own. The clergy can't do short sentences. I've the piece finished for the paper, though.'

'How much have you written?'

'About eighteen hundred words. Any more would have been overkill and Seán would have got cranky. I'll email it onto you now, if you'd like. It'll make a strong double-page centre spread if we include it with pictures of him with the likes of Constance Markievicz, Éamon de Valera, Amelia Earhart, Bob Hope, Jack Kennedy, Bill'n'Hill and John Major. I think there's one of him and Cameron as well. There was a pile of photos with Tony Blair, too, but Seán couldn't look at him after Iraq, so I gave them over to the *Leader*. There's another four pages of tributes and reminisces as well, but it's just reportage. Plus the front-page story: "Death of a Legend".'

'Nice headline.'

'Yeah, he'd have been mortified.'

'Modest to the last: it's the American in him. Did you tell any of the good stuff?'

'Not really. I alluded to it a little bit. But I'm pretty careful, given the Yanks are going to be holding the investigation and all.'

'Did you mention the videos?'

'Not specifically – talked about his memoirs but kept it vague. The last thing I wanted to do is announce that Seán spent a month in front of a camera while I put him over his life story – and the stories of quite a few other people besides. We'd start a stampede that would rattle cages from here all the way to DC and back.'

'So what do you think we should do with them?'

'Exactly what he told us – and told Tommy Bowtie – release them twenty-five years after his death, as long as everybody named in them is dead.'

'Does anyone know they exist, other than us?'

'More people than I'm comfortable with – but nobody who would ever want them seen. Officially, it's just you, Tommy, poor Seán, and me. But I'd reckon pretty much all the secret services know, or at least suspect, they exist. We've talked about them on the phones.'

'Would they have copies?'

'Very much doubt it. We managed most of it without computers – apart from when we transferred stuff from the SD memory cards to the DVDs. But we scrubbed that machine straightaway afterwards. And, as you remember, Seán insisted on us doing all the recording in the bunker.'

The bunker was a World War II bomb shelter in the grounds of Seán's old manse, which he had converted into a secure and soundproof underground apartment. Over the years, it had been used for everything from hiding refugees to negotiating with diplomats to filming his memoirs.

'I remember surely,' said Mo. 'No phones allowed inside, either, just in case. Seán was shouting about them being recording devices thirty years before mobiles were invented. So what about the tapes – or rather the DVDs?'

'We managed to get them security-coded and they're locked in the safety deposit box.'

'Really?' Mo was surprised at this level of efficiency. Editors of the *North West Chronicle* tended to talk a good trip, then fly home by the seat of their pants.

Maeve knew she was caught. 'Well, the originals couldn't be safer,' she said. 'But there are still Seán's own copies in a desk drawer at home – unlocked, I'd imagine. He wanted to watch them again last week, so I copied them onto that old laptop you got him for viewing DVDs. You know what he was like.'

'Ridiculous, the two of you. You're like a pair of children. Remind me to lock them away as soon as I get home. Are they at least coded?'

'Yeah. Password One-Two-Three-Four. It was about all he could remember after the stroke.'

Mo shook her head. 'I have to go back to the house to get the pearls out, so I'll do that all now. And don't forget to send me on the obituary. Somebody needs to check your grammar now he's gone.'

'Will do. And my grammar's just fine, thank you. That's a degree certificate from Harvard on the wall behind you, if you can read those big Latin words.'

'Yeah, but didn't they give one of those to George W Bush as well?'

'Touché. I'll send the damn piece on to you so you can bitch about what I've left out. Oh, and, Mo?'

'Yes.'

Maeve took a beat. This was important. 'I'm putting a picture of you, me and himself in the paper, too. Taken at the opening of the Peace Bridge. Captioned "Seán with his family". Hope you don't mind?'

Mo knew the picture well. It sat on the hall table of her flat at the manse and she touched it for luck every time she left the house. It was taken just over a year ago, on 25 June 2011, a fortnight before the stroke – all six-foot four of him, looking like a Hollywood star in a black suit and dazzling white shirt, perfectly set off with red silk handkerchief and tie. He just couldn't understand how anyone could ever want to dress down. Maeve in the middle – wearing a peach linen summer frock as a concession to him – arm-linking the group together. And Mo, the epitome of Betty Bacall glamour, in a svelte, navy velvet dress. It had been Seán's last public appearance as a healthy man. He never left the house afterwards – he didn't want to be remembered in his decrepitude.

The older woman dropped her head and tried hard to keep her voice steady. 'I don't know why you're putting me in the paper. The whole town will only start gossiping again about how I'm really your mother. As if I could whelp something as bad-mannered as you. I don't want it in. Get something else.'

She turned to leave but suddenly realised she couldn't move. Maeve had slipped up silently from her desk and wrapped her in a bear hug from behind.

'You were his best friend, Mo. And you're still mine. And you were his family, and you're still mine. And he loved you with all his heart. And so do I. The picture stays in the paper – and let the gossips choke on their own bile. Now go off home and hide the damn DVDs before the Brits break into the house again.'

CHAPTER 4

The City Hotel was booked out because of the funeral – the US political contingent had demanded the top two floors for themselves, 'in the interests of security', so Ally McCloud checked himself into the new Cunningham Lodge just across the footbridge at Ebrington.

And for a man with a reputation of being a slow starter, it took McCloud less than two minutes to hook up. A pretty blonde waitress in tight black livery – a Canadian exchange student, by the sound of her – asked him if he'd like a nightcap brought up to his room.

'You look tired after your trip. You're probably hoping for an early night if you want to sort out that jet lag.'

As an invitation, it was word perfect. But he was a little taken aback at how young she was – no more than twenty. Too young for anyone to suspect or look at twice. 'I'll take a whiskey and soda, Jameson if possible. And copies of today's papers.'

'I'm off duty shortly, sir. I'll bring it all up to you before I go home.'

He got to his suite – with the beautiful view of Ebrington Square and the meandering River Foyle behind it – ditched the cases in the bedroom and stretched himself out on the sofa in the living area. He was starting to get excited.

Virginia – or that was the name on her tag – duly rapped on the door of his small suite five minutes later, carrying a bottle of Jameson Special Reserve, a soda siphon and a manila folder bulging with press clippings.

'It's all in there, sir,' she said. 'Everything published on Madden – either online or in print – for the last three days. The bottle is a present from the Deputy Director, by the way. He says you're to make it last the full six weeks.'

McCloud laughed, wrenched open the bottle and threw the cap across the room and neatly into the bin. He then poured out two glasses, roundly ignoring the soda siphon he'd asked for, and offered one to his connection.

'I'm only nineteen, sir. I'll make myself coffee, if that's okay.'

He suddenly felt old and a little seedy. 'Good girl. You've passed the test. I guess I'll have to drink both these myself.'

'I wouldn't advise that if you're hoping to go to the funeral in the morning, sir. Liquor and jet lag are a bad mix. And given the state of your eyes, you had at least two doubles on the plane in from New York, and probably another one at Belfast Airport before you got your taxi here. So pour my drink back into the bottle, then go and fetch the cap out of the trash, sir. And yes, the DD has told me to keep a strict eye on you.'

'Is this your first assignment?'

'It is, sir. And my number one responsibility is to make sure you never exceed your quota.'

'And what precisely is that?'

'Three large measures a day; any more than that and you become reckless. Up to that point, you're still a high-functioning ...'

She stopped.

'A high-functioning what, precisely?'

He watched her flinch, worried she might hurt his feelings. She was efficient and professional, but was she cool enough to tell the truth to power?

'Alcoholic, sir. I have to make sure that you remain a high-functioning alcoholic, able to do your job to the Bureau's complete satisfaction. Any more than three a day – or six small ones, if you may – and you're in danger of becoming a lush again. I really shouldn't let you finish that drink in your hand, sir, if I'm being honest, but it's your first night here and I can't say for certain if you had the one at the airport. But I know the cut-off point on the plane is two, so I'm going to allow you this last one.'

He nodded graciously, accepting his fate, then necked his drink in one before she changed her mind. She was likeable, in a bossy sort of way, but he didn't want to push it. Truth is, he'd managed to charm a third double out of the Continental air stewardess to help conquer his 'fear of landing' and then had two more large ones at Belfast International waiting for the taxi he'd booked to come half an hour late, so he already had a pretty decent drunk on.

He held up the file but didn't open it. 'Anything new?'

'Not a thing. The sanitised Wikipedia account, with a couple of nice compliments and the odd nasty gibe thrown in. His own paper, the *North West Chronicle*, is out in the morning – Special Edition.'

'And what are they saying?'

'They'll have more than the others, that's for certain. But they're not going to give away too much. We'll know for sure in about half an hour. Maeve, the old man's granddaughter, refuses to work on an online

16

computer. Realises from experience that they're far too easy to hack. The *Chronicle* caught the Brits tapping their mainframe a few years ago – or rather the Brits outed themselves when they tried to stop Madden running a very embarrassing story about a sleeper they were running inside the IRA. So, the *Chronicle* now do most of their writing – and the page layout – offline. Much slower to produce, but it's rarely stale by the time it hits the streets – unlike most of the rest.'

'Have we a tap on their mainframe, too?'

'Of course. But the mainframe's only used for sport and ads, right up until the paper is ready to send to the printers.'

'So how do we get the *Chronicle*'s story, then? I take it we've a tap on the line to the printers? What time do they send?'

'Not till midnight. The printers handle dozens of different local papers and have quite a complicated queue system. But we shouldn't have to wait till then. Maeve has promised to email the main obituary on to Mo O'Sullivan, Seán's right-hand woman. So we'll grab it from the cloud as soon as she sends it.'

'How do we know she'll be emailing it?'

'I spent an hour this afternoon listening to the *Chronicle*'s offices on Waterloo Street through a directional mike. Kitted myself out like a CBC producer setting up for a shoot outside Seán's spiritual home. No-one batted an eye.'

He was impressed. 'And then, after that, you did a shift waiting tables here? Hats off to you, Virginia.'

'It all goes down as course credit, sir. Hours in the field. I'm just pleased to get some action. I'm getting paid double time, too, for this briefing session, and only right, too. The rest of my shift think I'm hooking. I've spent the past three months in Ireland, studying. It's good to get my feet wet.'

Seán reached for his glass, remembered it was empty and stopped himself. She saw the gesture, picked up the almost full bottle from the table in front of him and locked it in the safe.

She grinned. 'I've already emptied your minibar, and I've told the manager he's not to give you any more drink: it reacts badly with your medication.'

'You're joking?'

'No. Theoretically, I suppose you could walk across into town and get yourself a drink there. But I'll catch you for sure and dock it from your allowance tomorrow. You're just too easy to spot here. Have you seen my uncle, sir? Big, tall guy, a dead ringer for John Cusack, always cracking his damn thumbs?'

He immediately released his two thumbs from his palms and shook his head. Ten years of training but he still couldn't shake the habit. The drink he could quit anytime.

Back to business. 'They talk about the tapes?' he asked.

Officially, this question was above Virginia's clearance level. The investigation into the shooting, it was becoming apparent, was a blind to allow McCloud to shut down any and all stories in Seán's diaries that mightn't fit the prevailing narrative.

But Virginia didn't even blink. 'Yeah, they talked about them a little. They have them secured. We could maybe seize a set with a bit of finagling – might even be able to blame it on the Brits, too, if anything went wrong. Gotta ask ourselves, is it worth the risk, though? The family are happy to support our investigation into the shooting. The Consul rang Maeve to tell her about it – and she offered her full co-operation. But she's playing a longer game, I have no doubt. She has something else going on.'

'So we gotta be nice to them for the minute, then. And where's that likely to get us?'

'AFN, as they say at Quantico, sir. Absolutely nowhere. We're dealing with a particularly undomesticated animal here. Maeve has no discernible fear of, or respect for, anyone or any group, whatsoever. She's completely self-reliant.'

'Has she a temper?'

'Definitely, but I'd be more worried about her single-mindedness. She spent six days in jail last year for contempt, after refusing to hand over photographs of a dissident training camp to a judge – despite the fact she'd already published the pictures. The judge just wanted to see the originals, in case the guys in the fuzzy masks had left any clues to their identities that Maeve might have airbrushed out. Maeve told him that if there'd been any clues, she would have plastered them all over the front page, but that he couldn't have the pics, as it wasn't her job to collect information for the police.'

'So how did she get out, then?'

'The police raided the office and found the photos sitting on Maeve's desk, precisely where Mo O'Sullivan, Maeve's General Manager, said they'd be.'

Ally paused and cracked his thumb knuckles. 'She's the older lady, right? Seán's friend who was never his girlfriend? Would she be a better way in for us?'

'Strong indications would be no. She's as tough as Maeve and protects Maeve like she were her own daughter. Only reason she let them have the pictures was they'd reverse engineered them from the ones they had in the paper – they weren't the originals at all. The originals, of course, had been destroyed.'

'Had they been airbrushed?'

'Doubt it. Maeve doesn't do favours. It's a point of principle with her. Good journalists don't have any friends.'

CHAPTER 5

Virginia – who told Ally she preferred Jeanie – finished her report and was about to leave her boss to his coma when her phone pinged. She checked the message and smiled.

'It's through, sir. Turn on your laptop. I'll email it to you.'

Ally leaned back from his armchair to the desk behind him and flipped open his custom-issued MacBook Pro, which immediately sprang into life. As he readied himself to click open the file from derryfieldoffice@fbi.gov, it struck him that he was about to open private correspondence between two individuals of another country.

Jeanie spotted his hesitation. 'You're covered by the Patriot Act, sir. This search pertains to an attack on a US citizen.'

'Yeah,' he said, 'but how would you like it?'

He opened the file regardless, swayed by the thought of forced overtime out in the boondocks at just three crappy drinks a day. He scanned the obituary quickly, smiled a few times, scowled once and nodded slowly at the end. This was a man who'd led an interesting life – actually a very interesting life – and had a queue of people waiting to shoot him. Just like his second-cousin, Jack.

'Take a read of it,' he told Jeanie, flicking the screen around to her. 'If the granddaughter is anything like him – and I take it she is, given the way she's written the piece – this is not going to be simple.'

Death of a Legend

Seán Hannon Madden, Publisher

22 August 1922–27 June 2012

By Maeve Madden

As his lifelong friend Mo O'Sullivan said to him in the hospital back in 1994, 'The only mystery here, Seán, is that no-one shot you sooner.'

My grandfather, whose family set up the *North West Chronicle* one hundred years ago and have run it ever since, was, above all else, ruthless in his conviction to do the right thing. And I speak as someone who was grounded for three days after acquiring a petite tattoo. Aged twenty-three.

In his seventy-plus-year career in journalism, Big Seán – aka 'The Bank' – railed against every corrupting influence this city has ever met – and every power block that ever got above itself. He was the guardian, the watchdog, and the last of the checks and balances. He had, as his old headmaster once told him, no respect for authority – only people. And he had absolutely no favourites – only his readers.

Because of that, he was sued (regularly), boycotted, censored, suppressed, condemned in four different parliaments, rebuked from the altar, threatened, bombed, burnt out, and, yes, even shot.

Yet, conversely, every single group that he clashed with, from Blueshirts and clergies to revolutionaries and spooks, respected him. They may not have liked him – but at least they knew he wasn't on the other guy's side. The only side he knew was his own. And he stuck to his guns, even when he was wrong. Which, as he'd happily tell you, was about a thousand times a day.

Seán Madden, as he loved to boast, was born in Boston, Massachusetts, the day his hero Michael Collins was assassinated. His father, Johnny, a prominent anti-Treaty campaigner and this newspaper's editor, had been killed in a contentious road accident along the 'Provisional Border', six months before Seán's birth.

Seán's mother, Constance 'Connie' Hannon (1896–1980), a US citizen and full cousin of Rose Kennedy, returned to America immediately after Johnny's death and resolved to stay there to rear her child. Johnny's father, Mick Madden, however, had other plans. He had previously run the *Chronicle* himself for eighteen months, when Johnny left to accompany Éamon de Valera as his Chief Press Officer on a trip to America in 1919. But it was too much work for him on his own, so he telephoned Connie to tell her that he was going to sell the paper and send her over the proceeds – and that young Seán would have a far better life in the United States to boot. Mick knew as he was saying the words that she would come, but it was important to set up her narrative.

Sure enough, Connie set sail on the Queen Mary to take over the paper, leaving her infant son in the care of her sister back in Back Bay. It would be almost a decade later before Seán would join her. In the interim, he was educated with his cousins in Boston. But as soon as things became quiet in Ireland, Seán and his aunt, Mary Hannon, found themselves on a three-day Zeppelin flight to Europe. They then arrived in Ireland, from Berlin, just in time for the public launch of the *Irish Press* newspaper, where Seán was given his father's old seat next to Dev for the occasion.

He was a little better fed than the locals when he first arrived – 'full of

Boston beans', the headmaster at St Eugene's Primary School commented – though he soon lost the extra weight. An attempt by a fellow pupil to christen him 'Olly', after the movie star, failed miserably when Seán knocked his front teeth out with a hurl. He served a fortnight-long suspension for that and, characteristically, vowed never to hit another human being again.

It took Seán no time to adjust to Derry. And while he occasionally got hassle from the priests at St Columb's College – because of his mother's republican, American and, worst of all, secular politics – he was academic enough to survive their worst excesses. The Maddens also had a little money and, of course, their own newspaper, which always helped with the clergy.

By the time he was fifteen, Seán was six-feet four, and when he spoke, he rarely had to repeat himself. By that stage, he was already writing editorials for the *Chronicle*, along with match reports, council stories, and anything else Connie couldn't get cover for.

He read law at Queen's University, Belfast, in the early part of World War II. It came easily to him 'as a natural smartarse' and allowed him plenty of time for writing and his other great love – smuggling.

He agonised over whether to enlist in the US Army after he graduated in 1944 – but ultimately, he couldn't get past the immovable object. The British had been responsible for his father's death. So instead, Connie re-installed him as Chief Reporter at the *Chronicle* and he acted as Civic Liaison Officer for the thousands of Yanks stationed in Derry. Indeed, it was the GIs who first christened Seán 'The Bank', such was his ability to provide them with even the obscurest of materials – from smuggled Free State chocolate and butter (far better than the rationed Brit versions) to, on one occasion, a fully functioning radar system he salvaged from a scuttled German U-boat.

However, he fell afoul of the authorities *and* his family in 1947 when he was caught carrying a consignment of *poitín* into the North in the hollowed-out undercarriage of the *Chronicle* van. The Northern Customs had managed to turn one of his old girlfriends and Seán wound up paying a fine of £500 – the price of a house. His mother published the court report on the front page of the paper and issued a public apology on Seán's behalf – against his strong protests. The framed paper is still hanging over Seán's desk at home, with his petulant riposte scrawled in fountain pen across the bottom: 'Smuggling is not a crime – the only crime in Ireland is the border!'

A short time later, his American cousins decided it was time for a sabbatical and Seán spent the next six years as a congressional aide for the Democrats during Jack's first term. He never regarded himself as any more than a foot soldier there and was mortified when revisionists would suggest he had been a player. While in the States, he enrolled part-time in Harvard, acquiring a Masters in Classics and, more importantly, a beautiful young Radcliffe student, Amelia Jane 'Millie' Harrison (1932–59), who slapped some long-overdue sense into him.

It was Millie who persuaded Seán to return to Derry on their honeymoon in the summer of 1953. And they had barely landed at Ballykelly Airfield when Connie resigned as editor of the *Chronicle* and the shareholders (Connie, Aunt Mary and Old Mick) voted in Seán as her replacement. It was, of course, a complete stitch-up: Millie wanted her husband running his own Camelot and not as a bit player in somebody else's. That, and he had never stopped talking about Derry from the moment he met her.

Under Seán's leadership, the *Chronicle* expanded rapidly, opening new editions across Donegal, Sligo, Tyrone and County Derry. Later, he would open Radio North West and Derry TV.

Millie and Seán bought the manse, the garden of which straddles the border – 'let's see those whoring Water Rats catch me now' – and were determined to fill it with children. But Millie suffered heart failure and died during the birth of her first child, Amelia, aka 'Little Mill'.

The next few years were his angry phase, Seán taking his grief out on a cold world. He railed consistently against gerrymandering, vote rigging and the failures of the Unionists. He cut lumps out of the Nationalist Party for their appeasement and cowardice. He slated Belfast politicians for their failure to award Derry the new university and Derry politicians for their failure to stand up for their city. He fell out with the RUC when an informer disclosed that the IRA had used his bunker as billets during their Border Campaign; he fought with the British Government when he outed a visiting 'economist' as an MI5 spy; and he was denounced by his godfather, de Valera, and the Church, for sending his five-year-old daughter to a non-Catholic primary school.

Another trip to America in the mid-sixties, to meet black civil rights leaders, left Seán more contemplative and aware that his people at home needed to play a longer game. To that end, he set up the first 'Six-County Support Network' in Boston, which would fund civil rights groups in Derry and, later, political campaigns across the North. All done via 'The Bank'.

The CIA roundly disapproved of some of his actions, particularly as the Troubles progressed, and threatened to pull his US passport. But the British and Irish both found his business-minded independence a boon in securing temporary and lasting back-door deals with all the tribes. If 'The Bank' gave a guarantee, it stuck. And any transgressors found themselves nailed to the front page of his newspapers.

He actively avoided the limelight for himself – not out of modesty –

but rather because there was a risk of him being seen to run an agenda, be that a republican agenda, an anti-Catholic agenda, an American agenda or a Russian one. He knew well that to be an effective and independent watchdog, he could never follow a party line. So instead, he proposed and backed those who could speak best for him, and his readers, at a given time. Though those he backed never spoke as well as he did – unless he was writing their words.

Seán's full role in the endgame here will never be known. If anything, he was an anti-historian. He didn't regard his newspapers as the first drafts of history, but rather as the only true drafts of history. Everything after that was just revisionism and re-interpretation.

The Yanks, the British, the IRA and probably the Irish are bugging all before them – including the *Chronicle's* office and our home-lines – to try and get their hands on Seán's memoirs. But having witnessed the Boston Tapes debacle, 'The Bank' left us specific instructions to make public some very damning evidence about some very private matters, involving very senior players from each of these groupings, should they attempt to trawl through his ashes. And anyone who knows me, the granddaughter, will understand the joy that I would get in carrying out this particular deathbed request.

As a man, Seán was highly respected, if never quite popular, most of the time. His shooting, shortly after the sudden death of my mother Little Mill, shocked us all but wasn't an entire surprise. He had handed out a lot and refused to complain about a 'scratch on the leg'.

Seán, incidentally, was never a full pacifist – he viewed resistance to tyranny as an inalienable right. But he also knew that even the greatest idealists – be they religious, political or military – could become tyrants in their turn, without proper safeguards. The first thing any power learns, he would say, is how to protect and sustain itself. His job was to hold that power to account when no-one else would.

He tried to keep them honest. And that's why they hated him.

But, above all, he tried to keep them honest. And that's why we loved him.

Ar dheis Dé go raibh a anam uasal.

***

McCloud went to bed at midnight a completely happy man, hitting the pillow in a perfect mellow buzz. His employers could handle a few digs about their bugs from a delusional conspiracy theorist, but their fears that the family would demand a full public inquiry into Seán's shooting or, worse again, might embarrass old friends by releasing old stories to ensure some legacy-credit for themselves, were unfounded. The message coming from the *Chronicle* couldn't be clearer: leave us alone, and we'll leave you alone. And McCloud was okay with that. He would ask the precise number of questions necessary to tick all his boxes, while steering well clear of anything that might upset the natives. No-one was expecting him to solve a twenty-year-old mystery. And the triple-lock booby-trap Seán had rigged to his tapes meant McCloud could justifiably close down all further attempts to appropriate the memoirs.

That rare, warm and fuzzy feeling would last just a few hours.

CHAPTER 6

Jeanie's text pinged in at 5.05am, followed by one from the Deputy Director about twenty seconds later. Both said the same thing. The *Chronicle* had screwed them.

They had all been so intent in getting their hands on the obituary that they had paid no attention to what they assumed would be the bog-standard 'Death of a Legend' front-page news story. It was not.

McCloud knew better than to talk to the DD before he was fully briefed, so he gulped back a quick breakfast of bottled water and Tylenol while he called Jeanie.

'The Consulate in Belfast was contacted about an hour ago by the BBC's local overnight reporter,' she said. 'He wanted to know if we'd any reaction to claims that the US had sent a, quote unquote, Washington spy to Derry to try and seize the Madden Tapes. The *North West Chronicle* apparently named the spy as Ally McCloud.'

'Any wriggle room?'

'Not a bit. I got a copy of the paper straightaway from the service station. The front page has a big photo of McCloud standing at the bar at Belfast International Airport; looks like he's draining a large shot while signalling for another.'

McCloud knew better than to deny it. 'Must be an impostor – I got straight into a taxi. I have the time-stamps to prove it.'

Fair play to her, she laughed. Maybe she'd let it pass.

'You put it all into the system?' he asked.

'Yeah – I scanned it all in and emailed it to you directly.'

'Give me the bullet points so I can pretend I've read it.'

'I already have. Your cover is blown – and they're instructing the entire region not to speak to you. The tapes are the *Chronicle*'s private property and will stay as such for twenty-five years. They actually have a pretty full biography of you, too.'

'Hope the DD doesn't see it – my file's fat enough. Where did they get that?'

'Dead easy. Facebook.'

'But I hate the thing, it's just a bar with no beer. And besides, we're not allowed.'

'Yeah, but if you'd stayed awake for even one of the social media seminars at Quantico, you'd know how easy it is to scam all sorts of data by setting up dummy Facebook accounts. For my money, and I'll check it out now, they probably copied a picture of your father from your mother's Facebook page and then created a dummy account for him. They then started issuing friend invites to relatives. And after that, they started sending out "PMs", personal messages, as your father, inviting conversations about you. According to the *Chronicle* story, you're a disaster with women – couldn't score with a stripper in an ATM lobby, quote unquote – and you need to watch your drinking.'

'No secret there. It's on my Christmas card. Did they mention my brother?'

She paused.

'Yes.'

'How bad?'

'He did your SATs for you because you were sick. He was caught, thrown out of Berkeley, and was killed in Iraq. You, on the other hand, were forgiven and ended up with two Ivy League degrees.'

'Yeah, forgiven by everyone except my parents. Jesus, who in the hell are these people? I can see tomorrow's *Washington Post* now: "FBI get their asses handed to them by little-league hicks." How many international laws have they just broken – data fraud, spying on members of the Federal Government?'

'Let's not go there, sir. Not while I still have a directional mike and about a dozen fake reporter IDs under my bed.'

'Did they make you?'

'Not that I'm aware of, sir. 'Course, it helps that I look like I'm fourteen.'

'How did they do it so quickly?'

'They were waiting for us. They were ready.'

'How did they keep it from us – the front page, I mean?'

'We didn't anticipate it. We were too busy hunting down the decoy – the obit.'

Jeanie breathed out quietly. She'd been warned to expect this. It was the way he did business – dialectic reasoning. She was to be the sounding board. Question after question until he worked through his process. She was to give short answers, factual and to the point, with as little comment as possible.

'Okay, here's the big question. Why would they draw attention to the tapes?'

She took a beat to consider it. 'Everyone that matters know they exist already, sir. It's the final warning. They're acknowledging the tapes publicly exist to protect themselves – and tell you to back off, or else.'

'Or else what?'

'Or else, they'll publish whatever part of them you don't want published.'

'Why embarrass us, though? We're their compatriots. Why not the Brits? I'm sure they could have slapped them across the mouth just as easy.'

'They wanted to show us, and the Brits and the Irish, that they have no friends. They're prepared to burn whoever it takes.'

He nodded. 'But wouldn't the warning in the obituary have done the job for them? This front page will kick-start a rush to get the tapes now it's all in the public domain.'

'It would have been public, regardless, by the end of the week, sir. Either the Brits or the Irish, or some other group – IRA, maybe – who know what's on them and want some leverage, would have leaked the story. This particular crap-shower was coming no matter what – but this way the *Chronicle* controls it.'

Jeanie stopped herself. She had drifted too far into the realms of speculation.

McCloud closed his eyes and let out a sigh.

'Back to first principles,' he said, 'are we sure they exist? The tapes, I mean.'

'It's strongly probable, but with this crew nothing is ever certain.'

'Tell me what you know.'

'Couple of years ago, August 2010, Mo O'Sullivan bought a Canon HD camera and twenty-four SD memory cards, about a week before she and Maeve took a full month's leave. But they didn't go abroad. In fact, they barely left the manse – same with Seán.'

'Not enough. It could just have been one of those Overhaul Your Business symposia. Or Seán filming his will.'

'The day before their leave ended, Maeve rented a deposit box at the Oakland Bank across the border in Donegal.'

'Nope.'

'The same day, she drove to a mall in Omagh, about forty miles from Derry, and bought a stack of DVDs. She then asked the clerk if it would be easy to transfer material onto them from SD cards.'

'Still no.'

'The clerk was a girl called Paula Cunningham and she recognised Maeve. Paula's a bright girl and twigged something was going on. So she asked Maeve, all innocent, if she was transferring film – as it was very data-heavy and quite slow to transfer. She told her to make sure to use the proper software. Maeve, who was far enough from home to feel comfortable, asked in turn, how long would it take to transfer forty hours of film – they were putting together an oral archive of their family history, and her grandfather had rambled on a bit.'

'Warmer, but still no.'

'Paula rang her second cousin, David Cunningham, owner and editor of the Protestant paper, the *Londonderry Leader*, and told him the story. David, who sometimes talks to our Consul on the side, met Maeve at a press event that same night and decided to find out what colour her face would go when he told her old Seán was writing his memoirs. And the answer, if you're interested, was a very angry red. Followed by a direct threat to his physical and economic wellbeing.'

'I don't follow?'

'She told David it was lies, sheer lies, and if he printed a word of it, she'd cut his genitalia off and sell them on eBay. And then sue his ass off – or whatever remained of it.'

'Getting warmer.'

'On top of that, as you're aware we then have quite a few references to the tapes on our, ah, intercepts.'

'But as *you're* now aware, they know we're listening to them and are masters of the misdirect.'

'Yes, sir. But they're also well trained – and the vast majority of what they're saying will always be true. Otherwise we wouldn't be buying it. They're applying what they call the Ninety Per Cent Rule.'

'And what exactly is that?'

'It was an idea hatched by their lawyer, Thomas McGinlay – known as Tommy Bowtie to the locals to distinguish him from his late father, Tommy Senior. I read about it in a file back at base. Bowtie is a great believer, when you're under scrutiny, in telling ninety per cent of the truth. You then make up the other ten per cent to mislead the other guy, or give yourself plausible deniability, or even just to undermine your confession at a later date. Bowtie hit on the idea to counter the Brits' interrogation techniques. So a guy would confess freely to the nine bombings he'd committed – but then he'd add in a tenth he couldn't have possibly done because he'd been playing soccer in front of a crowd of thousands at the time. Then when his confession was read out in court, Bowtie just pulled on that one particular thread and the whole stitch-up fell apart.'

'Not bad at all – thank the stars the Taliban are too straight for that sort of thing. So where does that leave us with the tapes?'

'We work on the premise that they exist, sir.'

'So do we go after them?'

'Kind of hard now not to.'

'That's the killer, all right. To seize or not to seize. It's almost as if she's overplaying it – she's called us out into the yard, and asked her buddy to hold her coat. It's going to look really bad for us if we slope off out the gate. Is it possible that she wants us to hit her?'

'Why would she want that, sir?'

'Well, then she could break her own twenty-five-year moratorium and start kicking up some serious news-dust with Seán's stories. But could anyone be that cynical?'

'Absolutely, sir. She's a one-hundred-pound Machiavelli in a fifty-dollar skirt.'

He laughed.

'Okay, so. Well done, Jeanie. You batted back perfectly. And the bottom line is that the tapes are essential to us to find out who shot Seán and why. So we're going to go find them. Thank you. I think I'll get me a shave then do a little ninety-per-centing of my own.'

'How do you mean?'

'I'm going to wait outside the church and serve an injunction on Maeve Madden for wrongly calling me a spy.'

'But you are, sir.'

'Nope. I'm a Federal Agent, doing my job. I'm in Ireland to protect visiting US dignitaries at a funeral. I have never denied being a cop – or at least not to her.'

'Seriously, sir? You're going to drag her into court over semantics?'

'Absolutely not. I just want to slow her up a little, so we can grab a little air. She'll probably head off into Donegal to produce the paper from across the border – like she did the last time the Brits closed them down. But we need to teach her not to mess with us. And more importantly, we need to figure out what the hell we're doing here.'

CHAPTER 7

McCloud stood looking out the hotel window as a warm morning rose over Ebrington Square and the River Foyle. It was so peaceful and quiet; serene, even, if it hadn't been for the thumping in his head. This 20-acre site, according to the brochure in his room, had been a British military base for hundreds of years before it had been returned to the city about a decade earlier. Dozens of pearl-white Victorian buildings, including a landmark clock-tower centrepiece, had been perfectly restored to create a city within a city, while the former parade ground directly in front of him had been turned into a huge multi-purpose plaza, exposing long-hidden views of the other riverbank. For generations, the British had been the only people allowed to enjoy these views, which had been locked away, behind grotesque green iron hoardings, from the rest of the city. But today, the space was both open to all and spectacular. Without any fanfare, parade grounds had been turned into playgrounds.

McCloud reread the *Chronicle's* front page in full over coffee and a fried-egg roll, or 'bap' as the waiter had called it, in his room and was changing his mind about serving an injunction. They would only play it as the FBI Goliath trying to crush a quaint little newspaper. And he could never risk the wrath of the Irish lobby by following through with his threat and actually closing them down. Besides, there was a better-than-even-money chance that they had just listened to every word of his phone chat with Jeanie. He just hoped they wouldn't try to knock her out of the game as well.

The problem when you start chipping away at someone else's privacy is that you can't cry foul when that someone pulls down your shorts and takes pictures of your bare ass swinging in the air. Like the *Chronicle* had just done with him. Not that he was too worried. His position at the Irish Desk had always been unusual in that it required regular public exposure and an ongoing degree of abuse. Most other agents would have been ghosted out of Derry before their hangovers had lifted. But he was here for the duration. What he hated, though, was how easy it now was to become exposed.

The internet was too democratic and too open. He missed the early warning systems of the pre-Facebook days, and rued the disintermediation of serious, established authorities like reporters, editors and publishers. Today, every fourteen-year-old with a camera has the same power as a fully tenured newspaper editor. Indeed, in many cases, the kid is more powerful again, as he doesn't even have to pretend to be responsible.

Sure, transparency and accountability are essential in a free society. But too many levels of scrutiny meant no-one ever gets any work done. The Open Government Act in Washington, and the Brits' well-intentioned but ultimately self-mutilating Freedom of Information Act, allowed any crank with a chip on his shoulder to bring any public body to a standstill, just by asking the right, or wrong, question. How many perceived atheists have you working at your school, Monsignor? And how many of them are lesbian?

Even trying to organise a four-hand meeting was a disaster. The last briefing he was at in Belfast, the Brit officer-in-charge had to get three different prices from three different diners before he could order a lousy round of sandwiches. No beer, of course: it's years since anyone could claim for booze on an expense form.

But now McCloud's family, courtesy of Mark Zuckerberg and Bono, had been dragged into the mess as well, which would re-ignite all those awkward conversations about why he never contacted them. Jeanie had confirmed that his "father's" current Facebook status was a link to the *Chronicle*'s front-page story, with ten little smiley-faces attached. A final Up Yours to McCloud.

Happily, however, like many before, the *Chronicle* had completely underrated him. Because while McCloud was, like they had suggested, a card-carrying drunk, on his worst day he could sell off thirty IQ points to his nearest rival in the Intelligence Directorate and still have enough change to make Genius. And today, he was going to start getting himself those tapes – and no smarty-pants Irish *paparazza* was going to stop him.

***

After a seven-minute shower and another bottle of water, he climbed into his black suit and walked in the summer sun across the winding Peace Bridge to the Guildhall, Derry's nineteenth-century city hall, with its tower modelled on London's Big Ben. He crossed the square at the front of the beautiful red sandstone building, where Bill Clinton had three times addressed huge hometown crowds. He then headed up the hill to St Eugene's Cathedral to check out the security arrangements for the funeral. He'd been part of Clinton's detail during the president's 2010 visit and knew the city centre well.

There were only about a dozen security types and a couple of TV crews milling around the grounds of the neo-gothic cathedral when he arrived. Assistant US Consul Kenneth Foreman, a bald bear of a man in his late fifties, grinned broadly when he saw him approaching, earning himself a what-the-hell-can-you-do shrug in return.

Foreman signalled McCloud to join him beside the Holy Water fonts just inside the front atrium. 'You just need to get back on the horse, buddy. I've got a sister back home who's a fine looker, as soon as we can get her off the meth again. She's seventy-two, but she still has most of her own teeth.'

McCloud laughed. It would get worse if he didn't. 'Thanks, Ken,' he said. 'But it would only get in the way of my chronic drinking.'

Foreman knew to leave it there. 'The stuff about your brother was too mean. They're tempting you into striking first so they can publish their dirt – and then blame you for starting the fight.'

'Yeah. We made the mistake of thinking they were small-timers. But you can't take it personally – they know what they're doing.'

'Okay so, what do you need?'

McCloud pulled out his phone, opened up a blank text file, and began typing quickly. 'Need name of smart local who has serious beef with *Chronicle*. So who would love to see them closed down – and wd help do it? Get me a little intel on this individual, too. Also, cd we access *Chronicle* Facebook account?'

Foreman took the phone: 'Maybe post something on their behalf? On their page?'

McCloud nodded.

Foreman considered the request carefully and nodded back. 'When?' he said.

'Today,' said McCloud. 'While they're tied up with the ceremonies. This afternoon at the latest.'

McCloud quickly deleted the conversation from his phone.

'So that's a "no" on the injunction?' whispered Foreman, barely moving his lips.

McCloud clicked on his phone again. 'Leave it for the moment,' he wrote. 'Let them keep thinking we're a couple of days behind. Pretend like we haven't read the story – or that we haven't had the time to process it. No protests. No anger. And tell the Consul the same. Sort out the other thing, and meet me in the City Hotel lobby after Mass.'

Foreman nodded. 'Will do.'

McCloud turned the phone off again and smiled. 'Okay, so. I've got to go and open some car doors for a bunch of fake-Irish, bleach-toothed Boston WASPs. Bet my parents are real glad they gave me all that money for school. Those two law degrees sure come in handy.'

CHAPTER 8

Maeve knew they'd taken the bait when the US Consul hugged her warmly and said he was so sorry for her loss. She and Mo were standing in the receiving line outside the cathedral, conducting a running commentary on proceedings to each other out of the sides of their mouths.

'The Yanks are seething,' said Maeve. 'Too mad to even mention it.'

'Good. We want them like that. We want them pulling apart the offices before the day's out. We need them to get moving. Christ knows what would happen if the Brits got the tapes first.'

'Or the Irish.'

'The Irish wouldn't know what do with them. Fine Gael would fill their togs.'

They both laughed at the thought of the Taoiseach trying desperately to decide which of his big brothers' arses he'd have to kiss first. The Yanks, with their digital and pharmaceutical plants all over the country, owned about twenty per cent of the Irish economy. But ultimately, the Brits would bully the tapes out of the Irish even if the Yanks got a copy first. No. The Irish wouldn't look for the tapes at all: they actively couldn't stomach the hassle.

'I hope Seán's right about this,' said Mo. 'The Yanks could still hand over a few select pieces to the Brits. Throw them a bone. And the next time that Harry Hurley or some other reformed Provo threatens to throw his toys out of the pram, the Brits would pull out a skeleton from Seán's drawer.'

'Not as long as we've our own full copy – or indeed you and I are still alive. We'd just pull something from our own drawer about the Yanks.'

They both laughed again. But they knew they were dancing on a wire without safety nets.

An impressive-looking, shaven-headed piper in a traditional Irish kilt moved to the front of the cortège and began softly playing the Celtic lament *Táimse i mo chodladh*. It was the signal for the cars to begin leaving the cathedral grounds.

Mo and Maeve shook a few more soft, manicured hands, kissed a couple of well-powdered cheeks and got into the lead limousine. Their real friends – the ones who didn't need the photo-op – and the *Chronicle* staff had been invited to a private function in the Alexander Suite in the City Hotel that afternoon.

It was a warm day, so most of the procession would forgo their cars and walk the mile or so up the New Road, past John Hume's house, to the cemetery. A guard of honour from the local hurling club was lining the gate, sticks raised in salute, and two Police Service of Northern Ireland inspectors, in full dress uniform, were stopping traffic on Creggan Street to allow the cortège out of the grounds.

Maeve pulled out her phone and began typing as soon as she got into the backseat of the limo. 'When will we tell the staff?'

Mo took the BlackBerry – Maeve preferred the firmware keyboard to the iPhone touchscreen – and considered the message.

'We'll give them the weekend,' she said.

Maeve deleted the text and then began typing herself. 'What's the final count?'

Mo took the phone. 'The last two designers, all but one of the photographers and two advertising staff. Seven in all. The three reporters can double up with cameras and I'll start back on sales. They get treble the statutory redundancy, plus ten grand a person – Seán insisted.'

Maeve erased the text and spoke aloud. 'The generous old bastard. Easy for him to say, now he's dead and all. Can we afford it?'

'Yes and no,' said Mo. 'If we do it, it'll allow us to see the year out at least – as long as we don't take another hit. Bottom line, though, is we have to do it. It's either that or close. The *Leader* is in exactly the same position – except they've only half our circulation.'

Maeve produced the phone again. 'Do we have to do it now?' she typed. 'Can't we give them the summer? It would give us time to sell the building. Maybe then we could hold onto a few of them.'

Mo sighed. 'You poor, soft article. You're as bad as your grandfather. All tough talking until you have to put a man's lights out.'

'Good job we've got you, Mo, to stick the knife in.'

Maeve knew it was killing the older woman. None of them had ever had to do anything like this before, and they were all struggling with it. The damn internet was just screwing the newspaper into the ground. Money was leaking out from all ends. The advertisers had too many other options, and readers were demanding instant soundbite-sized news stories on their phones – and didn't want to pay for them. And despite huge investment in digitisation, no-one, from the biggest publishing giant down, had worked out how to monetise their online editions properly. The *Chronicle's* own e-paper cost them three grand a month to produce, before you even factored in how much it lost them in non-sales of the physical paper. And it brought in zilch. Maybe five hundred on a big month.

Ten years ago, the newspaper industry was at its zenith – multi-nationals were buying up local papers across Ireland at ten million pounds a turn. Now, they'd be happy to take ten thousand back for the same title. The *Chronicle* Group had been valued at thirty million at its height, and Seán, thankfully, had the sense to cash in a few large chunks of it. But the remainder was vanishing like steam off a fresh corpse. And they would soon be surviving off savings.

***

The Derry Diocese had, as expected, refused permission for a layperson to give a personal tribute to Seán inside the cathedral. They were particularly frightened that Maeve, who decried religion as a wishing-well for old women, wouldn't stick to a script. And they couldn't risk the embarrassment in front of so many TV cameras.

Maeve had warned them she would move the funeral to Brooke Park Community Centre unless the bishop, a born conciliator, agreed to give the speech she wrote for him from the altar himself. And he did. But the oration was straight down the middle, sincere and serious, and not remotely religious.

Mo O'Sullivan, however, as the senior in-house statesperson, was always going to deliver the real eulogy to Seán. And this took place behind the locked doors of the Alexander Suite at the City Hotel, in front of a select group of friends and family, without a single politician, cleric or cop in sight. Seán himself had agreed the guest list, comprising the *Chronicle* staff, his ten-or-so blood relatives, a couple of writers he trusted, and a pair of Grammy-winning singers who had travelled to Derry under the radar to play a few songs for their old friend.

After the dinner of stew and wheaten bread – vegetarian option, 'pick out the meat' – the waiters placed a fresh bottle of Tyrconnell Ten-Year-Old Port Finish Whiskey on every table and half a dozen glasses. Water, one guest was told, would be given to Brits, of which there were none present, and pregnant women. Maeve then stood up to instruct the gathering to fill their glasses and shut their damn mouths for two minutes for Mo.

For a woman who hated public speaking, Mo wasn't a bit nervous. This was her room, her family – and most importantly of all, it was for Seán.

'*A chairde is dílse,*' she began, '*tá mo chroí fíor-bhriste inniu.* Dear friends, my heart is truly broken today. I have lost my best friend.'

She paused and took a breath. That bit had to be said. 'But I'm under strict instructions from the man above – that's Seán, by the way, not God – not to be maudlin or sad. He had almost ninety years of a great life – and he wanted us to celebrate that life today. Though personally, I think he had another good fifteen years in him. If only he'd listened to his doctor and cut down the drinking and smoking – and, of course, all that Viagra …'

Declan O'Dorrity, Seán's favourite cousin and the only living *Chronicle* shareholder apart from Maeve and Mo, slapped the table in front of him and laughed. 'I always knew it. You're a fine-looking woman, Mo.'

Mo grinned in turn. 'How do you know it was for me, Declan? According to one of the MI5 dossiers we got our hands on, I was only a beard to allow Seán maraud through Derry's gay underbelly … seducing young musicians.'

'A likely story,' came a heckle. 'It was Gaelic footballers or nothing with Seán.'

'You're right,' said Mo. 'He even kept a mouth shield in his nightstand. That's why I'm supposed to have shot him, by the way. Caught him in bed with a twenty-year-old half-back … as if Seán would look at a half-back …'

Another heckle: 'And you wouldn't have shot him in the leg, either, Mo.'

They all laughed again. There wasn't a person in the room who didn't know who had shot Seán, and it was nothing to do with Mo. Maeve banged a spoon on her empty glass to quieten the mob a little.

'Bishop McNeilly did a fine job remembering the public Seán this morning. Or rather, he remembered exactly as much as Maeve would let him. And that was the big problem with Seán – he actively didn't want to be talked about.'

This time the shout came from the reporters' table: 'Unless he scored under-par at Lisfannon. Then he'd make us clear the back page.'

Mo smiled. Seán had once told her that golf was his real beard. It let people assume he was a bored fat cat who had nothing better to do with his time than walk around Donegal fields slapping rubber balls with an iron stick. So every time he got third place in a crappy turkey trot, he would ensure it got a mention in the paper.

'He took a lot of pride in his golf, all right,' said Mo. 'Not many men of eighty are still playing off single digits. But apart from that, he completely shunned the limelight. Harry Truman – Seán met him once while he was interning for Jack – used to say: "It is amazing what you can accomplish if you don't care who gets the credit." And that became Seán's way of life. Too many of his peers became so consumed with seeking credit that they stopped doing their job. Credit became their god. And the trappings of credit – money, status and power – became goals in themselves. But doing the right thing, your duty to your family, friends, neighbours and community, became secondary.

'The time of the first ceasefire in the 1970s, the British sent Seán a note congratulating him personally on an editorial he'd written and inviting him to drinks in the newly rebuilt Dublin Embassy. Seán wrote back politely and said he hadn't written the piece, but rather it had evolved from a series of discussions he'd had with the editorial staff of the *Chronicle*. But he said if the ambassador would like to send him up the price of two dozen stout, he would ensure that the reporters and subs would all get a drink out of it.

'In fairness to the Brits, they got the point. They sent up six bottles of vintage Black Label Whisky and a set of silver measures, to make sure it could all be divvied out equally. But, Seán, the hard-headed fool, raffled off the whole lot for republican prisoners.'

***

After Mo had sat down, Dan Conway, the *Chronicle*'s head compositor, took up an empty seat beside her.

Dan had been head of the *Chronicle*'s staff union for thirty years and was a world-class pain in the nipple, a guy who would cry all day if it rained and then cry the next when it didn't. 'Misery's mother', Seán used to call him. As ever, Dan looked like someone had just defecated in his pocket then stolen his hanky.

'We'd a union meeting in Sandino's last night after we left the wake,' he said. 'McCann came along.'

McCann? This could unravel quicker than expected. 'Jesus, Dan, not here. Could you at least give us to Monday?'

'Hear me out, Mo. I'm not here to whine. Well, not any more than I normally do. We'd like to help you out.'

This was unexpected. She braced herself for the rabbit punch.

He saw her face. 'No. Really. We know what's coming down the tracks – and we'd like to put an offer to you. Six of us – including myself – are looking to retire. We've all enough pension credits in the pot and we'll forgo our lump sums until the building is sold. It might give you another couple of months. Seán was decent to us, even if he was American. I never missed a Christmas bonus in forty-three years. And when I couldn't get the mortgage on my house, he sorted out the bank for me. We couldn't let his paper fall down round you and the young girl.'

Mo hadn't cried once over the funeral but was in serious danger of starting now.

'What if we can't sell? What if the bank sells the building from under us? You'll wind up screwed.'

'Yeah. We know. But we'd hate ourselves even more if we didn't give it a go. We don't need the money at the moment. The rest of you do.'

Mo looked hard at Dan, fought the urge to hug him, and lost.

'Steady on there, Mo,' he said. 'No offence, but I prefer my women with a bit more meat on their bones. I could never go for the scrawny ones … like Seán did.'

'I never liked you from the moment I hired you, Dan. Consider yourself sacked.'

CHAPTER 9

Downstairs in the spacious lobby of the City Hotel, Ken Foreman and McCloud were drinking coffee while the twenty-strong US delegation – minus a couple of cousins who had been allowed into the Alexander Suite after-party – got themselves checked out at the front desk.

Foreman had a little iPad in front of him and, after checking his watch a couple of times, clicked open the *Chronicle*'s Facebook page.

'It's up,' he said.

McCloud read the post, which was accompanied by a picture of two men kissing, and rolled his eyes in disapproval: 'David Cunningham and his young lover had lots to talk about at Club Thumpetty-Thump last night. Didn't see the *Londonderry Leader* editor at the funeral this morning. Wonder if he had to leave his new friend to school?'

Then, just to compound the libel, a user called '*Civis Quercetum*' had commented underneath: 'I know the young fellow that Cunningham is with. He's only fifteen.'

Foreman looked at his watch again. 'Jeanie is going to take screen-grabs of the page every five minutes or so and save any further comments. The longer the post is up, the worse it'll be for them.'

McCloud winced. He really didn't like this, but leverage is leverage. 'What happens when the *Chronicle* prove it wasn't them? And they will prove it.'

Foreman nodded. 'That's the fun of this. They can try all they want to prove they didn't put it up, but they've used the picture before. About six years ago. It was taken at David's fortieth birthday, and the *Chronicle* made a whole series of snarky comments not just online but in the actual newspaper as well. He objected, of course, but the lawyers said there wasn't enough in them. There is this time, though. They're clearly suggesting the other guy is underage.'

'Will Cunningham bite?'

'Definitely. He hates Maeve worse than you hate chocolate milk. The two families always got along before. There was no rivalry for sales: one paper was for Catholic clients, the other for Protestants. Then David's father, Edward Fredrick, better known as "EF", took over the business in the mid-1960s. A bitter, twisted and damaged bit of goods, he never met a wounded animal he didn't want to finish off. He's now in a care home in Donegal somewhere; the drink wrecked his brain. David was supposed to be the compromiser after him, but there was too much poison in the water by then. Someone is going to alert him to the piece about now.'

'What do the lawyers say?'

'Even with a full apology and *mea culpa*, it could run the *Chronicle* a hundred grand, plus legal fees. Worst case, if Cunningham proves aggravated libel or repeated libel, it'll be five times that.'

'Surely their insurance will cover it?'

'Not this time. They had two nasty payouts last year and refused to stump up the new premium. It's not the only paper in these parts flying like that, either.'

'Christ, we could close them down, so?'

'It's not "we" – it's Cunningham. And he won't. He would much rather take the title off them and run both papers as a little empire. Any other country in the Western world and the *Chronicle* would have a decent chance of fighting back, but Northern Ireland has fierce libel laws – very much in favour of the offended party.'

***

As the two men stared back at the screen, the Facebook page crashed. Foreman smiled, checked quickly it wasn't a Wi-Fi issue, logged back into Facebook and discovered that the *Chronicle* page was locked.

McCloud looked at his watch: 'Six minutes. Thought we might have got a little more time, with them all being at the dinner upstairs and everything.'

Foreman shrugged, unconcerned. 'It's plenty. The page will have gotten a couple of hundred views. Plus, it'll have been copied and posted by others. And I'm sure a few screen-grabs and photos of it will appear very soon.'

'And is that enough to prove libel?'

'You'd be surprised how little you need in these parts. About twenty years ago, one of the British tabloids wrote a nasty and very untrue diatribe about a couple of guys who'd been wrongly imprisoned. And in time, they were awarded full and proper compensation of about a million pounds. The same paper had a different edition in the Republic of Ireland, which didn't have the same rant, so the lawyers believed there was no case for libel in that jurisdiction. Then a friend of the guys discovered that a newsagent on the Southern side of the border sometimes stocked the Northern version of the paper. And they were able to prove that four people in the Republic had bought the paper there, and read the diatribe. The guys then took a separate case in the South and got themselves another million pounds.'

CHAPTER 10

McCloud was lying on his bed, sleepless and sober, flicking from channel to channel when there was a knock on the door. He assumed Jeanie must have forgotten something so, he quickly stopped scratching himself and shouted 'Use your own key' across the room.

'I haven't got one,' said an older female voice. 'I'm a visitor.'

Intrigued, he got up, crossed into the anteroom of the suite and closed over the laptop that was still lit up on the bureau. Nothing else was visible. He walked quickly to the door and opened it.

Out in the hallway stood a very elegant woman, still in funeral dress, carrying a forty-ounce bottle of Black Bush.

He laughed at just how brazen they were. 'If it isn't Mo O'Sullivan. Come in.'

He fetched two glasses out of the empty minibar – empty of liquor, that is – and they sat down in armchairs either side of the coffee table. Mo immediately kicked off her heels, 'killing me', and pulled her slim legs up onto the seat underneath her as casually as if she were in her own home.

She tipped him '*Sláinte*' with her glass and grinned. 'So how has your first day been?'

He toasted her back. 'Might have just got myself a draw in the end. Had to fight really dirty to get it, though. But I'm playing against some really dirty people. I think everybody underestimated them.'

'Ah, don't be saying that, Ally. We're nothing but simple rural reporters. No match for clever city folk like you.'

He shook his head. 'I wish. That photograph of me on your front page today? It cost me my minibar.'

'No, it didn't. The booze was taken out of here before you even landed. Medical reasons, I heard. Oh, don't look so surprised. Derry is a village, and the staff here are brothers and sisters, or cousins or second cousins, of the staff at the *Chronicle*. No money changed hands, and no laws were broken.'

'Well, it cost me my quota for today, then.'

'So I heard. Why do you think I brought you the present?'

'How did you get the picture, so?'

'Off the record?'

'Okay, I'll allow it.'

'A friend of ours accidentally heard Jeanie talking on the phone and we knew when you were coming in.'

His jaw dropped three full inches. They'd been tapping the calls. They owned him before he even touched the ground.

Mo raised a finger. 'Don't worry, though, we're not going to blow her cover. Well, not if we can all stop messing around and reach an agreement.'

McCloud's buzz was just settling in, enough that he was quite starting to enjoy the chat. Boozeless, he might have been arresting her for threatening a federal officer. 'We thought we were being subtle,' he said. 'Who's going to look at a Canadian student?'

'Soon as we heard you were coming over, we did an audit of all the Yanks in the area. They're obviously the people you're going to use to help you fish or maybe hide among. We actually threw Jeanie away in our first trawl – too young, too clueless – and then we realised that's exactly who you'd want. The person we'd never see. But there's no panic. No-one knows except Maeve, myself, Tommy and, well, the friend of ours who overheard her. You'll need to rethink her cover though.'

'Why's that?'

'She spent an hour in your room last night – and another two this afternoon. Her shift-team are convinced she's a prostitute. And the manager may have to speak to her. They reckon you're far too old to be a boyfriend.'

He grimaced. 'Whatever about the picture, Mo, that hurt.'

Mo stood up and poured them both another drink – a homemade treble for McCloud, as his needs were greater, and a splash-and-a-half for herself.

'Talking of hurt,' she said, 'that stuff on Facebook today was over the line.'

'That's a bit rich coming from you, Mo. And why do you think it was me?'

'Oh, stop it. Of course it was you. You were seen playing with your iPads in the City Hotel when the whole thing was going down. Just be thankful I'm here to call a pax. Because, while we're lovely people, Ally, and the best friends you'll ever have in the world, you don't want to fall out with us.'

'I don't want to fall out with anyone, Mo. And certainly not you. I'm just a guy trying to do a job, cleanly and quickly, and then get myself the hell back to civilisation.'

'David Cunningham did not deserve what you did to him today.'

McCloud was shocked. 'You're worried about Cunningham? I thought he hated you. What's the problem?'

'David is a very good person. I hold him in high regard. And his family have been our greatest allies ever since the *Chronicle* started. Maeve, though, and David have a major battle going on dating back about half a dozen years. Mostly down to her. David's father was a gulpin of the highest order and she ...'

'Sorry, a gulpin?'

'Apologies. A prick, I believe you Yanks might say. We're not as vulgar here. Anyhow, David's father, EF, was a nasty piece of work, and he had a terrible twist against the *Chronicle*, and old Seán in particular. But David, after him, was always trying to mend fences. Then when Maeve was appointed editor, she decided to restart the old battle – trying to show her muscle – and she and David fell out.'

'So she published the photograph.'

'She did. She thought it would be funny. Forgetting, of course, all about the internet's eternal tail.'

'Not very nice.'

'No. But it wasn't us who made the comments about underage sex. That was you.'

McCloud shook his head. 'Those words were published on your forum – not mine. That makes you liable.'

She nodded. 'We can go back and forth on this all night, Ally, but the bottom line is that we are now in a bit of a mess because of you. And all we're doing is trying to help you.'

He was baffled again. This Black Bush was maybe a bit too strong for him. 'You're trying to help me?'

'Yes, we were proposing to let you see the tapes, finish your inquiry into the shooting and get the hell back to civilisation. But we're probably going to have to sort out something with David on the side, too – a small payment, or a large favour, I would imagine – and you're going to have to help us with that.'

'You're kidding?'

'It mightn't cost as much as you think – just keep the damned lawyers out of it, or we'll be doubling or trebling the money.'

McCloud had no budget approval for anything other than incidentals – which might have included payments of a few grand for information. But he also knew well that, for the first time in his field career, he was no longer in charge. Resistance was becoming more and more futile.

Mo poured McCloud another double then stuck the remainder of the bottle under her arm. She gestured to the drink on the table. 'That should get you over to sleep. You'll get some more tomorrow, if you're good. Someone will pick you up at the Ráth Mór garden in Creggan in the morning at eleven. He'll drive you to a safe location to watch the tapes. You can walk over the bridge and up the hill to Creggan or get a taxi. We want to make sure you're not being followed – we can't afford to lead anyone else to the den. Also, don't bring any recording devices, or your phone – not even a pen. If we find anything on you, the deal is off.'

He was in too deep already and, while he could have argued the point, there was a handsome-looking glass on the table waiting for him when she left. God, these people were good.

'Where's this garden?' he asked.

'Don't worry,' she said, 'just keep heading up hills, and you're sure to find it.'

CHAPTER 11

He found the Ráth Mór garden easily. It was a beautiful little plot, full of sprouting flowers, vegetables and fruit, located outside a massive enterprise park they had passed on their road to the cemetery the day before. Jeanie, whom he had now decided to keep oblivious to all but the essentials for her own safety, had pinged him a full briefing on the place before breakfast.

Ráth Mór had been the site of King James's camp during the seventeenth-century Siege of Derry. Since the 1950s, it had become an industrial hive, home at different stages to a shirt factory, a car components plant, and Derry's former biggest employer, BSR, which manufactured record players and tape recorders. During the Troubles, the site had also, briefly, resumed its old role as army camp for the British – but smart people had reclaimed it twenty years previously to build a social-enterprise park for the community, and today three hundred people worked in sixty different businesses there. All life was catered for there: you had everything from a children's crèche to secure housing for the elderly to a funeral home. There was a mall with a large grocery store and liquor store, a bakery, a hairdresser's, a publishing house, a digital centre, a furniture store and a pharmacy. No bookmaker's shop or bar, though: Creggan Enterprises, who developed and managed Ráth Mór, wanted people making money for Creggan – not taking it out of it.

Creggan Enterprises was also very conscious of its social and political responsibilities to the community. Ráth Mór was used as a private venue for talks with various parties involving the Irish and British Governments during the 1990s and it had a role in the later decommissioning process.

Ráth Mór, Jeanie advised, was a prime example of Derry's recent drive to self-help and to self-improve. People like its director, Conal McFeely, had become tired of waiting for outside approval or assistance and had decided to build first and apologise later. Most of Derry's Georgian inner city, which had been badly damaged in the IRA's economic war in the 1970s, had been rebuilt and restored in a spectacular fashion by similar people in the Inner City Trust. A new, world-acclaimed hospice had been erected in scenic riverside parkland on the Moville Road; and the young people's media complex, the Nerve Centre – which had picked up Oscar nods and BAFTA nominations for its work – had been the prime driver in Derry's successful City of Culture campaign.

As McCloud came through the gate of the garden, a tall, bearded man in his late forties, who had been reading a copy of the *Irish Times* in the little summerhouse, came out to greet him.

'I'm your driver,' he said.

They shook hands.

McCloud pointed at a new bronze sculpture shining in the sun. It featured five children dancing. 'Stunning bit of work,' he said.

'That's a new piece by Maurice Harron,' said the guide. 'It's called "Celebrate", and it ties in with the city's big cultural revival. It was supposed to go up on the main square at Ebrington, but the powers-that-be couldn't agree the planning permission, so we snatched it up – and fixed it down with four tons of concrete before they could change their minds. Maurice is the guy who designed centrepieces for half the towns in Ireland. He has a studio here. You'll see his work at the end of Craigavon Bridge – the sculpture of the two men touching hands. And he did the huge representations of the Irish musicians beside the roundabout outside Strabane.'

'The Tinnies,' said McCloud. 'I remember them well.'

The guide's cell phone erupted in his pocket – the ringtone sounding too close to *The Internationale* for McCloud's comfort.

'Yes,' he said. 'He's here now. Yep, same guy ... Tall, good-looking fella, cracking his thumbs ... Yeah, the same guy that was on the front of the paper yesterday. No, no-one with him. I'll stick him in the jeep and bring him out. Do you want me to throw a hood over his head? No, he's not too big. I'll get Declan to help me. Or we can stick him in the boot if you'd like.'

McCloud, who had been pretending not to listen, looked over in a panic, but then saw that the guide was laughing. 'You had me going,' he said.

'All part of the service. Seriously, though, I hope you haven't got a tracking device on your clothes or in your shoes – they'll find it if you do.'

McCloud shook his head. 'Absolutely not. I'm not messing with these people. I'd sooner screw with the Tonton Macoute.'

'Good, so. Let's go.'

They got into a silver, middle-aged four-by-four, which began blasting Ry Cooder as soon as the guide turned on the engine.

'How do you know these guys?' McCloud asked.

'My cousin works for the *Chronicle*,' said the guide.

They turned up the hill towards St Mary's Church.

'Where are we going?'

The guide considered this for a second before answering. 'We're going out the back roads to the manse.'

'You're making sure we're not followed?'

Again a pause. 'Yes, but it's a bit more than that. The manse is right on the border, on this side – the Northern side. But if we cut out over the border into the South, and then come back in again, if anybody's surveilling us, it quadruples the amount of paperwork they have to do. It drives them mad. Most of them pretend they lost us – truth is, they don't want the hassle.'

McCloud laughed. The natives hated the mostly invisible border with a passion, but they played it for every advantage.

'Have you seen the tapes?'

'Who, me? I'm only a driver.'

'Do you know who shot Seán Madden?'

'I'm afraid I wasn't in the city at the time. I was in Buncrana that night.'

'Have you an idea, though?'

'I could give you some totally unfounded speculation like the rest of the country, if you'd like.'

'Well could you do so, please? It might make my journey home a day or two shorter.'

The guide grinned. 'There were a few people – mostly outsiders – who didn't like Seán at all. I thought he was straight, and a really great friend to a lot of Derry people. But if you fell out with him or did something that upset him, that was it. He'd gut you. No mercy, no second chances, and he wouldn't miss you and hit the wall – you were done. He didn't do it very often – or rather, he didn't have to. But some people thought he was soft and tried to take advantage of him – and learned the hard way. He had a way of talking that was so unthreatening, so polite – almost diffident – that it made him come off innocent. And he liked to play on that a little, let people underscore him. But, of course, he knew more than any of them and, in my experience, was usually the smartest guy in the room.'

McCloud processed this for a moment in silence and took in the view. They were leaving the hill at the back of Creggan, heading towards the border and McCloud could see the ancient hill of Grianán in the near distance. He reckoned they would travel out about another two miles then start to circle back in towards Glenabbey again.

He knew he was getting nothing from his driver, but principle dictated that he had to give it a final effort. 'Great answer. And many thanks for the recap. But who shot him?'

The guide laughed. 'At the time of the shooting, there was probably at least one Irish shoot-em-up group, one British shoot-em-up group and even an American outfit who had him on their lists. So pick a number. I'm paid to drive – not solve shootings. Except, of course, unless Mo has had a heart transplant and they've given her one, I'm not even getting paid ...'

CHAPTER 12

The bunker was a fully furnished underground flat – one of three properties McCloud knew to be on site, the others being a large country manse and a small, one-storey gate lodge.

His driver dropped him at the outer gate, shook his hand and told him he'd collect him at four. McCloud automatically checked his watch: 11.35am. The older man smiled and extended his hand again. 'You'd better give me the Rolex too,' he said. 'They're only going to take it off you anyway. You'll get it back. Or a very close approximation at least.'

He went down the concrete steps into the bunker, admiring the wheelchair access they had added after Seán's first stroke just a year ago. Mo was at the front door and ushered him into the spacious living room, which was perfectly lit by four corner sunroofs.

The 50-inch TV attached to the wall above the mantelpiece was already on, and the video-feed lined up on pause.

Mo handed him a remote control. 'Just play and rewind to suit. Some of the stuff is of a dodgy enough quality, so you'll have to shuttle back and forth.'

'Is it all there?'

'God, no – do you think we're mad? This is an edited version – but it's more than you'll need. You'd spend a month watching the whole lot.'

'I want the raw footage, Mo.'

'No. It's got far too much personal data on it,' she said. 'Not happening.'

McCloud smiled at how she used 'data', the professional spy's preferred term for information. He took the zapper from her hand and sat down in a comfortable black-leather armchair. They'd even left him out a little footstool.

'How much is here now?'

'A few hours for today – it'll take you from the opening of the *Chronicle* to the 1930s or so.'

'Is this historic bit important?'

'You'll need the background. And you'll also find that our man had enemies dating back eighty years and more – as did his family.'

'Is everything on these tapes true?'

'Doubt it. Have you ever heard of the Ninety Per Cent Rule?'

Tommy Bowtie's rule of the almost perfect, but fatally holed confession. He smiled. 'I have.'

'Well, the vast, vast bulk of it is true. But there are times Seán accidentally misremembers, or his nostalgia gets the better of him, or he tries to protect people, including himself. He's also conscious of the fact that there are people who might attempt to use these tapes in the courts or wherever against their enemies, so he has deliberately told one or two quite detectable lies, to undermine his own credibility. And in case people don't pick up on the lies, well, he carefully steered me as to where they were, and made me promise that I would blow the whistle if required. So no, this memoir is not all true. But it's probably as close an approximation as you're ever liable to get. Seán believed that contemporary accounts, such as newspapers, were the only real true drafts of history. Everything after that is written by revisionists, and he would certainly have included this memoir in that category.'

They were masters of the non-answer. He tried again. 'Will they tell me who shot Seán, why he was shot and let me get home?'

She laughed at his impatience. 'Possibly yes, possibly no. And that depends entirely on you.'

It served him right for trying a three-parter. Back to basics. 'Are there any major surprises in it?'

She thought a bit more about this one. 'To you? Not many. I think you'll be a little disconcerted at how different his account is to any current narrative. Politicians, scholars and the various players today will have you believe that everything we have today – old enemies in government, yada, yada, yada – was as the result of finely tuned strategies and plans. Almost as if it were pre-ordained. Like the stuff you teach about the Peace Process in Quantico, Ally. But the way Seán tells it, most of the people were flying by the arses of their trousers and then reinventing the story when they got lucky.'

First-hand accounts of history, if they're true, are always a mess of intrigue and contradictions. That's why McCloud loved them. This could be interesting. At least they weren't giving him a hagiography. 'And if I've any questions …'

She nodded. 'You will have. Save them until tomorrow and I'll deal with them then. I'm not going to sit with you while you watch – we're going to lock you in here. We'll set aside a half-hour debriefing session every morning.'

'Will Maeve be in on that, too?'

Mo gave him a broad smile. 'Do you really think you want to meet the heir apparent? Seriously? After the mess you've just landed her in? She's going to be stuck at the office for the next week dealing with a libel writ that was hand-delivered by David Cunningham's lawyers this morning. They're looking for seven figures – or alternatively the *Chronicle* title. She's storming round our offices at the moment killing dead things and slapping reporters' heads for sport. If you want to call into the Waterloo Street office anytime soon, I'll come around afterwards with the bucket.'

He was puzzled. Must be another local custom. 'What's the bucket for?'

'To pick up your teeth and mop up your blood.'

McCloud, as he wrote in his report later, took this all under advisement, smiled and said nothing. Like most rajas and self-appointed dictators, Maeve wasn't happy at being bested.

Mo noted the silence and returned the smile. 'And besides, we really don't need Maeve. I'll be able to answer whatever's needed in more depth. I mean this respectfully, but Maeve wasn't about for most of what went on whereas I, as you can tell from my laughter lines, saw a decent chunk of Seán's campaigns. She's actually not very happy with this arrangement: she did all the interviewing, so she still regards the tapes as her private property. I don't think she'd ever release them if Seán hadn't dictated otherwise. For me, maybe it's because I'm getting older, but I think they have to be made available for posterity. Not yet, though.'

Maeve Madden, McCloud had read, was fierce, impetuous and sometimes even a little tactless, as she'd shown with the Cunningham picture. He had no doubt that Mo was keeping her away from the Feds.

'I could really do with a pen,' he said, 'if only to remember what questions to ask you.'

'You'll remember what you need to. Trust me. But no pens. If you try to record any of this in any way, we will find out, and we *will* do whatever we have to, to stop you relaying it to other people.'

He knew well she wasn't kidding. They weren't letting this out of their iron grip. 'How many days of material in all?'

'Four or five days' worth. Six, tops. It was a lot longer before we cropped it back.'

Mo checked her watch. 'I have to go. There's coffee in the pot and sandwiches and snacks in the fridge in the kitchen. In case of emergency, there's an intercom through to the manse, where the housekeeper will let you out.' She pointed to a telephone fixed to the wall.

'One final thing,' she said. She looked at him as if a little embarrassed and he thought he detected real kindness in her voice. 'Do you need a drink?'

He shook his head. 'No. I try to leave it till after six. Unless I'm bored. But I have an idea I'm not going to be.'

'That's great. If you do, let Annie know up at the house and she'll sort you out.'

CHAPTER 13

The first few minutes of the tape were devoted to the set-up. Maeve could be seen in the picture quietly getting the old man comfortable in his armchair, sorting out his notes and testing his voice levels on the clip-mic. McCloud watched it all, intrigued. She looked much younger than he expected – slender and girl-like, barely out of her teens – though she must have been twenty-seven when the film was shot. She was wearing plain blue jeans and a white T-shirt, and was sporting a light tan but not a touch of make-up. Her voice, when she spoke to Seán, was sweet and chatty, like that of a young child trying to entertain a favourite parent. For a woman who had a reputation for respecting no-one, she clearly adored this man. She combed his hair, fixed his tie and told him he was the most handsome grandfather in all of Ireland. And yet, she never once compromised his dignity, even when she had to reach inside his ear and turn up his hearing aid. And just for a second McCloud found himself wishing that she would look at him for just one moment through those self-same, beautifully kind green eyes. Before, of course, he remembered that she was the devil.

It was apparent from the opening scene that Seán Madden was just starting to decline. He would have been eighty-eight then, and while he looked no more than seventy and hadn't a liver spot in sight no matter how much he deserved one, his movements were becoming a little slow and deliberate. His face was handsome and distinguished, a cross between what Jack Kennedy might have looked like if he'd lived and the little bust of the writer Sam Beckett, just visible on the shelf behind him. He had a full thatch of once-red white hair, expertly coiffed like a visiting ambassador's, and his eyes were as clear and blue as Maeve's were clear and green. He was dressed in a white satin shirt with black onyx cufflinks and a smart red silk tie, no jacket because of the heat, tailored blue chinos with a crease that would put your eye out, and a pair of new black loafers.

'Can we hurry this up, Maeve,' he said. 'I've a tee-time at Lisfannon for six, and if I'm late we'll end up finishing by the lights of our cars again.'

'You're not allowed to drive at night, Granda, remember? That dirty rat of a doctor made you promise before he gave you back your licence.'

He laughed. 'Can you get me a driver so? I'll be coming back in the dark.'

'I'll do it myself – I might even caddy for you, if you let me drive the buggy on the course. No more than one drink in the clubhouse, though. We'll be working at this again tomorrow morning.'

'Can we make it two? My engine never starts on one turn of the key.'

'No! You can have another one when I get you home. But I'll let you pour it yourself.'

'Sold. There's a couple of gallon jars in the garage; go out and fetch me one of them in.'

She laughed and slapped him playfully on the ear. 'Are you ready?'

'Never more so.'

'Well, let's begin.'

She disappeared from the picture and re-framed the camera carefully on Seán and the table beside him.

'Okay, then,' she said. 'Seán Madden, what can you tell us about the *North West Chronicle*?'

CHAPTER 14

1912: Dublin

Most of the stories I'm going to tell you about the early days, I got from Mom, Connie Madden. I'm sure they're on the money. As a source, she was eminently reliable, a straight-shooting journalist to her core – if a little protective of me. Even to the end. As I had no father, she tried hard not to over-mother me, but often, particularly when I was younger, she did hide away the darker stuff. And I hold her all the more dear because of it. I never believed in this tough-love business, where you expose your children early to the hardships of the world to harden them up. They'll have enough suffering to deal with in the course of their lives without practising early in the home. Better to rear them to believe in happy-ever-afters and encourage them always to hope rather than despair. And if people peg them for an innocent or an idiot, at least the child has a smile on their face. Tried this myself with Little Mill, my poor, darling daughter, and then you, Maeve. Though, in retrospect, I could still have been a little softer, particularly with you. You tend to forget, Maeve, that good also exists in the world.

Anyhow, Connie was born Constance Hannon in Boston, Massachusetts, in January 1896. Her mother, my grandmother Kate O'Hara, had been a bit of a trailblazer. The daughter of immigrant greengrocers from Mayo, she'd managed to win herself a scholarship to Radcliffe in the late 1880s before upping sticks to Europe after graduation. She ended up teaching art in London for a year before coming home to Beantown to marry Granda Pat Hannon, who owned a couple of pubs and a whiskey distillery. While she was in London, Kate became very friendly with one of her students, a Sligo woman called Constance Booth – they continued to write after she came home – so Kate named my mother after her.

'And that would be Constance Markievicz?'

Yeah – Auntie Con, they all called her. She was always 'Con'; Mom was 'Connie'. It turned out one of Auntie Con's relatives had actually loaned Kate's parents the price of their passage to America a couple of decades before.

Connie grew up in Back Bay in Boston in a big Georgian house like you'd get on Merrion Square in Dublin. Her father did very well, certainly well enough to send his two daughters to college – Radcliffe like their mother – with a little left over to allow them spend some time abroad. Granny Kate was ordered by the Church to stop teaching after she'd had Connie – it was the done thing in those times. And despite the fact she was one of the strongest women I ever met and was never given to taking orders from anyone, Kate didn't challenge them. Though she always resented the hell out of them for it.

Pat Hannon was well connected in Boston. His sister Mary was married to John Fitzgerald, who was a councilman and later Mayor. 'Fitz' was also father to Rose, who went on to become mother of all the Kennedys. Pat was very involved in the Democratic Party and was a big backer of his brother-in-law. He never wanted to run for office himself, though; he always reckoned too much politics was bad for business. No point in falling out with people if you don't have to, not while there's money to be made. But for all that, he was a genuine liberal – supported women's suffrage and votes for blacks long before the papers told him to. Sent money home to the likes of the Irish Volunteers. Had a fair heart – too fair for the times that were in it, perhaps. Fought against the Church when they wouldn't let Kate work in a Catholic school. Didn't go to Mass for years and even tried to persuade Kate to teach in a non-denominational school. But that was just one step too far for Grandma.

Connie first came to Ireland in the summer of 1912, when she was just 16, to visit Auntie Con in Dublin. And that's when she first met my father Johnny.

'Tell me about Johnny – what was he doing in Dublin?'

Well, for that, I have to take you back a bit – and again, most of this I'm getting from Connie, so it may be a little sanitised. Johnny was on assignment for the *Chronicle*, which had just opened earlier that year in the spring of 1912. He'd been sent on his first big field assignment by his father, Mick, ostensibly to report British Prime Minister Herbert Asquith's trip to Dublin. But as you and I know, the *Chronicle* had little business being in the capital for the visit; it was a small regional newspaper, after all, and could easily have picked up the story from an agency correspondent. While Johnny was there, however, he was tasked with building links with John Redmond's Irish Parliamentary Party, plus the various Sinn Féin groups and the trade unions, which were active in the city.

The Redmondites had just won a major battle in the campaign for Irish Home Rule, but the Unionists, who controlled Derry and most of the north of the island, were fiercely unhappy and were promising more revenge than the Famine. Home Rule meant a Dublin government rather than a London one. So Johnny and Old Mick were out to forge some strategic friendships in the South. They set up interviews with a whole lot of the players, including one of the main Gaelic revivalists, a guy called Éamon de Valera. Johnny got on so well with him they agreed to stay in touch.

'What age was Johnny then?'

Well, as far as I'm aware, he was born in 1892, so he couldn't have been more than twenty. He didn't go to university, as you know.

'Why was that?'

Mick would have had you believe it was because of money. But looking at it objectively, the family had a decent-sized farm outside Burt and owned a pub at Birdstown, so they should have been able to afford it. Johnny was an only child, after all.

'So, what's your theory?'

It's only a theory, but I reckon it was because of Johnny's mother, Peggy.

'She died in childbirth, didn't she?'

Well, that's the story, yes. But when I checked back in church records, there was no mention of her death. Nor could I find a grave. Anywhere. Johnny's birth certificate has no maternal name on it either. And anytime I mentioned Peggy's name, everybody would go quiet. The most you would get would be, 'Oh, that was a terrible tragedy, don't be bringing it up in case you upset your grandfather.' You know how these things are yourself, Maeve.

'So, the serving girl disappeared for a couple of months, then little Johnny appeared on a basket on his daddy's doorstep?'

You've a smart mouth on you, Miss Madden. But, on the balance of what we don't know, you're almost certainly right. And this background would have ruled Johnny out for a career in the Church or teaching. So there was little point in university. From what his contemporaries at St Columb's College told me, though, he was brighter than any of them. He read non-stop – politics, histories and the classics – was a skilled debater in both English and Irish and was a great, great singer. And he was also penning speeches for local Home Rule leaders from when he was in his early teens. Journalism wasn't so much a job for him as an extension of his personality. Loved sport, too, but preferred soccer to GAA, much to the chagrin of the priests. Good looking boy, too, over six feet tall, black hair, unbothered navy-blue eyes and a smile like Valentino, according to Connie at least.

After leaving school at sixteen, Johnny did three years of an apprenticeship with the *Irish News*, the main Belfast Home Rule paper – still is, of course – before his father convinced him to come back to Derry and they'd set up the *Chronicle*. Not that Mick had to push too hard. While the *Irish News* people were very good to Johnny, Belfast was a minefield of sectarianism in those days, and you wouldn't have reared a rat in it. That tallied with my own experience of the place, too, when I was at Queen's in the forties – it was a humourless, industrial town riddled with bitter and unforgiving people. I hated being there. Even when people were trying to be kind to you, you were forever watching over their shoulder for the other guy with the knife. Got a lot better in recent years, though; the younger generations are a whole lot smarter. Derry was always gentler, too gentle maybe. It was a small enough town that everybody remained mostly civil to one another. Because they had to – that, and we didn't want to end up like Belfast.

'Back to Dublin ...'

Yes. When Johnny got the chance to go to Dublin to see Asquith in action, he leapt at it. You've got to remember that Asquith was a heroic figure among Irish Nationalists back then. He'd just faced down Churchill and the Tories to bring in Home Rule. And there was a real sense that this visit was a historic step in Ireland's long road to freedom. Of course, as you know, everything went to hell in a handcart later that same year when James Craig rolled out his Ulster Covenant to keep his land British and then went and fired up his Unionist militia. But for a few short months in 1912, there were real possibilities – and it was in that brief window that Johnny travelled to Dublin.

Asquith's visit, however, would in today's terms be termed a PR disaster. The prime minister was followed over from London by a group of suffragette leaders, who weren't at all happy that he had actively opposed their cause. He'd even changed the law at one stage to enfranchise more men – at the expense of women. For all that, he always fancied himself as a ladies man. You wouldn't have left him alone in a room with a pre-boned, rib-eye steak, as Connie would have said. And, on the first evening of his visit, he was being driven along Harcourt Street in a carriage with Redmond when he told the hack to slow down so he could check out a group of young women waving from the pavement. Turns out they were suffragettes, however, and one of them fired a hatchet through the open window, which sailed past Asquith's head and nearly took the arm off Redmond.

I'd just note at this point that my mother strongly denies being the thrower – primarily on the grounds that she would have got him between the eyes and thus changed the course of world history forever. And besides, she was never arrested – nor was Auntie Con.

'You're joking. They were there?'

I have no evidence of that. The following night, Asquith was recovered enough to give a talk on Home Rule at the Theatre Royal, and my father got in good and early to get himself a decent seat by an aisle, near the front of the stalls. He wasn't seated more than a minute or two before a tall and slim, beautiful young woman with copper-coloured hair, racing-green eyes and pearl-white skin sat down in the seat beside him and smiled like she'd known him all her life. By all accounts, he was just about to turn on the charm when there was a loud crash behind them. They looked back to see a small fire in an empty, reserved section, where it appeared that a lighted chair had been flung down from the balcony. Then, up on the balcony, the projection box suddenly burst into flames, and there was shouting and screaming and smoke everywhere.

Cops started streaming into every aisle, and the order went out to round up the blasted suffragettes.

The girl put her hand inside her coat and was about to take what may have been a bottle of petrol out of her pocket just as a cop started closing in on their row. Johnny motioned his head 'no', put his hand on top of hers as casually as if they'd been courting for years, then said to her he'd better get her home or her mother would be worried sick. The cop, who hadn't seen the bottle, heard this, tipped his cap and waved the young couple out towards the street.

CHAPTER 15

1912–1917

The tape resumes with Maeve's voice heard off camera.
'I take it Connie was so pleased with Johnny saving her fine American ass that it was love at first sight?'

Au contraire, clever clogs. She felt totally humiliated and very angry. Or at least she claimed to be. As he guided her quickly along Wood Quay and back into the city centre, she looked back to see no police were following them, took her hand from his and slapped him soundly in the mouth with it. 'How dare you? I don't need no damn man to look after me.' It was the first time he realised that she was American.

'In which case, it sounds like he'd a lot of work to do?'

Not really. Strange as it seems, she told me many years afterwards that neither she nor Johnny felt they had any control over what happened inside the theatre. And while Mom never had any real religion, or believed much in fate, she said it was almost like they were being compelled to take part in a script, pre-written by forces much bigger than either of them. It was as if they were suddenly both aware of the huge confluence of incidences and co-incidences that had brought them both, strangers, to that specific spot at that specific time in history. She was transfixed. And so was he.

'So what did Auntie Con say?'

Here's the thing. Young Connie was really worried that she'd let everyone down by not playing her part. She was supposed to sprinkle her petrol over a few seats and set it alight. And yes, that is the first of about a thousand felonies you are liable to hear about over the next few weeks. But when they made it back to Con's house, which was busier than Times Square, they discovered that, rather than everyone being angry, there was huge relief that she'd gotten away.

Half a dozen of the protestors had been scooped up – mostly the English suffragettes, from what I remember – and the courts threw the book at them. Pinned the hatchet-throwing incident on them, too. They all got about five years each. But Auntie Con hadn't even known her favourite godchild was in the shooting party until it was too late to stop her, and she'd spent the past two hours worried sick she was going to have to cable her best friend in America with the worst of all shaggy-dog stories.

Of course, they all blamed Johnny for not letting Connie martyr herself and gave him a hard time for interfering – idiot Northerner sticking his nose in things he knew nothing about. But that was about saving young Connie's face.

Johnny took his shellacking with good grace – and even sang the company a set of Gilbert and Sullivan songs for his supper. Apparently, he brought the house down by improvising on *A Policeman's Lot Is Not A Happy One*. He changed one verse to [*sings*]: 'When the enterprising arsonist's not burning/When the suffragette's not occupied in crimes/She loves to watch Herb Asquith's coach returning/And listen to the Derryman make rhymes.' They even sang it at Mom's funeral, God love her. Connie got in on the act, too – as you know, she'd a wild streak herself – by rededicating her version of *Susanna* to Johnny, telling him: 'I come from Boston City with a banjo on my knee/And I'm going to Londonderry, a halfwit there to see.'

So for the rest of the night, Johnny kept pouring it on, ignoring all her insults, knowing well they weren't real. He even threw in a couple of Irish ballads to keep the Sinn Féiners happy. A thick hide will take you a long way in life. And by the time the evening was over, Auntie Con just loved him. And more importantly, so did Connie.

Johnny had never shown much interest in women up to that point. Five years in the junior seminary that was St Columb's had left him with some serious misconceptions about the fairer sex. But with Connie, their coming together was the most natural thing in the world. They exchanged addresses, promised to write every week, and he arranged to visit her in New England in five years' time, as soon as she was finished college, and take her back to Ireland.

'Hold on, you're telling me they got engaged on their first date – even though they weren't going to see one another for five years?'

Engaged is maybe a bit strong. But they just knew instantly and instinctively they would always be together. As did everyone else who saw them that night. They were then, and would always be, a couple. Little point in fighting it. It was about three in the morning when Auntie Con chased Johnny back to his hotel – and told him in future he would stay with herself and Casimir any time he was in Dublin. He was now family.

CHAPTER 16

The next five years flew by in a hurricane of social and political change. In 1913, Johnny took over as editor of the *Chronicle*, to allow Mick to concentrate on drinking his pub dry, and the paper was never busier. In the Home pages, Johnny issued warning after warning about the rise of the Ulster Volunteers, and fiercely opposed plans to placate the Unionists by excluding the six Northern counties from Home Rule. Dublin was selling us out even then. He encouraged all good men – and women – to join the Irish Volunteers to match the Unionist threat. And, of course, he was furious when all Home Rule proposals were shelved because of the outbreak of the Great War. He didn't believe for a minute Redmond's claims that the British would simply hand over power as soon as the fighting was over.

Abroad, he railed against the looming war in Europe, predicting that greed and imperialism would ruin the continent. He opposed conscription in Ireland and disagreed loudly that the Irish Volunteers should support the British regiments.

The *Chronicle*, as was traditional with newspapers then, was more radical than its audience, but as Old Mick would say, a bit of controversy is necessary for sales. And the paper's numbers went up and up, to the point where they launched a new Donegal edition, based in Ballybofey.

Naturally, as a newspaper editor, Johnny was also very much involved with the local political scene. And while Derry Corporation was Unionist controlled, there was a strong Protestant Liberal tradition in the city that backed Home Rule. At the time, there were thirty-three MPs in the House of Commons from across the nine counties of Ulster, the Unionists holding a razor-thin seventeen to sixteen majority of these. But when a by-election was called in Londonderry City, after the Unionist incumbent was elevated to the House of Lords on the death of his father, Johnny threw his weight behind the Liberal candidate, a Protestant shirt-factory owner called David Hogg. Hogg won by just a handful of votes over the outraged Unionist candidate, helped in no small part by Johnny's election slogan: 'Vote for Hogg, the Catholic Prod.' That victory gave the Liberals a majority in Ulster and was a major bat in the eye for Carson.

When Hogg died the following year, the Unionists wanted another election, but Johnny and others demanded a co-option, so Jim Dougherty, a Liberal academic who'd taught at Magee College, was appointed. And he served the city until the Sinn Féiners took the seat at the end of the war.

In 1916, Mick talked Johnny out of travelling to Dublin for the Rising, on the grounds that the provinces needed strong leadership, too. Johnny contented himself with setting up a connection between local IRA chief Paddy Hegarty and his old friend the schoolteacher Éamon de Valera. This allowed republicans to transport arms and ammunition smuggled out of the British Army's Ebrington Barracks – by Irish-born soldiers, naturally – directly to the streets of Dublin. I'm not sure who was the inside connection at the barracks, but Old Mick used to complain that the poet-soldier Frank Ledwidge, who regretted taking the King's Shilling, was forever hanging about the office. Frank was usually looking to get some poem or other published, but, of course, there's no money in poetry, and fewer readers. But in hindsight, he may well have been there for a whole other reason entirely.

'Was Johnny disappointed not to see direct action?'

Definitely. He had a real sense of adventure, no doubt. But as it happened, the Derry contingent heading for the Rising was stood down at the last minute by Eoin MacNeill. So he couldn't have gone anyway.

There are some really insightful accounts of this period in Johnny's letters to Connie. Letters, like newspapers, are the first draft of history and are often a lot more accurate than the revised version – like the one I'm telling you now. The pair wrote faithfully every Saturday night and at least one other time during the week, though it could be anywhere between a month and six months before the letters landed, often out of sync.

Connie completed High School and began a degree in History at Radcliffe. With the strong support of her father and uncle, she lobbied the Democratic Party to introduce the vote for women. And by 1916, the year before her graduation, the party had endorsed suffrage on a state-by-state basis. It wasn't enough, though she had high hopes for President Wilson.

She told Johnny all about her sister, my Aunt Mary, who was five years younger than her and pretty as a summer day. Mary was going to be a doctor, no doubt about it. She used to take the mice out of the traps and borrow Kate's kitchen knives to see what they were made of. The time she found a little set of baby mice inside one, Connie chucked up her dinner into the sink. And the next day, Connie made Kate buy a whole new set of knives. But as you know, Mary went on to become the first-ever female surgeon at Derry's County Hospital.

Connie wrote about the rise of the ATS – the American Temperance Society – and how a bunch of prissy old bible-rustlers were trying to put her poor, hard-working father out of business. Her uncle Fitz, and his new son-in-law, Joe Kennedy, were doing all they could to stop them, but they were up against it. Prohibition was coming down the tracks like a shooting train, and the Irish would all have to move to Canada.

Johnny advised her by return that her father could maybe purchase himself a few tons of potatoes, and a bit of remote farmland, and start making his own juice, like Mick had done when things got tight. Add a bit of tea to colour it, and tell them it's whiskey. And no, I have no evidence that the fifteen acres at Cape Cod were ever used for anything of the sort.

From time to time, Connie would let the mask slip and tell him she was tired waiting the full five years, and that he should come and get her sooner. And that she missed him and maybe even loved him. Stuff her degree. So he would write back and tell her he maybe loved her, too – but that if she really didn't need no damn man to look after her, she'd need to get herself qualified.

But they were both impatient. And towards the end of 1916, Johnny coerced Mick into resuming the editor's chair for three months, to allow him to head off to America to collect Connie in the New Year.

'How did she feel about this – him carrying her off to the old homestead in the West, like he was John Wayne in *The Quiet Man*? Not very feminist of her.'

Ah, you're getting ahead of yourself. Hang on a tick. In early January 1917, Johnny headed off to Liverpool to catch a liner to America. There was no direct route to America out of Derry during the war. He was nervous as a kitten on the trip across the Irish Sea; he'd never travelled on the open sea before, and he'd seen all the newsreels about the Titanic. But by the time he got to Britain, he was well mended. So when he got on the big liner at Liverpool, he threw himself on the berth in his little Second Class cabin and began to sleep the sleep of the just. 'Course, the huge feed of porter and crubeens he got dockside wouldn't have done him any harm, either.

'Oh, I know this story.'

Steady yourself; it's me that's telling it. Johnny slept like a top but was awakened seven or eight hours later by the biggest bang he'd ever heard. All the lights were out, the air was full of smoke, the horn was blaring and the ship was starting to lilt from side to side. Then, boom, another one. The liner, the SS *Laurentic*, had hit two mines at the mouth of Lough Swilly, not twenty miles from Derry, and was sinking like a stone. Johnny ran to the deck and got his bearings quickly. He was never putting himself onto a lifeboat – not while there was another passenger alive on board. So he took his bearings, figured that Rathmullan was the closer of the two beaches and pitched himself into the water. It was a full two miles away in the middle of winter. But again, he never doubted he would do it. He'd swum in the lough many times and knew well that there were men who'd made it right across. He was helped by the fact that the water at the Swilly is always warm because of the Gulf Stream coming up from the West Indies. But he made it to shore within an hour. More than 350 others died, and every one of the other 120 or so that survived came in on a lifeboat.

'What about the gold?'

Yeah, it's true. The *Laurentic* was carrying about forty-five tons of gold on the trip – the Brits were sending it to Canada to buy weapons for the war. Most of it was recovered over the next seven years, but about half a ton was never accounted for. And no, Johnny did not manage to stow a couple of bars into his breeches before he jumped. Connie used to tell that story to make believe he was mean. But he would have given you the shirt of his back. Indeed, we later learned his ticket on the *Laurentic* covered the price of a lifeboat seat. Old Mick used to say his son was the most generous man there ever was.

Johnny got himself a lift back to Derry the next morning, much to the delight of the *Chronicle* staff, who'd heard the news and presumed him dead. Not so his father, though. He knew his son was still alive, and still had miles to go.

In a break with tradition, Johnny composed a telegraph to Connie, in case she would read the reports and worry. It read: 'Trip postponed due to unforeseen circumstances. Have to rebook. Will be with you within the month. Will explain all in letter to follow. Love forever. J.'

Connie was not impressed. The blood rose up in her and she convinced herself he was blowing her off. Within an hour, she had replied: 'Don't trouble yourself. I told you a hundred times; I don't need no damn man to look after me. CH.'

Johnny knew well she hadn't put it all together yet and filed away the flare-up for future reference. And sure enough, within a few hours, she'd heard the news and sent a second telegraph. 'Hope you've dried off. Stay where you are. I'll come to you. You're obviously a danger to shipping. Will be with you for Easter, and for good. I love you. Connie.'

CHAPTER 17

1917–1922

Connie landed in Derry port at the end of March 1917, just a week before America declared war on Germany. She moved into lodgings with a cousin of Mick's on Great James Street and got herself hired as a reporter at the *Chronicle*'s offices on Waterloo Street. The Church tried to tell Johnny that this was 'inappropriate' work for a woman and warned that there might be a delay in getting her marriage banns cleared from Boston. A standoff developed, until Mick told Monsignor McKinley that he would march the young couple up to St Columb's Cathedral and convert them to Protestantism if they weren't married by June. The monsignor knew what he was dealing with and ended up officiating at a 'proper' Catholic ceremony himself, although he told Mick it was only to prevent 'another Madden bastard' from coming into the world. There's a picture of the pair of them on their wedding day upstairs in my study; you'll have seen it many times. They're so stylish they look like they've just stepped out of a Renoir painting.

They honeymooned in Dublin, staying with Auntie Con, who had recently been released in an amnesty after serving a stretch at His Majesty's Pleasure in England. And they spent their week renewing old connections and catching up on the news of the campaign. Independence supporters were planning to run candidates across Ireland in the next British general election – including in the North. Neither Johnny nor Connie was too excited at the plans to stand the Belfast academic Eoin MacNeill in Derry City – he was the dry old stick who had stood down the Volunteers heading for the Rising. But they were never going to get Dev or Collins, and Con had been picked to run in Dublin, so they sucked it up. Dev was impressed by the growing success of the *Chronicle* and spent hours talking to Johnny and Connie about the need for more pro-independence propaganda, until Auntie Con gently led the 'Long Fella' away.

Back home, the happy couple – and by all accounts they were supremely happy – managed to buy a three-storey merchant house on De Burgh Terrace with a long garden full of cherry trees, right beside Brooke Park. Alfie Cunningham, the editor of the *Londonderry Leader* and a great friend of Mick's, was registered on the paperwork as the nominal owner, because that was the way things had to be done. Connie didn't want to have children immediately – a decision she later regretted – as she needed to get some newspaper experience. Plus, she really wanted Johnny to meet her family first. Johnny, who'd grown up as an only child and was looking forward to a bit of noise, was a little miffed. But Connie had been well advised by her friends in the National Birth Control League in Boston, so he was able to live with it. And besides, it had the added bonus of ticking off the Church. Still, it goes to show that none of us was any good at big families. Maybe you, Maeve.

***

As a leading military port, Derry prospered in the war, if you can call the deaths of a thousand of the city's young men prosperity. And, of course, all the false promises about Home Rule were about to come back and bite the British the minute the Irish Volunteers got back home.

At the end of 1918, the Great War ended, and our next one started. In December, the British general election saw Sinn Féin take three quarters of the seats in Ireland – including one in Londonderry City for MacNeill, who squeaked home over the Unionist Bobby Anderson.

Johnny and Connie had long been of the belief that Ulster would be sacrificed in a heartbeat if the other three provinces were guaranteed their freedom. There was little advantage for the British in fighting to hold on to patently hostile territory in the South, but the Protestant North was a different story. They also knew that the Unionists would have few problems handling a weak and prevaricating Sinn Féiner like MacNeill. He wasn't strong enough for Derry. And so it proved. A couple of years later, the Unionists simply redrew the boundaries in the city to gerrymander a safe new majority for themselves, and MacNeill scurried back South.

Shortly after Dev broke out of jail in 1919, he telegraphed Johnny in Derry and asked if he fancied a special assignment. He was proposing to go to America for a few months to seek support for the new all-Ireland government and wanted a press officer to accompany him on the tour. Johnny accepted on condition that Connie could join them and, after some handwringing about the cost, Dev agreed – though Mick was to meet the price of Connie's passage.

It was, Connie said later, a honeymoon in a million. They even managed to negotiate themselves a month in Boston with the Hannons, after Uncle Fitz and Joe Kennedy organised a very lucrative series of fundraisers for the cause. The Hannon family loved Johnny: in the evenings he would play piano and sang operetta to Kate and Mary; during the day, he and Connie helped Pat prepare for the onslaught of Prohibition.

Connie arranged to stay on in Boston while Johnny went off with the circus on the rest of the tour. But they were able to meet regularly, apart from when Dev fell out with Irish-American politicians and Johnny had to go out and pour the salve. That was the hardest part of the job, apparently – that and being civil to all the bloody clergy Dev insisted on meeting.

The tour, while it raised a phenomenal amount of money, lasted longer than expected – over a year. And towards the end of 1920, both Johnny and Connie were itching to get back to Ireland. There were three reasons: firstly, Dev had blown it by backing the wrong horse in the presidential election; secondly, they were very concerned about how the war for independence was being lost in the North; and thirdly, and most importantly, they knew it was time to start their family.

**

They returned just in time to see Westminster ratify the 1920 Government of Ireland Act, which gave Northern Ireland its own Protestant parliament in Belfast to insulate it from the Southern Home Rulers. The act wound up consolidating Unionist control in the North for fifty years. And despite MacNeill's weak efforts to negotiate a better border for Nationalists at the Boundary Commission a few years later, Derry remained part of the new state, cut off from its Donegal hinterland and ultimately under British rule.

Sensing things going their way, hardline Unionists and ex-army personnel in Derry set about teaching the rebel Fenians exactly who was in charge. Supported by serving RIC police officers, they attempted a pogrom of the Long Tower and St Columb's College area of the city but got more than they bargained for when the IRA began shooting back. In all, eighteen people were killed and hundreds injured in ten days of fighting.

Connie and Johnny were in America when the worst of the trouble took place, but Mick kept them up to speed with what was happening. In a bid to keep a lid on things, the RIC attempted to ban the sale of the *Chronicle* for a month. But Mick simply moved operations to the Donegal offices at Ballybofey, then got gangs of youngsters to sell the paper around the Derry streets. It was a move that would be repeated several times in the ensuing decades.

The Unionists retaliated by putting out every window in the *Chronicle*'s Derry HQ and would have done worse had the *Londonderry Leader*, as a matter of conscience, not threatened to publish the name of every Protestant rioter its reporters could identify.

Mick had kept the *Chronicle* on a steady course. He never regarded it as his business, always Johnny's – or rather Johnny and Connie's. But he was tiring of life in the town and wanted to get back to his pub at Drumhaggart in Donegal, just five miles away as the crow flies, but light years away in terms of peace and quiet. And so, Johnny and Connie were barely ten minutes back at their Waterloo Street desks before he told them that Connie was being appointed deputy editor and that he himself was retiring. Little did Mick know then that it would be another thirty years before he could retire and mean it for real.

CHAPTER 18

The *Chronicle* had already established itself as diametrically opposed to the partition of the island long before the Treaty of 1921 formally ceded control of the North to the Unionists. Every Derry Catholic knew that Belfast, without the moderating influence of Dublin or even London, was too sectarian, and too preoccupied with Orange supremacy, to govern fairly. Even if Collins did say it was only a stepping-stone and that he personally would make the whole thing unworkable.

The *Chronicle* began openly supporting the anti-Treaty campaign and was threatened with another ban. But we had a new ally. Thanks to the introduction of the Proportional Representation voting system to Ireland in 1919, Derry Corporation had managed to elect its first Catholic mayor in three hundred years, the solicitor Hugh O'Doherty. He protected the *Chronicle* from Unionist ire and refused the motion of censure. A short time after O'Doherty's election, Johnny travelled to Dublin with him to meet Dev and tell him the Treaty would not do at all – and that Derry would not be excluded from the rest of Ireland. But they got the sense that Dev was trying to keep too many people happy and was turning lukewarm.

Mick's bar in Drumhaggart became a bolthole for the new anti-Treaty campaigners – including a group of anti-Collins IRA men who, if things went sour, were planning to form a guerrilla column under the leadership of the socialist writer Peadar O'Donnell. They'd regularly train in the field behind the pub and sleep in the stables at the back. Johnny would cycle out there most evenings to hear the gossip from the campaign and occasionally feed some news back down the line. Connie was worried that her husband would wreck himself on the roads – the only speed he knew was full-pelt – so she insisted he learned to drive the company's new delivery van.

As 1922 began, all eyes in the North West were focused on the proposed execution of three IRA men at Derry Jail. In a bid to shore up his commitment to the North, Collins himself sent a snatch squad to rescue them. They were disguised as Monaghan Gaelic footballers, heading to the city for the Ulster

Championship, but they were spotted by a keen-eyed RIC man, arrested and thrown in prison. This sparked even further anger among republicans, who reciprocated by seizing forty Unionists from their farms along the border. Again, this was at the instigation of Michael Collins.

The situation deteriorated rapidly, despite a reprieve for the men on death row in Derry, and, on 11 February, four RIC men were shot dead by the IRA in a bloodbath at Clones train station. An informer told the police that one of the shooters was from East Donegal, and the RIC quickly set out to even the score. The Chronicle's offices in Ballybofey were burned to the ground that same evening by a group of masked men, all wearing policemen's boots.

Shortly afterwards, Johnny got a telephone call at the Derry office to get down to Ballybofey to see what he could salvage and he was searching through the front desk for the van's starting handle when the telephone rang again. It was the bishop's secretary ringing from St Eugene's Cathedral to tell him that an RIC attack team was on its way to his father's pub in Drumhaggart.

His father had no phone, so Johnny leapt into the van. Connie, who could use the starting handle better than he, went out to help him. As ever, she told him she loved him and then instructed him to hurry back for his supper, as she was making a surprise for him. Johnny tore off north out of the city towards Muff. Just before the village, he took the sharp left up towards Drumhaggart and started racing towards the pub. With a bit of luck, he might be able to beat the police to the punch.

With just four hundred yards to go, however, Johnny's van hit a hole in the road, hurtled into a ditch and overturned. Johnny's neck was snapped in two on the impact. Mick, who was cleaning tables in the lounge, heard the crash outside and somehow knew immediately. And the RIC raid never transpired.

Johnny's surprise supper – a silver platter with a little pair of baby's bootees, in the American tradition – sat on the locker beside his coffin throughout the wake.

When the three days were up and Johnny's body had been returned to the ground, Connie announced she'd had enough of this pit of hell for good and was shipping back to America.

CHAPTER 19

1922–1923

The tape resumes with Maeve's voice heard off camera.

'So who was the informer who started all this? The guy who told the cops that it was a Donegal man who had shot up the Clones train – and what did they do with him?'

Straight to the chase. I love that about you, Maeve. You're a girl after my own heart. But, as you know, the truth is never simple. First thing you have to remember is the chaos of those couple of months in Ireland: no-one was entirely sure who was acting for whom.

Dev had been outvoted by the pro-Treaty supporters – the people who could live with the border – that January. And, unable to stomach partition, he had resigned as president of the new Irish parliament, pretty much leaving Collins in charge. But Dev had no army of his own yet, and full-on civil war was still about six months down the line.

Collins, as I said, was still trying to show his allegiance to the North so was sending in his IRA squads to wreck the establishment of the border. And from everything we know about him, he was genuine. After Collins was gone and the Civil War ended, the border was a *fait accompli*. The North was an embarrassment – a lost battle that no-one wanted to talk about.

'Enough of the *Four Green Fields*. Who set up your father?'

It turns out they got the man the same night Johnny died. A guy called Pius McGillicuddy, from Lenamore, the next townland to Drumhaggart, walked into Mick's bar and confessed.

'So, I take it he was executed?'

'No … it was a lot more complicated than that. McGillicuddy, who was known as 'Old Dog', despite the fact he couldn't have been twenty, was a committed O'Donnell man – totally opposed to the Treaty. He was part of the new flying column, preparing to fight against the 'official' pro-Treaty forces.

Old Dog and his comrades didn't accept the Collins contingent's sincerity; they believed that once the ink had dried on partition it was there for all time. So they had been working on a plan to destroy Collins's base in East Donegal, by getting the RIC from the North to roust them out, and thus do their dirty work for them. This would then leave the territory clear for the fledgling anti-Treaty forces.

Immediately after word came in about the bloodbath in Monaghan, Old Dog passed the address of the main Collins command house in Killygordon to the RIC and told them it was the home of one of the Clones gunmen. The idea was that the police would dive in and shoot all before them, and leave Collins without a functioning unit in the North West.

The trouble with this was Old Dog didn't count on the RIC having a few tricks of their own. They knew there was a risk of a firefight if they drove into Killygordon, so instead their unit headed on to Ballybofey, a few miles down the road, to burn down the much more vulnerable *Chronicle* building – and put the IRA's chief Donegal cheerleaders out of action.

'It wasn't very nice of Old Dog to try and wipe out his old comrades in Killygordon, was it?'

You're right. In fact, two of his own cousins would have been in the command house. But again, these were not very nice times. And a lot worse was going to happen over the year to come.

'So, what about Mick's bar?'

As soon as he heard the Ballybofey offices were hit, Old Dog was afraid the RIC would head for another soft target like Drumhaggart – he knew well the coppers wouldn't touch the *Chronicle*'s Derry offices for fear of reprisals. So he got a messenger to call into the cathedral to pass on a warning. And then poor Johnny died trying to save the day.

Old Mick had the final say. O'Donnell would have taken Old Dog out to the stable and shot him in the blink of an eye. And Old Dog wouldn't have lifted a hand to stop it, either. He knew he was responsible for the entire disaster – and would have been equally happy to die as to have to live with it.

'So, what did they do with him?'

Exile for life. Mick told the IRA, both groups, the last thing that day needed was another Irish body. O'Donnell got Old Dog working passage on a boat to New York and ordered him to disappear forever as soon as he got there.

'So, he was never seen again? Are you sure they just didn't stick him in a bog somewhere?'

'No. Mick insisted on putting Old Dog on the boat himself and gave him money to telegraph him as soon as he'd made it across safely. And actually, he was seen again, or at least we're almost sure it was him, in Philadelphia in the early 1930s. Wearing a cop's uniform, of all things. It was an old Irregular from the pub, who'd emigrated to get work, spotted him. Shouted across to him, 'Hey, Old Dog, you learning new tricks?' Old Dog flinched at first, then put his finger to his lips, like you'd hush a child, and walked away.

His mother never got over the son's rapid departure, though, and threatened all sorts of retribution on Mick and the *Chronicle* unto the fifth generation. One of the brothers, Terry McGillicuddy, even tried to put a dummy memoriam notice for Mick in the *Londonderry Leader* a few months later, but Alfie Cunningham caught him and threw him out. And eventually, they all calmed down – probably around the same time they started getting money back from Old Dog in America.

'What happened at Johnny's funeral?'

We don't know too much about it, to be honest. Connie never spoke about it, and Mick was always very cagey about it, too. Old Father McBlair, who had travelled with Johnny and the mayor to meet Dev the previous autumn, sermonised loudly against the indifference of Dublin and the dire danger of unchecked Belfast rule. But, according to the *Chronicle's* own report, which is the only historical account of the ceremony, his tone was that of loss and hopelessness rather than that of a rallying call.

The family insisted on no military or church trappings at the cathedral. Johnny was first and foremost an independent civilian. Nor was there an oration at the City Cemetery, despite several offers. Prior to the burial, the corpse had actually been transferred for a night to Mick's bar in Donegal so that several prominent friends could pay their respects without alerting the new Northern authorities and starting another shooting match. But when Dev suggested he might put a Tricolour on the coffin, Mick gently told him that, if it was all right by him, he would prefer not, as Dev's current Ireland was quite different from the one Johnny had hoped to see. Ultimately, the Madden family, like the rest of the North West, had worked out they were being left on their own when it mattered most.

***

The week after the funeral, Connie travelled back to Dublin with Auntie Con before heading on to Cork, from where she embarked to New York. She resisted attempts by both pro- and anti-Treaty campaigners to escort her home.

Mick re-installed himself as editor at the *Chronicle* and, with no great enthusiasm, continued his son's work.

He tried contacting Connie in Boston every week or so to check on the pregnancy by telegraph, and even by telephone, after the Hannons got one installed at home. But she refused to hear him. Kate and Mary would brief him a little when she wasn't about. Though there was never much to say. Pat was too grief-stricken at his daughter's loss to speak.

***

Towards the end of the summer, a little over six months after Johnny's death and just three hours after Michael Collins was killed in Béal na Bláth, I came kicking and screaming into the world at Back Bay, and changed everything.

Mary, who was acting as midwife, said to Connie: 'Enough feeling sorry for yourself, dear, you have a son to raise. It's time to get on with it.' I was immediately called Johnny, after my father, but after three attempts, Connie couldn't get the name out, so Pat quickly Gaelicised it to 'Seán', and it's been Seán ever since.

Christenings in those days were a lot lower key than they are today; they were private ceremonies rather than showcase events. So the following night, Mary simply wheeled me down to the Holy Cross Cathedral on Washington Street and the priest there did the formalities. Mary was godmother; I had no godfather – at least at that stage. Dev would later claim it was himself ... but only when it suited him.

By all accounts, I was a handful as an infant: I only slept during daylight hours and only smiled at women. But on the plus side, I kept Connie's mind occupied. She always swore she could hear Johnny's voice in my cries, so she was happy when I was noisy and relieved when I wasn't. As she slowly started to recover, she was astonished to discover that she really missed Derry. Mick and the close-knit *Chronicle* staff had become a second family to her – and then there was the bi-weekly adrenalin rush of producing a newspaper. Her life in Boston was serene but ultimately a little boring. And she made it abundantly clear to Uncle Fitz, in language not normally used by women on either side of the Atlantic, that she wasn't interested in entertaining any new suitors, no matter how high they were likely to ascend in politics.

The week of Johnny's first anniversary, Mick telephoned Mary to check how Connie was doing and was surprised when she picked up the receiver herself.

'I'm thinking of selling up,' he told her. 'I haven't the heart for it any more. It's been a year.'

It was, of course, a test. Kate had spotted her daughter needed to be fulfilling her purpose and had written to advise Mick that it was time to shake the tree.

A few weeks after the phone call, Mick wrote to Connie telling her that the Cunninghams had offered him a decent price for the title as a going concern and would retain about half the employees. He said he would send Connie over the full proceeds of the sale to pay for young Seán's education. And, maybe in a few years, the young fella could come and visit his Irish grandfather, when he got up a bit. But not to leave it too long, just in case. He was also going to ask Alfie Cunningham to sell Johnny and Connie's home beside the park, and would send on the equity.

It was, as he admitted later, exactly the right amount of guilt and about the same again more. Connie laughed for the first time in months as she translated the letter for her mother. 'If you don't come back to me, Connie, I'll be slinging fifteen of my staff out in the street and putting my paper in the hands of the Protestants. But don't worry, I'll send you all my money.'

The one sticking point was Seán. Everything Connie was hearing and reading told her Ireland was still too wild to be bringing a child there. Her parents knew it as well. The pro-Treaty forces, backed by the Church, were winning the battle in the South while the Unionists were already starting to crush all resistance to their new state in the North. So after a family conference, attended by Uncle Fitz, Connie agreed to leave Seán in Boston, with Mary as his legal guardian, until things got quieter.

The passage was booked, and on 1 June 1923, one week after the anti-Treaty forces formally surrendered, the newly appointed editor of the *North West Chronicle*, Mrs Constance Hannon Madden, set sail again for Ireland.

CHAPTER 20

1923–1928: Boston

It's fair to say that I spent most of the first twenty years of my life as a professional smuggler. Boston, Derry, St Columb's, Queen's – I was generally the guy who could get things no-one else could. I make absolutely no apologies for this. Smuggling is a basic human right. Why should people who live on one side of an arbitrary line be refused entitlements and privileges that people on the other side of the line can enjoy? If you live your life well, and you and your family work hard, you should be allowed to unwind with a glass of wine at the end of the day, whether you're from Montreal or Maine. And you certainly shouldn't be denied it just because some never-laid holy-roller waltzes in and starts singing hymns in the local saloon.

Likewise in Ireland, why should Mick be allowed to serve fresh butter, half an inch thick on the sandwiches at his pub in Drumhaggart, when five miles up the road in Derry we're being forced to eat greasy margarine that would poison the dogs? And yes, I understand full well about the need to pay tax and contribute to government, but what about when that government is completely failing to meet the needs of its citizens – or, worse again, ignoring them for expediency like the Free State?

My first memories in Boston are of Granny Kate pushing me around cafés in my big Silver Cross pram. It was the Rolls Royce of baby carriages – you could have got four of me in there. Which made it absolutely perfect to accommodate the dozen or so bottles of Today's Special, which Mary had brewed up in the basement still, and which were packed into pillow cases under the mattress and around my feet.

The bottles used to come in four different shapes, with four different labels, ranging from the very simple to the very ornate. I think Pat sold the Kentucky Rye at five dollars a throw wholesale, while a bottle of imported Tyrconnell Special Reserve could run you about twenty-five. The café owners would naturally have quadrupled that price and more, depending on what time of night it was. Needless to say, all the hooch came out of exactly the same bath. And Kate – who, you'll remember, had been an art teacher – designed the labels. Pat used to call her his 'Head of Marketing'.

The fact that Mary was training to be a physician was perfect cover for the home laboratory. At her peak, she was managing seven hundred gallons of 'hair tonic' a week, about half of which Pat sold through his pubs and the other half to customers like Frank and Stevie Wallace of the Gustin Gang.

Frank Wallace was a real pioneer and claimed to have been the world's first ever traffic-light bandit. He and his men would wait at intersections for liquor lorries to stop and then rob them. They became known as the Tailgate Thieves. In the latter stages of Prohibition, they would improve on this technique by wearing homemade Federal Agents' uniforms and flashing some pretty convincing badges. Yes, Uncle Frank was a very clever guy indeed, although sadly he was not as clever as Joey Lombardi, an Italian client of Granda Pat's from North End. After a series of misunderstandings in 1931, Uncle Joey called Frank in for a sit-down over some missing shipments and ended up shooting both him and his minder, Dodo Walsh, severely about the head.

From the age of about five, Granda had me working as his scout. I would walk a block ahead of the van, and if it was all clear, I would scratch my head; but if there were any cops or Agents about, I would bend down and pretend to tie my shoe so the driver would know to pull in and wait. For this I earned myself the sum of ten dollars a week and a free trunk call to my mother in Ireland. Though, of course, I could never tell her about the arrangement.

Before they moved to New York, Rose, my mother's cousin, would have sent her girls Eunice and Kathleen over to our house to play with me while her older boys went out on the boat with their father. Pat would always advise them to bring their dolls and prams so they could earn a little pocket money doing a light run or two for him. And they would smile more teeth than a Mormon choir when they got paid. No-one worried about flouting the law. Everyone, from Mayor Fitz down, knew it was completely, socially acceptable – the twentieth-century equivalent of watching TV from another country on your laptop. The cops knew well what was going on and, as long as it wasn't blatant, they were more than happy to live with it. They were all Irish anyhow, and had no respect for what was viewed as a WASP plot to stop the Catholics having any fun.

***

If I'd a day off school, Aunt Mary would take me to the hospital with her to watch her in action, and I loved nothing better than a trip down to the morgue to see the dead bodies. Not everyone was as hardy as me, however, and sometimes, if you were really lucky and a corpse had been left in a drawer too long, you might even get to see a young doctor vomit.

Mary could even tell you how long a body had been dead just by using a thermometer. Though not, she promised me, the same one she used when I had tonsillitis. She would stick the instrument into the dead guy's ear; the higher up the mercury went the fresher the corpse was.

One evening, Mary had just come in from work when she was telephoned at the house and asked to perform an autopsy in Southie, at Pat's speakeasy, The Hurler's Rest. A regular customer had dropped dead and the Chief of Police couldn't pull his men back to the station and leave the patrons alone to enjoy their 'coffee' until they'd established he hadn't been poisoned.

I'd say I was about five years old at the time and, as Kate was out keeping shop with Pat that night, Mary had no option but to take me with her. Not that I minded at all.

The dead guy was laid out on a table in the kitchen, and Mary knew almost immediately from the age, shape and colour of him that it was a heart attack. Regardless, she decided to do a mouth-and-pipes exam to check for burns or toxins. But as she was getting her kit out from her bag, I went in to see for myself.

Before Mary or the two cops could stop me, I had my pinkie jammed in the dead guy's ear and pronounced to the room: 'He's dead about an hour, Mary. His wax is still warm.'

Till the day she herself died, sixty years later, Mary used to warn people never to fall asleep in the same room as me if they didn't want to wake up with my finger in their ear. Thank God I'd never seen her using the thermometer in a rectal exam.

***

I did well at school and, thanks to Mary, was always top in science. The teacher, Miss Reid, did, however, send a note home after she asked one day if anyone in the class had ever seen a dead body. I told her, 'I'll give you better than that, Miss, my Aunt Mary let me see inside one. And they're really gross.' I was never allowed to speak about my trips to the cold room after that. Mary emphasised the point by taking me in and showing me the remains of a Sicilian gentleman whose tongue had been cut out and then arranged neatly in the breast pocket of his thousand-dollar suit. 'That's what happens to little boys who tell tales about their aunts,' she said.

Granda Pat knew I'd a head for business and was always honing my math skills. He taught me multiplication, percentages, averages, ledger sheets, and all the other bits and pieces you'd need to run a small-to-medium-sized distribution network. The math teacher, Father Devine, who was a brutal old so-and-so – far too long in the tooth to be teaching eight-year-olds – was always trying to catch me out by asking me increasingly difficult sums. But thanks to Pat, I usually gave a good account of myself. Then, one day, I made a cardinal error by advising the priest that I knew a quicker way to work out a problem than the one he was demonstrating to the class.

'Come up here and show me,' he said. So I did and, worse again, I was right. 'You're very clever, Derryman,' he said. 'You and your quicker way can take the rest of the class off.' But as I headed to the door, he pointed to the classroom window overlooking the playing field three storeys below. 'No, son,' he said, 'take the quicker way.' I was out on that window ledge for a full thirty minutes until Principal Flaherty was contacted by a passing policeman and ordered Devine to take me back in. But it taught me once and for all that the quickest way is not always the best way and is certainly not the safest way.

I was also very interested in engineering – and how things worked – planes, particularly. I had a secret yearning that someday I could fly to Ireland to visit Connie, who, though I barely knew her, was the centre point of my existence. Through work, Mary had gotten to know a social worker from Medford, just outside the city, who was a member of the Boston Flying Chapter. And for my sixth birthday, they arranged for me to go up in a plane out over Massachusetts Bay.

Mary's friend, as you now know well, was Amelia Earhart, and even then, she was quite famous, as she held the world record for the highest altitude ever reached by a woman. She'd also been a navigator on Wilmer Stultz's flight across the Atlantic earlier that year, but when I asked her about it, she just said it was boring and she'd much rather be piloting herself.

Millie, as she'd told me to call her, was incredibly beautiful, even by the standards of all the beautiful women who were raising me, and the first great love of my life. She tried to scare me by barrel-rolling the little plane a few times on her way back to the airfield, but I was too besotted with her, and the whole experience, to care. I screamed a little, just to keep her happy, but I wouldn't have cared if I'd never hit land again.

I told her about my mother living in Ireland and asked her if she could take me across to see her. Millie said she might take me someday, but it could be a bit dangerous yet, so she would check it out herself first and let me know. I assumed she was talking about the Protestants. So instead, I asked her if she would take my mother a note.

'We'll do better than that,' she said. 'We'll get a photograph of the two of us together and I'll deliver it myself when I see her.' So Mary knew a guy on the pier with a camera and we took that picture that's now up on the study wall. She also signed a copy of her biography for me, but I've promised that to Mo after I've gone, so don't be sticking it on eBay.

Before she went back to Medford, Millie kissed me on the cheek and called me her 'blue-eyed Irish boy', so ruining me for every other woman I met in my life.

CHAPTER 21

1923–1931: Derry

The *Chronicle*'s circulation grew steadily throughout the 1920s. It was respected, if not altogether admired, by both Orange and Green for what Connie described as its 'honest Nationalist impartiality'. Advertising wasn't so strong, however. The wars had left Derry poor. Not 1950s poor, but struggling regardless. The shirt factories, which employed more than fifteen thousand women in the city, were all that were keeping our boats afloat. Typically, you would have hoped for at least three-quarters of your paper's income to come from ads, but if Connie had been hitting sixty per cent back then, she would have been pleased.

They had two editions per week in Derry, Tuesday and Thursday, with the Donegal paper coming out on Friday. Both of the Derry papers were selling about eight thousand copies each by the middle of the decade. The Donegal edition had started off as a few switch-pages under Johnny's watch, but after Connie rebuilt the burnt-out Ballybofey offices, she officially registered it in Dublin as a separate title, the *Donegal Chronicle*, but retained the '*North West*' masthead. And it was one of the smartest decisions she ever made. They became completely different papers, right up until the time that Connie didn't want them to be. And this meant that any time the censors in one jurisdiction tried to shut her up, she simply moved shop to the other side of the border. The Donegal paper sold five thousand a week and, while it wouldn't have attracted as many ads, it still made a decent profit. In later years, I myself would start new editions in North Donegal, Tyrone and North Derry – but I was only following a well-laid road. Connie talked to Mick, who still minded the money, about producing a Sunday paper, in a bid to get their circulation up even further. But the market was too saturated and we couldn't afford the fees for the sports reports.

***

The *Chronicle*'s relations with the law were never good. One Thursday night in 1926 after putting the Donegal paper to bed, Connie was stopped on her way home and charged with Offences Against the State. The previous week's

82

front page had reported on an arrest in Stranorlar in which a supporter of Peadar O'Donnell had been badly beaten while handing out pamphlets calling for the seizure of British farms in the Free State. Four separate eyewitnesses had named the two Garda officers who had meted out the beating, so Connie named them as well. The victim had lost an eye.

After her arrest, Connie was transferred to Lifford Station, where a Deputy Commissioner from Dublin, in full dress uniform, was waiting. I think he was called Hasson. He was extremely pleasant to her, apologised for the inconvenience and said he knew it was pointless trying to muzzle her as she had another newspaper just fifteen miles down the road. But he had to be seen to go through these motions. He said he would release her now on her own recognisance, and that if she appeared at Lifford Court the following Tuesday, she would be given a nominal £10 fine for sedition and that would be the end of the matter.

'What if I don't pay the fine?' she challenged him.

His mood changed entirely, and she suddenly knew why he was there: 'That was my younger brother, you named, you smart-mouthed *striapach*, and he is now on every IRA death list from here to Bantry Bay. Please be advised that if you ever cause trouble for my family or me again, my friends and I will come for you and kill you. Just as surely as we helped the RIC kill your husband outside his father's bar three years ago. And no-one will be any the wiser about it. And no-one will ever write about it. And if for some reason we can't get to you, we will come after your children. Do you understand?'

Connie was a warrior, and she had more principles than any person I've ever met, but she let Mick pay the fine. And it was another five years before she sent for me to join her in Ireland.

The new Royal Ulster Constabulary in the North could be equally dangerous. There was one Derry sergeant, a hard-drinking bully – and a Catholic, as it happens – who started robbing passengers on the Derry–Donegal train. He claimed they were smuggling – as they certainly were – except he wasn't passing on what he seized to the Customs. Officially, he was only supposed to lift tea, sugar, and clothing – you had to pay an import tax on these when you were going into the new Free State. But naturally, if our man caught you for anything at all, he would take your watch, rings and even your wallet. Connie didn't name this fellow in the paper because she was afraid she might expose her sources, but she did write a pointed piece about 'military highwaymen on the Buncrana Express'.

The higher-ups in Belfast were forced to conduct an investigation. And, sure enough, our sergeant ended up confiscating a handbag from a District Inspector's wife. To compound his problems, he also insisted on giving her a body search, in case she had any tea stored in her undergarments. They ended up sending him to Larne, which, for a rosary-rattler, was a posting to hell. Did you ever hear of the phrase 'laying as low as a Larne Catholic'?

Before he left the city, the sergeant, a man by the name of Lynch, came into the Waterloo Street office and demanded to see Connie. Fearless to a fault, she came down to the front office to meet him but stood behind the counter, just in case.

'This was all your doing,' he told her. 'You're going to pay for this.'

She never backed down, no matter how big they were. 'You brought this all on yourself,' she told him. 'You stole from people you are sworn to protect. You let yourself down and us all down. You should count yourself lucky you're not being thrown in jail.'

With that, however, the cop, who was surprisingly agile for a drunk, vaulted the counter and rushed for Connie. He slapped her once on the cheek, knocking her out, before Harry Carson, our advertising manager, produced his demob pistol from a drawer and told Lynch he would love nothing better than to see if it still worked.

As he stormed out of the offices, Lynch told the packed room that if he personally didn't see to Connie, one of his many colleagues left in Derry would. And that she would do well to get herself a real husband to walk her home at night and not be hiding behind some Protestant dandy.

Incidentally, it was that same thief's son who caught me with the stuff in the van twenty years later at the end of the Emergency. And a rotten character he was, too.

***

I'd love to say that these incidents didn't influence the *Chronicle*'s editorial policies. But there is always a large slice of pragmatism involved in producing any newspaper. You never want to upset your biggest advertiser, for example, just as you never want to write a story that's going to lose you a big bunch of readers. And so it is with cops. You've got to work with them because, loathe them or despise them, they will always be there.

In saying that, while Connie may have been momentarily scared, she would write many, many more stories, holding public figures and public servants to account in the years to come. Lots of them threatened her, too, and I remember asking her if she never worried they would try to get her in the long grass. But Connie herself had already faced her worst fear with Johnny's death, so she was rarely truly worried. Besides, she was never one for holding grudges and, in her innocence, assumed that other people operated in the same way.

'They'll shout and scream for a few weeks and then they'll get over it,' she would say. 'And by that stage, we'll all be on to the next story.'

***

As the decade drew to a close, Dev began putting pressure on Connie to move to Dublin. He still had a bagful of money from his fundraising trip to the States ten years previously and was proposing to set up a new national newspaper. He wanted to counteract the Independent Group, which supported the partitionist Cumann na nGaedheal and the *Irish Times*, which still backed the Unionists. A whole lot has changed there, says you.

Dev was proposing to install Connie as deputy editor of his new paper to help shore up links with the Yanks. He knew Connie had the blood connection to the corridors of power there that he himself lacked. Truth was, though, Connie was no longer such a fan of the Long Fella and was starting to see through the mystique. The year after the ceasefire, Dev had made a fool of himself by stirring up a crowd in Derry for no purpose other than to pretend he was interested in them. He wound up serving a month in Crumlin Road Jail for his troubles. Moreover, Dev and Auntie Con had both agreed to swallow the oath and take seats in the new Free State parliament, under the banner of 'Fianna Fáil' or 'Soldiers of Destiny'. And while Connie appreciated this was a tactical step, she was seriously concerned that by accepting partitioned government in the South, they were legitimising the Orange State in the North. She wasn't impressed, either, that Dev was only organising his new party in the Twenty-Six Counties.

At the elections in 1927, Fianna Fáil wiped out the abstentionist Sinn Féin in the South and prepared for Opposition. The day after the poll, a very excited Auntie Con telephoned Connie and asked her to come down to Dublin to see her to discuss Dev's grand political plan. Connie refused – she was busy – but promised she would visit later in the summer. It would be the last time the two women ever broke breath. Before they got a chance to meet up, indeed, before Auntie Con even got a chance to take her new seat in Dáil Éireann, she was dead from a ruptured appendix.

***

Dev met with Connie at the Gresham Hotel the morning of Auntie Con's funeral and told her that plans for the *Irish Press* were well underway. He asserted that with 'virtually her last breath', the Countess had insisted he should recruit Connie as editor. Connie laughed at the flattery, knowing fine well that Frank Gallagher, who had done two terms in prison for Dev and was his Director of Publicity, was the only choice.

Out of loyalty to Auntie Con, and still heavy with guilt at having rebuffed her, Connie did agree to consider Dev's offer, which would start as deputy editor 'and we'll see from there'. There would be many advantages. If she wanted to pursue her interest in politics, she would be guaranteed a Teachta Dála seat, and maybe even a ministerial role, in future parliaments. She would be able to bring her young son over from America without fear of him being targeted. And she would become a leading figure in Dev's proposed new campaign to free the North and reunite it with its natural hinterland.

It was, as she later described it, her 'top-of-the-mountain moment' – and that Dev was showing her all the kingdoms of the world.

As she stood up to leave the dining room, Connie told Dev that she would think hard about his offer on the way home and get back to him with a definitive answer by the following week. But she knew as the words were leaving her mouth what her answer would be. She had just admitted as much – Derry had become her home. It was Johnny, it was Mick and, when the time was right, it would be Seán, too. It was high hills, long bridges, smuggling and Orange parades. It was sunshine, shadow, Sunday closing and the best singing in the world. It was smart and kind country people, who argued day and daily but who loved their city above all else. And most of all, it was her newspaper. Anywhere else she ever lived would only be a stopping point on her road back there.

***

The following week, she wrote Dev a warm letter politely refusing his offer on the grounds of Mick's poor health. But she wished him well on his venture and, in a throwaway line at the end, assured him that if she could help in any other way, she would. And that's how Connie became the Press's first North West Correspondent.

In the early summer of 1931, when Dev finally got the start-up money for the Irish Press cleared – Cumann na nGaedheal, the dirty dogs, had tried and failed to seize it for the government – Connie got a letter inviting her to the launch. The invitation told her the newspaper would begin publication on 5 September and mark the start of a new era in Ireland. Margaret Pearse, mother of Pádraic and Willie, was to be special guest and push the button to start the presses.

Connie, as a publisher and patriot, was delighted and resolved immediately to go. But she was even more thrilled when she read to the bottom of the letter and discovered that, at the owners' request, the Irish Press was inviting her son, Seán Madden, to travel to the ceremonies along with her.

CHAPTER 22

1931: Boston to Dublin

The original plan was that Aunt Mary would accompany me to Dublin, scoot up to Derry for a short visit to the *Chronicle* and then head back to Boston. But that was before she discovered that Abraham Bradbury, the thoracic surgeon she had been seeing for a year and who had asked Granda Pat for her hand in marriage, wasn't entirely serious about his intentions towards her. Indeed, Abe was so not serious that he had forgotten to tell Mary he was already married to someone else.

Say what you like about the Catholic Church, but they have an intelligence network second to none. The Hannons' family priest, Father George, a lovely and gentle old soul, had been contacted by a parishioner who spotted Honest Abe in Newport, coming out of a house with another woman. So George, who was as meticulous as he was protective, travelled down to Rhode Island to check the church records for himself and, sure enough, unearthed the proof.

Abe was unfortunate enough to be working for Carney Catholic Hospital in Southie at the time, which was run by George's bosses. And he woke up the following day to find himself transferred to Hillbilly Central in Kentucky, with strict instructions to bring his real wife along with him. God be with the days when it was that simple.

Mary, however, would have been turning thirty and getting to an awkward age, given that she'd always wanted children. So when Father George suggested that she extend her trip to the Old Country by a couple of months, to give herself time to mend her broken heart, she wasn't entirely convinced. But, of course, she was hardly in Derry a wet week before she bumped into the bright young headmaster Kevin O'Dorrity, and the rest is history. The fact that Kevin was George's nephew and had been quietly wired off to look out for the beautiful American doctor who'd been having a rough time is neither here nor there.

***

If I'm going to be completely honest, I was more excited about the mechanics of my trip than I was about meeting Connie for the first time – and with good cause.

We left Boston in mid-August, about a week before my ninth birthday, for our first stop in New York. Pat and Kate drove us to the station and hugged Mary goodbye like they were never going to see her again. In the years to come, Kate would travel across for the wedding to Kevin and both christenings, but Pat, whose liver was starting to go, never made it.

As we boarded the train, Pat shook my hand like a man and thanked me for being such a loyal partner. He then handed me a little package.

'I've one last job for you,' he said. 'This is a bottle of special reserve for your Irish grandfather. It's a very important present. I need you to guard it with your life on the trip and not let any thieving cop, G-man or customs man get a hold of it.'

I swore I would do my duty and I put the little bottle, hardly more than a naggin, inside the wooden pencil case Kate had got me for my new school.

'What about the runs?' I asked him. 'Who'll do your scouting?'

'I think your running days are behind you, Seán,' he said. 'Joe Kennedy says Frank Roosevelt is a shoo-in to win the White House next year, and he's promising to open all the bars again. Besides, it'll allow you more time to study your bookkeeping; that's where the real money is. Our Italian friends in North End say you've a real head for numbers.'

***

Pat then pulled me aside and gave me my last ten-dollar payment along with an extra four bills for which I was to take care of Aunt Mary. 'She's going to miss us. So anytime she has a little weep, just hold her hand, and remind her that her father will always be looking out for her. Oh, and be sure and tell her she looks like a frog when she's crying – and that no man will ever go near her with a face like that.' So I assured him I would.

We waved and waved from our compartment until the train rounded the bend and we could see them no more and, sure enough, Mary started to cry, so I took her hand. 'Your father says you're an ugly old trout, and no-one's ever going to marry you,' I told her.

She laughed so hard the snot came out her nose. Then she reached inside her purse and handed me another ten dollars. 'Pat bet me a sawbuck you'd have me in stitches before we got to New Haven.'

***

The Kennedys had offered to put us up in their new house in Riverdale, in the Bronx, but I wasn't going to miss my big chance. I begged and begged to stay in Manhattan, in one of the new skyscrapers I'd seen in the newsreels, and while it turns out they didn't cater for visitors, we were able to get a berth in the Astoria Hotel, just down the street from the Empire State. 'They're calling it the Empty State,' the desk clerk told us, 'because they can't rent out the offices. It's in the wrong part of town. The Chrysler Building and 40 Wall Street are filling up far better.'

I wasn't put off though – nor were thousands of others. And the queue for the lifts to the Empire State's Observation Deck was half a mile long. Even today, it gives me chills to think about that view. It was the highest I'd ever been on land – it really felt like you were on top of the world. It took me about five minutes before I would go up to the rail and look over, as I was convinced I was going to take a sudden impulse to climb out and launch myself into the street below. But when I saw the other kids up at the rail and happy as clams, I knew I had no choice – and I never stepped back from a dare before or since.

It's always struck me, too, when we can get nothing done in Derry – building a factory or whatever – that the only thing that really counts in this life is human will. If you are focused and determined, you can move mountains. The Empire State – which is more than half the height of Errigal, almost 1,500ft – was built, from start to finish, in just over a year. Yet it took us twenty years to build our little Peace Bridge; and fifty years on, we still have no university of our own. We're great, great talkers here in Ireland, but what I wouldn't give to have some of that American decision-making and follow-through.

***

The real highpoint of the trip, both literally and figuratively, was yet to come. I had been led to believe that Mary and I had been booked onto the SS *Bremen*, which was then the fastest liner in the world. But Uncle Fitz, who was friendly with the German ambassador, had managed to finagle a twin-berth cabin for us on the new Graf Zeppelin, which flew twice a month from Jersey to Berlin. Mary, quite cleverly, didn't tell me about it until we were en route to the airfield in Jersey, as I wouldn't have slept a wink.

To this day, I have never seen a more impressive aircraft. It was 800ft long – longer than three 747s – about 140ft tall, and inside featured two massive decks, all kitted out like a five-star hotel. It even had promenades along its inside walls and windows that you could open. Captain Eckener personally welcomed me on board and told me I could come join him in the Control Car anytime I wanted. He'd have been better off stapling his mouth shut, as for the next four days I lived with him on the bridge, asking questions from morning to night. He taught me how to use all the equipment – the rudder wheel, the gyrocompass, the gas valves and elevator wheels, so by the time we landed in Europe, I could pilot the thing like a pro. What were you flying when you were nine, eh, Miss Earhart?

The Zep only took fifty passengers, mostly older people, and so the crew adopted me as one of their own, even if they did have a little fun at my expense. There were safety notices everywhere about naked flames and smoking, as the hydrogen used to fuel the ship was highly flammable. In fact, no matches were allowed on board at all, and the smoking room was hidden away behind vacuum-sealed doors and contained just one solitary electric lighter.

The Head Engineer, Ludi Felber, who had fought in the Great War, told me stories about how the British had developed special exploding bullets to blow up the Zeps. But he warned me that even a small spark on the lower decks could be catastrophic.

'The other big danger is methane gas,' he told me. 'Even a tiny amount of that could react with the hydrogen, and boom! We'd be burnt as crispy as my wife's schnitzel.'

I had little to no chemistry training at that stage, as Ludi had worked out, and asked him if there were any methane anywhere on the Zep. And when he told me that it was a by-product of my own intestinal juices, I was horrified.

'Whatever you do, do not ever pass gas on board,' he said. The other crew looked around at me and nodded solemnly.

'But what do you do if you feel it coming on?' I asked.

'You must run and lock yourself into the smoking room as soon as possible,' he said. 'It is the only place that is safe.'

I was horrified and, for the rest of the trip, ended up saying the rosary any time I had to go to the bathroom. Just in case one would slip out.

I only realised they were hoaxing me when I wrote up the story of my trip for the *Chronicle* – my first by-line, aged nine, by the way – and Connie, who was subbing the piece, burst out laughing. Mary, the wretch, had been complicit in the lie and had assured me the reason she never had to run into the smoking room, as I did about eight times a day, was that ladies didn't do that sort of thing.

***

Berlin and then Paris, while more cultured and spectacular than any cities I had ever seen, were a little anti-climactic after New York and the Zep. I remember little except throwing buns to the bears in Berlin Zoo and throwing croissants to the pigeons at the top of the Eiffel Tower. But by the time we got to Dublin, my excitement levels were at fever pitch again.

Granda Mick hadn't been invited to the launch, but took the train down especially with my mother to greet us at the port. It was the most exciting reunion I'd ever had in my life – I can still hear my mother yelping with joy when she saw us. I don't think four people have ever talked, laughed and cried so much, all at the same time.

Connie was exactly like Mary except maybe a little slimmer and a little bit paler. But there was a warmth and sense of belonging off her that I had never experienced from any other human being. It was a completely new type of family. She kept her arm around my shoulder the entire cab-ride to the hotel, and then held her hand on my neck while we checked in and walked up to our rooms. It was as if we'd always been together. Nine years and two weeks old and I was finally on my way home.

The four of us sat chatting in the little suite I was sharing with my mother until the small hours. We were about to turn in for the night when I remembered the present Pat had given me for Granda Mick. So I ran to my case and, from inside my pencil box, produced the little package that I had successfully hidden from six different sets of customs officials.

Mick opened the naggin, toasted the group and knocked the contents back in one. The two sisters were shocked and were about to scold Mick for his recklessness when he started to laugh again.

'It was water,' he laughed. 'Pat wrote to me to tell me that our grandson was one of the finest smugglers he'd ever met, so we decided to put him to the test. But there was no way I was letting him risk his liberty for a half-pint of Mary's basement gin. His first suggestion was that Seán should carry over a Luger pistol. He said he never saw anyone as wide-eyed and innocent.'

Mick then put his hand into his pocket and handed me my first ten-shilling note. 'That's your delivery fee,' he said. 'I would advise you to put it in a place where no-one will find it, only I don't think I have to. Stick about, Seán, I think you're going to be useful around here.'

CHAPTER 23

McCloud's driver said he had some business in the city centre the following morning so would meet him outside the old Deanery next to the courthouse at 9.45am and take him out to the manse from there.

The American had dressed casually in polo shirt and jeans, better to blend in, so was surprised to see his guide appear in a three-piece striped suit, white shirt and a hand-tied polka-dot bowtie.

'Apologies,' he said. 'I was advising a client. The guy swears the light was orange, but the CCTV footage, and the poor man he left in the wheelchair, are strongly suggesting otherwise.'

'You're Tommy "Bowtie" McGinlay?' said McCloud. 'The lawyer?'

That earned him a big grin. 'One and the same. I confused you yesterday with the civvies and the old Jeep – you'd be surprised how many people walk right past me if I'm not wearing the bowtie. You should tell your people to update their photographs.'

McCloud laughed. 'Will do. You had no beard, either, in the pictures I saw. And you've lost a lot of weight.'

McGinlay looked a bit sheepish. 'I went off the beer,' he said. 'It was widely advised.'

He looked at his watch. 'Fancy seeing a bit of the Walls? We've got about five minutes to spare. I'll give you a pocket tour of East Wall.'

McCloud nodded, and his guide pointed to a set of steps between the Deanery and the courthouse leading up to St Columb's Cathedral and the Walls.

'George Berkeley, who founded Yale, was Dean of Derry in the 1720s,' said McGinlay. 'It was a very lucrative parish back then. When Fred Hervey – the man who put the spire on the cathedral there – was bishop in the late 1700s; his income, in tithes, in today's money was about eight million a year.'

McCloud whistled, impressed. 'Hervey was the builder, right?'

'Yeah – they called him the Edifying Bishop. He erected the first bridge across the Foyle and the Vespan Temple on the cliffs at Downhill, the one used in all the Irish tourism ads. He allegedly built that as a library, but it was really a knocking shop for him and his much younger cousin.'

'Sounds like quite a character.'

'He was. When he was interviewing potential curates for the Derry parish, he used to invite them up to his palace – that big Georgian building right across the street there – fill them full of sherry, and then make them strip naked and run a lap of the Walls. First one home got the job. They called it The Naked Mile.'

As they passed the entrance to the cathedral, McGinlay pointed inside at a cannonball displayed on a plinth in the vestibule. 'That big boy is actually hollow and contained the terms of surrender for the Williamites stuck inside the Walls at the time of the Great Siege. It was probably fired from up the hill at Ráth Mór, where we met yesterday, by the way. But James's men were bluffing – they didn't have the firepower to blast through the Walls. They were also riddled with disease and addled with drink, so when William's rescue team came sailing up the Foyle, they were easy fodder for them.'

***

They walked onto the Walls, passing the mound where the Apprentice Boys were commemorated, and began walking down the hill towards the river.

The massive fortifications, which form a perfect, complete circuit of the old city – and which, as McGinlay noted, are up to 40ft high and wide enough to drive two trucks around – were built in the early 1600s by London livery companies. The merchants had been ordered, under pain of imprisonment, to establish a new, colonial capital on the site of the ancient Irish city of Doire. The natives, as you'd imagine, were not on board with this plan – hence the huge bugger-off battlements, which are today one the city's biggest attractions. 'Life gives you lemons,' McCloud thought.

They passed over the newest of the seven gates to the Walled City – called, naturally enough, New Gate – which had been built in the early 1700s to allow easier access to the Talbot Theatre. 'This is still a big arts quarter,' said McGinlay. 'The Talbot building is still there and used now as church administration offices. But just down here before Ferryquay Gate, you have the CCA Gallery for Modern Art, The Playhouse – which does everything from drama to dance, and a hundred yards on down the Walls are the Millennium Forum Theatre and St Columb's Hall – both major events centres. Van Morrison is a regular at the Forum and Jim Reeves once played at the Hall.'

He checked his watch again and upped the pace. 'Here, we need to shift. I've just remembered the ticket on my car expires in about two minutes, and I don't want to be hauled up for slapping a parking attendant in the mouth. At least not twice in the one month.'

They crossed Newmarket Street and headed down quickly along the Walls towards Foyle Street and Tommy's big, black Merc.

'We'll go out the direct way today, past the Collon and along the Buncrana Road,' he said. 'I'll show you where the two bombs fell during the Second World War. You'll be hearing about it in the video before long, I imagine.'

McCloud knew, in that second, that McGinlay had seen the tapes – he'd probably helped the two Madden and O'Sullivan dervishes vet and edit them. But he also knew Tommy was not liable to offer up this information. So instead he asked about the libel writ. 'Are you handling the David Cunningham case?'

McGinlay grinned as they got into his car. He turned the key – this time it was Bob Dylan booming through the stereo – and pulled out of the car park onto the Foyle Expressway, heading north. 'Yes, I am. But it's going nowhere. I'll sort it all out. Seven figures, my arse. Don't worry about it.'

McCloud wasn't so sure. 'I think the editor is very worried about it; from what Mo is telling me, she wants to serve my *cojones* up with tonight's Bolognese.'

McGinlay shook his head. 'Naw. You've nothing to concern yourself about. And that's just how Maeve is with boys she likes. Which is very rare, by the way. She doesn't even realise it – she's just pulling your pigtails.'

'But I haven't even met her.'

'Yes. But you've a huge amount in common. Good-looking, major achievers, athletes, you both make your money as high-powered watchdogs – and you trust no-one. You're both ridiculously bright, and both drink a lot more than is good for you, too – and I speak as an authority in that department. Also, from what I can tell in the short time I've known you, you're both lonely people – like you're each missing another bit of yourselves. And you're both in Derry, at this very point in time and history, fighting to the death over, let's be honest, what is a minor historical footnote. The two of you could wind up married. You know she watched you on the spy-cam yesterday for about half an hour, when you were in the bunker?'

McCloud did a double take. 'Spy-cam?'

McGinlay laughed. 'Oh, hush,' he said. 'You knew well it was there – we watched as you tried to spot it. Don't pretend you didn't know. Either that, or you're the only man I've ever known, the late Seán Madden included, who doesn't sit scratching himself when he's watching TV on his own.'

These people were unbelievable – and so overt about it. They were running their own little empire. But he was intrigued that Maeve had watched him. Though, before he'd left the previous day, he'd rewound the video to watch her a second time, too. They probably had all that on their CCTV as well.

They drove in silence down the Strand, passing the hopelessly small university campus, which Belfast had been promising for fifty years to expand. At the roundabout, McGinlay pointed out the site of the old naval base, which the Germans had targeted in the bomb, and then he turned his car left along the Buncrana Road to where the parachute-mines had landed.

McCloud remained focused on his task. 'I have to meet David Cunningham, regardless,' he said. 'Will you fix it up, or will I do it myself?'

McGinlay nodded. 'It'll be easier if I do it. We might even be able to make a virtue out of it. Leave it with me. What about EF, the father?'

'I thought he was brain-damaged?'

'He's lucid some of the time. But definitely more out than in, as we say here. There are certain things that set him off, though. If we get a visit, I'll brief you on what not to say.'

'Point of order, Tommy – am I running this inquiry or are you?'

McGinlay smiled. 'Apologies. You're the Special Agent-in-Charge, sir. What would I know? I'm only a mere driver.'

CHAPTER 24

Mo had coffee and custard doughnuts ready in the little kitchen when McCloud arrived at the bunker. He sat down opposite her at the little breakfast table and absent-mindedly pulled out his phone to check his messages.

Mo extended her hand. 'I'm afraid I'm going to need that. Turn it off before you give it to me, if you know what's good for you. Maeve has a nasty habit of going through people's messages. I take it it's password protected?'

'God, yes.'

He briefly considered refusing, then complied. He needed them to think he was house-trained. At least, that's what he was telling himself.

Mo tapped her watch. 'Questions from yesterday?'

'Okay,' he said. 'The big one first. Seán says Connie protected him – maybe overprotected him. Is it possible that Johnny Madden, Seán's father, was murdered by either an IRA faction or the police and she didn't tell him?'

Mo sucked on her cheek. 'No. There were a few conspiracy theories – a couple of which the police and Guards liked to stir up to get into Seán's head, and maybe Mick's, too – but no. Mick told me the story himself: how he put Old Dog McGillicuddy on the boat, the poor lad crying with gratitude that his life was being spared. But the rest of the McGillicuddys hated the Maddens with a passion. I once went to a hurling match at Burt with Seán in the late fifties and, while we were there, a brother of Old Dog's slashed our car tyres in plain view. Seán never did a thing about it.'

'Would that hatred have carried down the generations, perhaps? Could one of the McGillicuddys have come into the office in 1994 and shot Seán? Maybe the guy who was forced out died or something – he'd have been, what, about ninety-one or ninety-two then – and a nephew or grandnephew decided to avenge him? It is possible.'

Mo smiled. 'I really love your thinking. Yes, we can carry grudges to the third generation here. What if it was Old Dog's own son or grandson who

96

came back from the States to do it? That'd be a real hornet's nest for you. A Yank shooting a Yank on Irish soil? But it's unlikely. And I'd imagine they'd have wanted to claim it – if they did it.'

He agreed. 'Funny name, though, "McGillicuddy". Isn't it a bit stage-Irish – a bit Darby O'Gill and the Little People?'

She laughed. 'What? You think this is all a figment of our imaginations, that we're making up fairy stories for you? Check through the *Chronicle* archives, you'll see Pius McGillicuddy mentioned in at least one court report for affray. I think he even gets a mention in one of Peadar O'Donnell's books as well. Also, if you were determined enough, you'd probably be able to find the manifest for the boat he shipped out on. And if you go out to Drumhaggart or Lenamore, you'll still find a couple of the family kicking around, though I think they call themselves MacLeod now – it's a shortened version.'

'Like me – "McCloud"?'

'No. Spelt differently. It's an Irish name. Yours, I'd imagine, is Scottish.'

'I don't know what ours is, to be honest. Mom and Pop always assured us we were Irish, but part of that was because it guarantees you favoured status back home. I envy you all your deep roots and long heritage; over in the States, most of us are nomads.'

Mo laughed and tapped her watch. She had to get into the *Chronicle* and he had a video to watch.

He closed his eyes briefly and remembered his mnemonic. 'M' for McGillicuddy, done. Now 'L' for Lynch. 'What about the crooked sergeant, Lynch? Seems like he had a real grudge against Connie. And the son then arrested Seán. Any chance it could have been a connection of theirs?'

'Would love it to be – if only so we could throw them in jail and settle a few old scores of our own. But no. Again, they were experts at nursing their wrath to keep it warm, but they're all dead. The sergeant died of drink, the son died of drink and, alas, there were no grandchildren, either drunken or sober. I can't see the cousins or extended family being that bothered. After all, it was hardly a shooting matter.'

McCloud resolved to get Jeanie to spend the night sifting through genealogy databases to check all this, though he doubted Mo was lying to him. She'd be saving her lies for bigger occasions and wouldn't want to give herself away on something stupid.

'H' for Hasson – the Garda boss. 'What about the Deputy Commissioner who threatened Connie and her family? Could someone connected to him, perhaps, have had something to do with this?'

Mo nodded. 'We might come back to that one maybe later in the week. All I can say is, I doubt it, because there's no history at all of Guards coming north of the border to do dirty work. In saying that, the Guards in Donegal were so filthy for decades that there was a state inquiry into their behaviour about ten years back.'

'That's right! The Morris Tribunal; I taught a module on it once back home.'

'That's the one. But I never knew them operate in Derry. We'll park it for the minute. Any others?'

'There are obviously other grievances that might have endured. The *Chronicle*, like any paper doing its job, got itself on a whole lot of shit-lists. You trod on a lot of toes back then: the Unionist Party, the Pro-Treaty forces, even the Catholic Church?'

'Yes, but none of them have reputations for shooting up offices in late twentieth-century Derry ...'

'So, that's a no, then?'

'Almost certainly. We'll revisit it if we have to. Anything else?'

He smiled at her. 'The *Laurentic* story – has it got a little polished up over the years, perhaps?'

She shook her head. 'No. And how dare you. It's all true. They're known swimmers, the Maddens. Seán did the Rathmullan to Buncrana pier-to-pier swim when he was seventy-four – five miles on that self-same Lough Swilly.'

He held up his hands apologetically. 'The courtship stories with Asquith and Auntie Con and the suffragettes, too?'

'Yes. All fact. If anything, Seán has downplayed a lot of what went on. Or rather Connie did. It wasn't half as civilised as it sounds there.'

'And what about the Boston smuggling? Was that civilised?'

'Completely. The Hannons were gentlefolk. Some of the Italians mightn't have been so genteel, but as you're aware, the Irish have always had a reputation for their manners.'

He laughed out loud at that and decided to leave it there.

Mo made her way towards the door. 'The fridge has your sandwiches and snacks. I'll be back at four thirty. It's all cued up and ready for you.'

'Thank you. Be sure and apologise to Maeve for my attire but tell her I'll wear my good jacket for her tomorrow?'

Mo smiled. 'She'll be happy to hear that. You interest her. The move with the Cunningham photograph was devious, effective and totally ruthless. She was genuinely impressed. Keep it up, soldier, and we might let you meet her at the end of the week.'

CHAPTER 25

1932: Derry

I slept through most of the *Irish Press* launch. Dev, while he was many things to many people, was never succinct. Connie filled up with tears when he mentioned Johnny and his vital contribution to the all-Ireland dream. But I had gotten to meet more than a few on-the-make politicians in my last hometown and wasn't convinced. Though I knew better than to say this. No-one ever went broke keeping their mouth shut, as Uncle Fitz would say.

The reward for my good behaviour was a ticket to my first hurling final at Croke Park the following day – Cork versus Kilkenny. We had played a bit with sticks on the street in Southie, but I'd never seen a real match and couldn't believe the speed and fury with which it was played. It made lacrosse look like a kindergarten game. I told Mick that I wanted to learn to play it properly when I got to Derry and he said he'd do what he could. But realistically, I was already too old.

After the game, which ended in a draw, we all got the late train back north. And I was allowed the rest of the week to get the lay of the land before starting school.

My first impressions of Derry were mixed. It was about ten degrees colder than Boston, which I'd been warned to expect, and when it wasn't raining, it was mizzling. The whole city, I worked out, had been built on the side of a massive mountain, and my calves were sore from walking up slopes for the first couple of days. Mick took me everywhere on foot: up the historic City Walls, down around the busy docks and across the Carlisle Bridge, which was just about to be replaced by the double-decker Craigavon Bridge being built alongside.

Whereas Boston had been quite impersonal, the people I met here were incredibly kind, as if immediately aware of my backstory. I quickly realised that Mick and Connie knew absolutely everybody and, while they clearly didn't get on with them all, it was for all intents as if I were moving into a 50,000-strong family. I was public property.

The house at De Burgh, while big for Derry, was small by Back Bay standards. Mary and I both got our own rooms, which I already knew was more than some entire families in the Bogside got. And the garden was full of trees and dark green grass, as was the adjacent park.

The *Chronicle* was a large operation crammed into two skinny three-storey houses in Waterloo Street that had been knocked together, right bang in the city centre. There were thirty workers on site – reporters, sales staff, compositors and typesetters – with another fifteen in the printing press off William Street. I was a little horrified to learn that Connie ran it like a social enterprise, ploughing her profits back into the business and the workers. All staff got profit-share bonuses and, in many cases, Mick would even guarantee their mortgage loans. Mick's philosophy was that a rising tide must lift all boats. But even at that very tender age, I knew that a fair-to-middling-sized storm could sink the entire fleet. Granda Pat had been a great believer in every man for himself, stuffing the mattresses with cash and bolting the doors to collectors.

Waterloo Street, before it became a shopping street, was still full of boarding houses where migrant workers from Donegal would spend their last night before catching the Scotch Boat to Glasgow. The landladies would regularly 'sub' the workers their board and dinner, trusting the men to pay off the ledger on their way back home. A number of these houses would become bars, taking their names from the different areas of Donegal where the workers had originally come from: Dungloe, Gweedore and The Rosses. And, now, more recently, we have the Peadar O'Donnell.

I started at St Eugene's Boys School in Rosemount, a short walk across Brooke Park and up another hill, and life quickly began to settle into a rhythm. Neil McKenna was my first teacher and I took to him immediately, even if he wasn't remotely impressed that my granda had money. It was a different sort of school entirely, servicing the entire community, not just the guys from the front three rows of the chapel. It used to annoy me that as probably the brightest kid in the class – and I say that with genuine modesty, given I was also the most privileged – I wasn't McKenna's favourite. And it took me years to work out that the reason he always sent the class hoodlums, wearing their third-generation hand-me-downs, down to the store or to his own home for 'messages' was so he could feed them – as he knew they weren't getting breakfast at home. Even when I won his annual contest to see who could hit a golf ball the furthest, he refused to give me the prize – a trip to the golf club in his open-top car – on the grounds that I'd played the game in America. And instead, he took Stevie Breslin, who'd never even been in Donegal before.

Initially, I didn't get on too well with the bulk of my classmates. I was too clean, too confident and, yes, too fat. This was the curse of having no father: every woman I ever met felt sorry for me and wanted to feed me up, although

I wasn't on my own in that regard at Rosemount. I'd guess about a quarter of the boys were being reared by their mothers alone, thanks to the wars, prison and, of course, that timeless old reliable – the drink.

One guy, however, Stanley White, the son of an RUC man, took a particular dislike to me. He was about a year older than me, a head taller and had his own gang. From day one, he made fun of my bright-coloured American clothes and took to calling me either 'Fatty' or 'Olly' because of my puppy fat. He would also spit in my books any time he passed my desk or wing my ear with his ruler. This went on for months, but I didn't want to worry Connie about it. And I knew from Aunt Mary what happened to little boys who told tales, so I learned to live it.

Then, one day, McKenna set us a math test, writing ten problems from his book up on the blackboard, like he always did. I had little bother with the first nine. But the tenth wasn't straightforward and, by my reckoning, needed us to work out the compound interest on a sum of cash – or 'the vig on the vig', as Granda Pat used to say. So I did the double sum, remembering, as I had been taught, to apply the second interest to the combined total of the first sum plus the repayment fee.

I wasn't sure about my method, though, as I'd never learned it in school, so I didn't share it with the class like I might have done normally, to curry a little favour. But Whitey demanded my answer before McKenna came back – on the basis that he would dust the board with my jumper, and me still inside it, if I didn't oblige. So I gave it to him and him alone.

McKenna came back into the room, and there were only two of us who had got the last problem correct, Whitey and myself.

'Neither of you should have known how to do this,' said the teacher. 'I haven't shown it to you yet. I just threw it in to worry you. Well done, the pair of you. I'm particularly pleased with you, Stanley. It's a great improvement. I wonder if you could now both come up to the front of the class and demonstrate how you got the result.'

I got up slowly from my seat and looked behind me to the corner, where Whitey was rooted in fear.

'Let Olly show you, sir. He's closest.'

Now McKenna did not like bullies in his class. But I did not want him making an example of Whitey on my account, so I moved quickly to the board and, without waiting for a cue, began scribbling out my work.

I was about three-quarters way through the problem, and had explained the method pretty clearly, when McKenna said that was fine and that Stanley could come up and take it from here.

Whitey staggered up through the rows of little desks and came to the board.

'Sir, I forgot, sir. It's just gone out of my head. I'm really sorry.'

He blushed with shame, fired me a look that presaged all manners of torture, and headed straight back to his seat.

About an hour later, after the bell went for home-time, I walked out into the playground, full of trepidation, to find Harry Carson, the advertising manager from the Chronicle, waiting. As he put his hand on my shoulder, he winked over at McKenna, who nodded back and smiled.

'I hear you've been having it rough,' Harry said. 'It's not your fault. You're being asked to pay back debts that have nothing to do with you. Young White's mother is a sister of that copper Lynch, whom your mother got sent to Larne. We didn't realise that the two of you would wind up in the one class.'

'Am I going to have to move school?' I asked. 'I like it here. In spite of him.'

Harry pulled a pained face. 'You might have to. We could probably get you into Foyle Prep, but I'm not sure that's a good fit, either. I went there, and it had a serious quota of awful little snobs. Sometimes it's better to stand and fight your battles.'

'But look at the size of him. And he has about six others along with him all the time.'

'You're right; you're never going to beat him. But that's not what you want, either. All you want is for him to know it's best for everyone that he leaves you alone.'

'I don't follow.'

'You will.'

***

The following day, McKenna took us out to the playground to teach us hurling. I'd been playing with the juniors from Burt village since I'd arrived and knew a bit, so was asked to captain one of the teams. Whitey, who was the biggest boy in the class, picked himself to lead the others.

The sliotar was thrown in, and we weren't going thirty seconds before Whitey had cracked me on the knee with his stick. McKenna blew a foul. Two minutes later, same again. This time he got me on the elbow. Again, another foul.

About five minutes later, the two of us went for a ball, and Whitey decided to swing at my ribs instead. This time, however, I stepped back, avoided the slap then smashed my own stick into Whitey's mouth as hard as I could. Got him right dead centre. It was cold-blooded, brutal and cynical, and was witnessed as such by the forty or so boys and teachers on the pitch. And, I have to say, I'm almost ninety years old now, but I never felt as good about anything in my life. It was pure, unadulterated power.

Whitey's mouth was a mess of blood; at least two teeth were broken and he was howling and crying in pain. But suddenly, in that minute, I saw him for what he really was – the unwanted son of a bitter, alcoholic cop, who would grow up just like his father and fail at everything he did. And I felt awful shame. I was the bully, and it had been the wrong thing to do. And I immediately resolved never to lift my hand to anyone ever again.

After the dust settled, I was sent to see Charlie Doherty, the principal. All the boys were whispering after me that I was going to get six of the best, or maybe even twelve.

Mr Doherty called me in, bade me sit in a chair and asked me right out if I'd hit Whitey deliberately.

'Yes, sir,' I told him.

He then wanted to know was there a history between us – if maybe I'd anything to say in mitigation.

'No, sir,' I said.

'Well, in that case, I have no option but to use the cane. And after I punish you here, your mother will take you home, and you will remain there for a fortnight, suspended. We will send your work home. Now, put out your hand.'

I closed my eyes and prepared myself.

'Okay,' he whispered quietly. 'Every time I hit the desk with the cane, you let a cry out of you. That was a policeman's son you lamped, so we've got to make it look good. And don't, for Christ's sake, let anyone see your hands on the way out the door.'

***

After two weeks in my room, spent reading Father Brown mysteries, I returned to the class and McKenna made Whitey and myself shake hands. We could barely look at one another but Whitey never targeted me again. In saying that, I could always feel the venom emanating from him. In my entire life, I have never met anyone who hated me as much as he did. That's the problem when you humiliate someone. Sixty-five years later, the day I got shot, Whitey was the first person I thought of. Though, of course, he was long dead by then.

CHAPTER 26

1932: Ballyarnett

In early 1932, the *Chronicle* suffered a severe setback when it wound up banned and slapped with heavy fines, on both sides of the border, for carrying statements from republican parties in the run-up to the Free State election. The Northern authorities were not at all happy that the *Chronicle* had given 'undue prominence' to de Valera's rising Fianna Fáil Party, while in Donegal, the Church – and hence the state – was furious that the paper there had carried factual reports of the 'illegal' but popular Saor Éire campaign. Connie and Mick had to dip into the reserves to carry the paper through its suspension, but Dev's subsequent election in the South meant at least the fine there would eventually be waived.

Dev's new anti-partition government in the South, while supported by virtually all Nationalists in Derry, was a disaster for business. An economic war between Britain and the new state broke out when Dev quite rightly said he was damned if he was going to continue paying back mortgages to London for land that the colonists had stolen from the Irish two hundred years earlier. Dev also whacked extra taxes onto British imports to allow his country to better compete. So the Brits retaliated with an iron fist, leaving Derry, as always, caught in the middle. With no money about, advertising at the *Chronicle* in both jurisdictions fell through the floor, but costs rocketed, particularly in the Free State, where we were forced to import all our newsprint paper and printing ink from Britain.

On the plus side, I was able to pick up some extra pocket-money at the weekends, scouting on the roads for Granda Mick and his fellow farmers from Drumhaggart. The thieving Brits had started charging them twenty cents on the dollar to move cattle, butter, bacon, eggs and cream into the North. So we set up a cattle run from Mick's farm in the South, along a couple of laneways and through a couple of hedges, to Larry McMahon's little holding in the North. It was mostly night work and could be tricky enough, as the Excise men tended to keep a tight eye on all the main players. But ultimately, there were never quite enough of them to plug all the holes, and we were never caught.

On our return trips, we would smuggle back cartloads of Welsh coal, which Dev had stuck huge tariffs on. 'Burn everything British but their coal' was the slogan. But coal burned longer, and hotter, than turf, so we had to give the Donegal people what they wanted.

**

After about three months of getting the bum's rush from the various infirmaries, nursing homes and doctors' practices in the city, Aunt Mary eventually managed to get herself a job as a locum at the city's lunatic asylum. You wouldn't remember it – it was situated between Northland Road and Strand Road but was knocked down in the 1960s and replaced with a police station. And yes, some jokes do indeed write themselves.

Mary, unlike most of the other staff at the facility, had studied psychiatry and was appalled at some of the primitive treatment being meted out to the inmates. She herself would regularly bring patients back to De Burgh, which was only a few hundred yards up the hill, to chat about their lives, under the guise of helping out in the garden. The asylum's trustees were furious when they heard about this experiment, and the Unionist chairman of the board demanded that Mary be sacked.

Connie, however, always liked to keep one in a drawer for emergencies. And she agreed not to publish two sworn statements, disclosing how the same eminent chairman had been tied up and robbed inside a knocking-shop, in return for his absolute silence.

If you learn one thing in your life, it should be this: there is no money in fighting with newspapers because, even if you win the odd battle, they will be the people ultimately keeping score. And, as Mark Twain reminded us, they buy their ink by the barrel.

**

In early May 1932, Mary asked her bosses for a week's leave towards the end of the month so she could travel to Paris to meet up with a friend who would be visiting from America. But this was an area in which Connie had absolutely no influence, so they refused point blank.

It was a decision they would later regret. On a beautiful early summer afternoon, two weeks later, Mary's friend, Amelia Earhart, accidentally cut short her solo transatlantic flight to France and instead pitched her Lockheed Vega plane down onto Gallagher's farm at Ballyarnett, four miles outside Derry.

'Where am I?' the aviatrix asked a farmhand, Dan McCallion, expecting the name of the country.

'Cornshell,' Dan answered her, giving her the name of the field. The spot where she landed is now the sixth green at the Foyle Golf Club, which is still run by the Gallagher family.

After Millie washed up and got a change of clothing, courtesy of one of the Gallagher girls – she'd brought no luggage or money with her – she was driven into the Northern Counties Hotel for a civic reception.

A rumour had gone around the wires that Millie had crash-landed in France and had been badly injured, so she had to telephone her husband George in the States to tell him that all was well. And, as chance would have it, the phone at the hotel wasn't working, so she called in and used the *Chronicle*'s.

Connie naturally used the opportunity to score herself a ticket to the reception and Millie told her she could bring a plus one. So Connie took a chance and brought both Mary and myself. And when the guest-of-honour saw us at the back in the cheap seats, she immediately broke away from her posse and insisted on the three of us joining her table at the front.

Millie remembered me well from my birthday flight in Boston and couldn't get over the fact that I also had flown an aircraft across the Atlantic, albeit with ninety other people on board. She insisted that Mary and I join her in about a dozen photographs, until Connie reckoned the point had been made and dragged us away. But as the dignitaries from the asylum board queued patiently to get their pictures taken with arguably the most famous heroine of the twentieth century, Connie nodded over to her cameraman. He then tipped the wink to his colleagues and they all withdrew their services *en masse* to give Miss Earhart some peace.

The asylum folk, to their consternation, were left high and dry. It is one of the oldest rules in newspapers: if there's no report and no pictures, it didn't happen. And their meeting with the most famous woman in the free world was never recorded.

I have to confess I pulled exactly the same stunt with a whole coterie of very important business people who had ticked me off the time that Clinton visited back in 1995. Every one of them wanted their picture in the *Chronicle* with Bill's arm around them; some were even offering us stupid sums of money. I refused the lot of them and, as you remember, just filled the pages with pictures of children who weren't working an angle but were just happy to see him.

The next morning, we travelled to see Millie off on a different plane; her 'little red bus', as she called the Vega, was in need of repairs. She kissed me again on the cheek, told me I was still her favourite blue-eyed Irish boy, and headed on to London for a few days R and R with the American ambassador.

All things considered – and I'm counting sieges, rebellions, Nobel Prizes, Eurovision Song Contests and presidential visits in this equation – Millie's visit is probably the most exciting and significant thing ever to happen in Derry. Why we've never named the city's airport after her, I can't fathom. After all, they can always name the new university after Hume. If this were America, they'd be erecting a billion-dollar theme park where she landed instead of a lousy little museum cottage that's never open. And if Belfast can make an industry out of the world's biggest sinkable boat, why can't Derry do the same out of this success story? It's a nonsense. As Millie herself once said: 'The most difficult thing is the decision to act; the rest is merely tenacity.'

***

Five years later, when Millie disappeared over the Pacific, I was brokenhearted. For about a year afterwards, Mary convinced me that she hadn't gone missing at all but was carrying out secret intelligence work for the American Government. And I secretly hoped that her husband would give up on her so she could return to Ireland and marry me; the pair of us would head off for a lifetime of adventures in the air. But deep down, I knew – just as with Jim Reeves, Elvis, Michael Collins and my father, Johnny – that no matter how hard you wish, some people were never coming back.

CHAPTER 27

1936–37

As the 1930s wore on, the Derry paper got back on an even keel – but Donegal continued to ship water. Circulation in both papers was steady, but advertising in the Free State was low to non-existent and costs were rising. So, increasingly, Connie was having to borrow money from the Northern account to pay the wages of the eighteen staff in Ballybofey. Several times indeed, Old Mick was forced to support both papers with the profits from his other sidelines.

You have to remember here, that during this time there was no money south of the border at all. None. What the Brits weren't grabbing in duties, Dev was lifting in taxes. There was also genuine fear of a new famine, and there were people still alive who remembered the effects of the last one in the 1870s. And they remembered what their parents had had to do to survive.

Mary's marriage in October 1934 to Kevin O'Dorrity was an expensive business, too, as the *Chronicle* insisted on paying the passage of a host of Hannon guests from America. They were having it tough across the pond, too: the stock market had collapsed and, with the end of Prohibition, they were all forced to resort to legitimate business, which was nowhere near as profitable.

The wedding 'breakfast' was a gala event at the City Hotel on Foyle Street, and the new couple were serenaded by a new dance band, featuring the vocal talents of the singing footballer Charles McGee and the cattle-dealer's son young Joseph McLaughlin. Twenty years later, McGee and his 'gay' guitar – God, we were innocent – went on to tour America, billed as the Irish Elvis Presley. McLaughlin, meanwhile, shortened his name to 'Locke', gave up a budding career as a policeman and became one of the biggest Variety stars in Britain.

The celebration made a huge impression on me. I already knew well that Derry was a musical Mecca. I'm not sure if it was down to the *Feiseanna*, the choirs, the hymn-writers or something in the water, but no other place I've visited in the world can legitimately claim as many singers per square acre. Connie, who, like me, remembered how flat and tuneless Boston was in comparison, used to say you couldn't throw a rock in Derry without hitting a musician – and the drummer tapping him for loose change.

I had started at St Columb's College the previous month and, encouraged by my new English teacher, had begun attempting to write articles for my mother's paper. Father Rennick was unusual for the College at that time: he wasn't a criminal psychopath hiding under a clerical collar, but rather a natural teacher who genuinely liked and understood children. Much later on, I discovered he had a lifelong girlfriend and, in normal society, would have got married – if he hadn't been the eldest son of the village publican.

I was already spending my Saturday afternoons at the *Chronicle* proofreading desk, looking for spelling and grammatical errors, and was acquiring a real taste for the ink. But up to that point, I rarely had the confidence to commit my own thoughts to paper. So when on Monday morning I told Rennick about the concert at the wedding, he insisted that I complete a review of it and return it to his desk before 3.00pm the following day.

I had the review finished within an hour of getting the assignment – and it was a joy to produce. And it was at that exact point I realised what I was going to do with the rest of my life.

Connie ended up printing the review in its entirety that same Thursday, though added the names of about sixty of the wedding guests at the end. 'People will want to buy a copy to keep if they're named in it,' she explained. And sure enough, there was a slight but noticeable bump in the sales.

The next week, I reported on a Gershwin musical being performed at the Talbot Theatre on Artillery Street, again accompanied by a list of about fifty audience members. And within a year, our new Arts Section had added about five hundred readers a week to our Thursday paper, and I was on a ten-shilling-a-week retainer as Music Reporter. I loved every minute of it, and I still do today. It was like Confucius said: 'Choose a job you love and you will never work a day in your life.' And, truth is, I've never really worked since.

Most days after school, I would head down Shipquay Street to HG Phillips's music shop to pick up the scuttlebutt on all the latest trends. The shop owner, the impresario Henry Phillips, had moved on to England by this stage to run an opera company and an orchestra, but occasionally he would return to regale us with stories of his glory days. I remember a customer scoffing at him when he said that he had once brought the legendary Italian tenor Enrico Caruso to Belfast.

'You're talking hogwash,' the customer said. 'Caruso was never in Ireland.'

The matter was finally resolved about a month later when Phillips brought in his scrapbook. But by that time, the spring of 1936, he had re-established his impeccable credentials to all by announcing – via my first ever exclusive in the *Chronicle* – that he had contracted the world-famous American bass-baritone Paul Robeson to sing at the Guildhall. Think Sinatra, only bigger, better and a far nicer guy.

The Guildhall had to build extra seating on the stage for the occasion, and the singer was mobbed everywhere he went – even when he tried to get in some light jogging along the Culmore Road. The event was described in the *Chronicle*, rather prematurely, as the concert of the century, but even now, seventy-five years later, I'm hard pressed to think of a better one. Several times, I actually thought the roof was going to come in during the applause after *Old Man River*, *Swing Low, Sweet Chariot* and *Joe Hill*. It was so good a night that the Unionists didn't even protest when the band forgot to play the British national anthem, *God Save the King*, at the end; we learned later that this was on the orders of Robeson, a card-carrying communist.

Despite an intervention from old Phillips, however, I wasn't allowed to interview Robeson, who was under strict contract to a film agency. But he shook my hand, posed for the obligatory picture and told me to write that Derry was the most musical city he'd ever visited. Which I did. It was only a month later that I discovered he'd also used the same line about New York – though significantly, he never said it about Belfast. Still, he was a complete star, who went on to become a world-famous civil rights leader, and his film *Showboat* is one of my favourite movies of all time. When I was interning for Jack in the late 1940s, the story went around that Harry Truman had stormed out of a meeting with Robeson when he demanded the president introduce new anti-lynching legislation. And, sure enough, he wound up getting blacklisted by that lying redneck McCarthy. They even erased his name from the All-American football records. Connie used to always cite him as an example of what can happen to you for doing the right thing. A man of real principle in an era when there were very few around.

CHAPTER 28

It was only a year or so after the Robeson concert that the *Chronicle* found itself in real trouble for a few principles of its own. Kevin O'Dorrity, Mary's new husband, had very quietly been refusing to administer the Oath of Allegiance to new teaching staff joining his school. Or to be completely accurate, he had been refusing to demand proof that they had taken the oath.

The oath had been introduced in 1923 by James Craig to weed out Fenianism in Catholic schools. Unless a teacher signed up to it, he or she could not avail of a full-time position, with retirement benefits etc, anywhere within the Six Counties of the Northern state. Senior priests from Dublin, who had no first-hand experience of the measure, instructed Catholics to hold their noses and sign it, but a small rump of ethical Northern teachers wouldn't stomach a sworn lie. And some of these ended up working for decades as temps, without a single salary bump or penny in a pension pot to show for it. The Act actually stayed on the books until the 1970s.

The Ministry of Education and Unionist Party at Stormont, of course, policed the oath like it was an anti-terror law. But the Unionists in Derry had more of a 'don't ask, don't tell' approach. Many of them feared Belfast supremacy as much as we did and were more concerned with putting bread on the table than poking their neighbours in the eye.

No good deed goes unpunished, however, and Kevin's penchant for letting the oath slide caught up on him when a teacher he fired for striking a pupil with a steel sewer-rod reported him to the ministry. Kevin was suspended without pay while the allegations were investigated and two months later was dismissed 'with prejudice' – no benefits, no references and no hopes of ever getting another appointment in teaching. Kevin was thirty-eight, and his first child, my cousin Declan, was just two weeks old.

Connie immediately did two things, one of which was very smart, but the other was to prove highly dangerous. She immediately hired Kevin as Chief Reporter at the *Chronicle* – to the delight of all the staff, including even those who had been coveting the job. Kevin had a brilliant mind, was a first-rate historian and could already write like a pro. His salary would only be half of what he had been getting as a headmaster, but Mary had just gotten a new position at the County Infirmary, so they would be able to manage okay.

The second thing Connie did was to write an editorial accusing the Church of 'rank hypocrisy'. She quoted letters to her paper in which priests, notably all Southerners, had argued that taking an oath, either under duress or without due cognisance, shouldn't trouble the conscience – and they wouldn't even consider it a venial sin. Connie, however, pointed out that, by that logic, every oath ever taken by, or for, a Catholic child – including baptism into the church – held no weight and that the whole foundation of their religion was a sham.

It was rash, it was bad-tempered, it was a line in the sand, and it was published without reference to either Mick or Kevin, both of whom nearly lost their breakfasts when they saw it.

As a *cri de coeur*, it was impassioned and inspiring. But as a newspaper editorial, it was a complete disaster. The Catholic Church was the only major power bloc in the North, other than the state itself, and Connie had just accused its leaders of being, quote, 'overfed cowards', unquote. Stormont was delighted – it was the best result they could have imagined. Instead of keeping the focus on Craig and the ministry and the injustice of their policies, Connie had gotten too angry, taken it too personally and turned on her own camp.

The response was quick and twofold. At all Masses in Derry and Donegal the following Sunday, priests read a terse four-line statement from the cardinal instructing the laity not to purchase the *Chronicle* or support it via advertising until further notice. The newspaper had caused grave offence both to Mother Church and to its community. The Church further demanded the resignation of the 'Editor, Mistress Constance Madden, and the Group Chairman, Mister Michael Madden'. And they announced they would be commencing legal action against the newspaper, and all its distributors, for libel.

Within days, it was clear that the bottom had fallen out of the *Chronicle*'s world. All newsagents and shops in the region – including Protestant-owned ones – stuck notices in their front windows to say they would no longer be stocking the paper. Advertisers cancelled their contracts, and the classified small-ads trickled away to nothing. Even some of the street-sellers refused to handle the paper.

The readership, needless to say, plummeted, with *Chronicle* staff reduced to selling the paper themselves from either the office counters or the back of vans. Within a week, our numbers were down by three-quarters and heading for the drain.

In a bid to fire a shot back in the Church's direction, Connie decided to reach for a story she kept in a drawer – a bishop with a bastard child. Mick attempted to overrule her, and when she wouldn't listen, he got Dev to telephone her from Dublin.

The Taoiseach was very sharp. 'You'll do us irreparable damage,' he told her. 'It's the wrong target. Apologise to the Church, pay them what they're due, and get back out fighting on the right side.'

'I'm apologising to no damn man,' said Connie. But she did accept there was a broader front to fight on and agreed to bury the story of the child.

The boycott went on for two months and the *Chronicle*'s reserves were almost eradicated. Staff were on half-pay and Mick was forced to put up half his farm for security. Connie quietly talked to Alfie Cunningham of the *Leader* to see if he would be interested in buying the titles. But Alfie didn't feel he could provide editorial leadership to both the Catholic and Protestant populations of the North West and graciously declined. 'I'd feel like I was talking out of both sides of my mouth,' he told her.

***

In the end, it was the weasels at Bank of Dublin who brought matters to a head. The Church's man in their administration department invited Connie in and told her she had two weeks to pay back all existing loans, including mortgages, or they would bankrupt her. Alternatively, she could resolve the matter by making a small gesture of conciliation to the Church.

'How small?' asked Connie.

'A twenty-thousand-pounds donation, a public apology and your resignation. Mick can stay where he is.'

Connie couldn't help but laugh — it amounted to a six-million-pound fine in today's money.

'We don't have that sort of reserve. As you know. And besides, I'm not going anywhere.'

'By happy accident, this bank would be prepared to purchase fifty-one per cent of your shares for that same amount.'

Again, Connie wanted to tell him to go to hell, but unfortunately she had seventy jobs riding on her back. So she had to hear him out.

'Would we still have to apologise to the Church?'

'Yes.'

'Would there be a buy-back agreement with the shares, say, if I could raise the money within five years or so?'

'No.'

'And I would have to resign?'

'Yes.'

Connie knew well that if she wasn't *in situ*, the staff didn't stand a chance anyway.

'Then we have no option but to close. You can tell your boss, Dev, for me, I'm done with him.'

The staff of both the Donegal and Derry papers met the following night at the Apprentice Boys Memorial Hall on Society Street, after the Church-run St Columb's Hall refused to let them hold their meeting there. They were there to consider a workers' buyout of the titles, but there were two main problems: money and Connie. Even if they raised the capital – and realistically they could only get about halfway there before they would have to run to the banks – there was the leadership issue. They wouldn't, and couldn't, go forward without Connie. She herself was more than happy to step aside if it meant the jobs could be saved, but the staff put it to the hands-up and the vote was seventy-two against, versus Connie's solitary hand for. Mick, who was chairing the meeting, abstained.

None of them had any problems with issuing an apology to the Church. As Kevin O'Dorrity quipped, 'It'll not be like we're swearing an oath or anything.'

And they could all see the merits in paying off the Church, as the boycott was going to kill them anyway. Yes, it was blackmail, but at least this way, the *Chronicle* would get to keep going. The meeting broke up with a vow to seek the additional buyout funds – and to contact the Church locally to see if there was wriggle room on the numbers and on Connie. They would reconvene the following Friday. But if the situation remained the same, they would produce their final edition the following Tuesday, then close their doors.

Word got out quickly about what had happened at the meeting – Derry always leaked like a sieve. And the local clergy, who had more spies than the Gestapo, recognised that their masters outside the city had overplayed their hand.

The locals realised the importance of the *Chronicle* as both a watchdog and a community voice in the North West, and were seriously concerned about losing it for good. So Monsignor McKinley, who had officiated at Johnny and Connie's wedding, telephoned Dublin and told them to wind their necks in. And quickly.

'If you sack Madden, the paper will close,' McKinley told them.

'What about the money?' the bishop asked.

'They can pay half. Ten thousand tops. But you're in danger of putting them out of business if they take another hit. You'd be better off looking for seven and a half. They'd be sore, but they'll survive.'

'It's twenty or nothing,' said the bishop. 'And the Madden woman goes.'

McKinley, who was a decent soul, took a breath.

'They buried the other story, you know.'

'What other story?'

'The one about your son and heir, Your Lordship.'

There was a long silence at the end of the telephone.

'They know?'

'They do – but they respect you enough never to publish. It would be

114

terrible if anyone else got it. And all of those journalists will end up at other newspapers – maybe even Protestant-owned ones.'

'You're a dirty, dirty fighter, McKinley. Leave it with me.'

***

The following Sunday, priests in Derry and Donegal read a three-line statement from the archdiocese, announcing that the *North West Chronicle* had humbly apologised for its egregious libel of the Church and would be making a substantial donation to the Derry Catholic Schools Fund by way of restitution. Copies of the newspaper would be available in local shops again from Tuesday. And the *Chronicle* would, from this point forward, be re-designated as 'an appropriate medium of advertising' for the North West community.

But even before the *Chronicle*'s workers could begin to gather up the £7,500 agreed damages for the Church, Connie called a snap meeting at the Waterloo Street offices and announced that, as she was responsible for the trouble, she would pay it all herself.

She then revealed that her father, Pat, had just died in Boston after a long illness, and, despite the fact it might leave him turning in his grave, her share of his estate would cover all the Church's costs.

CHAPTER 29

1937–38

Connie had little problem extricating me from the last week of the summer term to escort herself and Mary to the funeral in America. Kevin would have come, too, but Mary needed someone she could trust to run the paper in her absence. Despite the circumstances, it was a delight to be back in a country where an Irish Catholic could be both free and warm.

After the burial, we had dinner at Granny Kate's with Uncle Fitz and a whole bunch of cousins, where we enjoyed a spirited debate about de Valera's creeping appeasement – or pragmatism, depending on your corner – and the rising tide of Fascism. The Americans, who hadn't just gone through fifteen rounds with the Catholic hierarchy, were all for God, Fianna Fáil and Franco. In a move that the CIA would have been proud of, Joe Kennedy had just managed to block all US arms sales to the Spanish Government to better help the Fascist opposition. He was also a lot more neutral on Nazism than his biographers would have liked to remember.

The honest truth, though, is we were all a bit pro-German in those days. Not that Connie and I were anti-Semites, like some in the room, rather it was a case of Hitler being anti-British. And, as you know, my enemy's enemy is my friend.

The entire gathering had a fine time at my young expense, however, when I announced that I thought of myself as a socialist. I had heard Peadar O'Donnell speak at a number of events in Derry and was in awe of both his intellect and his compassion – think Eamonn McCann in a tweed jacket and a Donegal accent.

'How much savings have you currently?' Fitz asked me across the table.

'What do you mean?'

'From your work at the newspaper, and whatever else Mick pays you for running the roads with him.'

I had been careful with my money – I'd my eye on a car for when I turned sixteen – and was proud I'd been disciplined enough to save a tidy sum. So I told him: 'I've about two hundred pounds; roughly a thousand dollars.'

'Here's what we'll do so,' he said. 'There's twenty of us in this room. Despite the fact that you earned that money yourself, and not us, I want you to share

116

out your money equally – fifty dollars a head. Or alternatively maybe take us all out to a restaurant tomorrow night.'

I knew what he was up to. 'I've no problem with sharing,' I said, 'as long as you share back.'

He nodded and smiled. 'But I have a lot more money than you do – I've worked for a lot longer than you, and I've worked smarter, too. Why should I have to look after the other guy? I don't think I should have to share.' He stopped and pointed his fork at me. 'And that, young man, is why communism will never work.'

Everyone laughed, and I was mortified. I opened my mouth and was about to challenge him, but Connie motioned her head no. It was their table – and she didn't want me spilling secrets about how she was running the *Chronicle* like an anarchist cell.

So instead, I told Fitz if he loaned me a couple of sawbucks to go to the movies with the girls, I'd convert back again. And he appreciated my nerve and duly obliged.

***

That conversation rankled for a long time, as did Fitz's gentle mockery of me. And about a week later, when we arrived back in Derry, I asked Connie if she agreed that socialism was a dud.

'Not everything fits everywhere,' she said. 'And no system works perfectly. What I love about the socialists is that they put the common good first. O'Donnell is right in that Dev missed a real chance to redistribute property fairly in the South after the Brits left. And also when he says Fianna Fáil need to take the Church out of government. But the problem with the Reds is that they just can't stop themselves and will end up telling you what to eat for your breakfast. They become totalitarian and dictatorial. No system of government can be fixed in stone; they all have to grow and adapt. Success lies in finding the system that's right for your time and your circumstance.'

I only heard the last part, however, and was convinced that the system that best matched my time and circumstance was communism. Over the past year, Peadar O'Donnell had been relaying reports to all the newspapers in the area about the brave Irish who were fighting with the Connolly Column to protect the Spanish Republic from Franco. And I knew in my young heart that I had to join them.

That same summer, the leader of the Connolly Column, Frank Ryan, was recuperating in Dublin after having been shot in Spain. And he had just started a new left-wing newspaper, the *Irish Democrat*, which I read religiously. So at the end of July, I telephoned Ryan at the paper, told him I had heard O'Donnell speaking and wanted to join the fight. He instructed me to report to Connolly House on Great Strand Street the following Thursday, as there would be a contingent sailing out to join the XV International Brigade the next morning.

'What age are you, son?' he asked.

'Nineteen,' I lied.

'Have you been trained?'

'Yes, sir,' I lied. 'Two years with the IRA in Donegal.'

'Have you papers?'

'Not at present, sir – the police took them from me.'

'Don't worry, we'll get you a set.'

I quickly hunted down Mick and got him to advance me half my savings, telling him there was a second-hand Austin sedan I was interested in. And on the Wednesday morning, while everyone was busy putting the *Chronicle* to bed, I slipped off to the station and boarded the train to Dublin. It was three weeks before my fifteenth birthday.

***

The anti-fascist cause, while much feted today, was regarded as a fool's errand in Ireland at that time, and I knew better than to draw any attention to myself on my travels. The Church, the Blueshirts and even Dev were all supporting Franco's Nationalists, though our Taoiseach, of course, was cunning enough not to say too much publicly.

Late that Wednesday evening, I booked into a boarding house in Rathmines under the name I'd given Ryan, 'Seán Mac Gabhann' – the Irish for John Smith. The following morning, I went directly to Connolly House where I met with Ryan and a number of other men who would be making the trip the next day.

'You look very young, Seán,' said Ryan. 'Are you sure you're nineteen?'

'I am indeed,' I said. 'I've been working as a compositor with the *Donegal Chronicle* for three years now. Ask me anything you like about it.'

So he grilled me a little on newspapers and seemed happy that I knew what I was talking about. Besides, I was over 6ft tall, even then.

'Maybe I can use you to help with publicity when I get back out there,' he said.

We made an arrangement that we would all meet up at the offices the following morning at 7.30, so I headed back to my guesthouse for what would be my last night's rest between a pair of relatively clean sheets. I could barely sleep I was so excited – and proud that I would be serving both my country and my fellow man.

The following morning, I ate a greasy breakfast at my lodgings before walking in the two or so miles to Great Strand Street. I was the first one there – indeed, the office looked completely deserted.

I waited for about ten minutes and was starting to panic a little – maybe I'd got the wrong place – when I saw a car approaching from a distance. Great, we were on our way at last.

As the car got closer, however, I realised to my horror it was Mick's. Worse again, Connie was riding shotgun. They pulled up at the kerb without looking at me.

'Get in the damn back,' said my mother, 'and don't open your damn mouth till we get you to Derry.'

CHAPTER 30

1938-39

Young men, even the best of us, have little but feathers between our ears. Connie was beyond livid with me. But Old Mick understood. He had been a bit of an adventurer himself in his youth – hence Johnny. And he later confessed to me that there were many times he'd had to keep a tight rein on my late father, like when he tried to take a solo run to Dublin to help out after the Easter Rising.

It was Frank Ryan himself who had blown the whistle on me – never trust a revolutionary till he's a year dead. He knew by the softness of my hands that I'd never handled heavy machinery, or weaponry, of any sort. He was worried he might have a spy on his hands – the IRA had just tried to assassinate King George VI in Belfast and there was a major security clampdown across the entire island. So Ryan contacted Peadar O'Donnell about me, or rather Seán Mac Gabhann, and the Donegal man worked out in a trice what was going on: 'Gormless big young fella – talks like a Yank and dresses like Valentino? Don't, for Pete's sake, let him leave the city or his mother will blow me to hell.'

O'Donnell told me many years later that he had been impressed with my gumption in making it all the way to Ryan's door, but there was no way he was going back to Connie with a long face and a longer story.

I, of course, was humiliated – and hated Connie for months because of her interference. Mick talked her out of sending me back to St Columb's as a boarder – and effectively to jail – by assuring her that if they punished me too harshly, I'd head off again and never come back. But it was years before relations between the two of us returned to normal. God bless her patient heart.

And in fairness, it was never used against me again. The staff at the *Chronicle*, who had helped out in what Mick termed the 'search and seize' operation, regarded it as one of those things – 'a dose of the head-staggers', as Harry Carson put it. 'The trick,' he said, 'is to learn from it and never let it happen again.'

***

Over the next year, the *Chronicle*'s fortunes began picking up again – thanks to the ending of the Trade War between the Irish and the British. The Donegal paper, which had come very close to hitting the wall on a number of occasions, was starting to become sustainable. Every silver lining has a cloud, however, and our smuggling department suffered a serious lull, as import tariffs had been relaxed and all sorts of goods were becoming more widely available.

The *Chronicle*'s main editorial focus was on the fallout from the new constitution in the South. Unionists were outraged that Dev's new state laid claim to all thirty-two counties in the island and that it had enshrined the 'special position' of the Roman Catholic Church.

Buoyed up by Dev's harder-than-expected line, republican campaigners in Derry began lobbying Southern councils to frank all their outgoing mail with anti-partition stamps. And Galway, fair play to them, said that they would. Unfortunately, the Free State Department of Posts and Telegraphs took fright that this would lead to reciprocal action from the North, so they brought it to Dev, who quietly put an end to it. But if he was expecting fair play from the Northern postal service, he was naïve in the extreme. At least half the letters sent to 'Derry' until the 1970s wound up in 'Derby'.

✳✳✳

Unionists in the North were also incensed that British Prime Minister Neville Chamberlain had agreed to hand back the last vestiges of its empire south of the border to the Free State. These took the form of three Southern ports that had remained under Westminster jurisdiction after the Anglo-Irish Treaty of 1921. The Treaty Ports, as they were known, comprised three deep-water facilities, two in Cork and one in Donegal. And they had been retained by the British in the wake of the Great War to stop the Germans sneaking in the back door again. The Donegal port was at Lough Swilly, about fifteen miles from Derry, and was protected by two British-controlled forts at Leenan and Dunree.

In October 1938, I travelled with Kevin O'Dorrity to Dunree to report on the formal handover of the Swilly port to the Irish Defence Forces. It was a small but very significant ceremony. The Union Jack was lowered and, after centuries of conflict, the last British troops left Free State soil. Two months earlier, tens of thousands had watched the handover of the Spike Island port off Cork, but there were only about a dozen or so spectators in Donegal. It was the last time in history sovereignty over any territory was handed back to Ireland.

A major consequence of the port handovers would, of course, become apparent within the year, with the outbreak of World War II – or the

'Emergency', as the Southern government, and the *Chronicle*, called it. Ireland – and its ports – remained fiercely neutral, which meant that the British had to modify their shipping lanes and find other facilities at which to refuel. When the IRA started bombing Britain at the start of the Emergency, Dev claimed Churchill might use it as an excuse to seize back the ports – and he came down on his old colleagues like a ton of bricks. Dev also cut the British some slack by refusing to make an issue of access to the Allied port at Derry via the Irish waters in Lough Foyle. Nor did he protest too much when Allied aircraft flew over Donegal. Though even the Germans accepted there was not a lot he could do about it.

***

A few weeks after the war began, I enrolled in Queen's University, Belfast, to read Law. I had performed creditably at St Columb's, without particular distinction, other than in English, where I consistently scored highly. Though the fact that I was subediting my teacher's weekly Op-Ed column for the *Chronicle* couldn't have done me any harm. I had no intentions of practising as either a solicitor or a barrister, but my mother figured that another couple of years' education couldn't do me any harm before I joined the business full-time.

She also, I now realise, wanted to get me as far away from Old Mick as possible for a while, as the looming war held real potential for canny border businessmen like us. There was little she could do about my weekend trips home, though – and I negotiated my timetable so I could get at least one stopover in Derry during the week as well.

Mick was a dream to work with. He used to say that there were two very different types of smuggler: the showboaters and the pros. The showboaters were adrenaline junkies, who were driven by the thrill of the chase and the *craic* of telling the story in the pub afterwards. They loved nothing better than to taunt the Water Rats [Customs] and, more often than not, they took stupid, impulsive risks that wound up getting them caught. The pros, however, never told anyone what they were doing, never took chances or cut corners, and never, ever got caught. Everything was planned to the minutest detail and no outsiders were ever used on the jobs. Our team, and naturally we were pros – we wouldn't have had a showboater near us – was Mick and myself, and, if we needed a third, Harry Carson from the *Chronicle*.

And, because the border was so porous and the Customs on both sides were so stretched, if you applied a bit of wit and science to your labour, it was ridiculously easy. We used a variety of craft, depending on the size of the job: false-bottomed lorries on the main roads, advertising reps' cars on the side roads, and bikes on lanes.

We had legitimate reason to be crossing the border regularly, so when we were stopped, our papers were always in order. And while others would abuse the Water Rats for delaying them, we would always give the same Customs Officers complimentary copies of the *Chronicle* and thank them for their service. And then drive past them with a hundred sides of leather for Bertie Downey's shoemaking shop beside the Derry naval yard.

***

Both sides of the border had their shortages. It was our job to end them. In the North, where rationing had been introduced, our customers were crying out for eggs, sugar, nylons and poultry. In the 'State', it was fuel, tea, tobacco and white bread. Oh, and contraceptives, which were banned in the South. Old Mick wasn't at all keen on the 'dirty stuff' – he was past that sort of thing – but Connie knew what her delivery fleet was being used for her, and it appeased her social conscience.

Our cut varied wildly depending on demand. When the South stopped exporting Guinness in the early 1940s because the Brits wouldn't sell them farm machinery, one Derry-based American battalion agreed to pay us six times the price of a normal barrel if we could get them a regular supply. And we did.

You have to realise that, unlike what was going on in the States a decade earlier, we never regarded what we were doing as in any way criminal or in contravention of the law. We looked on it as our right, if not our duty. 'The biggest crime in Ireland is the border,' as Old Mick used to say. The Church, likewise, never regarded smuggling as a sin – even a venial one. Priests used to be hoors for it, altogether, until the Free State grounded all their cars as non-essential during the fuel crisis. And the *Chronicle* never reported on smuggling cases brought before the courts; we weren't hypocrites, after all – until a few years later, that is.

And because we never talked about what we were doing, and had no interest in talking about it, we were never caught. We were only interested in making money and, for a time, we were making mountains.

CHAPTER 31

1940–41

The *Chronicle*'s neutral – or, more pertinently, non-jingoistic – stance on the new war would soon run us into more difficulties with the Northern state. From the outset in September 1939, Connie took an editorial decision that any coverage of the war in Europe would be precise and objective and that we would leave the adjectival cheerleading to the rest. Words like 'glorious', 'heroic' and 'daring' were forbidden, as were 'dastardly' and 'cowardly'. It was not our job to support either Germany or Britain; it was our job to deliver the news. And so we spent our days subediting increasingly hysterical propaganda from war correspondents, trying to sort the facts from the hype.

We were warned a number of times by friendly Unionists in the city that their colleagues in Belfast were just looking for an excuse to close us down – particularly when we refused to lie about how badly things were going for the British. They couldn't see outside the justness of their cause and genuinely believed that anyone who looked over the other side of the fence was doing Goebbels's work for him.

Eventually, in early 1940, our Derry edition found itself banned, though not for its war reportage – or at least not directly. The banning order, from the NI Ministry of Home Affairs, came after we condemned the hanging of two Irishmen convicted of a bombing in Coventry during the IRA's so-called Sabotage Campaign. In an editorial, written by me but commissioned by Connie, we praised the men's bravery in the face of a 'witch-hunt'. But we stopped short of calling them 'martyrs', as we didn't want to give any further credibility to what was frankly a reckless and ill-timed caper.

Northern Unionists and – to a lesser extent – the British establishment were apprehensive that the Germans would invade Ireland and that the IRA would help them. The IRA commander Steven Hayes at one stage even drew up a plan to team up with the Germans to invade the North. But, as we know now, the Germans worked out quickly that the IRA had neither the numbers nor the military capability to be of any real use to them.

Nonetheless, neither Stormont nor the British wanted us giving the IRA any quarter whatsoever in our columns and they whacked us with a six-month ban. We immediately made plans to print our Derry edition in Donegal, then sell it on the streets of the city via our network of paperboys as we had done before.

Alfie Cunningham of the *Londonderry Leader* knew, however, we would be risking serious fines if we continued to butt heads with Stormont, so he decided to take matters into his own hands. And before the first of our proposed 'underground' editions even hit the presses, he set up a meeting with Northern Minister for Home Affairs Richard Bates for us.

We travelled with Alfie to a hotel in Coleraine, where the minister was waiting in the manager's office. And to be fair to him, despite his reputation as being an appalling anti-Catholic bigot, he was civility itself. He accepted our assurances that we had been fiercely neutral and dispassionate in all our coverage. His problem was, however, that this was no longer enough.

He then produced a huge back catalogue of our papers and challenged us to find any single positive comment we had written about the Allied forces. He knew well we couldn't.

'We don't do comment on the war,' Connie told him. 'My readers are intelligent enough to make their own moral judgements.'

'I'm sure they are,' he told her, 'but I think you need to consider becoming a little more Redmondite.' Redmond had encouraged the Irish to enlist with the British in the Great War. 'Your own home nation, the United States of America, will be joining our cause soon – and I wouldn't be surprised at all to see major changes in this neck of the woods as the war goes on.'

We – Connie, Kevin O'Dorrity, Alfie and myself – were intrigued. We all believed that Bates was alluding to speculation that the British would seriously consider an end to partition after the war if Ireland joined its corner. In other words, if you play nice with us, we'll look after you when it's all over.

What we didn't know at that time was that the British and Americans had already struck a private agreement, before the war ever began, that the Yanks would make Derry their primary European base. And within a year, our entire city would be swamped with GIs.

Connie, naturally, declined to give Bates any guarantees as to her future conduct. But, as we were leaving, he told her he accepted her *bona fides*, and would recommend the lifting of the ban – as a gesture of good faith.

'Any friend of Alfie Cunningham has to be honourable,' he said.

We thanked him. He had made his point, we had made ours, and he had graciously put his gun back in his pocket.

***

On the car-ride back to Derry, the thing that rankled Connie most, however, was the fact that Bates clearly knew a lot more about what was going on than she did. She was used to being the most informed, and smartest person in any room she walked into. And she realised how little she knew about America's prospective role in the war, despite the fact that the new US ambassador to Britain was married to her first cousin.

The following week, we set sail to London to visit Ambassador Joseph Kennedy for a full briefing at the embassy, disguised as a catch-up lunch. But within about five minutes, it was apparent that Joe wasn't interested at all in involving America in Europe's affairs.

'Britain is defeated,' he told us. 'It just doesn't know it yet; it's got six months left, a year at the most. America should be talking directly to Hitler to discuss relations going forward. The current war gives America a chance to decide what it needs to do next. But I don't think fighting in Europe should be part of it. We'd be risking too much.'

Joe had always been an isolationist, but, according to the wires we read every morning, the public mood in the US was changing. And it was apparent, even to us, he was unlikely to last in London for too long. One of the jokes doing the rounds in Whitehall at the time was: 'I thought my daffodils were yellow until I met Joe Kennedy.'

As you know, Joe was accused of appeasement, fell out with Roosevelt and by the end of the year had been forced to resign his position.

***

It wouldn't be long before the *Chronicle* was up before the minister again, though this time he was offering more carrot than stick. He had been concerned about our reportage of a Luftwaffe bombing in Derry in April 1941 and wanted us to downplay the pandemonium it had caused among civilians.

Derry had always regarded itself as pretty safe up to that point. The city was located right beside neutral Éire and, despite the fact it had become the British Navy's temporary North Atlantic Headquarters, it was so far from mainland Europe that few German bombers, if any, would risk the trip here and back.

The River Foyle, however, was packing up with ships – both battleships and escorts – to such an extent that at one stage, you could actually walk across the river hopping from boat-deck to boat-deck. Extra anti-artillery guns had already been installed, and giant helium barrage balloons on winches had been deployed across the region to deter low-flying air attacks. Other than London, Derry was the most protected city on the islands.

At the height of the Blitz in April 1941, Belfast took a bad hammering, and one night, either by accident or design, a Luftwaffe plane made its way as far as Derry and, we believe, attempted to drop two parachute-mines onto the docks. The bombs both missed their target. But one of them landed at the Collon, smack bang in the middle of a row of houses built for servicemen who had served in the Great War. Thirteen people were killed, four of them ex-soldiers.

The fallout was extraordinary. I never witnessed fear like it. Thousands of people from across the city left their homes for Donegal that same night, some never to return. And despite the fact there was never another attack, others would only return to Derry during daylight hours, to work or go to school, and then would sleep in billets arranged by families or the Church in outlying villages like Muff, Killea and St Johnston. Rows of shanty huts and temporary homes sprang up on the Donegal side of the border on land gifted by sympathetic farmers.

Those who didn't join the exodus – such as Connie and myself – spent many of our nights in bomb shelters, as the sirens tended to go off with every flock of passing geese.

In the immediate aftermath of the bomb, the *Chronicle* reported how more than a thousand Catholics, many believing the world was coming to an end, had queued up outside St Eugene's Cathedral to receive confession. Indeed, priests were reduced to hearing the penitents in the aisles of the chapel because all the boxes were in such demand. And it was this detail in particular which had alarmed the minister.

Again we met Bates at Coleraine, and again Alfie agreed to come as arbiter.

'We need to put a lid on the fear and panic,' he said, holding up a copy of our report. 'It's harming morale. And while I appreciate that's not your concern, it is mine, and I'd very much like some help. And specifically, I need your help, Mrs Madden, and Seán's.'

Connie studied him carefully for a couple of seconds, a little puzzled. 'How can we help you exactly?'

He took a deep breath, then looked at us cautiously over his reading glasses. 'This is all still classified, so can I have your word that it will remain such for the time being?'

We all nodded solemnly.

'Thank you,' he said. 'In just over two months' time, three hundred and fifty American technicians are going to arrive in Derry to begin work on a new US naval base, with at least the same number again expected to join them before Christmas. We would like very much if you and Seán could help us welcome them and help them acclimatise.'

I could see that Connie was genuinely thrilled to be in the loop but she wasn't going to let Bates know that. So instead, she went fishing. 'Where's this base going to be built?'

'In about ten different locations across the North West as far as I'm aware,' said Bates. 'They're going to make preparations for between five- and ten thousand American service personnel in total, across a range of disciplines. Initially, they'll be based at Beech Hill House at Ardmore – but they'll also be in Springtown and Caw, and at various sites along the river. These technicians – note, not soldiers, at least not yet – will spend the next year building depots, radio installations, a new quay at Lisahally and a new ship-repair dock.'

This was eight months before Pearl Harbour, but Connie and I realised immediately what this meant. After years of dealing with treacherous Free Staters, perfidious Brits and hostile Orangemen, things were finally looking up. The Americans were coming in to save us.

CHAPTER 32

1942–47

It was clear, though Bates never spelt it out, that the main plank of our role as liaison officers would be procurement. The Yanks – or 'Leathernecks' as they were sometimes known – were not generally short of supplies, but when they needed to get their hands on materials quickly, from gravel to gravy, they called on us and we sorted it out for them. Fresh produce was always in demand – particularly good meat and dairy products. And yes, it's true, I once persuaded a diving team to salvage a working German radar system from a scuttled U-boat and sold it on to our friends for a king's ransom.

Our work for the base was an open secret, tolerated by both the Water Rats and the police, who, like the rest of us, had fallen in love with our Hollywood visitors. For the next three years, not a single *Chronicle* van or vehicle was ever searched at a military or customs checkpoint. They were sacrosanct – we might as well have had big red crosses painted on the side of them.

The newspaper itself benefited greatly from the connection, too: advertising revenue doubled in 1943 and again in 1944, and we never suffered newsprint or ink shortages, like many of our compatriots. The soldiers and sailors all read the paper religiously – they appreciated that we would never blow smoke in their faces about how well, or badly, things were going. So our circulation shot up as well. During the latter part of the war, Derry's population was nearly twice what it had been pre-war, thanks to the 20,000 British service personnel, 10,000 Canadians, 6,000 Yanks and many other assorted nationalities who had turned our little city into a cosmopolitan melting pot.

Our special status also won our reporters access to American concerts and VIP receptions and landed us interviews with visiting stars like Bob Hope, Paul Robeson and my own fantasy lady, Merle Oberon. When I told Hope that I edited the *Chronicle*'s Arts & Culture Section he quipped: 'Culture is the ability to describe Jane Russell without moving your hands …' We were also invited for coffee with Eleanor Roosevelt at the Ardowen Hotel on Northland Road, later blown up by the IRA – the hotel, that is.

The one downside with the Yanks was that because they were enormously generous, and had the best cigarettes and 'candy', other soldiers could get a bit jealous. It wasn't unusual for a British Tommy to dance all night with a local girl at the Corinthian and for a GI Joe to swoop in with a pair of black nylons or a pack of Camels at the last minute and wipe his eye. This, as you'd gather, did not generally go down well. And I spent many an early morning at the police barracks, with fistfuls of ten-shilling notes trying to post bail, pay fines and occasionally pay off witnesses.

The Americans weren't always fully aware of what was going on around them, either. On one occasion in 1943, I took a posse of junior officers down to Moville in County Donegal for an ice cream. The neutral South had by then adopted a very practical approach to visiting soldiers in that if they didn't announce themselves, they didn't get hassled. It was known as 'taking off your hat'. My Yanks were in the lounge of a local hotel finishing off a drink when I got chatting to a man who was leaving the restaurant and who wanted to know where the clerk was. He was a very polished looking guy in his early forties, I'd guess.

'Are you Irish?' he asked me. I detected a bit of an accent.

'I am indeed,' I replied proudly.

'Are you with the Americans?'

'I'm just showing them around. What about yourself?'

He pointed through the front door down towards Lough Foyle. 'I'm a visitor here myself. I've just stopped in for a meal after a few days at sea.'

It took me a few seconds to understand what he was saying.

'I think you might be moving on now,' I said.

'I think you might be right,' he said and flashed me a big grin. 'Auf Wiedersehen.'

And he disappeared out the door and hurried straight to his waiting U-boat.

***

In 1944, after I finished my degree, I took a fit of conscience about the fact that I was living a very privileged life and wasn't risking my skin like most others of my age, and I began seriously considering enlisting in the US Marines. There was no way I could join a British regiment, or serve under Montgomery, after what they had done to my father and my country.

Connie sensed I was bothered and set up a meeting with a visiting general, who had agreed to brief the *Chronicle* on recent movements in France. The real purpose, as I worked out later, was to talk some sense into me.

At the end of the session, I asked him how I could best go about enlisting, and where did he think my legal or journalistic skills might be best employed.

'You're not going anywhere, Seán,' he said, 'even if I have to shoot you myself. You're the man who keeps my troops in Guinness and butter.'

And with that, an aide entered the room and hurried General Dwight D Eisenhower away for his next meeting.

***

The last year of the war went by in a blur, with tens of thousands of personnel passing through the city on their way to Europe for D-Day and the follow-up campaign. In early May 1945, while Dev visited the German Embassy in Dublin to pass on his condolences, Derry celebrated along with the Allies as victory was secured. Then, a week later, the world descended on the North West for the formal surrender of the German U-boat fleet on the Foyle.

Business boomed during that final year – the city had full employment for the first time ever – so, like all local employers, we found ourselves hiring in outside talent from Donegal and Tyrone. But ultimately, none of us was prepared for what followed next.

As things quieted down in the months after the war, and the fleets that had floated the town on their money for the past five years departed, commerce in the city ground to a halt. And the serious social problems, which had been simmering before 1939, re-emerged.

It quickly became apparent that the housing shortage in the city was worse even than in London – half of which had been razed to the ground. Only two houses in total were built in Derry between the years 1939 and 1944. In January 1946, the *Chronicle* reported that one house in William Street had forty-nine registered residents – all of whom were expected to share the one toilet. Things were dire. It wasn't uncommon for a family of ten to have to eat and sleep in the one room. Health officials lost count of the number of young children and elderly people who developed lung complaints and died.

When the Yanks set sail for home, squatters immediately began moving into the metal Nissen huts they had vacated in outlying areas like Springtown, Belmont and Creggan. All electricity and water supplies had been stripped away, so conditions were worse than primitive: they were freezing in winter and saunas in summer. But thousands flocked into them regardless and, in some cases, people ended up staying in the camps for more than twenty years. One of the saddest sights I ever saw was a bailiff evicting families from huts at Belmont to clear the area for new houses for policemen. It was a dispossession of those who already had nothing.

***

Politically, it was anathema to Unionists in Derry to build new houses. They had expertly carved up the city's electoral boundaries to give themselves a majority of council seats – despite the fact they were outnumbered almost two to one – and they knew that any tinkering would wreck that fine balance. Also, the housing crisis was forcing at least a thousand Catholics a year to emigrate from the city, thus improving Unionists' chances of holding onto power in the long term.

This, I am happy to say, wasn't the position of ordinary, decent Protestants in the city – people like Alfie Cunningham – but rather spoke to a particular, hidden section of the political class, who would later become known as 'the faceless men'. And it was their short-sightedness and casual cruelty that led to the social upheaval in the 1960s.

My contemporary, the excellent young journalist Frank Curran, wrote a short book about the situation in 1946, along with the Nationalist MP Eddie McAteer, entitled *Ireland's Fascist City*. And by 1948, the Unionists had been shamed into building three thousand new houses in Creggan. But, of course, this was in the already Nationalist South Ward and so wouldn't affect the overall Unionist majority.

***

The *Chronicle* had done well in the boom years, but Connie and Mick were slow to adapt to new peacetime realities and insisted on retaining all their new staff, despite the fact there was patently no work for them. A number of the advertising department, who were unused to finding doors shutting in their faces, stopped trying so hard and revenue figures quickly plummeted.

That number, I'm ashamed to say, included a bright and bossy junior manager, Tish Brehony, whom I had escorted to the pictures on a number of occasions and who, in retrospect, might have had designs on the boss-in-waiting. Though, of course, I had not picked up on this at all, because, as you're aware, I never had eyes for any woman except your Grandma Millie. Anyhow, when I dared mention to Tish at a management meeting that the figures were down, she told me it was none of my affair and that I would need to watch myself, as at least it was honest money.

I was astounded, as was Mick, who was chairing the meeting. But as is the way with these things, we agreed to let it slide for the sake of a quiet life and pressed on with the day's agenda. Big, big mistake. A short time later, Tish barged into my little office and started with the 'How dare yous' so loud they could be heard the whole way to the top floor. And Connie, who had missed the morning meeting, came downstairs and ordered Tish home to compose herself.

Tish sent for her cards the following morning and vowed never to put her nose over the door of the *Chronicle* again. So Mick and I congratulated ourselves on our lucky escape and on getting rid of a lunatic. But naturally, we decided not to tell Connie about Tish's quite pointed threat.

Up to that juncture, I had little to no experience of womankind's sharper edges – having largely subscribed to the 'sugar and spice' theory. It was one of the joys of a single-sex education. For all my adventures on the roads, I was a complete innocent abroad. And so, the following night, while I was driving a van full of Donegal papers to the shops in Derry which stocked both editions, I was astounded to be stopped by the police and advised that my 'former fiancée' Tish had outed me as a smuggler.

To my great relief, I knew the van was clean. I had been hoping to collect a large consignment of butter and chocolate in Killygordon that evening, but the supplier had rung the office to say it wouldn't be ready for another couple of days. So I was travelling with nothing but perfectly legal newspapers.

One of the cops was Mousey Lynch, son of the thug who Connie had gotten sent to Larne twenty years previously. And he demanded the keys to the back door, which I handed over with a smile and an instruction to search high and low, as he would find damn all.

But as he moved to the rear of the van, I looked out the window and, sitting on the ditch, I saw six crates full of bottles, gleaming in the moonlight, and my heart sank. Because I knew, sure as eggs, that four policemen were about to swear under oath that the biggest haul of *poitín* they had seized so far that year had been resting in the hidden compartment of my van.

CHAPTER 33

1947: Derry to Boston

Give a dog a bad name and it sticks. Howl at the moon one time and you're a wolf. Or, as Old Mick, God rest him, used to say, you only have to shag one sheep … And now, despite the fact I had been completely set up and framed, the whole world had me pegged as a smuggler.

It was after midnight by the time Connie bailed me out of Victoria RUC Barracks – fifty notes, no less – and we walked in terrifying silence up Waterloo Street to the *Chronicle* offices, where Old Mick was waiting.

Connie sat herself down at the head of the boardroom table and looked down coldly at the two of us. I hadn't seen her so angry since Peadar O'Donnell told her that her little boy had run away from home.

Mick and myself huddled together for protection at the other end of the table, heads down as if in the headmaster's office.

She gave us about twenty seconds' silence to let the fear sink in properly and then began. 'I warned you both,' she said. 'It was always going to happen. I warned you to stop when the Yankees went home, but you wouldn't listen.'

Mick raised his hand to interrupt. 'In fairness to Seán …' he said.

That was as far as he got. Connie shut him down with a single look.

'Don't play the innocent with me, Mick Madden. You'd smuggle sinners out of hell if you thought it would make you a few pounds.'

'But we couldn't have known the girl was serious,' he said.

Connie froze. Mick had just broken the cardinal rule of never opening your big mouth and making a bad situation worse.

'What girl?' she asked quietly.

Mick decided to rip the bandage off all at once – off me, that is. 'The Brehony one. She told young Casanova there that she knew what he was up to at nights when he wasn't with her.'

Connie's face got even darker. 'And how do you know that, Michael?'

He started to stammer. 'Ah, ah, ah, well, I may have heard her.'

'And you didn't tell me? And you let me throw her out the door? Of all the addle-headed idiots I have ever met, you two win the parish draw.'

I hadn't said anything up to then as Mick was doing just fine on his own. But my conscience got the better of me. 'It's not his fault,' I said. 'I didn't know she'd a notion for me – I thought she was being friendly, just enjoying a laugh.'

She scowled furiously at me over her glasses. 'I'm sorry to tell you, son, but your jokes aren't that funny.'

That was unnecessary. 'But besides, this isn't entirely my fault. It was your old pal Lynch's son who fitted me up.'

Her eyes widened. 'You? You're blaming me for this? Are you serious?'

'No, ma'am. I'm not.'

'The inspector says they're going to throw the book at you. Maybe even send you to jail. I should let them do it – teach you some humility. But Paddy Maxwell reckons they'll not want to risk a battle with a newspaper, so they'll make do instead with a helluva fine. I hope you have the money saved, Seán, because I'm not paying for it.'

Maxwell was the local Nationalist MP and also our solicitor.

'I'll pay the fine,' I said. 'But I'm not apologising for what I did. I'm not going to buy into their lies. We have to take a stand.'

'Take a stand? Take a stand? You'd make us a laughing stock. You've evaded more tax than Capone. You know it, I know it – the whole country knows it. This newspaper lives and dies on its integrity. You got caught, so you're now going to pay the penalty. And better again, we're going to report on it all in the next edition of the paper.'

'You can't do that – we don't do smuggling cases. Smuggling is not a crime, remember?'

'Oh, yes, it is. As and from now. And *poitín* is a poison that blinds people. We're going to start covering cases from Tuesday and, to show we're serious about it, you're going to be the very first. We need to try and restore some credibility ...'

'In which case, I'm resigning. I've had enough. I'm not going to be treated like this.'

There was another silence for about thirty seconds, and when Connie spoke, her voice was ice cold. 'Okay, Seán. We'll do it your way. Don't for a minute think you're irreplaceable. None of us are. And you're not resigning – you're fired. No severance. Kevin can run the paper when I'm done.'

Mick lowered his head and was just about to remind Connie never to make a decision when you're mad. But it was too late. She was already out the door.

***

I know now, sixty-five years on, that my mother had no option but to make an example of me. A good watchdog can't just bark when it suits. You have to do exactly what Connie did – suck it up and stick the story on the front page, if only to make sure everyone and anyone knows you have no favourites. The number of friends I lost over the years since because they wanted me to drop drink-driving cases or petty assaults runs into the hundreds. And I've always warned my family and the *Chronicle* staff alike that if they, or their families, ever get into trouble, the paper is going to dish it out to them on the chin, like it does to everyone else – only, perhaps, more so.

But for all that, I was left with a real sense of injustice in that I had never lived my life other than by Connie's principles, and yet here she was bringing a new set of rules into play. It's like when you become good at a game and all of sudden they stick you with a handicap.

Connie had turned fifty the previous year, and the plan had been for her to become chairman within the next year to allow Mick to retire. I would then assume the editorship, with support from both of them. But there was no way I could work with her now. Or she with me.

After I quit, I kicked up my heels at home for a week, skulking off to my room any time Connie came back. I was actually considering asking Alfie Cunningham for a job on his newsdesk when, out of the blue, I got a call from Granny Kate in Boston.

'Mick tells me you're getting a raw deal,' she said. 'Why don't you come over here for a few months to clear your head? They've got some graduate courses across the river in Harvard that might interest you.'

'Thanks, Kate, but it would look like I'm running away. I'm not going to let people think I did anything wrong.'

'No-one thinks that. But your mother's not going to appreciate what she has until you've gone – nor, more importantly, will the *Chronicle*. And to be honest, I could do with the company. You could have your old room back – and you can have Pat's old car. I'm a bit lonely since Pat passed, and your cousins don't call as much as they did. Was I telling you about my operation?'

Classic Irish mother stuff and, of course, I lapped it up like milk. Truth was, Derry had gotten a little too claustrophobic with its sneaky coppers and bi-polar stalkers, so it was time for a change. More importantly, perhaps, it was time to grow up.

CHAPTER 34

The next day was the last Friday of term and McGinlay again had business in the courthouse. It was a beautiful, sunny morning, so he rang McCloud's room at the hotel to tell him he'd meet him at the Apprentice Boys Memorial Hall at quarter after ten.

'What's wrong with your mobile phone?'

McCloud sighed deeply. 'They haven't given it back to me. Apparently, Mo dropped it shortly after she took it from me and has taken it to get the screen repaired.'

McGinlay laughed. 'Your own fault. You were warned not to carry it. I once left a laptop in Maeve's office by accident; had to get a court order to get it back. But don't worry, I'm sure they'll give you your phone eventually.'

***

McGinlay was five minutes late and out of breath when he arrived at the 'Mem'. 'Apologies,' he said. 'It never helps when the client has been pouring vodka onto her cornflakes.'

McCloud had passed the time reading the info-sign outside the massive gothic building, which commemorated the apprentices who saved the city from King James by slamming shut the gates. The Mem contained both a Siege Museum and a social centre, and twenty years ago, McCloud remembered, had been the scene of a standoff between Protestant would-be marchers and Catholic would-be march-stoppers. But Derry, typically, had resolved its marching issues shortly after that, long before the rest of the prehistoric North. And the Mem now regularly partnered with the Bogside-based Museum of Free Derry on various projects. McGinlay pointed to a little church, set in a perfectly maintained country garden, on the higher ground to their left. 'That's St Augustine's – known as "the wee church on the Walls". It's built on Derry's oldest Christian site – where Colmcille erected his monastery back in the sixth century.'

McCloud pointed to a big empty plinth on a bastion out on the Walls. 'And what's that?'

McGinlay grinned. 'That's where Walker's Pillar used to stand, before the IRA blew it up in the 1970s. They did the same to Nelson's Column in Dublin. In their defence, it was a bit triumphalist to stick a statue of the man who kicked the Jacobites' arses on a seventy-foot obelisk overlooking the Bogside. I think we're all a little more sensitive now.'

The pair ambled down the hill towards the river, McGinlay pointing out the various landmarks – First Derry Presbyterian Church, the Calgach Interpretative Centre, the Nerve Centre and Magazine Studios.

'Before I forget,' said McGinlay, 'I spoke to David Cunningham and, all being well, he'll take you out to meet his father at the nursing home in Dunavady next Monday evening. EF should have had his dinner and a couple of drinks and will be as together as you'll ever get him.'

'Are you coming?'

'Oh, yes. I wouldn't miss it.'

'You're still friends with David?'

'Absolutely. He's a client when he's not fighting with the *Chronicle*. The links that bind the Maddens and the Cunninghams go back more than a hundred years. The families have bailed each other out so many times that we're never going to allow what EF did to wreck that.'

'Why? What did EF do?'

'We'll come to that in due time. Suffice to say, you'll have your questions well ready for EF by the time you get to meet him.'

'But I thought David and Maeve hated one another, too?'

'Yes, and that's why you planted the photo. And they do, a bit – but only because Maeve doesn't know any better. We'll work it all out.'

As they reached the steps that led down to Magazine Gate, Bowtie fell back a step to admire McCloud's new white linen jacket. 'She'll love it,' he said. 'Very George Clooney in *Ocean's Eleven*.'

McCloud laughed. 'It's like I'm in a shop window.'

'*Like*? You are in a shop window, comrade; live with it. How's the drinking panning out? Have you got your quotas regularised again after your jet lag?'

McGinlay wasn't just fishing. The guy had been through it, and McCloud knew he was offering his help. 'I only had two last night. Well, two large ones. Slept like a log, too – it helps when the brain is getting real work to do. That gives me an extra one for either tonight or tomorrow night.'

'She lets you carry it over?'

'God, no, I've it hidden in an empty aftershave bottle I brought with me.'

McGinlay gave him a sympathetic smile. 'If you ever get tired living from buzz to buzz, just let me know. I've walked in your shoes.'

CHAPTER 35

Back at the manse, Maeve was threatening not to give Mo the keys to the bunker.

'Let me meet him,' she said. 'I'll be good.'

Mo shook her head emphatically. 'No. You're still too angry. You're wearing your patent-leather DMs this morning – like you do when you want to stomp on someone.'

Maeve laughed and threw Mo the keyring. But her guardian wasn't done. 'You're going to have some serious making-up of your own to do before this is over, too.'

'Why? What did I do?'

'Don't play innocent. You started it all – with your smarty-pants CV of him on the front of the paper. I told you that stuff about his brother was too nasty. The poor fellow's dead. Do you not think McCloud feels guilty enough?'

Maeve flushed. Seán's one rule about decisions was: if there's any doubt, sleep on them. And Mo had begged Maeve to sleep on those lines. But, of course, she hadn't, and she knew now she was wrong. Badly wrong.

'I didn't think I'd like him. I didn't think he'd be a good guy – one of us.'

'But he is.'

'So it would appear. And I've blown it again. What is it with me and smart men?'

Mo had struggled with the same problem for years; she smiled supportively. 'They're the only ones who interest you – but the problem with that is they're also able to dish back whatever you give them and more. There's a reason for the phrase "more than a match for you".'

Maeve's last serious boyfriend, indeed her only serious boyfriend, had been her college sweetheart at Harvard, seven years previously. Interestingly, Leo had also been a 6ft-plus, dark-haired Irish-American lawyer. By the time they broke up, he had almost taught her how to trust another human being. But she felt it just wasn't right for her, took fright and ran back to Ireland.

'If you had to do Harvard again,' asked Mo, 'would you leave Leo behind?'

'I wouldn't have left him so quickly. I think I might have asked him to come here. The problem is, though, he might have done just that.'

'You could always ring him up now.'

'I may just do that. His wife and two children would really like it here.'

'You're kidding?'

'No, I Facebook-stalk him all the time – or rather his wife. That particular Elvis has left the meat-market. I'm probably better off. He was a bit too buttoned-up. Never once got a speeding ticket, never once got drunk and never once asked me to do anything kinky …'

Mo smiled. 'This new guy drinks a bit, though. Could you handle it? You sometimes have bother handling your own.'

Maeve shrugged. On a good week, she doubled the recommended intake; on a bad week, she could quadruple it. 'I only drink when I'm unhappy or when I'm bored,' she said.

'Well, you must live a dull and dreadful life, then, princess. I think I'll get Tommy Bowtie to talk to you – maybe get you a sponsor.'

Maeve raised a warning finger. 'Drunken physician heal thyself. You say one word to Bowtie and I'll tell him how you and Seán filled your coffee-cups with whiskey during his intervention for Marty Corrigan.'

'Yeah, we mightn't have set the best of examples. Just take it a little easier, that's all. You're too young yet to be getting a big red whiskey nose and liver spots.'

'I haven't had a drop since the funeral. I need the real sleep – not the comas.'

'Keep it up. We're going to need clear heads over the next few days to keep an eye on McCloud. Talking of which, there's Tommy Bowtie's Merc coming up the drive. I'll go down and meet them – I should be in Waterloo Street about a half-hour after you. Try not to slander, libel or otherwise offend anyone until I get into the office.'

'I'll do my best, you fat old slapper. See you later.'

CHAPTER 36

Mo also admired the linen jacket but thought it was more Pierce Brosnan than George Clooney. 'Tommy Bowtie used to have one,' she said, 'but he couldn't quite pull it off. We used to get little children to go up to him on the street and ask him for an ice cream.'

They had spoken in the kitchen the previous day, but she now was guiding McCloud directly into the comfortable seats in the TV room. 'Better spy-cam coverage in there?' he asked.

'Close,' she said. 'For whatever reason, we can't pick up sound in the kitchen.'

'Do you let other guests know about the surveillance?'

Mo was genuinely startled. 'Of course we do. Do you think we'd watch or record people in a private place without their knowledge? For a start it's illegal, and secondly, and more importantly, it's morally repugnant.'

It was his turn to be surprised. 'But what about the other day? You didn't tell me.'

She laughed. 'You're a paid Federal Agent – a full-time spy, here to snoop on us. You expect us *not* to watch you like a hawk? Come on, man, be sensible. But civilians are completely off limits. And rest assured we're the only ones who have any surveillance inside this bunker. We can render the entire place completely impregnable at the touch of a few buttons – shutting off our own security systems and anybody else trying to piggyback inside ours. Seán designed this thing to be a bulletproof, leak-proof pod.'

He shrugged. 'Very impressive. But you've got a very opt-in, opt-out view on morality, Mo, particularly given what you did to me on the front page of your paper on Tuesday.'

She nodded. 'It should never have happened. I apologise unreservedly – and I've already spoken to my charge for doing it. We're better than that, Ally. Really. She just got overheated with Seán's death and made a mistake. I've told her she has to apologise to you herself. Now, let's get on to business – do you remember your mnemonic?'

He smiled. 'Thank you, and I accept you at your word. No mnemonics today. Just a couple of small queries.'

Mo kicked off her summer flats and rested her feet on a leather footstool. 'Shoot.'

'I've heard some of the Joe Kennedy stuff before. Are there any suggestions in the unedited tapes that he was more than a passive supporter of Hitler?'

'That's hardly germane to your inquiry, is it?'

He waited her out. Eighteen seconds before she resumed. 'No. Seán never suggested there was outright collusion, like there was between Joe and the Spanish fascists.'

'Did Seán himself ever collude with Germany? Hiding personnel, smuggling weaponry or supplies, anything like that?'

'Absolutely not. Seán's business during the war was making money – nothing more. And taking sides with anyone meant you generally couldn't do business with someone else. Connie and he both would have had sympathies at the start of the war – no doubt about it. But they never crossed the line. And then when the Americans came in, it was about supporting the extended family.'

'Thank you. Second query – and it's a quick one – de Valera. Seán sounds disappointed in him. Why didn't he do more for you?'

'In retrospect, I suppose he couldn't. He had no money – and not enough energy, or space, to fight a war in the North while building a country in the South. He didn't betray us outright, in the way that Fine Gaelers do when they claim that all the problems in the North are of our own making. They intellectualise their moral cowardice and inaction by convincing themselves that the Northern Irish are a race apart. Whereas we in the North tend to see ourselves as the child they abandoned. A bit naïve of us, if I'm to be honest. The British have always had little-to-no respect for the Irish, but Dev's crew kept them a little more honest. The Irish elements to the peace settlement faded away to very little a few years back when Arnie O'Reilly was thrown out in the South.'

McCloud wished he could get this on tape for his students at Quantico. Maybe he would ask Mo for a copy of hers when this was all over – or better again, she might come out and talk to them.

'Anything else?' she asked.

'Final thing,' he said. 'It won't take long. Tish Brehony – was she a one-off, or was there maybe a line of women waiting to shoot Seán?'

Mo gave him a sideways look. 'Between ourselves?'

He nodded.

She smiled. 'He always did attract the crazies. Connie once told me that when he was only fifteen, a fistfight broke out between two typists in the

142

front office over who was going to marry him. Apparently, he bought them both buns every Friday, and that made them special. After that, Connie used to run point for him, without him ever knowing it. Derry mothers can be very protective. And she blamed herself for letting Tish slip under the radar.'

'Was Seán really a bit innocent?'

'Definitely – at least he was before he went back to America and got a bit wiser to the ways of the world. He never said as much, but I think he spent his first years back in Boston learning from the guys in the office and hunting women for sport – until he started to get hunted in turn. And he didn't like that at all. But then he met Millie and all that changed.'

'What was she like?'

'I only knew her for a few weeks. But she was an angel. No woman would ever be enough for him after her. Not a chance. She was just so perfect for him – and the two together were the most amazing force. They lit up every room they went into.'

'And after her?'

'It could never happen again. You don't get that lucky or blessed, or whatever it is you believe in, twice in the one life. Seán knew that and, for a long time, he didn't bother at all. I was his beard. Everybody assumed – completely wrongly – that we were together. But he was halfway between a big brother and a young father to me. It would have been obscene.'

'Did he ever date again?'

'Well, after I took up with Johnny, we had to get him protection as, for a while, it was like he'd a huge target on his back. Every mother thought their daughter would be perfect for him; every widow was sending him chocolate cakes; and every married woman was thinking "if only". I put it down to the American mystique – and the bit of money didn't help, either. So Connie and I had to be strategic about finding cover for him. Over the years, we found him a lesbian headmistress, who was perfect for a couple of years until she wanted to live free in London; a much older widow, who died; and a young divorcee, who, unfortunately, fell in love with him.'

'How did that work out?'

'Joe McGinlay wangled her a public appointment in Belfast and she moved on. It was a bit messy, but we managed all right.'

'She didn't shoot him, then?'

'I really don't think so – she was devoted to him. She'd have shot herself first.'

'Any crazies – other than Tish?'

'Not that I knew of.'

'He never looked at anyone else at all?'

143

'The odd time you'd see a female researcher – generally code for spy – from Dublin or the US stay over at the manse. And I did wonder if he'd ever considered it. But they never stayed in his quarters.'

'What about boyfriends?'

Her eyebrows nearly shot through her forehead. 'You believe that stuff in the paper? No. Not his form at all. Truth is, in the last thirty years the only time Seán ever got excited was when his first three numbers came up on the lottery. It was that simple with Seán: he never got over the love of his life and never wanted to. As far as he was concerned, Millie's death didn't part them – it just delayed them reuniting.'

McCloud believed her. It was a rarer and rarer phenomenon in modern society, but his parents had it, too. And he knew if either of them died, it wouldn't cross the other's mind to look for someone else.

Mo looked at her watch. 'Okay,' she said. 'Your turn, McCloud.'

'I'm sorry. My turn for what?'

'Why aren't you married? You're thirty-one, very good looking and have pretty decent job prospects. Other than your drink problem, I'd say you're a catch. What happened?'

He froze.

'What's the matter?' she asked. 'You think you're the only one who gets to ask personal questions?'

He started looking around the room desperately for the cameras.

'Don't worry,' said Mo. 'Maeve's probably away to the office already. If she's not, she'll be a little distressed to hear me tell you that she is a disaster with men – and hasn't had her relic rubbed in seven years.'

'Her relic rubbed?'

'Yes. Have you ever seen those religious scapulae that the bible-thumpers wear next to their skin? Like the guy in *The Da Vinci Code*? They're known as relics here – and they need to be rubbed regularly.'

He sighed. He had nowhere to go, and he knew it. He shook his head dejectedly and decided to face the music. 'I'm not much of a man for relic rubbing, either,' he said. 'My mother and two sisters used to vet any girls that came around when I was at school. And they were fierce, too. I eventually got myself a stunning high-school sweetheart who followed me to college in Yale, so robbing me of the chance to get some desperately needed man-about-town experience. And at the end of my post-graduate year, she left to marry my best friend. The year after that was when I learned how to drink whiskey, if you're wondering.'

'Rough. Was he better looking? Had he more money?'

'Neither, it was just the right fit. I was embarrassed, shocked and hurt and very lonely, as I lost the two of them. But I knew on another level that it was completely the right thing. I was sleepwalking – and the jolt of it woke me the hell up.'

'Better looking, so. And since then?'

'I refer you to my father's comments on the front page of your own paper. I couldn't disagree with a word of them. The Deputy Director back home calls me "Belgrano" – because women will travel two hundred and fifty miles out of their road to torpedo me.'

She laughed. 'The old Thatcher joke. And now – anything on the go?'

'Nothing in the pipeline. But my mother has a hotline to St Jude of the Hopeless Cases – so it's going to happen any day now.'

'We've all been there,' said Mo. 'Never give up. The best things in life are worth waiting for.'

CHAPTER 37

1948: Boston

I didn't speak to Connie for the first year I was in Boston. I refused all her calls, didn't open her letters and, when I did eventually break my silence, it was only with a view to torturing her.

She came over to Boston in 1948 on the pretext of helping manage a series of press events for Dev along the East Coast; Kate insisted I meet with her. It was only after I had a child of my own that I worked out that seeing me was the whole point of her trip.

Dev had been demoted to Leader of the Opposition after sixteen years as Taoiseach and was attempting to shore up his hard-man image among the diaspora – and hit them up for a few dollars while he was at it. But it was now a full quarter of a century since he'd guaranteed us an un-partitioned island, so most of us weren't buying. Not even Connie, who admitted over supper in Kate's dining room that the trip was a tough sell. Though she added that when it came to honesty and sincerity, Dev could fake them better than anyone she knew.

After we'd cleared the plates, Kate retired to bed to let us catch up, so I figured it was time to stick my fingers into some old wounds. I told Connie that, while it was nice to see her again, I'd had to resort to seeing a psychiatrist to help me with the trauma I had faced from having been left as a baby. 'Abandonment issues' was what the head-shrink called it. And while it would take a couple of years to get me through my problems, he was confident that I would have an adequate standard of mental health eventually. Though it might take me a few more years before I could form any appropriate and healthy relationships with women. This was all a big fat lie, of course, and I was reading from a script a Psych major had provided me.

Unfortunately, Connie's face started to crumble and she dropped her head in her hands and started to sob uncontrollably. I had never even seen her cry before, and the shock of this sent a charge of guilt through me that made me choke up myself. I had overplayed my hand, been incredibly cruel to my mother and was the lousiest louse in all the world. Though again, it wasn't until I had a child of my own that I realised that I mightn't have been the only one there playing a hand.

Regardless, I quickly made with the 'There theres', and before the end of the evening, we were lifelong buddies again. And there was no further mention of psychiatrists or botched smuggling operations.

At the end of the night, she asked me if I would ever consider returning to Derry.

'Of course,' I said. 'It's my home. But not yet. I need to do a bit more exploring first.'

'Maybe find a nice girl?'

'Possibly. Old Mick tells me Tish Brehony's off the market. Pity. I do like them wired to the lights.'

'Too soon to crack wise about it. She's promised to shoot your eyes out if you ever come home.'

I dropped it immediately. 'What about the *Chronicle*? Will there be a job for me?'

Her eyes lit up. 'Kevin's made it clear he doesn't want the editor's chair. There's too much politics in it for him – and with Mary working full time as well, they'd never get to see one another.'

'Anybody else in with a shout?'

'Not a chance. It's yours, son, whenever you're ready. It was made for you – no-one else will ever fit. Realistically, I'm good for another few years – though the paper is in poor enough shape.'

'Are you just saying that to get me back sooner?'

'God, no. It's the times that are in it. Derry has hit a real slump. It's had seven years of great abundance, with the war and all the money it brought in, and now it's hitting a seven-year famine. There's no cash, no houses and not a lot of hope, either. We've stopped replacing staff when they leave or retire – we're down to fifty between the two papers. Mick has stopped taking a dividend, and I'm down to a half-salary.'

'So I'm un-sacked, then?'

'You were never sacked, you big baby.'

We spent the following days sightseeing, and I told her then about all my adventures in the biggest Irish city in the world – even the neighbourhood I worked in was called Old Dublin. Upon my arrival I'd registered for a Masters in Classics at Harvard – cue the old joke: *amo, amas*, am at it again – but it took only six hours a week. And there's only so much granny-sitting a man can handle, so I'd quickly gone looking for a job. Uncle Fitz had gotten me a start at the *Boston Catholic*, filing sports reports, which had been perfect for the first glorious summer. Who doesn't want to watch baseball and get paid for it? But Fitz knew it was several steps below where I was aiming, so he'd also put the word out on Beacon Hill to see if anyone needed an aide.

To the surprise of us all, Mayor Jim Curley was first to express an interest. He had just returned to office after a stretch in jail for mail fraud and was looking to reinvent himself. And what better way to start than to recruit as his front man a good-looking Irishman whose father had died for the Auld Sod.

Curley's magnificent star, however, was on the wane, as Uncle Fitz knew well. The Kennedys had recently persuaded him to give up his seat in the House of Representatives, and instead serve a fourth term as Boston mayor, to allow Jack a run-out in Washington. And while nobody doubted that I could do a fine job for Curley, it might take a little time afterwards for the stink to clear from my clothes. So instead, the Democrats installed me over the river in Cambridge as a junior constituency aide for the new Congressman Kennedy. And, just to clarify, in the five years I was there, I saw Jack about a dozen times in total, and spoke to him on the phone maybe twenty more. I was like a modern-day intern only with less access. But to read the newspapers in Ireland, you'd have sworn I was standing between him and Jackie when he took the oath of office on Capitol Hill.

***

The next couple of years flew by in a whirl of perfume and politics. The first I will say nothing about, as it's none of your business, and the second only a little, as it's mostly penny-ante stuff. Dev's visit did manage to excite a little interest in the Irish cause. And groups like the American Association for the Recognition of the Irish Republic and the American League for an Undivided Ireland began priming Jack to ask increasingly awkward questions at the House Committee for Foreign Affairs. Jack even called publicly for an all-Ireland plebiscite – a risky enough move for a man depending on Boston Protestants to carry him over the line on Election Day.

When Uncle Fitz died in 1950, it prompted probably the biggest funeral Boston had ever seen. The Kennedys, quite rightly, viewed this as a major vote of confidence in their new dynasty, and they began planning for the future.

During the Great War, Fitz had run for the Senate against the Republican Henry Cabot Lodge, whose grandson Henry II currently held the seat. And there was a belief that if anyone were going to dislodge Boston Wasp royalty, it would have to be Boston Catholic royalty. Lodge himself was doing us a big favour by neglecting the home nest to run Eisenhower's campaign for the Republican presidential nomination. So it was agreed, or pretty much decreed, that Jack would run for the Democrats, and that Tip O'Neill would replace him in the congressional race for the Massachusetts 11th district.

And while Tip's selection process was relatively straightforward, it wasn't without a few critics. But I didn't mind that, as his campaign would also provide me with possibly the most important moment in my life. Because it's where I first met Millie.

CHAPTER 38

1952: Boston

Connie always said she knew immediately that Johnny was the person she was supposed to be with, right from the second she first met him inside the theatre she was trying to set fire to. But I never truly believed her. I just assumed it was a story she'd dreamt up to make life a little kinder for me. Connie was hard-headed, practical and not in the least romantic, three attributes I both shared and admired. So, during our weekly phone calls, when she would talk about not always being in control of events or your own destiny, I would tell her she'd gone soft in her old age and remind her I was bulletproof.

'Tougher men than you have fallen,' she'd warn me. 'Sometimes the world lets you think you're the lead actor when in reality, you're only a bit player in a much bigger production.'

Post-war Boston with a little money in your pocket was a privileged life for a bachelor, even a good Irish boy living with his grandmother. There were four of us, all the one age, who worked out of the one office in Cambridge for the Democrats. We spent our weekends, and often midweeks, dining, dancing and dating, like the princes we imagined we were. But never the same girls for more than a week or two. Nor did you date anyone smarter than you – there were rules about that sort of thing.

Personally, I blame Jack for starting the rot. Although we moved in different circles, he was a big influence on us troops, and when he started taking Jackie seriously, it had a domino effect. In the summer of 1952, all three of my office-mates began doing steady lines – I blamed the heat. But I also started to notice that all the set-ups being thrown my way were a lot more loaded than they had been in the years gone by. It had become less and less about the charm and more and more about the breeding lines.

For a couple a months, it got so bad I stopped playing entirely. I let them at it and concentrated instead on the autumn campaigns: Adlai's for President – Christ help us all; Jack's for the Senate; and Tip O'Neill's to replace Jack as Congressman for Cambridge. Tip had been the majority leader in the Beacon Hill senate since successfully leading the campaign to oust the Republicans in

1948, and was a Boston College alum. In other words, the perfect candidate.

I loved O'Neill from long before I ever met him. He had fought, albeit unsuccessfully, against Boston's own oath for teachers, an anti-Communist measure which required educators to swear loyalty to the State of Massachusetts. And this had earned him the wrath of both the Catholic Church and the American Legion.

Jack was never quite as troubled by his principles as Tip was. And we were all a little disillusioned when he struck a side-deal with Joe McCarthy, a fellow Catholic, who agreed not to back the Republican candidate Henry Lodge, a Protestant, in return for Kennedy support for his witch-hunts.

So one day in early autumn, when Tip called into our office to ask if anyone would have a couple of hours to head over to Radcliffe to recruit some younger volunteers for his campaign, I signed up immediately.

After some tricky negotiations with a bursar, a closet Republican, I managed to get permission to set up a stall outside the minor hall close to the main drag. And I wasn't there two minutes when it happened.

'I'd like to sign up to help Mr O'Neill,' she said.

I glanced up and knew immediately I was in trouble. Cropped black Audrey Hepburn hair; quizzical green eyes shining with mischief; and a fresh, confident smile, teeth as white as God's sheets. She was dressed, as was the fashion that year, in blue jeans and a white shirt, like one of Kerouac's beatniks, unadorned with a single drop of lipstick, powder or paint. She was about five-five, slim as a deer, and was undoubtedly the most beautiful woman I'd ever seen in Massachusetts, America or Ireland.

It wasn't so much love at first sight for me – or at least I kept telling myself that – but rather a realisation that, whatever happened next, my old way of life had gone forever. It was as if I'd woken out of a dream into something entirely different, entirely better and entirely important. I had met many women before who were completely out of my class – but I had never met one who I actually needed to be with. Not because I desired her or lusted after her – but because it was in the script of my life, and also in the script of hers. And despite all my previous promises to myself, I knew I had no option but to play out this scene.

I was damned if I wasn't going to go down swinging, however. It was too much of a risk – and what if I failed? My survival instincts worked out that I still might have a chance, if I could get rid of her quickly. All I had to do was annoy her to the point where she would hate me on sight and storm off. Granted, it was not the best plan I'd ever come up with, but it was all I had in the moment.

I pretended to concentrate on the application form. 'Name?' I asked.

'Amelia Harrison,' she said.

'Age?'

'Twenty-one.'

'You're lying,' I told her, without raising my eyes. 'You're not old enough to vote. Go away.'

'I am so twenty-one,' she said.

'No,' I said. 'You're twenty, tops. You were named after that crazy lesbian pilot, Amelia Earhart, who nobody had ever heard of until 1932, which, incidentally, is only twenty years ago. I'd say you were born a month or two after her flight across the Atlantic – say June 1932, so you just turned twenty at the start of the summer.'

She glared at me, burning with embarrassment. 'How could you possibly know that? And Amelia wasn't a lesbian, she was married.'

'You Radcliffe women are totally predictable. Now move along please.'

'What do you mean, predictable?'

'You're either stuck-up, slappers or spinsters. And you're clearly a stuck-up Republican snob over to make fun of the working-class Democrat on the stall. So move along, please, and let some of the slappers and spinsters in. They mightn't be as pretty as you, but at least they're sincere.'

'Take that back.'

'Okay then, you're not that pretty. I'm just saying that to get rid of you. Now, move along.'

Up to that point, I hadn't noticed that Millie was carrying a hardback copy of a new short-story collection, *Runyon On Broadway* – measuring approximately nine inches by six inches by three inches, and weighing in at about a pound-and-a-quarter. And, in hindsight, if I'd spotted it, I might have moderated my tone a little. But as Old Mick used to say: 'If ifs and ands were pots and pans there'd be no call for tinkers.' And so, I had only myself to blame for my poor observational skills when I woke up on the concourse floor thirty seconds later, wearing a book-shaped lump on my forehead. Runyon was lying beside me.

Amelia, needless to say, had disappeared.

CHAPTER 39

I'm a great believer in telling the worst stories about yourself first, before anyone else has a chance to put a spin on them. The guys in the outer office – the bullpen – were as merciless as I could have expected. But, of course, I left out the part about how the Harrison doll had completely turned my head before attempting to separate it from my shoulders. There is little point in handing over live grenades that are just going to be lobbed right back at you.

O'Neill, though, who was a little older and smarter than the rest of the mob, was curious as to why I had sent Amelia packing.

'She was only twenty,' I told him.

'We can always use campaigners – doesn't matter what age they are. It looks great to have younger people around the polling stations.'

'I'm pretty sure she's a Republican, too,' I said.

'Then why did she speak to you?'

'To yank my chain and waste my time. You know the type.'

'Yeah, but they normally back off when you call them on it. This one knocked you clean into the cheap seats. Sounds like it got personal.'

'I don't follow – it was about politics, pure and simple.'

'Never be fooled. Politics is neither pure nor simple. All politics is personal. And cracking someone on the head with a book is as personal as it gets. Anyhow, I want you to get back up to Radcliffe again next week. And this time, come back with a few volunteers and not a sick-note from the doctor.'

***

I was sure I'd see her again. As sure as toothache. And the following Monday, when I landed to set up my one-man recruitment stall, there she was, waiting in my spot. Behind a desk of her own, signing up volunteers under the Republican banner. She had dressed up a little more for the occasion, and was wearing a white halter top and a matching pair of late-summer pedal pushers. To this day, I'm convinced my heart actually stopped when I saw her.

This time she was ready, though, and stood up and shook my hand as I approached her table. 'Good morning, sir, would you like to come and work for our next president, General Eisenhower?'

Truth is, I'd met Ike and liked him a lot more than Adlai, but I was never going to admit that. And I still had a big red lump in the middle of my head. She was going to have to work for it.

'No,' I told her. 'I'm afraid I'm already taken.'

'Actually, you're not,' she said. 'Your grandmother has been telling me all about you. She says you've never looked at another woman since Amelia Earhart kissed you on the cheek the day she landed in Derry.'

Busted. I laughed. 'Lies. It was from when she took me up in a plane for my sixth birthday. But, yes, I did get another kiss in Derry. What were you doing talking to my grandmother? Where did you meet her?'

'I called round to your house to collect the book you stole from me, and we got chatting.'

'How did you know where I live?' Christ, what was going on here?

This time, it was she who laughed. 'Yeah, it's like Tish Brehony all over again.'

'She told you about that? I'll kill her.'

'Don't panic yourself; Kate plays bridge with my mother. And it was my mother who insisted I went around to check on you. Apparently, she heard you left a little pool of blood on the concourse there, and she was frightened you might tell the police. Anyhow, I ended up having a great conversation with Kate. She worries about you – thinks it's time you stopped making an ass of yourself, squiring every young filly that floats up the Charles. Said you should settle down with someone smart. Someone like me, she said. She thinks I could save you.'

'And could you?'

'That depends. Do you want to be saved?'

'Sorry. You're not my type. I don't go for bossy women.'

'Actually, we're the only type of women who have a chance in hell with you. Kate also told me that herself and your mother are both Radcliffe graduates. So, tell me, Seán, are they stuck-up, are they slappers, or are they just spinsters?'

Caught.

'Please tell me you didn't ...'

'Of course not. You didn't mean it – you were testing me. You were just a little too convincing, though.'

'I'll know better the next time.'

'But more importantly, Seán, even if I were to save you, why would you deserve me?'

I needed a beat. 'I wouldn't. Not in a million years. You're far too good for me. One look at you and I completely lost my breath. That's why I was mean. I was scared – and I'm so sorry.'

'Correct answer. Well done. You can collect me from my house – Kate has the address – on Friday for dinner, and maybe we'll take in a show afterwards.'

I looked at her and couldn't stop myself smiling. And neither could she.

'Are you sure about this?' I said.

'Yes. But I'm not sure I've much to do with it, Seán. Neither of us is writing this particular story. Now, go off down the concourse and set up your stall somewhere else. This is my spot.'

CHAPTER 40

1952–53

About three weeks after I first met Millie, towards the end of October 1952, I was in Brattle's Specialist Bookshop in downtown Boston when I chanced upon a first edition of Damon Runyon's debut 1932 collection, *Guys and Dolls*. And there on the inside page was the author's signature, along with his quote: 'She has a laugh so hearty it knocks the whipped cream off an order of strawberry shortcake on a table fifty feet away.' It was perfect.

Every evening as we were saying goodnight, Millie would remind me that I still hadn't returned the Runyon book she had whacked me with. So I would promise to return it after school the following day, thus giving us another excuse to meet up. And naturally, I would forget to bring it.

The Brattle book was wrapped in a protective cover, so I assumed it would cost a healthy welt, but I was delighted when Pete Gloss the shop owner said I could take it with me for fifty dollars. Though, bless his heart, he knew well I wasn't buying it for myself.

I had to have it for her. But I also knew what it meant, and so would she.

Millie had completely turned me around since our second encounter on the concourse. And getting to know her, without labouring a point, was the happiest time of my life. The one thing we couldn't agree on – or at least we pretended not to agree on – was politics. She had been reared in the leafy confines of Newbury Street – the Georgian enclave not far from Kate – and her folks were very much in the Brahmin blueblood mould. They had, naturally, thrown their weight, and not a little money, behind Henry Lodge for the Senate against 'that criminal Joe Kennedy's son'. Or so they told me at my first dinner at their home. I suspected they had been primed to get a rise out of me, so I told them that my Uncle Joe was no criminal, or at least not a convicted one, and that I wouldn't hold it against them when Jack punched Lodge's clock on Election Day.

They knew as well as I did that Kennedy had the momentum – their man had spent too long running around the country with Ike, and his Boston base had suffered. So they let me away with it. The Kennedys were slowly but surely stitching the whole thing up. They had just spent half a million dollars buying the

Boston Post newspaper to guarantee themselves a tamer press. And the family were hosting huge campaign tea parties all over the state, so that Jack could meet and charm the socks off every woman on the east coast – or at least every one he hadn't yet met.

'Who are you going to vote for in the presidential election?' Millie's father asked me.

Unfortunately, I have a tell. I tend to look down when I don't want to answer a question. Or at least answer truthfully. Sam Harrison spotted it and laughed.

I looked over at him. 'Strictly at this table?'

He grinned like he already knew.

'Adlai's a drink of water,' I said. 'And Millie's been working on me since the moment she met me. So I'll probably go for Ike. But you cannot say a word or they'll fire me. I reckon about half our bullpen in Cambridge is going to do the same.'

They nodded. 'It's all right to use your own head, Seán,' said Millie's mother, Grace. 'We're all going to vote for your man Tip in the House race. Millie convinced us. Says he's a really genuine guy.'

I had taken Millie into the office to meet Tip about a week after we'd started dating and for devilment, he told her he didn't need no damn highborn Yankee help, thank you all the same. And if she tried to hit *him* with a book, he'd stick Rose Kennedy on her, and the Legion of Mary besides, God help her Protestant soul.

Millie had assured Tip in return that she would rather cycle naked through Boston Common than vote for a 'damn Dem donkey', particularly one who couldn't get into a decent school like Harvard.

***

The morning after the election, I called around early to Newbury Street for a post-game catch-up; Millie was sitting out on the stoop with the early editions of the papers.

'Here's your book,' I told her and handed her a little bag with a parcel inside.

Her face fell. The election was over and so was our game.

She opened the wrapper. 'It's the wrong one,' she protested.

I shrugged like I didn't know any better.

'Smartass,' she said. Her face was still cross but her eyes were curious.

'The police want to hold onto the other one for evidence,' I replied. 'But you haven't answered my question.'

So she turned over the cover and read the inscription.

She tried and tried to play it straight, but after about five seconds she finally gave in and broke into a smile. And it was the greatest smile I ever saw in all my life. Full of love, hope and happiness. Just like my own.

'Okay, Seán Madden,' she said, 'the answer is yes. Let's get married.'

CHAPTER 41

Kate was ecstatic at the news, and doubly so when I agreed to let her inform the Irish connection. 'This time it'll be me who'll be first with the Derry news,' she said, giving it the old *Chronicle* marketing slogan.

The Harrisons were mostly pleased, too. I say 'mostly' because Charlie, Millie's older brother, who we all knew was unlikely to breed, wasn't happy at all that I was a Catholic. Thus the family money, after his demise, would pass into sullied and undeserving hands. He refused to have anything to do with the planning and, as you're aware, he refused to stand in for any of the photographs. 'It's nothing personal, Seán,' he told me, 'some of my best friends are Catholics.' But it was. Sam and Grace couldn't have been better about it, though – indeed Sam took Charlie aside the night before the wedding and warned him that he'd cut him off entirely if he didn't call home his petted lip.

We waited until Millie finished her exams to get hitched – she scored *summa cum laude*, naturally, while I got myself a gentleman's pass in my Classics post-grad. Before she'd even telephoned the Derry office with news of our engagement, Kate had arranged for Father George to conduct the ceremony at the Cathedral of the Holy Cross at the end of June. Kate, as you're aware, was never gospel greedy but she knew that if the venue were presented to us as a *fait accompli*, it would stop any fighting over whether it should be a Catholic or Anglican church. In turn, I was very happy to assure the Harrisons that I would leave the religious instruction of any children to their mother. Not that they, or we, were too worried about this, but sometimes you have to throw a nod to the optics. I loved Millie so much I'd have got married on the Twelfth of July to an Orange band playing.

Connie, of course, came out to Boston for the wedding, along with Aunt Mary and Kevin O'Dorrity; Mick stayed at home to run the ranch with Harry Carson, who was now the all-round VP.

In all, we did well to keep the numbers down to sixty – we started off trying to restrict it to the immediate families, but it got away from us slightly when we forgot to muzzle Kate. We're also pretty sure that it was her who tipped off the society pages, who crashed the chapel steps and snapped a half-page photograph for the *Boston Post*. Connie was livid, but only because she hadn't thought of it herself and it would be another week before the same image could appear in the *Chronicle*. And yes, as I've told you before a thousand times, there has never, ever been a more beautiful bride.

***

The plan was to honeymoon in Europe for a month and then Ireland for a fortnight before returning to the States, where both of us had been offered new postings in Washington in the fall. The Dems had rewarded me with a speechwriting job, working halfway between Tip's office and Jack's, while Millie had gotten a start on the newsdesk at *The Post*.

We took a leisurely rail-tour from Paris to Budapest, hitting about ten capitals in the first fortnight. But Millie sensed I was itching to get back to Ireland – to show her off, if I'm totally honest – and when we reached Berlin on the homeward leg, she suggested flying directly back to London. We stayed a night in Pimlico, walked down the embankment to Big Ben – which I explained had actually been modelled on Derry's Guildhall – and the following morning headed to London Airport for the daily flight to Belfast.

We were in a queue at the airport for something or other when I got a hefty slap on my shoulder and looked around to see Harry Carson's son Henry – now an RAF pilot – standing before us.

'Happy wedding,' he said. 'I saw the picture in the paper. Can I offer you folks a lift?'

'We're en route to Belfast,' I said.

'I figured as much,' said Harry. 'Your mother published your itinerary. But we all knew you'd get homesick about halfway through. I'm flying into Ballykelly – any use to you? You'd have to rough it on a couple of wooden benches, but you'd only be a thirty-minute drive from Derry when you land. And I'll radio ahead and get someone to come and collect you.'

Millie laughed at the serendipity. 'Sold,' she said. 'The quicker we get you back to God's country, Seán, the better. You're boring the pants off me with all your damn whining about how great it is.'

***

Things happened very quickly after that. Just an hour and a quarter later, we were in Mick's car, heading back in the Limavady Road towards Derry. Connie was in the driver's seat and Mick, whose eyes had started to falter, was riding shotgun while Mary was in the back with Millie and me.

158

We were passing through the dark forest at Walworth when Connie looked back over her shoulder at us, grinning all over her face.

'We had a board meeting last night,' she said. 'I've resigned as editor.'

Mick nodded in agreement. 'Your mother's going to become chairman,' he said. 'I mean chairperson. I'm retiring for good. I can finally take a drink in peace and not have to get up in the morning.'

Mick, who was over eighty, had been drinking all his life and had never missed a 6.00am start.

Mary, who had been quiet up to this point, then looked around at me. 'And I forgot to tell you,' she said, 'Kevin's got a job lecturing in English at Magee University – doesn't have to swear an oath or anything. Starts next month.'

It was at that precise point I had a sudden rush as I put it all together. I turned sideways to look at Millie, expecting her to be as alarmed as I was. But she was smiling hard, too hard. Like a smarty-pants who knew a lot more than I did.

'Washington was never a goer, Seán,' she said. 'Your days as a bit player are over. This is where your life is.'

I was genuinely astounded. 'But what about you?' I asked her.

'I'm the new Leader Writer and Copy-Editor. Kevin interviewed me when he was over for the wedding. He said I'd be great – but that I was to take no nonsense from the new boss. He said I was a whole lot brighter than you anyhow.'

They all started to laugh. It was a done deal, and we all knew it.

I would never have asked Millie to come – it was too much to ask anyone. To give up Boston, or Washington, for Derry? But she had done it all in a heartbeat for me, without ever having visited here, and without me even knowing. That was the measure of the woman. A real angel. And while I'll be forever grateful to her, there isn't a day goes by I don't wish she hadn't done it.

CHAPTER 42

1953: Derry

The newspaper landscape in Derry and Donegal had changed considerably in my absence. The most significant difference was that the *Londonderry Leader* was circling the drain. A new, supposedly middle-of-the-road weekly, the *City Bugle*, had opened and was tearing lumps out of the *Leader's* advertising and circulation figures.

Alfie Cunningham, Mick's contemporary, had died at the start of 1953, leaving the *Leader* to his son Jackson, a fine and honest gentleman in the cut of his father. There had been consternation among the younger Cunningham clan, however, when it emerged that Alfie had actually purchased Connie's house in De Burgh Terrace for her – as Catholics weren't supposed to buy in that area. And there was uproar when they discovered he was now leaving the house to her in his will, as agreed when they shook hands thirty years previously. Connie had, naturally, paid the mortgage off years before.

Despite protestations from the young guns – particularly from his son, Edward Fletcher, or EF as he was known – Jackson Cunningham refused to contest the will, so ceding the land to a Fenian. This, you have to remember, was in the days when Protestants could be ostracised and even attacked for not safeguarding the purity of their inheritance. Jackson's younger brother, Irvine, who was still Connie's escort to official functions, backed him one hundred per cent, however.

Worse was to follow when Millie and myself went looking for a new home. Connie was proposing to give us De Burgh and move into a cottage in Donegal down beside Mick, but I knew my grandfather needed a little privacy for his drinking and occasional entertaining. So we gave her a straight no. We'd find something. There still was a major housing crisis, however, right across Derry. The Unionists were holding onto their gerrymandered majority for grim death and were refusing to allow Catholics move anywhere except the South Ward. Unfortunately, this ward was almost full to bursting point. So Millie and I were stuck in the guest room at De Burgh for the duration.

Then one Thursday morning in early December 1953, Jackson Cunningham telephoned me from the *Leader* to ask could he meet both myself and my wife at the *Chronicle* office. It wasn't unusual for us to visit one another – indeed in earlier times, Mick and old Alfie would have edited one another's papers while the opposite number went on holiday. But Jackson wanted Millie in the meeting as well, which meant it wasn't business. Or purely business.

He was a worried man as he sat down opposite me in the little office, Millie to his right.

'We're about to go under,' he said. 'The *Bugle* is undercutting our advertising prices to the point we can't compete. We're running losses like you wouldn't believe – and I'm certain so are they. What they're doing isn't sustainable for more than another month or two – at which stage they'll go to the wall themselves. But they only have to hang on longer than us, and if we crash first, they can claim the ground and ratchet the advertising prices right back up again. Then we're gone, and they're the only Protestant paper left in the town.'

The Catholic populace, as you'd expect, had spotted immediately that the *Bugle* was a bigot posing as a liberal and had refused to buy it.

The Cunninghams, setting aside all nonsense like politics and religion, were our oldest friends and had pulled us out of the ditch when we needed them. So there was never any question but that we would return the favour.

'How can we help, Jackson?' I asked him. 'I'm happy to loan whatever we can afford. Give, if necessary.'

He smiled and shook his worried head.

'Much appreciated,' he said, 'but I'd rather not borrow, if you don't mind. I'd like to sell you something. How would you like to buy the manse? I'll sell it to you for half the rateable value if you can get it done before Christmas.'

The manse, as you know, was, and is, a thirty-roomed behemoth set in ten acres of orchard on the border at Glenabbey. It had been built in the early 1800s by a Cunningham ancestor who had survived the Napoleonic wars, and the family had lived in it ever since. Officially, they were forbidden from selling it to outsiders under a primogeniture agreement, but before his death, Alfie had modified the clause to allow Jackson a back-door exit if things got tight. Jackson and his wife Winnie had taken Millie and myself down to dinner in the manse the week after we came back, and Millie had raved about it ever since.

'So you want us to buy the manse and then sell it back to you?' I asked Jackson.

'No,' he said. 'We still have Alfie's old town house up beside your mother, which is more than big enough for ourselves and the two children. The manse would be yours to keep. I don't want it any more. It's a noose around my neck. Every penny I make is spent maintaining it. And ultimately it's pointless anyway, as EF is only going to squander it all away after I go.'

EF was then nineteen years old and, while a promising journalist, he was already a thoroughly twisted character. Even then, the whole town knew he was going to come to a sticky end.

'When do you need the money?' I asked.

'By the end of the month,' he said. 'Sooner if possible. If the *Bugle* see I've deep pockets, they might just pull the plug on their paper.'

'What's the rateable value then?'

He told me – and it was quite a sum, even then.

Millie then spoke for the first time.

'We'll buy it,' she said. 'At its full value. My folks in Boston will help with the mortgage. And they're good Protestants to boot, so your buddies won't throw you out of the Lodge.'

'Small odds if they did,' smiled Jackson.

'What about EF?' I asked him. 'Have you told him?'

'Not yet. And he's going to hate you forever, Seán. He sees it, and has always seen it, as his entitlement. But if it's any consolation, he doesn't deserve it – and he's going to hate me even more when I have to tell him that.'

The *Leader*, as is apparent, survived, the *Bugle* went to the wall, and we got the greatest house there ever was. The garden ran right along the border until I approached the farmer next door and asked him could I buy a couple of extra fields – so getting myself a foothold in the South. The whoring Water Rats warned me, though, to leave the fence up – and never cross the line – or they'd come and build a checkpoint in the middle of the land. And, naturally, I obeyed them to the letter.

CHAPTER 43

1957

As I warned you earlier, for different reasons, I'm going to lie to you sometimes in the course of this memoir. I'm also going to withhold – particularly some of the stuff of which I'm less proud. A lot of it is best forgotten and, unfortunately, most of us are only remembered for the worst ten minutes of our lives. And yes, you're right, that is generally the way we start the obituary. Nonetheless, there are times, as you will have worked out, that the *Chronicle* had to pull some unsavoury stuff to survive. And the mid-fifties were not at all easy times.

Connie had wanted to expand the paper since the 1930s – even in the darkest points of the economy, but there wasn't the money then, and we were all far too busy during the 1940s, what with the war and me being sent off to the naughty step. But shortly after Millie and I arrived back, Connie began warning us of the dangers of just ticking along. She was, understandably, frightened of another *Bugle* springing up, this time on the Nationalist side. So when the *Derry Messenger* opened its doors in Maghera – at the outer edge of our reach in the county, and began clipping a few shillings off our rural advertising, she called me into the boardroom.

'I think you need to open another edition,' she said. 'You have to drown the *Messenger* at birth.'

'But it's forty miles away and has a totally different market – what happened to live and let live?'

'We are the professionals, Seán. We have the best staff and best connections of any paper outside Belfast. Moreover, we have seventy to eighty homes in Derry and Donegal reliant on what we pay. You can't put all that at risk to allow a bunch of know-nothing amateurs sweep in and start stealing our turf.'

She was overselling it, way overselling it. We were leaking a little, but there was absolutely no need for lifeboats.

'We've no extra money for new staff,' I told her.

'You're right. The people here and in Donegal will take on extra duties. But we'll need a base out there, so I'll make money available to open offices in Dungiven.'

'How much more are we going to pay the staff?'

'Not a thing. We don't have it. We currently have far too many on our books anyway. Fifteen at least. If they don't like it, they can go – and in fact some of them will have to.'

Connie saw my face fall. A wet week in the job, and I was about to become the man they all hated.

'Don't worry. You won't have to do it. The board is commissioning a time-and-motion study of all our operations, to check for inefficiencies. They'll report back to Harry. He's bringing in a personnel officer from the *Ulster News*. She's a real piece of work; loves nothing better than doing the dirty work. If you ever see her smiling, it's because she's just made a little baby cry.'

'So if our staff don't work their socks off for the new paper, they're out the door?'

'We're not running a charity here, Seán.'

'What happened to protecting the workers?'

'We are – we're protecting the people who want to work and who will work. We need to grow if we're to protect them. But we can't afford to pay four copy typists to sit and do their nails and sneak telephone calls to their boyfriends. Not now it's a prerequisite that every member of our reporting staff can type fifty words a minute. We have no room for luxury. For the *Chronicle* to keep going with the same revenue, even if we could guarantee it, isn't enough anymore. It's not an option.'

It was the sign of things to come. Being a manager is great until you have to close the hospitals.

'So, effectively you're proposing more newspapers with fewer staff?'

'We're also going to invest in new technology. Instead of us running printing presses in both Donegal and Derry, we'll have one big press here in the city. Why we haven't done this years ago, I don't know. We reckon about half a dozen of the printers are ready to retire anyway – and we'll make sure they're well looked after. They've worked damn hard.'

Connie had a big soul, and I could see this was as hard on her as it was on me. The *Leader*'s near collapse had put a fear in her, and she was absolutely determined her *Chronicle* wouldn't go the same way.

I tried one last Hail Mary. 'Is Mick on board with this?'

'The former chairman, like yourself, I suspect, is none too happy. But he knows that if you don't clip the wool, the sheep will go blind. We can fight them now, Seán, or we can do it at the point of a gun, like Jackson did, in a couple of years' time. It's up to you. But my advice is, stop the rot now.'

***

164

The *Messenger* was little more than two men, a dog and a small bank loan – and we had them on the rack within a month. Why would anyone pay £100 for an ad in a new paper no-one reads if they can get one in the *Chronicle*, on special offer, for half that? In fairness to Connie, she let me buy them out rather than put them to the wall and they went on to become our South Derry edition, which is still running today. We also started Limavady and Strabane editions within the year, as soon as we had built our new printing press. And a couple of years later, we struck out for Sligo.

The personnel officer, an evil little Dubliner who hated Northerners, took a grand total of eight scalps from the *Chronicle* – all early retirements, and Connie did the decent thing and made up their full pension. Even the copy-typists survived, although we switched their telephones to incoming calls only. And all staff got a five per cent raise, paid to them, untaxed, as an annual Christmas bonus.

And yes, I love telling this story because it shows that even when we were being mean, we were the good guys. Only this wasn't always true. Sometimes you have to be nasty, if only to survive. This is why I regard newspaper journalism as the only possible accurate draft of history – everything afterwards is too easily revised.

CHAPTER 44

1959

I blamed lots of people for Millie's death.

Firstly, it was Mick's fault for getting old and demanding a great-grandchild to secure the empire before he passed. Millie and I dearly wanted children but it wasn't happening for us. Eventually, after two miscarriages, we went to a private doctor in Ballykelly, on the advice of Mary. He told us – and he used these words – that Millie was 'very probably barren'. He suggested that a pregnancy to term could be very dangerous, as Millie also had a heart flutter, and we should consider adoption instead. Of course, we said nothing of this to Mick, and promised him a Gaelic team before his liver packed in.

Kate was also making enquiries on a weekly basis from the States as to when we were 'getting started', as were Sam and Grace, Millie's parents. Her brother, Charlie, was unlikely to get much started on his own.

Connie was less bothered, but there was pressure nonetheless. She had taken on the Catholic Church a number of times about its stance on contraception, and she saw a major opportunity for change with Pope John's announcement in January 1959 of the Second Vatican Council. But it didn't help her arguments that the laity were suffering and oppressed when her own son was clearly choosing to ignore Church teaching and use birth control anyway. When they were later proved wrong on that one, a number of priests put it about that Millie's death was 'God's will', as she had said she would be rearing her children outside the one true faith.

Mary and Kevin were very supportive. But their son, Declan, who was fourteen years younger than me, was already married with a child. And there was talk, albeit in a jokey fashion, that at least the *Chronicle* dynasty wasn't going to end with me.

I did, and still do, harbour a large slice of blame for the hospital doctor, who refused to countenance saving Millie's life before the child's. Yes, it was policy, and, yes, he wasn't even a Catholic, but we were never allowed to be part of the conversation. And I can't forgive that.

I blamed the Unionists for us not being allowed to buy a house in the city – where we might have had a chance of getting Millie to the hospital in time, after she took the seizure. By the time I'd covered the five miles into town from Glenabbey, over bad country roads in an icy November, Millie was three-quarters dead. Maybe, indeed, that was EF Cunningham's revenge on us for stealing his home?

The RUC, while they mightn't have been responsible for Millie's death, had no right to disrupt the funeral by moving in to wrestle a tricolour from a standard-bearer. And the IRA had no business being there in the first place, either. It was my grief – not theirs.

We should never have left the States. The Democrats should have made me a proper offer in Boston – maybe a seat on Beacon Hill. And we would have had proper grown-up doctors in the delivery room.

Moreover, Millie had no business working eight hours a day while she was pregnant. She should have rested up and let me take care of her, like I asked her. The shock, the void, and the sudden end of all that love, it was completely unfair of her. She had shown me that the world was a kinder, lighter and more beautiful place, but without her, it was all a lie. What right had she to blaze into my life, set me on fire and then leave without so much as a goodbye? It was crueller than if I'd never met her. And where was she now when I needed her most? What did I know about looking after children? I'd been looked after like a child my entire life.

And, of course, what I really wasn't saying out loud, but which I knew to my core, was that it was all my fault. I was being punished for my useless life by a god I didn't believe in. I could have gone to Washington with her, I could have refused to have children, and I could have driven faster to the hospital. Coulda, woulda, shoulda …

Millie's brother, Charlie Harrison, knew it was my fault, too – and wrote me a stack of letters to tell me so. I was never worthy of her, which I wasn't, and that, if he had his way, I would die an equally horrible death. I hoped he was right.

Yes, they were all bastards. Every last one of them. As was I. And the world, as I'd suspected all along, was just a warm-up for hell.

The only person I never blamed for Millie's death was Little Mill. I loved her from the moment I set eyes on her.

She was her mother incarnate.

CHAPTER 45

It was Mo O'Sullivan who saved my life.

She was the seventeen-year-old girl Millie had recruited in the last couple of months of her pregnancy, to help out when the baby was born. She lived just a bike ride away, across the border in Bridgend and, without a word from me, took over as Little Mill's minder from the day after the funeral. As natural as if it had been ordained. She'd arrive on the last pip at eight o'clock to let me away to the office. And she'd stay at the house until six, seven, eight at night, or whatever time I pretended I had to work to. Six days a week. Either Connie or Mary, or Mary's daughter Katie, would do the Sunday shift while I hid out at the *Chronicle*. And for about six months, everything was fine, if not exactly dandy.

I was clever about how I tried to kill myself, even if I say so myself. I didn't try to pretend to the world that I was okay. I let it be known I was heartbroken but that the passage of time was making everything a little more bearable. And, of course, I had Little Mill to look after, and she was such a joy, even in the midst of everything. It was an early version of Tommy Bowtie's Ninety Per Cent Rule – you tell people so much of the truth, they wrongly trust that everything you're saying is true and fail to spot the bigger lie.

What I wasn't saying is that my mind had quietly convinced itself that if I wanted to find Millie again, I had to enter the same dimension she was in, the spiritual dimension in which, of course, I had never believed. But to join her now, I had to put my own lights out – or have them put out for me.

I wasn't brave enough to do it by myself. But I saw an opportunity to get a bit of assistance – and to take out an old enemy along with me.

At that time, the IRA was waging a not very successful campaign against partition, blowing up checkpoints and the like. So, one evening, I rang the RUC Victoria Barracks and reported that a *Chronicle* distribution truck had been stolen, and that I feared it was going to be used in a bomb attack.

The truck was actually hidden in my garage, and the plan was that, when I drove it rapidly towards the Buncrana Road checkpoint at 6.00am the next day, the waiting police would fill it, and me, full of holes. Everyone would be happy. I would be an innocent martyr reunited with my wife, there would be outrage at the recklessness and corruptness of the cops, and Little Mill would never have to know that her father was broken.

At 5.30am, I went into Little Mill's room and kissed her on the forehead before heading out to the garage to get the van. I had arranged for Mo to come in at 6.30am, telling her I'd an early delivery to do in Donegal.

I took the truck out of the garage, said a quiet goodbye to the house, and slowly made my way along the twisting 400-yard-long drive. But when I got to the big iron gate, it was bolted. From the outside. Mo must have locked it on her way home. There was no other way out. And even if I had been able to get a decent run at the gate, the truck would barely have made a dent in it.

So I reversed back to outside the house and waited for Mo, growing more impatient by the minute. I'd never really spoken much to her to that point – other than to ask about Little Mill. She was smart, reliable and, most importantly, terrific with the baby – Mill smiled every time Mo came into a room, and she went over to sleep every night like a charm. Mo, I'd also noticed, was very determined and afraid of no-one – she never let telephone callers bother me: 'Mr Madden is in a private meeting and cannot be disturbed, not even for you, Your Eminence.' I'd been impressed at how literate she was, too – both in English and in Irish. On occasion, she had taken some very accurate, and nuanced, messages from some very important people. She told me once when she was reading to Mill that if she hadn't become a nanny she would have loved nothing better than to be a journalist. She'd left school at fifteen, but only because she had to – she was the twelfth of twelve children and was grateful that her parents had carried her so long.

At 6.30am, I heard a vehicle at the gate and drove down to investigate. It was Connie's car, but it was Mo who was standing in the laneway unlocking the gate.

'I'm sorry, Mr Madden,' she said through the bars. 'But I couldn't let you do it.'

I was afraid to look at Connie in the car. But as soon as the gates swung open, she simply got out of her seat, ran over to me and hugged me.

For the first time since Millie died, in the privacy of my own driveway, I sobbed my heart out, and so did my mother.

We stood there for an age until I could cry no more, and then we looked over at Mo, who was also a mess but was pretending to keep it together.

'How did you know?' I asked her.

'You have a tell, sir,' she said. 'You look at the ground when you're lying. So I knew whatever else you were doing this morning, you weren't doing a delivery. Then, on my way home last night, there must have been thirty police at the checkpoint – and they asked me had I seen a *Chronicle* van. Every one of them had guns and they were very edgy. So I cycled back here and locked the gate. Just in case. And then I went into Barney McLaughlin's bar and rang Mrs Madden.'

I shook my head in disbelief. 'But how did you work out what I was planning?'

She took a beat. And her voice, when she spoke, was both measured and serious. 'I don't mean to offend you, sir, but you're not that complicated. You've been seriously hurting and trying to make it all go away. Hiding in your office, drinking too much, not talking to anyone – or when you are talking, lying through your teeth. But there's still a whole lot of people watching out for you – and a whole lot who need you, too, like Little Mill. So if you're going to try another stunt like this, sir, you're going to have to fire me first. Because I hate to say this, but you're not bright enough to get one past me.'

Connie started to laugh, and so did Mo, and eventually so did I. Mo was right, of course.

After that, I cried every night for a full year, grieved for another couple and brooded for at least another five after that. But I never tried to harm myself again. And I never lied to Mo again, either – or very rarely, at least.

CHAPTER 46

1964

I once interviewed a very wise doctor about hypothermia and the elderly. He was providing our readers with all sorts of tips about quilts and heaters and how often to check in with their neighbours. It was an annual puff piece we did coming up to Christmas.

When we were done, I thanked the doc and told him it had been very useful.

'No problem,' he said. 'But what I should really be saying, although, of course, I can't, is that each of us gets our three score years and ten, then winter comes and carries us off. And no amount of blankets or hot-water bottles is going to make any difference.'

Both Kate in Boston and Mick in Drumhaggart did a lot better than average and had seen past ninety when the grim winter of 1960–61 finally carried them off.

Mick died first, in November, happy in his own bed, with Connie and myself beside him. He'd taken 'queer' about a fortnight previously while changing a ten-stone beer barrel at his pub and casually asked us if we might take turns waiting for him until he passed. He lived just long enough to hear word of Jack Kennedy's election on the wireless.

'A Catholic in the White House, Connie, and your cousin to boot – you'll have to take me over to meet him.'

Mick had been promising to go to America for forty years. It was a running joke that Connie would take him to visit Kate and maybe fix the two of them up. But he never made it.

The funeral at St Eugene's Cathedral was enormous. The *Chronicle* estimated 2,000 people were there, including the archbishop, three bishops and four government ministers – Southern ministers, that is. Unionists couldn't darken the door of a Catholic chapel or they'd get thrown out of the Lodge, and maybe the country – though, in fairness, all the local representatives visited the wake-house and were genuinely sympathetic. Mick had always been fair to them, if never particularly easy.

Mick left four-fifths of his fifty-per-cent shareholding in the *Chronicle* directly to me. Connie owned the other fifty per cent and had already made provision that this would pass directly to me on her death. But Mick had greatly appreciated Kevin O'Dorrity's major contribution at the paper, and Mary's many sacrifices for his family, so he left them ten per cent of his total, which amounted to five per cent of the paper.

'Their experience and wisdom will be a real asset on the Board,' he told me.

Mick's remaining shares were left, in trust, for Maureen 'Mo' O'Sullivan, for when she turned twenty-one. No explanation was needed or was given.

***

After Mick's death, Connie, understandably, felt a very strong need to visit her own mother. And when the telegram arrived inviting her and Mary to the inauguration in Washington on 20 January, they seized the opportunity to make the trip stateside.

Kate had been becoming a bit forgetful but knew enough that she wanted to go to Washington, too. She loved it, too, in spite of the cold, and was never as proud as when the new president gave her a big hug and told the photographers that she was his 'favourite Irish auntie'. Kate told Connie that in all her ninety-one years, she had never felt as hopeful for the future.

Sadly, however, it was all a bit too much for her. Kate took to her bed with a cold the next day and succumbed to a chest infection before the week was out.

'It was typical of her,' said Connie. 'She was always so considerate. Mary and I didn't even have to change the dates on our return tickets.'

The day before she died, Kate asked Connie to give me her author-signed copy of the Kennedy inauguration poem, in which Robert Frost welcomed the shape of things to come. She said it inspired her, and she hoped it would inspire me as well. I still have it in the safe along with Millie's Runyon book – the one she hit me with, not the signed one.

So, at the first meeting of the new Board after Kate's death, we voted unanimously to change the newspaper's masthead from '*Veritas Lux Mea*', which was always a bit too Catholic for my liking, to the one we have now, from her Frost poem.

It's been there ever since and will remain there till the day I die. And it still speaks to me every time I read it: 'Firm in our free beliefs without dismay/In any game the nations want to play.' Just like the poet and the president said.

***

Even while Jack was scaring us to death with the Bay of Pigs disaster and the Cuban Missile Crisis, his new, 'golden age of poetry and power' was filling our hearts with excitement, if not a little optimism. After all, if an Irish Catholic could hold the most powerful position in the world, then surely it was only a matter of time before some of his influence began rubbing off on this side of the Atlantic as well.

The civil rights campaigns in the US had a profound influence on the Derry public, who lapped up any and all coverage and opinion writing that resonated with them. The *Chronicle* reported faithfully on the integration of the schools and universities, the Freedom Rides in the Deep South, the desegregation of buses and restaurants, mass voter registration, and, of course, on the march on Washington in March 1963 where half a million demonstrators listened to Reverend King deliver his 'I have a dream' speech.

Understandably enough, there was frustration among Northern Nationalists that change wasn't happening quickly enough here – certainly not compared to what we were reading about in the papers and now, for the first time, seeing for ourselves on television. We identified completely with the Negroes except, unlike us, they had found their voice.

When it was announced that Kennedy was to visit Ireland in 1963, Nationalists saw a chance to get partition back on the international agenda. Just a decade previously, our favourite cousin had announced to the Senate that the US must be 'placed firmly on the side of a united Ireland'. But things had changed, and our brothers and sisters in the South left us languishing again by refusing to allow the discussion as part of the visit. Nationalist MPs who tried to organise a meeting with Kennedy, even off the books, were blocked from doing so by the Free State's Minister for External Affairs, Frank Aiken.

I privately extended an invitation to Jack to visit his 'family' in Derry, if he felt like making a symbolic gesture. He had called in before in 1947 during a tour of Ireland as a young US Congressman, just as Tip O'Neill had dropped by in the late 1950s en route to his Granny Fullerton's ancestral home in Buncrana. But the Unionists threw a spanner in the works by formally inviting Jack to inspect the NATO base in the city here – thus emphasising the point that Northern Ireland was America's military ally, unlike the quisling South, where he had no business going anyway. The British were furious with the Unionists, and Prime Minister Harold McMillan put the kibosh on any cross-border visit at all after that. Dev, naturally, said not a word – not that Jack would have listened to him too much anyway. He had long considered the Long Fellow a lunatic.

The visit, as the *New York Times* said later, was a triumph – during which the people of Ireland were entirely 'willing to forget that six northern counties are still under British rule'. I got myself an invitation to a garden party at Dev's new palace, Áras an Uachtaráin in Phoenix Park, but had no desire to be part of a free-for-all and didn't go. That, and I would only have spent the time wishing Millie were with me to make fun of all the grasping cap-tippers. Connie and Mary said it was an embarrassment and so badly organised that they only got to wave at Jack across the room.

The *Chronicle*, naturally, devoted acres of space to the visit – flawed and all as it was. It spoke to unstoppable, momentous change, and it was vital we showed it as such. It was probably the most important thing that had happened in our lives to that point. To this day there are people in this city who have Jack's photograph up on their living-room walls between the portrait of the Pope and their picture of the Sacred Heart.

When Jack died in November, my own heart broke again, both for what might have been and for the fact that I hadn't gone to see him. But by now, there was no quenching the fire that had been lit. We were on the march, and we would overcome.

CHAPTER 47

'Bowtie', as the natives called him, was waiting for McCloud at the summer seats outside the Tower Museum in the Craft Village, reading his *Irish Times* and drinking a coffee. It being Saturday, he was back in his civvies – painting clothes today – and was barely recognisable.

The Craft Village was a maze of beautifully restored inter-connected courtyards, winding their way between Hangman's Bastion on the old Walls and Shipquay Street. It was like a trip back in time – old-style shopfronts with dressed windows and canopies to the front, and baskets of purple flowers hanging from ornate nineteenth-century lampposts.

Bowtie pointed to the coffee he had gotten for McCloud and bade him sit down.

'Why are we meeting here today?' McCloud asked him.

'I'm looking for a first-edition Heaney, *Wintering Out*, which I heard they've got around the corner in Foyle Books. It's signed – though, as my father always says, an unsigned Heaney from back then could be worth an absolute fortune.'

McCloud laughed – a man is never a hero in his hometown.

'How's the head this morning?' Bowtie asked him. 'Your eyes look a lot brighter.'

'The head's crystal clear. Only had the one last night. I was too tired. My aftershave bottle is full to the brim – and I've a little in my vitamin bottle, too. It's easier here. Even though I'm under scrutiny by the two *Chronicle* witches twenty-four hours a day, I feel totally at ease.'

'I get that,' said Bowtie. 'And you've nothing to worry about. They're appraising you – not judging you. They were a bit rough to begin with, but they weren't sure what they were dealing with. They like you now, though. You ask the right questions. They know you're one of them.'

'I'm not sure that's a compliment …'

'It is, of course. They know you're straight. And even if they don't like what you find, they know that you'll handle it properly.'

'Just like you're handling me now …'

Bowtie laughed. 'You give me too much credit. Look at me, I'm only a humble painter.'

McCloud laughed and let it go. But he was privately convinced that Bowtie knew more, and about more things, than any other man he'd ever met with the possible exception of the Director.

'How did you get on yesterday?' Bowtie asked him.

'Okay. But there's a couple of questions I mightn't be entirely comfortable asking Mo. Would you be able to help?'

Bowtie nodded. 'These would be questions about Mo, I imagine. And yes, that's completely fair. You wouldn't be doing your job if you didn't look at her, too. After any shooting, the first person you speak to is the wife – or in this case, Mo.'

'Okay, then. Did she do it?'

Bowtie shook his head emphatically. 'No way. Not at all. No. For a whole bunch of reasons. First and most important of which is that she couldn't have done it, she was away that weekend.'

'Away where? Any witnesses?'

'She was in Dublin, at a business conference – where she was seen by hundreds of people the night before the shooting and the morning after.'

'She couldn't have slipped home in the interim?'

'She could have. But Paud Devlin, who was sharing a hotel room with her, would have told me …'

'You're kidding! Paud Devlin the IRA leader?'

'Yes, one and the same. Paud, God rest him, and Mo had a very discreet and very loving friendship after Paud's wife died. I knew about it, Seán knew and now you do, too. Maeve never did, and I'd really appreciate it …'

McCloud dismissed his concern with a simple wave of the hand. 'No problem. What happened Paud?'

'Drink, eventually. He had to do some rough stuff over the years and some of it did not sit well with his very Catholic conscience.'

'Like what?'

'Well, you'll hear a lot in Seán's tape – if you haven't heard already – about some very twisted people doing very twisted things. Though generally, they tend to be people on the different side of the argument from Seán. The dirty little secret is that some of his own friends, or associates, could be equally twisted and ruthless. I'm not sure that makes them bad people necessarily. As a lawyer, particularly as I get older, I put more and more down to circumstances, and less and less down to character. I think we're all capable of terrible things if the pressure is on us.'

'So what sort of things did Paud do?'

176

'Let's just say his eyes were the last eyes a lot of people ever saw. He never ordered another man to do a job he wouldn't do himself.'

'Did Mo know that?'

'Almost certainly. But don't get me wrong. She seriously disapproved and challenged him on it all the time. This wasn't some feather-headed maiden chasing after the handsome warrior. She plagued him relentlessly to do the right thing. I firmly believe that she, and she alone, is the reason he eventually signed up for peace talks.'

McCloud was once again incredulous at just how little he knew about anything. 'So Mo couldn't have done it,' he said. 'Would she ever have wanted to shoot him, though?'

Bowtie shook his head. 'No. She fought with him every day about everything from headlines to finances. But she loved him more than any of us. She has spent her life caring for him and his family. And even when they fell out, which did happen from time to time, there were too many ties for them to stay mad for too long. She had absolutely no motive – she was in charge of the empire while he ran the newspaper, and she was getting well paid for it. She had no ambition to be editor, the titular head – she had done her stint in the limelight and much preferred the anonymity. And again, and importantly, she loved him.'

'But that doesn't mean she couldn't shoot him. What if she, or he, wanted more?'

'I've played all this out over the past eighteen years, Ally. And the bottom line is that they didn't want more. They were two very smart people who had found a relationship that you or I might think peculiar but worked perfectly for them. And they were never going to change that. Also, I kept a very close eye on how they interacted after the shooting – and it barely changed a beat. If anything, she just became more worried about him.'

'But ...'

'Let me save you some time, Ally. I investigated all the staff immediately after the shooting – and then I reinvestigated them all again a month later. I did the same with the extended family as well. Even Maeve, though she could only have been about twelve or thirteen. And none of them wanted to shoot Seán, and none of them could have done it. They had solid alibis and genuine friendships.'

McCloud downed a big mouthful of latte while considering this. 'What happened the police investigation?'

Bowtie cast his eyes to heaven. 'They got nothing. Though in fairness, there was little to work with. A masked man, a scuffle, two shots and a minor leg wound. There was a lot of other stuff going on around then, you know – it would barely have qualified as a domestic. And let's face it, there were one or two in the RUC back then who wouldn't have been too worried that Motormouth Madden got what was coming to him. So, it was never pursued too vigorously.'

'So who, then?'

'Who do you think? You're about halfway through the tape.'

McCloud bit his lip for a minute. 'EF Cunningham?'

Bowtie grinned. 'And why would you think that?'

'Well, I certainly think you're all trying to steer me that way. And it's interesting that you've already lined up a meeting for me with him next week – a meeting, incidentally, that I didn't ask for. So why would he do it?'

Bowtie stood up, drained his coffee and pointed up the hill towards Foyle Books. 'If I told you that, Ally,' he said, 'you'd be able to go home straightaway. And we're only starting to enjoy your company …'

CHAPTER 48

To McCloud's surprise, Mo was also wearing casual clothes: jeans, a hooded top and sneakers. She pointed McCloud directly into the living room. 'So I've been cleared, then?' she said.

Bowtie had never once left McCloud's presence, nor had he phoned or texted anyone in the last hour. He hadn't even spoken to Mo when he dropped him off in the driveway – and had just given her a solitary nod.

McCloud grinned. 'You're all just showing off now. Try to throw the poor Yank off his game.'

'I told him to brief you,' said Mo. 'You'd have been irresponsible not to ask him about me. You'll not say a word? Not even to herself.' She gestured with her thumb towards the manse.

'Not a word,' he said.

For a second, Mo looked a little vulnerable, frail almost, and the professional tone shifted. 'It's not that I'm ashamed of it – I'm honestly not. It's just, well, I discovered late on, too late on, that he had hurt someone who was most dear to me. And it didn't end particularly well. And it was very sore. That's all I want to say about it for now.'

'You can take it to the bank. I heard nothing.'

'Thank you.'

She poured them both coffee and sat down on the armchair. 'Now, we'll have to be quick today. Maeve and I have promised Bowtie we'll go and help him paint his boat out at Fahan Marina. He's cashing in his chip for all the running about he's being doing with you this week.'

'Why wouldn't he get a professional painter to do it? Surely he's not short of a dollar?'

'Same reason we didn't hire a taxi driver. If you were Tommy Bowtie, would you want some stranger working at your property? God knows what they could take – or leave?'

McCloud laughed. 'To be honest, I'd be more worried about hiring you and Maeve.'

Mo motioned as if to slap him. 'So? You want to recap on yesterday?'

He nodded. 'A few things. I checked up on some of the Kennedy references, and State won't necessarily like them, but they can live with them. His reference to Dev as a "lunatic" is probably top of that list.'

'Yeah, Jack made that comment in his diaries when he was travelling as a young correspondent in Ireland in the 1940s. The *Irish Times* has published it at least once; it's not going to ruin any relationships, so don't worry.'

McCloud had long dropped the pretence that the shooting was the only thing he was interested in. 'Good to hear. Tell me about the suicide attempt after Millie's death. Did he ever try to self-harm again? Is there any chance what happened in 1994 …'

'You're wondering if he could have become a bit unstable and maybe shot himself? Invented the whole masked-man bit?'

McCloud shrugged. 'It is possible.'

'No. He stopped bottling things up after that. And if Connie or I ever detected him becoming moody, we'd make sure to up his quota of Little Mill. Spending time with her always brought him around.'

'Was he self-destructive?'

'Yes. But within limits. He was careful not to burn too many bridges.'

'Bridges? Surely you mean "boats"?'

'Apologies. It's an old joke of Seán's, "I'll burn that bridge when I come to it".'

McCloud furrowed his brow. 'You say that his mood was better when Little Mill was around – but what about after she died, in 1994? And you weren't about, either, when he got shot, you were out of town. Is it at all possible that he went back to a very dark place? Chickened out at the final moment and shot himself in the leg instead?'

Mo stroked her chin for a moment. 'No. His anger after Little Mill's death took a very specific direction – and it wasn't towards himself. The *Leader* published an awful hatchet job on Mill – EF Cunningham's doing – shortly after she died. And, well, if Seán were going to shoot anyone, it would have been EF. But he got his wings clipped before he could try anything. I'm sure of it.'

'And how can you be sure?'

She paused, closed her eyes then took a big breath. 'Because when Seán asked Harry Hurley for a gun that same week, Harry contacted me directly to warn me. And he then put out an edict that no-one, repeat, not anyone, from the chief-of-staff down, was to give Seán Madden a pistol or there would be hell to pay.'

'Could he have got a gun anywhere else?'

'No. Seán played tough, but in matters like that he was totally hapless.

Besides, there is no doubt that there was another person in the room when Seán was shot. There was certainly a struggle of some sort. Seán would never have thought to bust up the pictures on the wall – certainly not the ones of Millie Senior and Old Mick at least.'

'So you think it was EF wearing the mask as well?'

She shook her head. 'I think you really need to watch the rest of the tapes. Maeve would be very disappointed if you were to hand in your report just now. She told me to tell you she loves your blue polo shirt today – it goes so well with your eyes. She's really looking forward to meeting you when all this is over. The two of you might take in a movie together.'

Maeve, naturally, had said no such thing, but it would set up about five or ten minutes of smart remarks later at Bowtie's boat.

McCloud smiled gently. He knew well he was being ribbed, too. 'You didn't answer …'

'Okay, yes,' said Mo. 'I think it could well have been EF. He was a bully and had form for violence. He'd been nipping at Seán since old Jackson sold off the manse in the fifties – and there were some awful threats bandied about. But I'm still not one hundred per cent convinced – and I think we would need to establish the why as well.'

'Fair enough. But did EF not appreciate that Seán had helped save the *Leader* when it was about to go under?'

'He didn't see it like that. EF was a Unionist dinosaur – the Basil Brooke variety, who wouldn't have a Catholic about the place. His bigotry let him ignore his own inadequacies and blame all his problems on lesser mortals.'

McCloud had spent eight months training in Georgia, where he had encountered supremacists of a similar ilk.

'What sort of financial shape was the *Chronicle* in at the time of the shooting?' he asked.

'Very healthy – not quite its zenith, but approaching it.'

'And its zenith would have been when?'

'Early 2000s. That's when Seán sold off the bulk of the titles. He was one extremely astute, or extremely lucky, guy. Within about three years, the bottom had fallen out of the newspaper market, and as we know all too well, it's taking its time coming back.'

'You think it will?'

'The *Chronicle* and the *Leader* are different from most of the traditional press across the water or in the South. They're very much the voices of – and guardians of – their communities. So, if anyone has a chance, it's us.'

'The money Seán made from the sales – fifteen million sterling, according to my notes – will you reinvest some of that in the *Chronicle*? You're not going to let it go to the wall, are you?'

'God, no. And we're not liable to reinvest either – or at least not much. Seán had Tommy Bowtie primed to make sure we don't throw good money after bad, and he'll be executor of the trust.'

'So what next for the paper, then? A financial hit could close you down. And you're still facing a serious libel from young Mr Cunningham.'

'I'll let Maeve worry about the writ. I'm certainly not going to. It's her own damned fault, feeding the internet like that.'

'What might happen, though? Could there be a takeover?'

'No-one's taking over the *Chronicle*,' she said. 'We'd shut it down first. But it wouldn't necessarily be the worst thing in the world if the two papers merged. Financially, that is, not politically. They need to retain their separate identities – if only for sales. But a merger would keep costs down and allow us both to fight on for a few years more.'

This sounded to McCloud's ears like more than idle speculation. 'Have you ever spoken to young Cunningham about this?' he asked.

Mo looked at her watch, deliberately not answering. Maeve could still be listening across the driveway. 'We're way off topic here, Alistair,' she said, 'and I have a boat to paint. We can continue this tomorrow. Tomorrow's Sunday, isn't it? If you're very good, I might get Annie to send you down a bit of the roast. See you then.'

CHAPTER 49

1965

There is no better place to hide a spy than in a newsroom. It is the perfect cover. Your mole can sit all day asking questions of whomever he wants, get all the information first, and report it back to HQ while the newspaper picks up his cheque.

My vetting was usually too thorough for them. Though in saying that, they tended to stick out like a sore thumb because, ultimately, they were outsiders who came out of nowhere. And, as a smart old Sinn Féiner told me, people who came out of nowhere came out of somewhere.

To gain your confidence, they might pose as being a little radical and will quietly admit to you that they were a member of a left-wing party or grouping in their youth. They need a bit of buy-in with the rougher set, otherwise it won't work. But anybody who includes you in a secret at your first meeting will have ten more that they're not telling you. So run.

I'm sure one or two got past me in my time. And it's not just governments who like to plant. We had at least a couple of Provos in our ranks in the 1980s, which was no great harm as it got us great access to stories and gave us a bit of street cred. They were also, I have to say, terrific journalists. And at least one of the supposedly new republicans we had working with us in the 1990s was very probably working for the other side as well. You couldn't watch them. At times it was like an episode of *The Man from Uncle*.

Some didn't consider themselves professional spies, either, but would describe themselves as advisors or consultants. Still others didn't even realise they were being used as spies – instead, they got invited to boozy dinner parties by friends in the business, where they couldn't stop themselves from spilling all the inside gen. I met a British ringmaster once and challenged him about a guy who had briefly worked for us before we weeded him out – I said he had to be one of his. But he just laughed and asked me why he would bother paying him when the guy was of 'a like mind' to him anyway.

Sometimes, however, they just tell you outright.

***

I didn't realise for sure that I had correctly spotted the CIA's new man in Derry until our second meeting.

The first time I came across him was a fortnight after the Kennedy funeral. I'd just returned from the ceremonies in Washington to discover we had lost one of our junior reporters to the *Daily Mirror* in Belfast and needed a replacement in a hurry. We advertised with a very short deadline, less than a week if I remember, and got two applicants: a local youth in his early twenties with no arse in his trousers and a distinct smell of last night off him, and a perfectly turned-out young American graduate with a journalism degree from Stanford. The suit must have cost him two hundred dollars and the haircut another fifty.

Connie was doing the interviews with me, and it didn't take us thirty seconds to decide.

'The Yank is very good,' I said, 'it's a pity he's a plant. Great stories about the freedom marches – you'd almost believe he'd been on one. Will we re-advertise, so?'

Connie shook her head. 'No. Young Doherty from Creggan will be perfect. He knew everything that was going on in every pub in Waterloo Street. The characters, the political players, the musicians and the business operators. He's related to half of them, too, so they'll trust him. He'll bring us more stories than the bible – as long as we can keep him to a timetable and maybe run a hose over him.'

The Yank – who called himself Danny Given that particular day – was outraged when we sent him a Dear John letter; he called into the office to protest.

'This is discrimination,' he said. 'I'm better qualified, better presented and I have a reference from a United States Congressman. What has Doherty got that I don't have?'

'Local knowledge,' I told him. 'The lifeblood of any local paper. And no judge in the land is going to disagree. Thank you for your interest, Mr Given – be sure and give my regards to the State Department.'

He glared at me for the last dig. And although he couldn't have been more than twenty-five, he worried me a little. 'We're not done here,' he said. But I pointed him to the door, and we were.

CHAPTER 50

In early 1964, a schoolteacher called John Hume published an article in the *Irish Times* in which he threw down a gauntlet to the Nationalist Party. Hume, who was inspired by the American civil rights movement, argued that it was no longer enough to sloganise against partition, and that if Catholics were to achieve unity in Ireland there had to be engagement, and consensus, with Unionists. It was time to get out of the armchair and make a difference. The *Times* board weren't happy at all at this new line on the North – they called their own editor a 'white nigger'. But the playwright Brian Friel wrote a letter to the *Times* supporting Hume – asserting that there would be 'no real unity in Ireland until both sides come together voluntarily'.

Hume's proposals were radical and energetic, if not entirely new, and the *Chronicle* was kept busy discussing the decline of the older Nationalist Party and the rise of the young guns. Occasionally, Irish government officials and visiting British industrialists, who may have been wearing a couple of hats, would ring, or call in, to discuss the shifting political landscape. And there was a real sense, given all that was happening in the US, that major change was in the air.

One Friday afternoon in June, just as I was preparing to leave to take Little Mill to Lisfannon Beach, the telephone on my desk rang, and like a fool I lifted it.

It was Maria in reception: 'There's a man here insisting on seeing you,' she said. 'He's an American, and he's the new Head of Public Relations with Dunavady Council. He's rung about five times over the last week but you kept refusing his call. He says his name is Donald Grover, but here's the thing – he's a dead ringer for that guy you interviewed for the reporter's job at Christmas, the one Johnny Doherty got.'

This was intriguing. 'Give him five minutes and then pull me out – emergency of some sort. And ring Mo to say I'll be a bit late.'

I knew I'd been right about him first time by the way he came into my office without any apology for the intrusion and took a seat without being asked.

'You were supposed to hire me,' he said. 'Instead, I'm now stuck twenty miles away in a Hicksville so remote the hillbillies write songs about it.'

'You're with the government, so, Dan or Don.'

'Of course I am – and the name is Don. But understand, if you ever so much as breathe a word of it, I will cause serious problems for you and anyone else you tell. Or worse.'

I gave him a big smile. 'No problem. And I will give you five seconds to retract that threat before I call in my photographer, take your picture and put it on the front of my paper with the words "Intelligence Officer" underneath it. I did it with a so-called British economist two years ago and would have no hesitation doing it again.'

He was young and brash, very much in the Napoleon Solo mould, but he wasn't for bending.

He nodded like he understood and ignored me. 'When you were in Boston before Christmas, Mr Madden, you met with a group of Irish-Americans and prevailed on them to establish a Six County Support Network.'

'I did. We need funds and international media support for our campaigns: for decent housing; a university; one man, one vote. Basic human rights. We're not talking about setting up secret societies, here.'

'Four of the people you met are on a watch-list of suspected IRA members.'

'Only four of them?' I said. 'I was wasting my goddamn time, so.'

'You can be as big a smartass as you want – it's only going to take longer, and I've got all day. How's your daughter, by the way? Five now, isn't she? No, she'll be five at the end of the year.'

'Okay, you've read my file. And rest assured, I will have yours by return post. What do you want? And for the record, I had no idea any of those guys were IRA men. It strikes me as an easy smear to make if you don't like someone's argument.'

'You also met with some black leaders, when you were in Washington?'

'I did – that was the primary reason for my visit. It had actually been in the pipeline before poor Jack was killed.'

'You met with Malcolm Little, also known as Malcolm X?'

'Yes, briefly – I didn't like him. He was too sore on Jack. He didn't realise that it takes time to turn a tanker – and that it doesn't help when you shoot the captain who's trying to steer the thing the proper way.'

'And Reverend King?'

'Yes – he struck me as a very moral man. He could see well the links with Ireland.'

'We don't like either of them.'

'There's a surprise. The ghost of Joe McCarthy is back writing his lists.'

He smiled and pretended I'd scored a point then pulled some paper out of a little attaché case he had along with him.

'Just a couple of final bits to tidy up while I'm in the neighbourhood. The inheritance your grandmother left to her daughters – your mother Connie and your aunt Mary – has it cleared yet?'

I paused and took a breath. And there it was. He'd found my button. Every penny Patrick Hannon ever made from bootlegging, and no doubt an awful lot more besides, would be struck out of Kate's will if I didn't start taking this guy seriously.

Rest assured, everyone – no matter who you are, or how much integrity you think you might have – has a button. For most people it's easy enough to find – it boils down to either sex or money. And the Brits and the Yanks were masters at catering to both. On two or three different occasions, I was sitting in hotel lobbies in London in the late eighties or early nineties, after meeting with negotiators, when gorgeous women came up out of nowhere and offered to buy me a drink. I used to tell them they weren't the right fit for me – which is probably where those rumours started. But I know other guys who weren't so careful and ended up leafing through a series of ten-by-eight-inch glossies while their position on the issue *du jour* did a rapid *volte-face*.

Money is the other great corruptor. If you have none, they will show you how to get it – and if you have any of your own, they will show you how they can take it all away from you. If you're a good dog, you might get a tip to buy something low, which will immediately shoot through the moon. But if you're a bold boy and don't do what they tell you, your business will suddenly find itself facing three legal cases and a full audit. And, of course, they keep records of any and all payments and favours they do for you, just so they can leak them any time you thought you were done. There's nothing very skilled about any of it. It's about leverage pure and simple, and it's how the world works.

For a few unfortunates who try to keep themselves clean, their button will be their children – or their children's dirty little habits. And occasionally, it's done out of the noblest of intentions. One pol I know had a very sick daughter, terminally ill, and he switched his vote when the Brits arranged for her to see a top Harley Street specialist. Direct threats can work to a certain extent, too – but they're risky in that people can react badly to them and turn on you. They tend to use them when all else fails.

But, as I say, Don had found my button with just a few gentle pokes. So instead of reaching for the paper knife, which was my original impulse, I took it on the chin like a big boy. Or at least I pretended to.

'I hear what you're saying, Mr Grover,' I told him. 'How can I help you?'

CHAPTER 51

1966

There is a hair's breadth, if even that, between collaborating with someone and working independently, in parallel with someone, towards a common goal. It is the difference between being an informer and being a negotiator. It is the difference between being controlled and being in control.

If you are going to run any sort of a paper in Derry, even now, you are going to have to have a working relationship with all the political groupings – plus the likes of the Irish Government, the Brits, Stormont, the IRA, INLA, the various loyalist gunsels, the police and, yes, the Yanks. And while frequently, you – as the watchdog – will have radically different views from any or all of these parties, at other times you will be entirely on the same page. But you can never be in their pocket – or be seen to work for them. If your readers are to trust you, to take you seriously, they must always believe in your independence and integrity. Because, otherwise, as my old friend Runyon might have said, they will spot that you are trying to sell them the old 'phonus balonus'.

I realised straightaway that, whatever else he was, Don Grover was now our pipeline to official America. My family connections would always be there, but he was Route One.

It didn't take me the rest of the day to accumulate enough 'data', as the spies call it, to have Don sent back to the States. Three telephone calls, to his hotel, his new employers at Dunavady and the parish priest at Drumvale, had established that Don couldn't handle his drink and that he liked to play cards, but not very well. He also had been seen three or four times in the company of a married woman – possibly innocent enough, but her husband owned a shotgun.

I didn't want to make an enemy of Don, however, for a number of reasons. For a start, I'd realised from our last meeting that Don bore that extremely focused, psychopathic zeal you see in certain people who have been so damaged by life that they will burn anyone and anything to get what they want. I have no doubt if I'd had Don sent home, he would have spent the rest of his life ensuring Connie and Mary never got a cent of their inheritance – and he would have come after the *Chronicle* and our friends, both here and in America, to boot.

188

Whatever had happened Don in his childhood or youth, he was completely devoid of empathy and, possibly, humanity. But he also had, as was evident by his anger at not getting the *Chronicle* job, a real fear of failure. Even though he was only hoping to establish a cover story, the fact he didn't get the job badly hurt him.

Moreover, I knew well that if Don left, he would be replaced in a heartbeat, and that Mark Two could be worse again. Except this time, whoever it was would not only visit the same again on me, but they would also know me to be treacherous and spend their days watching me like a hawk. And I certainly didn't want to wreck my lifelong connection with a country that had taken me in and sustained me, a country that I loved.

No, as I said, I didn't want to make an enemy of Don. But neither was I going to work for him nor do his bidding for him. If he wanted my help, it would be on my terms, not his. So, the morning after he made his big shakedown pitch, I rang him at his Dunavady office and told him to meet me at the *Chronicle* that afternoon.

***

Don strode into my little office like he owned the place, glanced disdainfully at the scuffed leather chair that was waiting for him and eventually sat down.

I had one card, but it was a good one.

'I've thought about your offer, Don,' I told him. 'And I'm rejecting it. You've completely overplayed your hand. It's like the way you play poker, or so I hear – all bluff and bluster in the wrong places, and then when you've got all the aces, people see right through you and don't want to play. You didn't have to threaten me – most of what you were suggesting editorially is totally in line with what we're doing anyway.

'Our agenda – social change, equality, an end to discrimination, new housing and better education – is no more radical than the one President Johnson is pursuing with his new government. Probably less so, if we're to be honest.

'Your one big complaint, that we have been in some ways inflaming the situation is, frankly, a huge overstatement. The Southern national broadcaster, RTÉ, filmed a totally factual documentary here in Derry last summer, but they're too terrified to broadcast it in case it would offend the British. Well, here's the difference – we can't afford not to tell the truth. People, here and abroad, need to hear what is happening here – and we have to do it because no-one else can, and no-one else will. We're not being irresponsible, we're not starting fires, and we're not bringing people onto the streets – at least not yet. We're just doing our job.

'So I called my former employer, Congressman Thomas O'Neill, and asked him for his advice. I told him about all your blackmail, too. Boy, he laughed hard at that – and said he hoped nobody ever looked at where the Kennedy money came from. But Tip, anyway, said that he would be happy to raise the issue of coercion against American citizens in Ireland by the CIA if I wished …'

I paused for effect. Don stared really hard at me for about five seconds, went through at least four of the five stages of grief, then shut his eyes. He'd finally met a fellow traveller, someone who would scorch the entire earth, not to get ahead but rather to protect the things he loved.

When he spoke, it was in a whisper. 'Don't do that,' he said. 'Please.'

I pretended I hadn't heard him. 'So I told Tip, if the guy had only come to me, first day, and asked me if I would be interested in some official American briefings, guidance, advice – call it whatever you want – on a voluntary basis, I would have taken the hand off him. Of course I would love to hear what the biggest player on the planet thinks – and of course I would want to help inform and, at times, challenge that thinking. We need that now more than ever. But that doesn't compromise my paper – it just makes it, and me, better informed. But instead, this guy decided to play five rounds of who's got the biggest mickey and wasted everybody's time.'

Of course, I hadn't rung Tip at all. But it wasn't like Don was going to be in a hurry to check.

'So, Mr Grover, your options here are simple. I am happy to meet with you for a cup of coffee here once a week, for say an hour or two, where we can catch up like two old American friends might do. Or you can go back to Dunavady, pack up your bags, and tell your replacement I'll meet him with the same offer in a couple of weeks' time.

'But before you leave this office, you will withdraw any and all threats against my family. There will be no duress – and any hint of the same will end our relationship. I won't wear hostile takeovers. Do you understand?'

We both knew I'd broken him. And we both knew I had to – it was either that or he broke me.

But he respected me for it. I later learned that he had pulled the same stunt with a series of other local outfits – including a number who should have known better – and they had all rolled right over to let him tickle their bellies.

He flashed me the grin of a man who had got a result he could live with.

'Look forward to a coffee on Friday afternoon, Mr Madden. And please, believe me, I would never wish any harm on you or your family. It was a complete misunderstanding.'

'That's what I thought,' I said. I shook his hand. 'Welcome to Derry, Mr Grover.'

***

190

Over the years to come, they all sent their messengers, envoys, attachés or emissaries to the *Chronicle*. Some came with guns drawn, others with sugar. But they all got the same arrangement. We will listen to you and we will talk to you. And if we are on the same page, great. And if we are not, it's nothing personal. But you will not tell us what to write. And if you lie to us, you are demeaning us, and our readers, and we will roast you so hot you will never lie to us again.

Most of them only wanted to know about one another – but that was another of the rules. No talking out of school. You want to talk to the Brits, we'll set it up for you. But we're not carrying your bags. We're not your middlemen.

There were some very decent, sincere people involved, and there were some rogues, men who would ride two horses until they were sure of the winner. I fell out with quite a few of them, too. Though not Don. He and I had an understanding that would last for more than twenty years – and from that day on, he was always straight with me.

What happened between us in the end was my fault.

CHAPTER 52

1966–67

At this stage, I'm going to have to start using dummy names – and maybe move about some of the minutiae of what went on. This archive's not supposed to be released for twenty-five years after I'm gone. But when you see how the Northern state kicked down every door, and threw aside every legal challenge, to get their hands on the tapes from Boston College, we have to assume they're going to try to get their hands on this, too. And, there are a lot of people I admire who, for different reasons, might be greatly embarrassed, or hurt, or feel left out, and you don't want their relatives coming over and putting in your windows.

The next few years were extraordinary times, and people did extraordinary things – but sometimes those things were extraordinarily stupid, and I'm not sure it helps anyone for us to poke fun at them or judge them too harshly. In fact, deep down, I'm not entirely sure that this account should ever be made public at all. The only reason I'm doing it is to try and keep a few people honest.

***

The *Chronicle*, largely because of our friendship with the Cunninghams, had always been respectful of the Derry Unionists. Far too respectful, if I'm to be frank. But a number of things changed rapidly in the mid-1960s, which changed the relationship radically.

For a start, EF Cunningham took over the editorship of the *Londonderry Leader* after his father, Jackson, spent one late night too many at his desk and took the dive. And not to put too fine a point on it, EF was as big an asshole as his father had been a gentleman. He was an out-and-out bigot, who spent his time pandering to Unionism's worst excesses, railing against moderates like Stormont Prime Minister Terence O'Neill and cheering on lunatics, bible-bashers and anti-Catholic firebrands. At least in Alabama, they wear white hoods and robes so you can pick them out easier.

In 1967, after O'Neill's friend, mid-Ulster MP George Forrest, publicly supported Unionist talks with Southern Taoiseach Seán Lemass, EF and a group of his drinking buddies travelled to a Twelfth of July demonstration in Tyrone, tore Forrest off the speaking platform and almost kicked him to death.

EF and the *Leader* had, on the face of things, supported the campaign for Derry to get its own new university in 1965 after the Lockwood Report scandalously advised that the facility should be sited in Coleraine. But privately, the little toad had worked with a group of faceless Unionists in the city, including several councillors, to ensure that their own home city, four times the size and about twenty times the need of Coleraine, was passed over. They couldn't risk an influx of Catholics into their citadel, not when their obviously stacked voting system – which still gave them control – was starting to come apart at the seams.

It was sneaky and it was outrageous, and when the *Chronicle* caught EF and a senior corporation official lobbying against the city in a private letter in late 1967, it exposed the duplicity on the front page – and the guilty parties were quite rightly vilified. I even coaxed Connie out of retirement to write a furious leader column.

***

EF attempted to sue the *Chronicle* for printing his confidential correspondence with the Stormont and British officials. He sent us two letters from his solicitors, followed by a writ from a barrister, which I returned with a one-line reply on our headed paper. It read: 'Does a man of your character really want to take us on in court?' And we never heard another word. We didn't have anything specific on him, but it wouldn't have taken us five minutes. In fairness, he could technically have won his point in a courtroom run by his mates, but he would never have been able to put his head outside the door again. And even if he was a rogue, he was too well rooted in the city to risk that.

***

The *Chronicle* also took on the Unionists over housing. We took to embedding our reporters with the sit-down and sit-in demonstrations at the Guildhall – and started sending more and more copy to the increasingly interested Irish and British national press.

There were two big issues – both related. The first was the ongoing gerrymander, which meant that there was no house building at all in areas like the North Ward, in case the Protestants would lose their slender majority both there, and then in the Council overall. Virtually that entire area, from Pennyburn to the Donegal border, was undeveloped in those days, but as you know, the area today is full of housing and densely populated. To give you an idea of the scale of abuse then, today there are 40,000 Catholic voters in that one area alone and roughly 2,000

Protestants. But up until 1968, all four councillors for the ward were Unionist. The South Ward, meanwhile, had become a gigantic Nationalist ghetto. It was bursting at the seams – no land was left at all for housing – but Unionists were refusing to extend the city boundary. Two thousand Catholic families – up to fifteen thousand people – were waiting for houses, whereas there were practically no Protestants living un-housed in Derry.

By shining a light on the housing issue, the *Chronicle* in turn exposed the second prong of the most corrupt voting system in Western Europe – deliberate disenfranchisement. In Britain at that time, anyone over the age of twenty-one had a vote – but here in the North, it was only the householder and his wife. So by denying a family (a Nationalist family) a house, you were stopping them voting. Coupled with this, you had a provision which allowed business owners – the vast majority of whom were Unionists – up to six additional votes, depending on the number of companies they owned.

***

Unionist hardliners bristled at being exposed on the bigger stage. It was okay for it to be Derry's dirty little secret, but they didn't want the rest of the world to know. The leader of the backroom boys – an angry little ex-military man, who was a slum landlord himself – rang every newsroom on the islands to complain about us. But he only got the editors more excited. Later, during the Troubles, the same guy would regularly drive up and down to Donegal to play golf, impervious to the mayhem his policies were causing at home. Instead of shooting him, though, the IRA used to wait until his back was turned and stash weapons in the boot of his car, and let him smuggle them back into the North on their behalf. He was never stopped at any checkpoint, until of course the time he was caught, about five years into his new career. And by that stage, the Provisionals had already re-equipped about a brigade and a half. Or so they claimed.

One of the big problems 'The Colonel' and other Unionists faced was that, for the first time, they were facing highly-educated Catholics – often more educated than themselves. Catholics, out of necessity, had taken great advantage of sweeping changes to the British education system in the mid-1940s, which the Unionists had then reluctantly introduced into the North. These changes gave children the right to stay on at school until at least the age of fifteen, ended fees for secondary schools and grammar schools, and provided grants for university study. Education was no longer the preserve of the rich. And a new generation of bright young Catholics were standing up and saying we want the same houses and voting rights as you've got. And we're not going away until we've gotten them.

CHAPTER 53

1967: Mo (Part I)

We knew from the very off Mo would end up running the *Chronicle* newsroom. She had three great attributes: she was honest as a saint, determined as a devil, and she was afraid of nobody. I often think if she hadn't stayed with us, and if it hadn't been for Johnny Doherty, she'd have ended up running her own country.

A couple of years after Little Mill started school, it must have been 1967, Mo came into the business. She was supposed to be part-time at first, mornings and Sundays only. As far as Little Mill was concerned, Mo was her mother, so that was always her real job.

On Mo's first day in the bullpen, I asked Johnny to take her up to Bishop Street to show her the ropes at the Petty Sessions Court. The reportage wasn't a terribly complicated process back then – who, what, where, when, why, and how much blood – but there are lots of internal protocols you have to get used to. And the first and most important of these is that you must never turn a word in the Resident Magistrate's mouth.

Mo knew this rightly, of course. But she also loved to push boundaries and, as I said, she knew no fear. Because of her soft accent and the fact she had little formal education, a lot of people thought she was just a simple rural hick with buttermilk on her chin. And she played up on this a little – used it as a weapon, even. She tended to get away with saying things that politer society might have considered blunt, or even plain insulting. But she would then get herself a pardon, as a know-nothing boondocker – at least the first time.

RM Donald 'No Holds' Barrett wasn't so slow, himself, however. And when Johnny came into my office at lunchtime after Mo's first trip up to the Petty Sessions, without her, I knew immediately something was wrong. For a start, Johnny never visited me voluntarily; largely out of fear I might give him something else to do.

'We have a small problem, boss,' he told me. He was looking at his shoes – always scuffed, as you'd expect.

'What did she do?' I asked him. I was used to Mo's directness – I loved the way she unsettled people. But if she was going to start hassling Johnny about his drinking, then we were going to have to find her a new mentor. He was, as we knew when we hired him, a functioning alcoholic – though in the sixties we just called it being able to handle your liquor. Every newsroom had one or two Johnnys back then – and the stories they generated from guys dropping their guard in public houses more than made up for the occasional late start the next morning.

He looked up at me nervously, then picked another spot on the floor. 'She got a bit out of hand.'

'Did she have a go at you about the smell off your clothes?'

'What? My clothes? What's wrong with my clothes? No, no. She's far too nice for that. In fact, she's promised to take me shopping for a new suit at the weekend. Says she's going to talk you into giving me a sub. She knows I'm not that flush …'

He was trying it on. But Johnny knew how to pick his times well.

'Chancer. We'll see. Out with it. What did she do?'

'Well, actually, boss, she's in the holding cells and will be until you go up to the magistrate and apologise for her behaviour.'

I glared at him over the rims of my new glasses, suddenly aware that I was turning into both my mother and my grandfather. 'This is a joke, right? This is some weird Donegal tradition of pranking the boss on your first day?'

He went back to the shoes. 'It's no prank, Mr Madden. But the worst part of it is – I don't think that you're going to want to apologise. So she could be there for a right while yet.'

'Oh, Jesus, did she call him on his sentencing record?'

'She did indeed – in open court. And caught him beautifully, too.'

Johnny pulled a little shorthand notebook from a torn and shiny jacket pocket and proceeded to read. 'Amy Watson; aged twenty-four; Bond Street; unmarried and unemployed; three offences, all related to the one incident; stole a bottle of whiskey from WG O'Doherty's pub; public drunkenness; and common assault of a police officer. Long record of previous stuff. Sentence: fine, one pound no shillings. Three months to pay. Quote: "I would love to be able to get this poor girl some help."'

'Don't tell me.' I knew what was coming. Ninety per cent of the Petty Sessions stuff was drink related – still is, as you know. No Holds Barrett had great sympathy for women drinkers; he believed it was down to stress. Protestant women drinkers, that is.

'Twenty minutes later, they called up another woman, this time from the downstairs cells. Big black eye and a bruise on her neck. Sinead Keddy; aged forty-one; Old Bogside Road; mother of twelve and supervisor at the City Factory; one offence – public drunkenness. Found asleep outside her home, after her husband beat her out the door. No record. Sentence: three months in jail, plus a ten-pound fine. Quote from Barrett: "Disgraceful behaviour. She

196

should know better at her age. Maybe if she'd drunk a little less when she was younger, she wouldn't have had all those children.'"

We had all become so used to this type of double standard again and again that we barely recognised it for what it was anymore. But Mo had caught it with a pair of fresh eyes.

'So what did she do? And stop looking at the carpet, Johnny – I'm not blaming you. I know very well what she's like.'

'I did try to stop her, Mr Madden. But she put up her hand, told the judge it was her first day, and asked him all innocent-like, if the sentencing guidelines were different for Catholic and Protestant defendants across the whole of the United Kingdom or just in Northern Ireland. Just a query, Your Honour, she wanted to know for her future court coverage … She was smiling at him so sweetly, and batting those big soft brown eyes, I thought for a second he was going to let her away with it. But instead, he just smiled back at her and said to her, "Miss O'Sullivan, I'm afraid I have to hold you in contempt – and I think you know full well why. You're going to spend a few hours in the cells, while Mr Doherty goes and fetches Mr Madden up here till I talk to him." Which is what I'm doing now, boss.'

I detected the beginnings of a grin on Johnny's face, so I asked him if he found this whole affair funny.

He couldn't contain it any longer and smiled all over his face. 'Not at all, boss. I think it's terrible that you have to get up off your comfortable armchair and re-enter the real world to rescue your protégé from a bigot. And, by the way, those are Mo's words, not mine.'

I tried to make an angry face but instead heard her saying them, and started to laugh. 'All right, Johnny, what are we going to do now?'

He pursed his lips and rooted about in his pockets absent-mindedly for his thinking aids – unfiltered Woodbine cigarettes. Johnny wasn't just a first-class reporter; he also had a very solid reasoning process.

'You've a few options. You could apologise, get Mo out of the clink, and then I could write a verbatim report of what happened in the courtroom – word for word, and show them up. But then, of course, No Holds will simply jug me for contempt the next time he sees me – and almost certainly sue you.

'The safest bet, of course, would be to apologise and leave the whole thing alone. You could argue, if you were challenged – which you won't be anyway – that the Chronicle can't afford to risk another legal mess. And we would all pretend it didn't happen and return to tipping our caps.'

I shook my head, but Johnny had stacked the deck to make sure I would. I held my hand out to bid him continue.

'Or we could do the right thing and ring Joe McGinlay, and fight this tooth and nail.'

McGinlay was our lawyer, a slightly crumpled young man of Johnny's vintage and habits. But he was an excellent performer on his feet and a political star in the making.

'Mo mightn't like that,' I told Johnny. 'She could be stuck in Armagh Jail for a week or two if they dig in their heels.'

Johnny took a drag of his fag and shook his head. 'She wouldn't mind at all, boss. It's exactly why she did it. We can't pretend to hold up a mirror to society and simply screen off the bits the establishment don't want the public to see. It's better to be a starving watchdog than a well-fed lapdog, as Connie always told us. If we don't fight this one, Mr Madden, we might as well, pack up our desks and go home. Because no-one else is going to fight it for us.'

He was right. 'I better ring Granny Connie, so, and tell her she's on babysitting duty this evening. And maybe for a little while after that, too.'

CHAPTER 54

1967: Mo (Part II)

Such were the machinations of the Northern Ireland legal system at the time that the *Chronicle* couldn't risk reporting on why Mo was in jail. To repeat her comments would have been construed as so libellous by the courts that they would have fined us so heavily, and so repeatedly, that we would have had to close down. Instead, on Joe McGinlay's advice, we simply printed the Watson and Keddy court cases together on our front page, side by side, under the headline: '*Chronicle* reporter jailed for passing comment on these cases.' It was, even for the dimmest reader, completely self-explanatory.

I refused to withdraw the supposedly contemptuous remarks on Mo's behalf, or apologise for them, as I was not responsible for them. That was Joe McGinlay's first major victory. Mr Madden did not make the comments, he did not sanction the comments, and they were not made on behalf of the *Chronicle*, even if he agrees one hundred per cent with what was said. So the court had no comeback on the newspaper – which I'm pretty sure Mo had figured out before she went off on her solo run.

Mo, of course, had no intentions of withdrawing her comments, not because she wanted to be in jail – she was no martyr – but quite simply, this was a point of principle, and she knew she was right.

The case was tremendous fodder for the civil rights campaigners – or Civil Justice Group, as I think they were called then. It received national and international coverage, and the bigger players weren't afraid to publish what Mo had said – or, more importantly, pass judgment on how right she was. The Unionists were incensed, the final ignominy coming when the BBC – *their* BBC – reported that a question had been asked at Westminster about the row.

As the days ran into weeks, I worked out just how big an influence Mo had become in my life. The manse, despite Connie's efforts, had become shambolic. Little Mill was restless and lonely – and so was I. Mo had, without me knowing, quietly assumed the role of my adult daughter – the person I talked to more in my life than any other; the person I complained to about my day; the person who with bluntness sometimes bordering on brutality always reminded me of the right thing to do – from politics to homework; the person I trusted with both my life and Mill's. And no – despite what you may have read, and despite the fact that, yes, we did share rooms when we were travelling – I never looked on Mo like a wife. My wife is Millie – it doesn't matter that she's dead.

I did feel guilty, though, that Mo had no time for a family life or friends of her own. So I was delighted when she started at the *Chronicle*, as I figured this would give her a chance to broaden her horizons.

At first, it struck me as a little odd that she put Johnny's name down for the prison visits and not mine. But Johnny explained that only relatives were allowed in – and he was able to pass himself off as her fiancé, whereas I wouldn't have been plausible. And my presence at the jail would have added fuel to the Unionist complaints that this was all a *Chronicle* plot to begin with.

Then at the end of the first month, I caught Johnny about to set off on a visit – and he was wearing a new suit and new shoes. I'd seen the letters coming in every single day – and had noticed him staying in after his shift to do some writing of his own. So I called him into my office to throw him on the griddle for a while.

'Love the new clothes,' I told him.

'Ah, don't be giving me a hard time, boss.'

'I thought Mo was going to take you shopping? She'll not be happy that you went without her.'

He was back looking at the feet again. The new shoes were intriguing.

'She, ah, told me what to buy, where to get them – and how much discount to ask for. I'm kind of afraid that I mightn't have got the right ones. Do you think I did okay?'

I started to laugh. 'So it's like that?'

He shrugged his shoulders like he didn't believe it himself. 'I never saw it coming, Mr Madden. The very first day. It was as if we had known one another all our lives – or maybe it was in our other lives before – whatever way it was, it was the most natural thing in the world. And for all my scepticism, I neither wanted, nor saw, any reason to fight it. It is what it is – and we both know it. We haven't even had a date yet – if you don't count holding hands over a prison table – but I'm pretty sure we'll be getting married. Though, of course, I'll wait until she tells me. It'll be a few years yet – she wants to be running this place, first.'

'You know she's far too good for you?'

'God, yes, she reminds me of it in every letter.'

'And that she's going to knock at least some of the drinking out of you?'

'That's fine. I don't need it so much now that she's around.'

'Will you always be good to her?'

'Always.'

'And who's going to look after Little Mill?'

'Mo is. She wants to buy the little gate lodge at the manse from you.'

Mo was still travelling in and out to her parents in Bridgend every night. It wouldn't have been appropriate for her to live in the manse – despite the fact I'd converted a corner block at the west side into a separate apartment for visitors. She no longer had to cycle, though – Connie had gotten her a company car the previous year when it became apparent that it would save us all, and me particularly, a whole lot of time and money.

The gate lodge would require a bit of work but, like most of Mo's ideas, it was a sound plan – and hadn't been voiced until it was fully thought through.

'You know she'll become even bossier to you when she gets out of jail.'

'Not possible. And don't try to put words in my mouth.'

I laughed. Johnny was a good, smart kid. He posed as a cynic but had the heart of a romantic and idealist, and would be a good match for Mo, who had the same values but perhaps the other way around. He was a great reporter – full of passion – and was ideal for the *Chronicle* at this point in history. And he had stepped up immediately to take care of Mo when she got into trouble. Connie used to say that he reminded her so much of her own late husband Johnny that it hurt.

***

It took us three months and two weeks to spring Mo from Armagh Jail. In the end it required a direct intervention from Stormont Prime Minister Terence O'Neill to the Lord Chief Justice. They couldn't risk any more international scrutiny. O'Neill had just about managed to ignore pressure from both Westminster and Dublin, but then my American chum Don Grover got his friends in the State Department to include a mention of Mo's plight in a civil rights speech being given by Hubert Humphrey. And as soon as that happened, the Unionists knew they had to circle the wagons and release the hostage.

Typically, they did it with no grace. The first we knew Mo was coming home was at 11.30pm one wet Saturday night, when the warden rang me at home to say he was about to throw an unwanted Fenian troublemaker out into the street if anyone wanted to claim her.

I collected Johnny from his mother's home at the top of Beechwood Avenue – he hadn't been out on the town for a change, he was saving up for a homecoming gift – and we drove straight to Armagh. Before we left, I managed to reach Barry McCorry from the *Lurgan Tribune*, who lived about six miles from the jail, to lift Mo and take her to his house.

She looked dreadful – I immediately noticed that she had lost at least a stone on the crappy prison diet and was pale and gaunt from the lack of any summer sun. Her fine dark hair looked lank and matted – and her clothes were torn, ill-fitting and filthy. She had refused to wear a prison uniform, so they hadn't given her a change of clothes. But as soon as she saw Johnny, her face and aspect seem to transform entirely. It was as if she was being lit from within – her skin seemed to glow, her eyes started to shine and all of a sudden her face could not stop smiling. And neither could his.

She hugged me quickly, but only so she could hug him long and properly without me noticing.

'Jesus, your clothes smell awful,' he said to her. 'I know this shop in Derry gives great discount. But you'd need to give yourself a bath first.'

She punched him in the ribs then kissed him lightly. 'Did you wait for me?' she asked.

'Of course I did,' he said. 'And not just because I was too afraid not to, like the boss there said. I'd wait forever for you, Mo.'

She shot me a look. I wasn't supposed to know. But he'd dropped it in beautifully, and nobody was annoyed.

'What do you think?' she asked me.

I smiled at her and nodded slowly.

'I want fifteen hundred words on the hell-hole that is a women's prison in modern Ireland by Monday morning,' I told her.

'It's already done, boss,' she said. 'I've actually done about three thousand in all – it'll make a two-parter.'

'Good. And in case I'd forget, I've never been more proud of you in my life, Mo. You did more on your first day in journalism than most of us do in our entire lives. Take the rest of the weekend off.'

CHAPTER 55

1968

The competition between Mo and Johnny to be top dog in the newsroom is undoubtedly the greatest thing that ever happened to the *Chronicle* – but it is also one of the most important things that ever happened Derry as a city. In their attempts to outdo one another, the young couple also informed and improved the political landscape of a radically changing city.

Mo's two-parter from the jail was the start of it – a brutally frank insider's account of a sectarian and sexist regime sponsored by the state. It was powerful, prosaic and I didn't have to add a comma. The story was reprinted in full by the *Irish Press* in the South and by the *Guardian* in Manchester, which nominated her as its Woman of the Year. And, in an unprecedented move, the Department of Justice in London appointed its own Prison Visit Inspection Team to the North in a bid to improve standards. Though, significantly, none of the Northern Ireland inspectors was sacked or even sanctioned.

Johnny, who had a couple of years' head start on Mo in journalism, couldn't have her stealing his thunder, and the following month asked me for a week off to prepare a special feature on housing. I agreed, and his report 'My week at the Camp', which exposed the conditions at the Springtown huts twenty years after the US departure, is still used in textbooks today as an exemplar of social journalism. Again, it was picked up by the national and international press, and the BBC sent a crew down from Belfast to produce a documentary about the camp, which left the Unionist Party both humiliated and apoplectic. They knew that the historical inertia, which had protected them for decades, was being shifted aside by a newer, cleaner energy.

The *Londonderry Leader*, under EF Cunningham, attempted to strike back, and labelled Mo and Johnny the *Chronicle*'s new 'Fifth Columnists' – out to destroy the great Unionist entitlement. But it only spurred them on more. They asked for, and I immediately gave them, their own joint op-ed page to target corruption and force social change, which they simply called 'The Fifth Column'. And it is my understanding that within weeks it was being read every Thursday morning not only in Stormont but in Downing Street as well.

It was a joy to manage as an editor, if occasionally a bit terrifying. At least once a month, I had stand-up shouting matches with them in the bullpen after I removed names or unproven allegations from their page. Unproven to my satisfaction, that is; it did not mean they were wrong, as they often showed me later. Their competition for the front-page lead story also sparked the occasional row, though generally only when Johnny got it, as he was a far more gracious loser. And he never once accused me of sexism for spiking his material or suggested that the mayor's wife carried around my man-parts in her handbag. Don Grover walked in once in the middle of one such row and remarked to Mo that she had a very 'salty' tongue on her. And for years afterwards, if we ever wanted to get a rise out of her, we called her 'Salty'. Mo had the last laugh, though: she christened Grover 'Don the Spy' in turn, and it stuck.

In the early days of the housing demonstrations, I would have assigned one or the other to cover whatever event it was – a sit-in, march or meeting. But I quickly learned that the other was only going to sneak out to it anyway. So, instead, I let them double up and, in turn, I got double the value. Johnny, the quicker writer, would script the news reports while Mo would handle features and comment. Occasionally, they would switch berths to keep themselves fresh or if Mo felt she deserved another front-page by-line. Johnny worried a little less about seeing his name in lights and generally let her away with it.

Mo got a bit shirty with me when I put Johnny in charge of the paper for a week while I accompanied Connie to Bobby Kennedy's funeral in June 1968. Johnny had the cooler head and more experience. But she forgave me when I handed both Johnny and herself a contract to write 'corr' – contributed news correspondence – for a host of US foreign desks on my return. So they got to spend the rest of the summer travelling across the North, reporting on the burgeoning civil rights campaign and got paid decent wages for doing it ... for a change.

They were becoming more and more widely known. And it was no surprise when they were both arrested in Dungannon, after a housing march from Caledon, for inciting 'sedition' – a charge I hadn't heard since I was a cub. But Joe McGinlay, one of the leaders of the protest, quickly sprung them by quietly asking the District Inspector if he really wanted Mo O'Sullivan doing another exposé of Her Majesty's facilities.

The *Chronicle* itself, however, wasn't so lucky. In July 1968, we were hit by another two-week Stormont ban for printing 'fabricated' allegations against the RUC. And typically, it wasn't Mo or Johnny who caused the problem but me, myself and I. The two blades had been reporting on a blockade on the Lecky Road where a man who was living in a one-room caravan with his family of ten had pulled the structure across the street for forty-eight hours. Hundreds of people had come out to support him. Johnny remarked in his news report

204

that the protest had been broken up 'in typical fashion' by the RUC. This was our in-house code for 'viciously', though it gave us a little deniability as it could also, theoretically, be construed to mean 'efficiently'. I, however, accompanied the front-page piece with a photograph of a cop swinging a baton at a demonstrator's bloodied head, which I captioned: 'A member of the police strikes a protestor on Lecky Road.' But within two hours of the paper hitting the streets, both the policeman's personal lawyer and the Unionist Party had written to me to inform me that the cop pictured had actually been pulling his baton away from a protestor who had seized it. They also claimed that the supposedly wounded party, a fifteen-year-old boy, was a 'known subversive' who had 'self-injured' minutes before this incident was said to have taken place. And, by the way, there were four police witnesses to this effect. It was enough of an argument for both the courts and the Stormont Parliament and I ended up paying the cop the price of a car. I hope the bastard died in it.

The Unionists warned us that if we tried to circumvent the ban by using the traditional trick of printing in Donegal and hiring newsboys to distribute the paper across the city streets, they would stick us with another month. So, on Joe McGinlay's advice, we adhered to the letter of the law. We did, however, open pop-up shops just across the border in Donegal and passed fliers around the city encouraging people to travel across to buy our special *Ulster* edition. This led to cavalcades along the Buncrana and Letterkenny roads, and to a fifty-per-cent increase in sales. And, of course, Mo and Johnny got another great story.

***

Police violence, however, was getting worse and worse, and matters came to a head one day when I refused to allow Mo to cover an unlicensed civil rights march from the Waterside Railway Station to Guildhall Square.

And on Saturday morning 5 October, I called her into the little office, where she would have no backing other than her own tongue, to deliver the news.

'You might be my finest reporter, as you say, Mo – you're certainly in my top two – but you're also the closest thing my child has to a mother. And I'm not letting her lose a second parent. And before you start, this isn't a sexist thing; I'm not going on this march, either. We know for sure they're going to beat and batter all before them. I can't stop you going as a civilian, but I really hope you don't. But rest assured, if you do go, you're not getting a by-line – and I'm damned if I'm paying for your funeral. You can stay here instead and co-ordinate all the reaction to whatever happens.'

Of course, the only bit of my carefully thought-out plea that Mo heard was 'I can't stop you going as a civilian'. And it was as well she did, too.

Three hours later, she was back in the bullpen, shaking like a leaf and covered with blood. I went quickly to grab the bottle of brandy from my office, sat her down and handed her a full glass.

'They beat Johnny up and down Duke Street,' she said. 'He's in the hospital and will be there for a few days. He's in and out of consciousness, though the medics say he's out of danger.'

'Did they single him out?'

'No. They hit everybody – the women got a little less, maybe, but only because they screamed louder. I've welts all down my back. Joe McGinlay was badly split, though he was still walking at the end. Fitt got whacked, too, as did all of the committee. A couple of our guys stood in under shop awnings and pretended they were bystanders, and for whatever reason didn't get touched.'

'How many of our lot were there?' I asked, meaning civil rights supporters.

'A few hundred, tops,' she said. 'Though, you know what Derry's like, twenty thousand will have been there by the time the pubs are closed tonight.'

'Someone needs to put manners on those cops,' I said. 'So, Mo, you'd better get writing.'

She drained her drink and headed for her desk. 'But here's the best bit,' she said. 'For the first time, they'll not be able to cover it up. RTÉ was there and filmed the whole thing. McGinlay was interviewed afterwards with the blood pouring out of his head. Someone offered him a hankie to stem it, but he refused – he wanted people to see what had happened. For once, there'll be no suggestion that the protestors seized the batons and beat themselves up.'

With that, she sat down and began typing. Her first-hand reports would lead dozens of late editions across the islands that evening, and a host of the Sundays the next day.

I, meanwhile, went out the front door, through Castle Gate and across to Radio Rentals, where I bought the bullpen their first television. They deserved it. And more and more, I knew they were going to need it.

CHAPTER 56

1968: Johnny

As soon as Johnny got out of the hospital, I promoted him to full-time news editor. The incumbent, a Southerner who'd arrived just three months previously to get himself some tough-guy credentials, had run screaming back to Dublin. I explained to Mo, who obviously had designs on the post herself, that News Ed was an office-based job, and we needed her in the field. She knew as well as I did that the RUC attack on Johnny had left him gun-shy and that we had to rest him from the front line.

Johnny was happy enough to play along, particularly when I finally sorted out a permanent lease to the gate lodge for the pair of them. And no, they had no intentions of getting married yet, and yes, they were proposing to live in sin, but I didn't see any of that as a problem. The surprising thing is, though, dozens of *Chronicle* readers were quite upset when the pair moved in together – not just the crazy Christians either – and wrote to the paper to tell me so. At first, I was angry and a little alarmed, but when I raised it with Connie she was delighted.

'People regard this paper as their own,' she said. 'The *Chronicle* isn't just our business – it's an institution for them, a public touchstone and a community focal point. And your staff, whether they like it or not, are public figures. They're role models, even – they're seen as respected, and trusted, arbiters of our society. And our society has very few of those. And with the best will in the world, Catholic-Derry-Mother-of-Ten doesn't want to have to explain to her children what exactly a twenty-six-year-old woman wants with a twenty-eight-year-old man if they're not having babies.'

'Any tips on how to handle it?'

'Put it about quietly that they sleep in separate rooms but that they are secretly engaged. Blame the cops. Say Johnny and Mo don't want them to know in case they use it against either of them.'

'You're kidding?'

'No. Sometimes, in the world outside newspapers at least, all you need is a story that might not be untrue. It doesn't even have to be plausible – just enough to give you a bit of cover. Back to your Mother-of-Ten, all she has to say is there are two bedrooms, they're engaged but the cops can't know about it. Now shut up and eat your breakfast. It's how the Unionists have got away with it for so long here: of course Catholics have the vote, Your Honour, well, most of them do anyway – and the ones that don't, well, that's their own fault for breeding so hard that we can't build enough houses for them.'

***

Johnny's first front page as News Ed was perhaps one of the most optimistic we ever had. On Friday 22 November 1968, Mo, Connie, Johnny and myself were sitting in the bullpen, planning the next Tuesday edition of the paper when Joe McGinlay rang in and told us to turn on the television news. They were reporting that the Northern prime minister had announced the dissolution of the corrupt Derry Corporation. A nine-person Development Commission would take its place in the interim. O'Neill had also said he was ending the Company Director Vote and would be introducing a standardised points system for housing allocation, based on need.

It was electrifying. We had won – Unionist bullying in Derry was over for good. Within seconds of the broadcast, McGinlay telephoned the office again to say that the Derry Citizens Action Committee was considering suspending demonstrations for a month to give O'Neill a chance to steer through his reforms.

I'm not sure if it was the brandy we'd all drunk while watching the TV or the fact that we all felt we owed Johnny a particular debt, but within seconds, we were planning a special edition of the paper, a four pager, for the following morning. Connie and I began calling in all the troops and discovered to our delight that about half of them were already making their way to the office.

Johnny and Mo started pounding the phones for reaction to the O'Neill speech – tracking down clergy, civil rights leaders, Nationalists, the IRA, and, importantly, local Unionists, both the liberal and the head-banging variety. Within an hour and a half, we had the four pages drafted. And within another hour the pages had been designed, copy-read and set.

We were just about to send to the printer when the freelance photographer Tommy McBirney burst through the door of the newsroom with a roll of negatives he'd taken of 'The Colonel' and three of his fellow faceless men skulking out of the Guildhall. We knew immediately they would be worth a thousand words. Ten thousand, even. And I was delighted to pick out EF Cunningham as one of the skulkers.

Needless to say, the traditional row broke out when the printers discovered they'd have to hang on another half-hour until the negatives were developed. But McBirney, a Protestant, threatened to go down and kick each and every one of their useless Catholic arses if they didn't wait, so they conceded. And they all ended up going out for a drink together when it was over.

That's the thing about newsrooms – anything that is said or done in the heat of the moment in the run-up to a deadline is forgiven instantly as soon as the work is finished. It can get very, very rough at times, but no grudges are ever carried. Everyone in the trade knows that it is the room that is boiling, not the individual, and not to take it personally. McBirney, by the way, like the rest of us, had long left his religion behind him – he was a newsman first, foremost and only.

We decided to print 20,000 copies – at full price – though, in hindsight, we could have doubled both the print run and the cover charge. Copies were sent all over the world. It was about three in the morning by the time we got the first run back from the printers, and the little paper looked terrific. I'd resisted Mo's tongue-in-cheek headline – 'RATS DESERT SINKING SHIP'. And we went instead with Johnny's line, borrowed from Reverend King: 'FREE AT LAST'. Though in a triumph of hope over experience, I deleted the question mark Johnny had inserted at the end, to leave it as a simple statement and not a question.

And yes, in retrospect, it was possibly far too ambitious and, in years to come, we would get laughed at many times for our innocence. But that was how we felt. It was monumental, the biggest political shift in the city any of us had ever witnessed. We had done what every good newspaper should do that night: we had written a true draft of history. And for that brief moment, we spoke for our city and it felt wonderful.

CHAPTER 57

1969

It didn't take the Unionist monolith long to regroup. They showed their teeth again in early January 1969 when they confronted a People's Democracy march from Belfast just outside Derry at Burntollet. Their logic was that the civil rights 'rebels' were breaking the truce they had offered O'Neill for his reforms, so all bets were off. To that end, three hundred of them, including about a hundred off-duty cops, armed themselves with a full lorry-load of gravel, iron bars and clubs studded with nails. They then waited until the demonstration was passing across the tiny bridge at the bottom of Burntollet valley and charged the marchers in a pincer movement.

We had got wind of the proposed attack from Nigel Lyons, a sympathetic young police inspector, who rang the office to advise me not to send Mo out to witness what was euphemistically being termed a 'counter-demonstration' on her own. So, reluctantly, I let Johnny go along with her. It was a mistake. He was battered to a pulp trying to protect her, and then got thrown into the river. For the second time in the space of three months, his job had nearly got him killed.

That incident, more than any, spoke to the redrawing of the lines. Liberal unionism, or conciliatory unionism, was finished – the old ways were back. Sensing the mood, the RUC charged into the Bogside that same night to teach the residents a lesson. But the locals responded by fighting back with anything they could lay their hands on. They sent the police packing and erected barricades around the entire neighbourhood to keep the forces of Unionism out for good. The end gable at the corner of Fahan Street and Lecky Road marked the dividing line – inside of which the Northern state was no longer welcome. Liam Hillen and John Casey painted the slogan 'You Are Now Entering Free Derry' on the wall, and a version of it is still there to this day, although both streets of houses are long since gone.

As soon as she'd established Johnny was going to be all right, Mo embedded herself in Free Derry for the week. And her 'Barricade Bulletins', painting a picture of how an independent utopian republic had suddenly constituted itself in the middle of a United Kingdom city, were syndicated across the globe.

I was very conscious, however, that both Mo and Johnny had become household names – and was aware that there were serious risks associated with this. I had received numerous threats about the paper in the past, but now they were more pointed and more specific – one of which advised me that both Mo and Johnny were now on police watch lists. So I rang our one decent cop, Nigel Lyons, and asked if I could come see him at Victoria Barracks.

Lyons met me in his little windowless office, every inch of which, from ceiling to floor, was covered in paper. He saw my face taking it all in and laughed. 'And these are just the files I've got on you,' he said.

He cleared an armful of folders off a chair and bade me sit down. 'What's troubling you?'

'My News Editor and my Chief Reporter – are they on a list?'

'Off the record?'

I nodded.

'They almost certainly are,' he said. 'They're known in here as Bonnie and Clyde – and there is no shortage of volunteers looking to send them to a similar end. You can't expect to bring down a city government and for the powers-that-be not to notice. You're being watched, too, Seán – as is your mother. They'd be crazy not to. And you'd be crazy to think that every move you make isn't being recorded – and every call listened to.'

'But we're a public watchdog. Surely this is a violation?'

'Like it or not, you're not impartial. You're a player in this drama – and one of the largest ones at that. The Church and the various political parties may have influence, but you're the public voice of the campaign. Or at least that's how you're seen. You're the public record.'

'Can't we establish any boundaries in this? Can we, for example, be allowed privacy at home?'

'Doubt it. Everything will be fair game. And I mean everything. I'm pretty confident that we've already got at least a couple of Derry staff, and three or four in your regional offices who are feeding back stories into us. That's in spite of all your vetting. For the rest of your days, you should automatically assume that anything you ever say into a phone or write on a notepad is being copied into these headquarters. Keep your private stuff private.'

'Are you telling me this to frighten me?

'No, no – it's a warning from a friend. You're dealing with a dangerous element here. They feel dispossessed and abandoned. And they'll do anything to protect what they genuinely believe is their birthright. You make the mistake of thinking they're bad people – or that they're greedy. They're not – they're more scared than you are. Except they've woken up to find they're suddenly on the wrong side of history, and that it's all starting to slide away from them. That way of life – of supremacy, of dominance, of entitlement, of we're better than you, of two caste systems – is gone. And they're living in terror that the sins of their fathers are all going to be visited back on them. That they're going to be punished.'

'Is there anything we can do to, how can I put this, improve relations with the police?

'Not at the moment and, take it from me, you don't want to. They'll see right through you, think you're weak and become convinced they should kill you off. But I will say this: we don't all think the same way. Some of us even believe in Joe McGinlay's united Ireland by consent. And we're not going to be part of a lynch mob – we simply want to keep this city, and the people in it, safe. All of them.'

'And so do we.'

'I believe you, Seán. Which is why it's important we're talking now. Listen, the police have serious issues here, between self-interested politicians deciding all our strategy for us and the madmen in our ranks – particularly the B Specials. Whoever thought that it was an idea to arm the neighbourhood drunks and wife-beaters deserves his backside kicked for half an hour every thirty minutes. Over the weeks and months to come, myself – and others of a similar mind – we're going to need people in the Nationalist community that we can trust. We need to keep a lid on things. As partners.'

'Sounds like you're asking me to work for the police, Nigel.'

'Christ, no. The police are the last people you'd want in this. As Brendan Behan said, there is no situation so bad a policeman couldn't make it worse. Listen, these others of a similar mind I'm talking about, they're not police and they're not from Derry either. Nor Belfast.'

His eyes fixed on mine briefly to make sure I wouldn't miss the nuance.

'Whitehall?' I asked.

He nodded. 'It's coming from Westminster, yes. But it's very much at an early stage. Harold Wilson and Jim Callaghan are seriously worried that the Unionists are going to get out of control, and with cause. We've already got a local businessman, we call him 'Mr Smith', who's helping out on the republican end of things – with their approval, I hasten to add.'

'Are the Irish involved?'

'Smith covers that bit – he has his own connections there.'

'Sounds like you've quite the committee.'

'Absolutely not. You will never see these people sitting down at the one table ever. It's not how it works.'

'So where do I come in, why are you telling me this?'

'We know you have the American connection already. I've spoken to Don Grover, but he's been briefed only to liaise with you. But he knows we want you helping us – and he's happy for you to proceed. You know what their cypher for you is?'

'Yeah. They call me "The Bank". It dates back to my smuggling days – before your lot put an end to them. They used to say I was as reliable as the Bank of England. If I gave a guarantee, it stuck. But that was when I was playing Cowboys and Indians, Nigel. This is a whole lot different.'

'Will you think about it, at least? We're not asking you to sacrifice a single principle, compromise anyone or put anyone at risk.'

'So what do you want from me?'

'Your wisdom, your experience, your insights, your influence, your recommendations – pick any one of them. This isn't about following an agenda. This is about trying to set a better one.'

'It's all very altruistic. But ultimately, you're talking about dealing with the British – the single most perfidious race on the planet.'

'We Irish are no saints, either, Seán, despite all our marketing strategies. But officially – inasmuch as anything about this is official – you're neither British nor Irish. You will be the American representative in the room.'

'And they're okay with that?'

'It's my understanding the Yanks are prepared to give you plenipotentiary negotiating powers. Talk to Don, he'll fill you in.'

'Why me – why not him?'

He laughed. 'Don the Spy? Sure everything he knows he gets from you anyway. Much better to be hearing it from the horse's mouth.'

I said I'd talk to Don and stood up to go. 'I can't be coming in here to see you again. It doesn't look well for either of us. I'm only really here to register a complaint about the beating Johnny took at Burntollet …'

'And it is duly registered,' he said. 'I would imagine, though, that your News Editor provoked the entire incident and there are already sworn statements to that effect. I'll check it out regardless. If it's any consolation, I'll deploy the rogues who did it to the Falls Road for a few months – it might knock some manners into them.'

He took out a little notepad and I could see him scribble an address and a little map.

'Thursday mornings – your quiet day at work – I have coffee at a friend's house outside Dunavady. It's secluded there and you can cover your absence by saying you're out doing some scouting for the county edition.'

I took the sheet, slipped it in my pocket and said nothing. As I turned to go, Lyons fixed his eyes on me again.

'I love this city, Seán,' he said. 'I grew up here, went to school here and am now rearing a family here. It is my city as much as it is your city. And I'm not going to stand by while the Unionist Party sticks us with another fifty years of shanty housing and Prod-only industries.'

He was sincere, he was good-hearted, and I could see he was totally dedicated. I could also see, however, that for all his determination and all his connections, he was going nowhere without my help.

'I'll think about it,' I said. 'But the first time someone tells me what to write, I'm gone.'

CHAPTER 58

1971

The Yanks, if anything, were always bit players here. In the later stages, we had our uses, yes, but not back then. I'd love to put us, and the *Chronicle*, in the middle of things, but we existed at the fringes, if even there – as did many other people who are claiming the credit now that no-one has proof to the contrary. This may not fit in with the current narrative, or indeed any narrative, but I'm too old to worry about being tactful any more.

Mr Smith was the real player – he was the guy you went to if you needed anything done. If your son was serving six months for rioting, the standard at the time, Smith could get him out early for a funeral. If your grandmother was under pressure to hide guns under her floorboards, he would go the IRA and instruct them to leave her alone. If you needed to get a meeting with a Prime Minister, Taoiseach or an IRA commander, he was the man.

Everybody was in charge of their own little empire, but the only power blocs that mattered, as time wore on, were the British and the IRA. And Smith was the only person both the Brits and the republicans had confidence in – correction, would talk to. Most of the time. He was a born diplomat, and often, to keep one or other lot on board, he had to be very resourceful. So sometimes he upset them. 'There are days I have to stretch like an elastic band,' he once told me. 'And my great fear is that one or other will pull too hard and the whole thing will snap.' He came at his task from the perspective of a republican pacifist, although he wasn't a complete altruist, either, and would confess that, as a property developer, the war was a disaster for business.

Inspector Lyons was the British linchpin initially – they filtered their stuff through him and the Dunavady coffee house. But in late 1971, the first in what would be a series of 'strategic development advisors' arrived from London with a brief to try and settle the natives.

The new arrival introduced himself at Waterloo Street as Aubrey McCallum. He claimed he was considering building a textile factory in the North West, and he wondered if he could pick my brains about a few things. He was upper class, Oxford or Cambridge by the cut of him, about forty, dark-haired and very good-looking, and had a lingering tan that suggested a recent posting in a much hotter country. His was a plausible enough story and, while I normally tend to assume that any Englishman in Ireland is a spy until I have evidence otherwise, he was so skilled that I thought for a few seconds he might actually be genuine.

But just as I was preparing myself for a ten-minute diatribe on the virtues of synthetic carpets over wool, he smiled and asked me if I had seen much of Nigel recently – meaning Lyons.

'Not for a few weeks,' I said. 'He's in the doghouse. He recommended that a soldier who shot an unarmed civilian in Creggan should be prosecuted for murder. But, apparently, that's just too dangerous a precedent for your lot.'

'Yes,' he said. 'Your paper stuck it to us for that one. Quoting Gandhi in the editorial: "There is a higher court than the courts of justice and that is the court of the conscience – it supersedes all other courts. But it's becoming increasingly clear that the British people, or the people they send out to represent them, have no conscience." A bit laboured, and preachy, do you not think?'

I had no time for a lecture or tit-for-tat. 'Listen, Julius,' I said, 'it's deadline day, as you know, and I'm far too busy for this ...'

'My name is Aubrey,' he stammered, 'not Julius.'

'Highly unlikely,' I said. 'And if there's one thing I've learned from my friend Mr Smith, it is that it saves us all time if we give people the names they deserve. You, Julius, are an agent – just as sure as your namesake Julius Rosenberg was. And if I'm going to deal with you, this will remind me exactly, in all our dealings, that you are not my friend – but rather exactly who you are.'

Smith was always very on the money about ascribing names to people. Two local political leaders were always privately referred to in correspondence as 'Walter' and 'Knickers', thanks to Smith; Walter because he was a fantasist who spun outrageous lies like Walter Mitty; and Knickers, well, let's just say he was easily distracted.

The newly christened Julius tried to look offended but couldn't quite manage it and started to laugh. 'Julius?' he said. 'Could you not have picked something a little more glamorous, like Bond?'

'I could have,' I said, 'but Bond was never a Roman emperor.'

CHAPTER 59

Julius had actually called in to do me a favour, or at least that's what he was claiming at first. So I shouted out to the bullpen to Johnny to make us a cup of tea, saying I'd be out on the floor in ten minutes, thereby giving my visitor his deadline.

'Your News Editor is an exceptional writer,' said Julius. 'But I think he's in over his head.'

'I disagree entirely. He's more than competent in the job. In fact, I don't think there's a better-run newsdesk in Ireland.'

'Funny you should mention that, but my good friend is a director of the *Irish Evening News* in Dublin and they're looking for a deputy editor. It might be time for Johnny to consider moving up in the world …'

'But I thought you just said he was in over his head?'

'He is – but not in the newspaper domain.'

'If you mean the beatings he took, he's more than recovered. He's back playing Saturday morning football.'

'No, I'm sure he's physically fine. Though he does drink a lot.'

'You do whatever gets you through. What about it?'

'Have you noticed it's got worse recently – the drinking, I mean?'

Something was going on here. Mo had been complaining about Johnny only this morning – a real rarity from love's young sweet dream.

This was too important to dance around. 'What's going on here?' I asked him.

Julius dipped his head, as if he were uncomfortable, though he was so nuanced in everything he did, it may well have been an act. 'We have information that Johnny has accidentally found himself compromised.'

'What do you mean – has he another woman? Christ, those first two batterings will feel like a picnic by the time Mo's finished with him.'

'No, no, it's not a woman. It's actually more serious than that. Johnny was recruited to sit as an independent member of a tribunal. They thought he'd be ideal, given that he has years of court experience – he knows all the procedures and has a very solid head on him.'

'I didn't know about this. What tribunal?'

'Well it was more of an inquiry, really. A private hearing into information sharing by IRA personnel to, well, British personnel.'

'Christ, no. What happened?'

'A friend of ours was taken outside at the end of the proceedings and shot dead. Or should I say, *one* of our friends was taken outside. We had another friend advising the tribunal panel. Had no option but to convict, I'm afraid.'

The whole thing was filthy – even then.

'Had Johnny done this before?' I asked.

'Not to our knowledge – which is pretty extensive, as you must appreciate. And he did everything he could to save the poor guy's life. But they had a tape recording of the guy, from a telephone box, ringing Ebrington Barracks in the Waterside – and he was naming names, giving dates and, to cap it all, looking for his pay cheque. There was nothing could be done.'

This was awful. I was going to kill him, and then Mo was going to stitch back the pieces and kill him all over again.

'Did Johnny know what he was letting himself in for?'

'Definitely not. He was sick as a dog at the end and said if anyone ever asked him to do anything like that ever again, he'd sink the lot of them. He didn't care who they were.'

'He said that?'

'Yes. So, realistically, he will now be seen as a threat to them, too. And you can pull all the strings you want with Smith and Joe McGinlay, but for his own safety Johnny needs to get the hell out of Dodge immediately. Before his name starts appearing in the wrong sort of dispatches.'

After Julius had left the office, I composed myself for a few minutes before summoning Johnny in from the bullpen. He knew instantly, and by the time he came through my door he was sheet white.

Without any bidding, he sat down and opened up. He was as honest a man as I ever came across.

'I'm sorry, boss,' he said. 'They convinced me I was a big shot, told me that they needed my expertise, and the next thing I was witness to the execution.'

I handed him the telephone number Julius had left. 'The *Irish Evening News* has an opening for a deputy editor. You can start on Monday. I'm really, truly sorry – but it's the only way out of this. You can't stay – either at the *Chronicle* or in Derry.'

He hadn't been expecting the lifeline – just the bullet, so I saw his eyes fill up with relief. And then, suddenly, he remembered Mo and the fear set in again.

'Does she know?' he said.

'No,' I said. 'Mo and everyone else will be told that I'm firing you for repeated drinking on the job. So I suppose you'd better reach into that press behind you, get me the brandy and the glasses, and we might as well make it true.'

***

Mo never forgave me – nor did Connie. Not ever. But I couldn't tell them. They wouldn't have rested until they had personally eviscerated every IRA man and British agent in the city. The two of them barely spoke to me for a full year – and even then it was business only.

Mo's anger at me was only surpassed by her rage at Johnny for not telling her why he was going to Dublin. She broke off their engagement and said some things he didn't deserve, but she didn't know the full story and couldn't be held accountable. Even at this remove, I know too well the pain she will feel when she hears this tape.

Johnny went on to become a star at the *Evening News*, winning all sorts of plaudits and awards for his work. But he never got over Mo, or his Derry experiences, and died in his Dublin bedsit four years later, a bottle of Courvoisier in one hand and a fistful of sleeping pills in the other. I sent Julius a copy of the obituary I wrote for the *Chronicle* – with a note advising him to add it to the hundreds of others he was responsible for.

CHAPTER 60

1972

In the immediate aftermath of Bloody Sunday, I'd estimate that a quarter of the *Chronicle* staff attempted to join the IRA. And if it hadn't been for a very diplomatic intervention by Mr Smith, I would certainly have lost Mo to their Communications Department. Mo was approached while covering a memorial event at Guildhall Square in February 1972, but such was the state of Derry at that stage that I knew about it before she'd even got back to the office. One of Nigel Lyons's men had spotted her in deep conversation with the recruiter, Fatman O'Reilly, and Lyons warned me immediately.

Mr Smith rigorously avoided involving himself in, what he termed, the tittle-tattle of how the IRA worked. He was a strategist and a politician – and he was careful never to pick up gossip or 'data' that other people could try to shake out of him. It was always better if he didn't know. And so when I went to him for help, he apologised politely and refused.

I was a little surprised, as Don Grover and myself had lined up a number of meetings for Smith during his recent visit to America and felt he owed me one. And I told him so.

'Leave it with me,' he said. Classic Provo-speak for 'I'll do what I can'. But he wasn't happy.

Two days later, he rang me back. 'I spoke to Thumper,' he said. I assumed this was an IRA commander. 'I told him you were stuck for experienced staff and couldn't afford to lose another one. He mentioned job-sharing, but I didn't think you'd be on for that either. So I proposed another idea.'

'What was that?'

'Suffice to say, there are about sixty recent English graduates from Queen's and UCD, who want nothing more than to avenge what happened here. You don't need to know any more. In fairness, it was nearly a stampede.'

'I take it I now owe you, then?'

'You take it correctly. And I will call it in.'

I was seriously grateful to him – and with cause. In the years to come, three of the *Chronicle*'s production staff wound up in jail with sentences ranging from six months to life. And one of the printers, whom I'm not naming, was shot while on active service with the IRA. The Brits actually couldn't convict him, despite the fact they knew he was hit and had seen him fall, as they couldn't find the bullet wound. He denied all, and walked – or more correctly limped – out of the barracks after three days. It turned out he had been shot in the sole of the foot as he was being chased. But every one of the doctors missed it.

All those who served time were rehired, without loss of benefits, after their sentence. It was company policy – and another reason why we lost so few staff over the years.

***

Five months later, in late July 1972, Smith cashed his chip. He demanded my presence at his home in leafy suburbia then told me he wanted me to go out for a drive with him.

I was a little surprised when he pointed to his work van, rather than his shiny new sports car.

'Julius has been in touch,' he said. We had all adopted the codename by now, and Aubrey, or whatever he was really called, had no option but to play along. 'The army is going to clear out the no-go areas tomorrow.'

The no-go areas were republican-controlled zones such as Free Derry, which had successfully resisted any foreign military presence for the past couple of years. It was no secret that the British were planning to invade these areas. They had deployed extra soldiers to the North, and two colossal battleships, full of troops and tanks, had sailed into the River Foyle.

'The IRA have already pulled out,' said Smith. 'They're regrouping in Buncrana. But there's still a consignment of weapons left in the Bogside. And Lyons is really worried in case some younger ones might get their hands on them. They might get a rush of blood to their heads and try to fight back.'

'So what's this to do with us?'

Smith smiled. 'You and I are going to go and lift the weapons now, and transport them somewhere safe where they'll be out of harm's way.'

I looked at him, very puzzled. 'But don't the Brits want to seize them? What's Julius playing at?'

'It's a gentleman's arrangement,' said Smith. 'The last thing they need is another massacre here.'

He then drove us into the city centre and through a barricade onto Lecky Road, stopping outside a little house. A woman was waiting at the door.

'Mr Smith,' she said. 'And it's yourself Mr Madden. I wouldn't have thought you'd the bottle. They're in there.' And she gestured over her shoulder to the front parlour.

The room was packed with crates – containing fifty rifles wrapped in blankets – which we quickly transferred to the van.

'Where to now?' I asked Smith.

'Your house,' he said. 'Back down to the manse.'

'You're kidding.'

'No. We're going to stash these in your old air-raid shelter.'

I don't know what arrangements Smith had made, but he was waved through two checkpoints, one army and one police, despite the fact that the bottom of his van was scraping the road under the extra weight.

As we unloaded the crates into the old bunker, Smith remarked on how large it was – and quite well appointed to boot.

'How did you know about this place?' I asked him. 'I never mentioned it to you.'

He laughed. 'Your late wife let a friend of mine stay here in the 1950s, when he was, how can I put this, under a little scrutiny for his role in the Border Campaign.'

Millie had told me she'd lost the keys, fair play to her.

'I'll tell you what, though,' he said, 'after we've returned these to their owners, we might think about doing a little conversion in here. Private space like this is hard to find.'

I would have done anything for Smith, because, all things considered, he was the bravest, most selfless man I ever knew.

Sure enough, the army cleared the no-go areas the next day, 31 July, in Operation Motorman, killing two young Derrymen in the process. Neither was offering any threat.

About a month later, my production manager called at the manse late one night, driving a *Chronicle* delivery van.

'I've been told to pick up something here, boss,' he said.

I nodded and handed him the key to the shelter. 'Not a word,' I told him.

And that was how it worked. All of a sudden, we were all complicit at different levels.

Some republicans got the wrong idea about my actions, however. And, soon afterwards, the Six County support group I'd helped set up in the US was approached by the IRA about sending over crates on a much larger scale. Again, such was the curse of the Irish that Don Grover knew about the request before I did.

I told him, however, the same as I told Smith to relay back to Thumper, that this was not my role. If the Yanks needed a broker, at any stage – and they would – I would have to have clean hands.

CHAPTER 61

Jeanie was surprised to see the three doubles of whiskey, still sitting in the clear plastic cups where she had left them, when she called in to McCloud's suite for a debriefing before his meeting with Bowtie on Sunday.

He caught her looking at the shelf and smiled. 'Don't worry,' he said. 'I haven't found myself a secret supplier. I just didn't have a drink last night.'

'So how come you didn't pour it into a medicine bottle or an aftershave bottle like you did before?'

He glared at her, a little peeved at the smart remark but mostly impressed. 'I'm taking a breather for a couple of days. You can take those glasses away with you when you're done, or empty them down the sink. And if I do fancy another drink, I'll go wherever I want and buy one – and you can tell whoever you like.'

It came out a little sharply, so he immediately held up his hand to apologise. 'I didn't mean it like that. My brother's anniversary was the day I landed here, so I leaned a bit too hard on it. It was easier just to stay numb.'

Jeanie said nothing but stared at him, curious.

He smiled. 'Between ourselves, I let them think I'm worse with the drink than I am in reality. It gives them something to put in their reports. And it also keeps them out of the rest of my life.'

She was suddenly worried he was about to go off the reservation. 'So you're not a functioning alcoholic, sir?'

'No, I very possibly am. But I'm not at rock bottom, and I'm going to be very careful to make sure that never happens. I've had a shaky few days, that's all. And this is a much nicer city when you've got a clear head.'

'I'm sorry about your brother, sir. It was unforgiveable of the paper to print that story.'

'I don't know about that. What they reported was true. It was no more unforgiveable than my father turning him in.'

She was confused. 'Excuse me?'

'It was my father – he was a Fed, too – who caught us cheating and handed us in. In truth, though, he had little choice. Terry, my brother, had sat an exam for me the same day I was having an appendectomy fifty miles away. How we thought we'd get away with it, I don't know. When my father saw my results, he knew immediately, and Terry paid hell for it. Literally.'

'But not you?'

'Terry told him I knew nothing about it. Said to Pop he was just trying to save me delaying college for a year, to do one lousy re-sit. Didn't think anyone would worry too much about it. I was a straight "A" student and would have had no problem with the test anyway.'

'Did you know that Terry had taken the test for you?'

'Of course I knew. I begged him to do it. My girl and my friends were heading for Yale and I didn't want to miss out. And I told Pop all of this. But for whatever reason, he chose not to punish me. Terry was older – and always got it a bit rougher. Pop thought he needed to set an example. But he couldn't have predicted how badly it would work out. Terry was sacked from Berkeley for gross misconduct. And, in a fit of pique, instead of transferring to another college, he enlisted as a marine. He lasted just two days in Iraq. The entire disaster took less than five months to unfold from start to finish. One minute we were planning a spring break together in Florida, the next I'm in an aircraft hangar with my mother and two sisters waiting to bring his body home.'

'Where was your father?'

McCloud's face softened. 'He blamed himself, as did the rest of us at the time. He couldn't face it – either us or the funeral. He moved back to Philly, on his own, for a year. But he's back working things out with Mom now – he could never really leave her – and things are improving. In fact, I hear he's opened a Facebook account.'

Jeanie smiled at that. She then noticed him eyeing the glasses still on the shelf and decided to keep him talking until she could get him back on safe ground.

'Why did he go to Philly?'

'That's where he was from originally. His father was a cop there. I never knew him, though. He died before we were born. Apparently he was one hard bastard. "Thumbs" McCloud he was called.'

'Because he would break guys' thumbs to get them to talk?'

He laughed. 'That's what I always thought, too. But no. It was because he was always cracking his damn thumbs anytime he was thinking. A ridiculous habit I know, but one that his son, and then his grandson, inherited.'

He paused then pointed to the clock on the desk to indicate he was running late. 'I know now, of course, that Terry's death was nobody's fault – but rather just a consequence of living in the world. Or a "bastard fact of life" as my old Psych lecturer at Quantico would have it. Young people, all young people, think they're bulletproof. They have no idea how fragile life is until it's too late. That's why it's so easy to persuade them to go off and fight wars.'

CHAPTER 62

Bowtie, barely recognisable in his boat clothes, was already sitting at the table in Fiorentini's on Strand Road, tucking into half a tableful of breakfast served with chips, when McCloud came into the café. The other half-table was covered by his companion's food, so the pair did some quick re-arranging to give McCloud some room at the table while Bowtie signalled for the same again.

Bowtie's visitor, also in boat clothes was a tall and wiry, distinguished-looking man of about fifty-five, whom McCloud immediately made as a Yank.

'McCloud meet Patrick; Patrick meet McCloud.'

McCloud could hardly believe it. 'You're Patrick O'Lennon, the ambassador, aren't you? What brings you to Derry? Christ, I hope you're not checking up on us. These locals are making a horse's ass of me.'

O'Lennon returned the smile. 'I saw your picture in the *Chronicle* all right,' he said. 'But you played it brilliantly. You ignored it publicly, hit them a large slap in private and got on with your job. Well done.'

'Thank you, sir. So what has you here?'

'I came up for Tommy's yacht-painting party.'

McCloud looked at Bowtie accusingly. 'It was a party?'

Bowtie held his hands up. 'It was a dinner party. Only sixteen of us. That's all the boat can sleep.'

McCloud was incredulous. 'You have a yacht that sleeps sixteen people? I thought the way you were talking it was a row-boat.'

'No, it's a yacht, all right, and a pretty decent one. Seán sold it to me for a song when the *Chronicle* decommissioned it. They used it to broadcast pirate radio for about half a dozen years. Right out on the high seas. I get friends up to help me paint it at the start of every summer. It's a standing invite – but I'll count you in next year as my token Yank. Patrick here is taking another posting.'

McCloud nodded. 'I'm sorry to hear that, sir. Where are you off to?'

'The UN. My wife and I love Dublin, but my daughters really want to get back to New York. Bright lights and Broadway. Do you like Ireland, Ally?'

McCloud was suddenly struck that O'Lennon had used his first name, despite the fact Bowtie hadn't referred to it at all. This breakfast was no accidental meeting, so the question required a considered answer. 'I do, sir. I think the people are all quite mad, but in a kind way. They tend to look out for one another and even for strangers like me. They've emerged from their war a lot more reflective, mature and optimistic than before. They can still be a bit lawless when they have to, but if the Brits can't civilise them after eight hundred years, I think we're just going to have to accept them as God made them. Oh, and I prefer the climate here, too – DC is about ten degrees too hot for me in summer. I like it milder.'

O'Lennon smiled approvingly. Something was going on. The ambassador looked over at Tommy, who nodded, and then back at McCloud. 'We're opening a new consulate here in the North,' he said, 'somewhere west of the Bann. Possibly Derry. Would you be interested in a job? It would be reporting to both Dublin and London. It would save you from some of those sixty-hour weeks the Deputy Director tells me you put in back home. And you'd get your weekends back, too.'

'That sounds very interesting. Doing what precisely, sir? Heading up security?'

'God, no, man. You're far too useful to be searching through bags. We need a new consul. Someone who knows the ground, knows the politics and can pass themselves with the locals. You've been here three times now. And Tommy here says you might be a good fit. You don't have to tell us right away. Take your time. Finish your coffee first.'

They all laughed at that.

McCloud was genuinely flattered, but it was very sudden. 'Would you give me a week to think about it, sir?'

The ambassador nodded. 'You want to finish this case and see where it takes you first, don't you?'

'I've kind of bought into it at this stage.'

'No problem. A week it is. Here's my card – the cell's on the back – ring me as soon as you've decided, one way or the other.'

CHAPTER 63

He could smell the roast beef cooking in the oven in the bunker's kitchen as Mo let him in the door. He hoped he'd be hungry again by the time it was ready. The Fiorentini's breakfast had left him in need of an early nap.

'Jeans and a crew-neck shirt on a Sunday?' Mo asked him. 'Maeve will be very relieved. We were worried you were going to turn up in your Mass clothes. Your credibility would have taken a serious hit.'

He pulled a pretend frown. 'Maybe I should have worn my deck shoes? I might have got myself an invitation to a party.'

'Oh, don't pout,' she said. 'Feeling left out, are we?'

'Not at all. Afraid to let me talk to your friends, are we?'

She laughed and pointed him into the TV room. 'So what's on the agenda today?'

He sat down on his armchair and loosened his belt two notches. 'Only a few little things. Spies mostly. American and British. Seán seemed to have spies on the brain; were there really as many as he suggests? Never trusting a man with an English accent – that seems a bit extreme.'

Mo considered this carefully. 'It was extreme. And he was wrong a lot more often than he was right. And he accepted that himself. But it was okay to be wrong a lot of the time, because if you're caught – and we were caught a few times with people telling tales out of school – it does an awful lot of damage. So, yes, we were paranoid; but yes, they were out to get us.'

It is hard to argue paranoia with people who have been both shot and bombed, so he didn't even try. 'If we could talk about the official agents first,' he said, 'the ones we know were real: Don and Julius. Did relations with them end well? Could either of them have borne grudges?'

'No, relations did not end well,' said Mo, 'and yes, they could well have borne grudges. He fought with both of them, particularly when he thought they weren't doing their jobs. And there's no doubt his actions damaged Don's career at the later stages. He had a lot of respect for Julius, generally. But Seán had a huge falling out with the guy who came after Julius.'

'The fights – who was at fault?'

'All sides. It was always the same damn thing – like little boys trying to see who can pee highest up the wall. Seán was generally less volatile – the others were younger, fiery and more eager to show off who was boss. But if they rankled him, he would flatten them – and he had no hesitation using the *Chronicle* to do it. Neither of them shot him, though.'

'And how do you know that?'

'They would have got a message to us somehow – to let us know it was them. They would have got no satisfaction out of a hit-and-run. Like the time the Brits petrol-bombed the office, they made sure we knew it was them. And when you Yanks were turning the screw on us, like with the threatened audit into Granda Pat's estate, you told us exactly what you were planning – just to intimidate us all the more.'

'Could any of the junior spies have had a go at Seán?'

'No. They didn't have the authority.'

'The relationship between Grover and Seán, was it widely known? Could anyone have targeted Seán because he was feeding the Americans?'

'Very unlikely. Any communists and anarchists here tend to be unarmed and not-at-all dangerous. None of them to my knowledge has ever spent forty-eight hours in a holding cell in Castlereagh – unlike many others we've had dealings with. And Seán wasn't feeding the Yanks, he was advising them … and he was a Yank himself, remember.'

'Can you say unequivocally, then, that this was not a political attack on a US citizen?'

Mo pursed her lips and thought for a minute. 'What was it Tip O'Neill said? All politics is personal? Well, this was certainly a personal attack, and there was certainly politics in there somewhere.'

He waited quietly. Silence is a great weapon for the interrogator. Most interviewees can't resist the need to fill the void. She cracked. 'But I don't think he was shot by a spy of any colour. No.'

He nodded. 'What about the IRA, then?'

'We'll come back to them tomorrow,' she said. 'You need to see the latter bit of the tape before we talk. The IRA in the 1970s was very different from the IRA in the eighties and nineties – they had different leaderships, different goals and a lot of very different personnel. So we're better to be dealing with that in the round.'

She looked at her watch. 'Are you not going to ask me about Johnny?'

He had been hoping to pick his moment. He lowered his eyes. 'I'll just come right to the crunch then – is that why it ended badly with the other man?'

He didn't mention the name in case Maeve was listening. But he had spent most of the previous night considering Mo's relationships first with Johnny and then the IRA leader Paud Devlin, and was confident that he'd figured out the common factor. It had been Paud who compromised Johnny.

Mo looked at him directly and nodded. 'Johnny was the love of my life. He was an innocent, and they used and abused him. I didn't realise it was the same people until it was too late. I'm not sure it makes them bad people, or good people who did a bad thing in a terrible time. Regardless, they were wrong to think I wouldn't find out – or that I wouldn't take it personally when I did. And they were so, so wrong to involve themselves in my life after what they had done to me – without ever making me aware of it. Up to then, I'd always tried hard never to blame everyone in an organisation for what one person does. Now, I'm not so sure. It was like I got a private lesson in the need for corporate responsibility.'

'If Johnny had told you what he'd done, would you have gone to Dublin with him?'

It was a dumb question, and it was out before he could stop himself. It was none of his concern. But it was right there.

She took it on the chin. 'I try very hard never to ask myself that question,' she said. 'But the reality is, I never got the option. So I played the cards as they were dealt. For years, I thought he'd rejected me, which was very sore. But when I learned then he'd been exiled because of a stupid mistake, because of someone else's cynicism, I hated myself again for not doing more for him.'

He needed to lower the pressure, to change the mood. 'Did Don Grover really used to call you Salty? I found a reference in an old CIA cypher to a "Salty O'Sullivan" – is that genuinely you?'

She laughed at the distraction. 'Don was an old woman when it came to language and protocols. He heard me telling Johnny to eff off one day – it was purely affectionate, don't you know – and nearly had a stroke. So, yes, for a few days I was "Salty". But it didn't stick.'

McCloud grinned. 'What would he have made of Maeve?'

'Christ knows,' said Mo. She looked at her watch again. 'And talking of salty, she's waiting for me upstairs – and if I keep her back from her food, her language will make mine look like something out of *The Princess Diaries*. Your roast beef will be ready in an hour, by the way. But if you were trying to keep up with Bowtie at brunch, you might want to leave it a while. Just turn it down to about a hundred and it'll keep.'

CHAPTER 64

1974

I would love nothing better than to claim that the *Chronicle* always remained an honest broker, or at least a force for good, during the 1970s. By and large, we tried to be, but time and time again, we found ourselves compromised. Lying and chicanery had become the national pastimes, as people grew more and more afraid and distrustful. All media were being manipulated, corrupted and abused by one set of players or another, or indeed by several at the one time.

I like to think we were caught less often than others on the grounds that we operated a strict no-second-chances policy – zero tolerance, they call it now. But then, as time wore on, we often had to re-engage with the people who had burned us and give them second lives. And yes, we often got burned again.

Some of the transgressions against us were very serious – and I'll come to those in a moment. But others were almost comical in retrospect. For example, the *Chronicle* had a policy of refusing to name kneecapping victims – guys that had gotten shot in the leg by paramilitaries. This was invariably as a punishment for stealing cars, minor touting or behaving in a manner unacceptable to women, as the bishop used to put it. More serious crimes were left to the social services – note, not the police – or the nutting squad.

But a large part of any rehabilitation process requires public acknowledgement of your crime – typically via a published court report. The thinking is that the shame of your crime, coupled with the fact that everyone now knows where you live, will make you a little bit more circumspect about your behaviour the next time. And so republican and loyalist paramilitaries could never understand why we, the press, wouldn't name the reprobates they had dealt with so justly – and the heinous offences of which they had been convicted.

My standard reply was that the *Chronicle* would be happy to name the defendants, as long as we could publish the identities of all the other people involved in the trial as well, including the prosecutors, judges and firing squad – as we did with regular court cases.

I was pleased with this answer and more pleased again that it was respected by the various shoot-em-up groups.

One day, however, Mo came into my office, looking worried.

'How long have we been running the results of the Felons' raffle?' she asked me.

'More than a year now, I'm sure,' I told her. 'Eighteen months, probably. Why do you ask?'

'I've just had an irate mother on the phone complaining that we have identified her son as a car thief. Apparently, the IRA are using the draw results to name and shame all the wee hoods they're kneecapping. And the whole town knows about it.'

I was stunned. 'How do they do it?'

'The Felons have been running three separate prize draws every month – one with a car as top prize, another with a state-of-the-art stereo radio system, and the last one is a holiday. And they can each have up to ten runners-up prizes.'

'Don't tell me …'

'Yep – the car raffle is for car thieves, the stereo is for guys who are fond of broadcasting stories, and the holiday is for guys who like exposing themselves to the sun. And all the lucky winners and runners up get their full names and addresses published in the paper.'

I had to laugh. It was ingenious. 'Absolutely brilliant,' I said. 'Shut them down – and tell Dara Devlin at the Felons Club he's just got himself a five-year ban.'

***

While the Felons had managed to make fools of us on a repeated basis, we cottoned onto most other hoaxes right away. The dummy memoriam notices were a case in point.

We had always allowed families to submit the copy directly, along with a cash payment, and never really felt the need to vet the messages. Until that is, one week, Nigel Lyons rang me and asked me if I realised we had just named two active Special Branch informers in our 'In Loving Memory' column. Sure enough, I checked the page, and there, in the midst of the genuine notices, were two well-known and still-breathing middle-ranking republicans; both pronounced dead – one five years ago, the other three. Needless to say there was no official complaint nor libel suit – but to be honest, the guys might as well have been dead for all we ever saw of them after that. And obviously, that led to a major rethink of the entire classified-ads section, including a demand for photographic ID before any and all insertions.

***

Bomb warnings were another quagmire. At one stage, we were getting at least one a day – and our ethics bound us to notify the police and army, who would cordon off whatever street had been targeted. Except, quite often there was no bomb at all – it was just an invitation for the Brits to turn up and get shot at. So, effectively, the *Chronicle* was being used as the starting pistol for a gun battle.

But if we didn't notify, and a civilian got hurt or worse in a blast, we – and we alone – would be to blame.

We'd frequently get hoax warnings from civilians, too, wanting to miss a morning's work – or, more often than not, school. So we developed a code-word system with the various groups that worked fairly well for a time, until a nervous bomber forgot his cypher and came within a hair of blowing up a dozen old-age pensioners in a city-centre café. The Provos had to handle that evacuation themselves.

The police and other forces of good were constantly monitoring our connections with anyone and everyone. They tapped our phones and bugged our cars and our homes. We all knew that the only way to hold a safe conversation was to head for a Donegal beach or, at a push, write shorthand notes to one another, which we would then burn.

Our biggest rows with the cops, however, weren't over us disclosing sources – they knew we had a modicum of protection under the law. The biggest fights were about photographs. And there were two particular issues: we wouldn't give them ours and we wouldn't use theirs.

Unlike the 'security forces', we could have our pick of dozens of views of any riot or incident. Our cameramen were able to walk among the crowds with both impunity and immunity, whereas theirs quite clearly couldn't. But there was no money for us in publishing pictures of stone-throwers, even if they were daft enough to do so unmasked. So we didn't. But that didn't mean we hadn't got the pictures, as the cops well knew. And a number of times – if for example a well-aimed petrol bomb had set fire to their newest Land Rover – they would raid our offices, demanding all negatives. For a brief period, our photographers took to doing all their developing in the Donegal offices – until Lyons negotiated a shaky pax. The police grudgingly accepted that we weren't in the business of working for anybody but ourselves – and we let the rioters know if our pictures were seized, and they were unmasked, they would have to take their medicine. We didn't do propaganda for any side.

Difficulties would also arise when the police needed help from the public – and perhaps wanted to talk to individuals to eliminate them from their enquiries. They were so keen to eliminate these individuals, that they would issue us with large photographs of them, accompanied by some pretty serious aspersions about their characters to boot, and then pressurise us into publishing them.

Unfortunately, however, when we asked the police, in turn, to identify serving RUC officers or soldiers we had photographed firing loaded weapons at civilians, they tended not to co-operate. So again, we agreed with Nigel Lyons to settle on a scoreless draw and left the taig-kicking to EF Cunningham and the *Londonderry Leader*.

Sometimes, however, it wasn't so easy. Mo, who was, by a mile, the toughest person in the building, had a near breakdown when she discovered she'd pronounced an informer dead twenty minutes before the poor soul had actually been shot. She was given details about his transgressions for the Thursday paper and wrote up her story, and various allegations about the man, assuming that he was already dead. But the *Chronicle* came off the printing presses a little earlier than normal on Wednesday night. And the victim wasn't dead at all – or at least the shots that killed him weren't heard until after the paper had been distributed to a couple of all-night garages.

The police had all sorts of questions about that one – as did our own lawyers. And Mo, who refused to say where she'd got the information, was held for two days for obstructing a murder inquiry. Eventually, Lyons brokered her release, but Mo was badly shaken at how she'd been played and then left swinging. And she refused to deal with single-source paramilitary stories after that point.

She blamed herself, entirely. 'I was so intent on getting the exclusive on the story that I didn't ring the police for comment,' she told me later. 'In case they might tell another paper. But if I had called them, they could have pulled him out and he could still be alive.'

Sadly this story was not atypical either for the *Chronicle* or for the dozens of other local papers across the twisted North. There were many days you just wanted to go straight home and take a hot bath.

CHAPTER 65

1975

It's hard to explain how quickly society, or normal life, call it what you will, can disintegrate so completely. Just when you thought that we had plumbed the depths of humanity, someone, it didn't matter who – usually the other crowd – would bring it to a whole new level of low. I wouldn't describe it as evil; that would suggest that there was a moral standard somewhere, which we were failing to meet. It was more that there was an absence of any morality at all. There was no sliding scale of venial and mortal sins any more. And no-one, not any side, had the authority, or respect, to dictate what was right and what was wrong. There was no centre, and there was no plan. Anything and everything was permissible – until most of us gradually found ourselves inured, impervious and immutable.

Empathy and sympathy were in short supply if they were ever apparent at all. The only abiding emotions were anger, at your powerlessness to control what was going on around you, and fear. Fear for yourself and your family every time you heard a bomb or a gunshot, and fear of what you might say – or, in our case, write. Print one wrong word, and someone would end up dead. And sadly, it happened. Frequently. From wannabe big shots shouting their mouths off about the wrong thing, and us giving them all the space they wanted, to older hands using our columns to pick off their enemies, nice and subtly, so that no-one but a triggerman might notice.

In time, the amorality became completely normal. And the *Chronicle* continued producing papers, kidding ourselves that we were at one remove, as if little had changed. Again, I'd love to say we were better than the rest – but it's hard to find new tears, or provide leadership and understanding, when every building in the city has been blown up, children have been killed, hundreds of young men thrown in jail, and it's going on and on, day in and day out, for decades. As the poet said, 'Too long a sacrifice can make a stone of the heart.' And so, we became the hardest of the hard. It was as if the city had lost its soul.

***

234

In that context, any hope at all, even false hope, can become very important. The 1975 ceasefire had many flaws. It allowed the British time to regroup and gather intelligence. It undermined the middle ground and the middle-classes by sidelining the political process and letting the IRA negotiate directly with government. And its ultimate collapse convinced the younger guns on all sides that negotiations were pointless, and that we'd be better off digging in for a long war.

At the time, though, we were desperate. You look around this city now, and see beautiful, refurbished Georgian streets, riverside walks and peace bridges. But back then, Derry was a living battleground. As Eamonn McCann said in *War and an Irish Town*, the city looked like it had been bombed from the air.

There had been lots of talk about a ceasefire for the last few months of 1974 – indeed, there had been so many rumours that we'd all stopped believing again. But I knew that something serious was afoot when one Monday morning in early 1975, I got a call from reception to tell me 'Johnny Walker', the then code-word for the IRA, was here to see me. A minute later, Paud Devlin and Blanaid Cullen, two veterans of the Border Campaign, were shown into my office.

Paud sat down and casually picked up a copy of the previous Thursday's paper that was on the desk. 'So,' he said, 'what's your big story tomorrow?'

I knew well from the way Paud was pretending to be relaxed that he was fishing for something. So for badness, I decided to throw a rod in the water myself. 'We're going to run with Father Falloon's statement at Mass yesterday,' I told him. 'The one where he said that the ceasefire was actually coming into effect from last night – and that the Brits and the IRA are going to sit down together later this week.'

Father Falloon had one of the biggest mouths in the town and I wouldn't have dreamt of leading a paper with one of his pronouncements. But the staff in the bullpen had mentioned that the priest had been grandstanding again at the weekend. So I figured it would be fun to see if I could get a rise out of the Provos.

Blanaid nearly fell off her seat. 'Jesus, Mary, you can't do that,' she said. 'It'll ruin everything. That fecking Falloon can't hold his water.'

This time, it was me who was shocked. 'So it's true, then?'

Paud stared at me hard. Warning me. 'Off the record?'

'Yes, of course.'

'Yes, it's true. Or rather, it will be soon. As you're aware, we've been talking to the Brits through a third party for the past while now. We know he briefs you, too, so that you can brief the Yanks – not that they're a damn bit interested.'

I ignored that. 'So what's the problem with Falloon?'

Blanaid shook her head. 'He went a week too early. The ceasefire's not due to be announced until Sunday coming – he thought it was coming yesterday. But the Derry Command haven't approved it yet.'

'How can that be?'

'The whole thing's being handled by the national leadership, through Mr Smith, back to the Brits. But while the truce talks are going to be handled in Derry, it's not our game. And, to be frank, there's a lot of the younger ones here aren't happy at all about that.'

'Are you going to veto it?'

'No. Not at all. But it wouldn't do any harm for Smith to show a little local accountability once in a while. It's not good for myself and Blanaid to be hearing the war is over at the same time as the rest of the parish. It makes us look bad.'

I paused and looked back at him. 'So you want me to sit on the story?'

'No,' he said. 'I don't want you to – I absolutely need you to. I really need the week to settle some heads. If it breaks tomorrow before they've been properly told about it, they could easily say, "To hell with the lot of you", and come out shooting.'

His point was a good one and I had plenty on my conscience already. 'No problem,' I said. 'We'll hold the story.'

The two visitors visibly relaxed into their chairs. Paud then looked at me again, a bit more sheepishly this time. 'I don't suppose you could do me another favour, could you?' he asked.

I grinned at him. 'What? You want the keys to my car – and I can't alert the cops for an hour?'

'Not quite,' he said. 'It's a little more complicated. Derry is in charge of the travel and accommodation arrangements for the first big meetings next week. Smith is handling the main show – just outside the town. But we also need a bit of back-up.'

'I don't follow.'

'Two things in particular,' he said. 'There's some of our team that the Brits aren't comfortable with. They're happy enough talking to Michael and Billy – they reckon they're the moderates. But they won't be in the same room as Thumper and Mr Kelly. And we need them nearby, in case there are decisions to be made.'

I didn't really know who he was talking about – as was often the way with Smith. But I knew what he was looking for. 'You're thinking the manse?'

'Yes. There'll be no danger of raids or the like. And Nigel Lyons will get them safe passage in and out from the South.'

'Okay – for how long?'

'Could be months.'

'How about the bunker? I've converted it into a little apartment now, you know.'

'I know full well,' said Paud. 'My cousin did the plastering for you.'

I laughed at the presumption of the man.

'And the second part of the cover?'

Blanaid took this one. 'We need to set up a series of Sinn Féin meetings with the Brits to run in parallel with the IRA talks.'

'So you're going to run a kind of kiddies' table to keep the focus away from the main party?'

'Not how I would put it,' said Blanaid. 'But essentially, the main business wouldn't be done there. No.'

'And you need a venue?'

'Yes – we'll only want it for a week or two, at most …'

'You can have the dining room at the manse. I rarely use it. Though you probably knew that as well. Give me a day or two to clear it out.'

'It's not just that …'

'Jesus, do you want dibs on my firstborn as well?'

'We need the media to know that the Sinn Féin talks are taking place here in Derry. Sell the decoy a little. It'll explain why the various personnel are milling about the roads, without raising too many awkward questions.'

This was a little less passive. But I was being hung for a couple of lambs anyway, so I nodded to them I'd swing for the sheep, too.

'And in return I get?'

The smile left Blanaid's face, and for the first time she looked sad. 'The eternal gratitude of a generation of tired Derry mothers,' she said.

CHAPTER 66

1976

I never asked any of the guys their given names – neither the Irish nor the British. It was safer, as Smith said, not to have that sort of data, then no-one would ever try to shake it out of you. Anyhow, Smith simply made up names for people as he went along – the sarky little sod used to call me 'Bing'.

It was only after 'Mr Kelly' had been staying in the bunker for about three months that I realised that it wasn't his name at all. I saw his picture in a London paper, accompanied by some very interesting biographical notes. Not that I said anything about it, mind. Mo and I privately referred to the same guy as 'The Furnace' because he chain-smoked – and not, as Mo once joked, because he invented the car bomb.

It was Kelly who first tipped me off that the 1975 ceasefire was becoming rocky. I had been asked to drive him and Smith to a meeting in Galway to give 'friends' of theirs an account of what benefits had accrued four months into the truce. Smith stayed the night in Clifden, in the beautiful cliff-top house which had been supplied for the meeting by a well-known actor. But I had to get back to Derry to put a paper to bed, and Kelly wanted to visit a niece in Ballyshannon, so I took him up the road with me.

As we wound our way through Mayo, along the N17, he lit up yet another cigarette, rolled down the window and gave a big, sad sigh.

'Where do you think it's all going?' he asked. It was a tried and trusted Provo technique – better to be asking questions than to be answering them.

It was also an editor's technique. 'What do you mean?' I replied.

He laughed and tried a second open-ended question. 'Are we winning, Mr Newspaper Man? In your humble opinion?'

'And what exactly would be your definition of victory, Mr Kelly?' Connie Madden had not raised any children dumb enough to tell the IRA where they were going wrong.

He nodded like I'd said something significant and then cut to his point. 'To be honest, I don't know what the win looks like this week, Seán. But I do know I need a bit more help getting there. We have a big personnel gap, for a start. We need a second point-of-contact with the Brits. Smith is great, don't get me wrong, but everything – every negotiation – is going through him, the whole lot of it, and we can't risk something happening to him. Also, a second pipeline would assure us that we're getting the correct amount of petrol out of the first.'

So after Smith had thrown a perfect game, they were in the market for a relief pitcher. But I wasn't so sure. 'Do you really think you could get more with someone else?'

'We don't know. But we have to try.'

I didn't like where this was heading. I didn't have Smith's diplomatic skills, or tolerance – or time.

But Kelly was reading my mind. 'Calm yourself,' he said. 'We're not thinking of you. And you have your own connection to look after anyway. We were thinking about Mo.'

'What about her?

'You know that Julius has a bit of a thing for her? He asks about her every time he's in Derry.'

'You're kidding? But he's married! He wears a ring!'

'Yes, but he has an eye for the ladies. We're pretty certain of it. Strike that, we know it for certain. And Mo is one strong individual.'

'Christ, Kelly, what are you suggesting? You want Mo to pull a Mata Hari?'

He shook his head quickly. 'God, no.' Kelly was a regular Mass-goer, and hardly a Saturday night went by that he didn't have me running him out to Burt chapel for Confession. 'I'm talking psychology here, not prostitution. Men like Julius love nothing better than to impress beautiful women like Mo. They can't stop themselves – they want to spread the "cloths of heaven" under them. There's one or two on our side with a touch of the same condition themselves, though they would never act on it. But if something like that could ever give us an edge, then we certainly should use it.'

I needed not to be talking about this anymore. It was too dangerous. So I switched the topic. 'How bad have things got? Is the truce in trouble?'

'We'll be back to war in a couple of months. Thumper is running out of patience with Julius and company. And the younger ones are just raring to go again. If we were to lose a couple of the older leaders now, we could be in real trouble.'

We drove in silence the rest of the way to Ballyshannon. But as I pulled in on the hilly main street to let him out, he paused before he opened the car door.

'So, you'll talk to Mo, then?' he said.

'We'll see. I'll chat to you in Derry later in the week.'

For good or ill, the plan never came off. Two days later, before he ever made it back to Derry, Kelly was arrested by the Gardaí and spent the next four years in jail. Despite the fact the IRA leaders had been granted limited immunity in the North, the Southern authorities were still hell-bent on eradicating them. The British were never going to allow a second channel, though; the IRA tried three or four times after that, via the Irish, the clergy and even the Yanks, but Whitehall shut them down straightaway. There would be no double-tapping the well. Smith knew these attempts were going on, and wasn't remotely annoyed. It was a massive job for one man. And, like Kelly, he had spotted Julius's weak spot and worked out how to get him to go the extra mile. And while Mo was never interested in doing it – or ever approached again – in later years, I'm pretty confident Smith found someone else who was.

CHAPTER 67

1980

It was a privilege to get almost sixty years with my mother – or fifty, if you count the nine we missed at the start when she left me in Boston, and the one when I wasn't speaking to her.

Typically, as Paud Devlin quipped at her funeral, she died from injuries sustained while on active service. She was furious that our lawyer, the formerly radical politician Joe McGinlay, had accused supporters of the Hunger Strike of 'blackmailing' the British Government. So at the tender age of eighty-four, Connie decided to take part in a massive Trade Union march to the Guildhall in support of the prisoners, where she tripped trying to keep up with the pace and broke her leg. This led to enforced bed rest and ultimately pneumonia.

Hunger striking has been the ultimate Irish protest against injustice since pagan times, when accusers would fast at the doorsteps of their offenders. It is a weapon that strikes directly at your transgressor's honour, or lack of it. And it was the weapon Connie's godmother used successfully when she led a hunger strike of almost one hundred women rebels locked up by Free Staters at the end of the Irish Civil War. So there was a real issue when Joe McGinlay stood in judgment of a new generation of IRA and INLA men and women who were being held, not as prisoners of war, or conscience, but as common criminals. And yes, there was only black and white with Connie – she was too old to worry about shades of grey any more.

The Hunger Strikes affected everything and everyone. They consumed and overwhelmed the entire city. For month after month, there were marches, protests, walkouts, stoppages, school closures and riots. Derry was as fearful a place as we had ever known it. My abiding memory is that for two entire years the sky was always dark, either from rain or from the smoke of the city burning. There was a sense of imminent, inevitable disaster hanging over every plan, every conversation and every future. This was embodied in a large billboard, visible over all the Bogside and most of the city, featuring a calendar counting the number of days the seven hunger strikers had fasted, and their growing proximity to death.

***

Connie had managed to get herself on a prison visiting committee in the late 1970s and had written feature pieces for Irish and American papers about the appalling and brutal conditions in Irish jails. The British press, significantly, wouldn't publish them. Even as she lay on her deathbed, she was ringing London editors to shout at them.

As Connie grew more ill, Smith called to the house at De Burgh to visit her and assured her that he and others were doing all they could to stave off the cataclysm. The British officials, he said, were mostly decent and attempting to reach an accommodation but had problems with the new prime minister, Margaret Thatcher, who was keen to show off what Smith termed her 'lady-balls'. The Americans, as we knew from Don Grover, were actively disinterested in what they regarded as an internal British matter. And Grover was a big supporter of Reagan, the new president-elect, which compounded the problem. Connie told Smith to stick with his task and never worry about what the damned Yanks thought.

In mid-December, Smith called to the office, under the pretext of buying advertising, and briefed me that a settlement to the entire prison issues would be announced within the next two days. I relayed that news directly to Connie at home – and she was so relieved that she started to weep.

The next night, just hours after the breakthrough was officially announced, she died, peacefully and happily, at home, with myself, Mary and Little Mill beside her. The photograph of her husband, Johnny Madden, was on the bedside locker where it had been for the past fifty-eight years.

***

The funeral, at St Eugene's Cathedral, featured an embarrassment of self-serving politicians but, in line with Connie's strict orders, not a single photographer. She refused to consider herself a public figure. Her coffin was draped in both the Tricolour and the Stars and Stripes; I don't know who organised that. And the Colmcille Ladies Choir – the best ensemble in the entire world, according to the Clintons – softly sang her home. As the cortège came down the aisle at the end, a group of two dozen eighty-year-old women in purple and white Suffragette sashes filed out of the back two rows of the chapel and formed a guard of honour at the exit. The visiting bishops were clearly taken aback and glowered at the tribute. Which was exactly as Connie would have wanted it. As she always said, the world needs more smart women to stop asking permission.

While we were standing in the cathedral grounds, receiving the mourners and imposters, Paud Devlin pulled me back from the throng and, out of the side of his mouth, told me he wanted to talk to me as soon as possible.

'Politics?' I asked him.

'No. Well, not entirely. It's about Millie – Little Mill. And it's important.'

'Can you do the office tomorrow before opening? I'll be in from eight.'

'No problem. I'll see you then. Say nothing in the meantime.'

**

I haven't talked at all about Little Mill – or Amelia Jane Madden, to use her full name – up to this point, because I've been hoping if I rip the entire bandage off quickly, it won't be so bad.

In my life, I have lost a mother, a wife and a child. And while I know you're not supposed to grade these things, each death hit me very differently. With Connie, I can honestly say she had a long, healthy and fulfilling life, and it was her time – even if it was shorter than I would have liked. I missed her, I mourned her, and at times the loss was overwhelming, but in the end, it was the natural passage of life. With my wife Millie, the pain was wrenching, tearing and destructive – leaving bitterness that took years to shake and a lifetime thinking of what should have been. I never accepted it and I still complain to her every day about it. But with Little Mill, the loss was simply unspeakable. And the only way I manage is to try not to think about it, or her, at all. Even now.

One of the things you never learn until it's far too late is that parents – even the richest, smartest or best meaning of them – can't protect their children from the world. The best you can do is hope to all the gods that they don't make the same mistakes you did. But between all the genetic programming and environmental programming you saddle them with, the odds are stacked against them.

There was nothing I could do about Mill's actual death in 1994 – it wasn't in any way pre-ordained. It was unforeseeable, and I've never blamed myself for that. My guilt stems from the mistakes I made when she was alive. Like in 1980.

CHAPTER 68

I once read a Mary Lavin short story – I wish I could remember the title of it – which had two endings. In one, a son is rushing home to tell his widowed mother he passed his big exam, but as he comes to the house, a chicken runs out onto the road in front of his bike, he brakes to avoid it, falls and is killed. In the second ending, he kills the chicken, enraging his mother, and the two never speak again. So either way, the mother loses the child, and her heart is broken.

The outworking of Paud Devlin's visit to my office always puts me in mind of that story. And my chat with him also, I imagine, was uncomfortably close to the same conversation my own mother had with another revolutionary forty years previously.

Paud was standing outside the office at 7.55am when I arrived to open the shutters. Two men in a car, parked outside the bookies about fifty yards up the hill, were watching his back.

We walked up the stairs to my office in silence and sat down around the desk.

He closed his eyes and looked weary. 'Mill has asked to join up,' he said.

I froze in terror. I didn't care who he was; he wasn't taking my little girl. 'No. No way. Get out. Get out now before I say something I can't take back.'

He ignored me. 'And while she's now twenty-one, and it's not your call, given that we have done a lot of business, I thought it would be sensible to take a sounding from you first. Though, naturally, I'm not telling her about this.'

Mill had turned twenty-one just the previous month. She had only months of her degree at UCD left to finish and had already signed up to become Mo's deputy news-editor at the *Chronicle*.

'I can't just turn her down flat,' he said. 'She'd be a real asset. She's a great speaker, a fierce debater and a first-class writer. She could do a fine job for us, whether in Sinn Féin or elsewhere. And that's before you consider the connections she'd bring with her. All your American friends, for a start.'

I got a sense from his tone that there might be just a little wriggle room, so I kept him talking. 'How did this all come about?'

'She's friendly with a couple of girls whose brothers are in jail. She got herself a visiting pass to see one and couldn't believe how desperate the situation was.'

Mill's stupid big heart, the curse of all the Hannon women – and men. And in this case, I couldn't blame her. 'But does she not understand, that's exactly what she could be looking at twenty-four hours a day if she signs on with you? With all respect to you, and your plans to keep her in politics, you can't help yourselves. She'll be dead or in jail within a year.'

He nodded and looked sad. 'She's ashamed that she's off out of here enjoying a comfortable college education in a free country while men and women the same age as her are filling the jails back at home. She just wants to help out, Seán, and that's no bad thing.'

Paud had four children of his own, and I knew well he was working hard to keep the politics out of his home. There was a big card I needed to play. 'If it were you ...'

'If it were me,' he said, 'I'd probably tell the IRA leadership that if they took my daughter, I would resign my office, then go to the nearest barracks and give away each and every one of them. I shed real tears every time a seventeen-year-old comes in our door. It's not right for us to inflict it on every generation below us. We have to sort it out. It has to end with us. You and I knew some peace in our lives, Seán. We remember what it's like not to be afraid. Our children don't.'

'So, if I threatened to do the same – to blow the whistle on you all, I mean?'

'We wouldn't touch her. We couldn't. We couldn't afford to make an enemy of you. Your paper is the nearest thing we've got to a social conscience for this city – not just for us, but for the other crew as well. I don't like a lot of what you say – you've been propping up Joe McGinlay for far too long – but you allow everybody a right of reply, which is what democracy is about. But we don't take kindly to threats, either. So, officially, we'd blacklist you for a while. Though it won't be as long as you gave my brother Dara for running his dummy raffle ...'

I laughed at that. I'd refused to let Dara in the door of the *Chronicle* for three years, after he'd caught me with his hood-naming scam. I'd given him five, then knocked off two for good behaviour.

'We're not stupid, Seán. We need soldiers, sure – but if we're ever going to have a better society, we also need architects, teachers, nurses, lawyers, bakers, and even journalists. We don't answer every knock on our door.'

'She's going to hate me forever for it.'

'Yes, she is.'

He hesitated. 'And there's one more thing. I need you to return the favour.'

'Name it,' I said. Truthfully, I'd have hidden the IRA's entire arsenal under the kitchen floor of the manse I was that relieved. Though I knew by him he wouldn't put me in that position.

'Don Grover is no help to any of us anymore. You need to find some other way into the American mainstream.'

He was pushing on an open door. But he didn't need to know that. So I pointed him to the clock to let him know we'd better wrap it up and gave him the classic Provo answer. 'Leave it with me.'

CHAPTER 69

1982

The first time I knew that you, Maeve, even existed was from a solicitor. Tommy McGinlay – Tommy Senior, that is, Joe's brother – who worked out in Dunavady, made an appointment to see me at Waterloo Street for a Thursday morning in late November, when we would have 'a bit of time to chat without rushing to a deadline. I figured he wanted me to keep a lid on some of the wheeling-and-dealing his young fella, Tommy Junior, was into. Junior had plans to become a lawyer himself and, as you're aware, eventually became a very useful one and now represents us. But back when he was eighteen or so, he would have sold the eye out of your head and then stuck up a For Rent sign on the socket. Of course, all his stuff was being smuggled either in or out of the North – cigarettes, booze, cheap TVs – and he was acquiring quite a reputation. So, Senior, I believed, was calling in to appeal to my former nature.

The *Chronicle*'s just-recruited news-editor, Gerry Corrigan, from Letterkenny, was in my office for a post-production review when Tommy landed, so I asked him if he minded if the new guy sat in. Mill's departure had forced us to restructure – Saul Doherty, the late Johnny's brother, was recruited as deputy news-ed, we brought in Gerry as news-ed, while Mo shifted out of the bullpen upstairs to become general manager. She was, as she said herself, getting too long in the tooth to be chasing every loud bang in the city – and there were just too many of them.

Tommy shifted uncomfortably in his seat. 'No. I'd rather this was kept to the two of us. No offence, Mr Corrigan.'

Gerry, who as you know went on to become group editor, nodded seriously. 'Of course. How could I argue with the man who knows where Paud Devlin's bodies are buried? Literally.'

It was Tommy's first experience of the big Donegal man's refreshing directness, and he laughed. Gerry closed the door behind him and crossed the big room back to his chair as King of the Bullpen.

Tommy looked at his fingers and then inspected the bottom of his tie. He did anything but look at me. 'This isn't easy,' he said. 'It's about Little Mill.'

I was suddenly frightened. I hadn't heard a single word from Mill for almost two years, ever since she'd packed her bags and left the manse. I knew she was in Dublin and had scored a good subediting job at the *Irish Press*, but only because they rang me – on the quiet – to check if she was my daughter before they hired her. She had already got the job on her own merits, though, needless to say, had never mentioned the connection. She had interviewed under the name of Hannon. But an older head said I bet she's related to Seán, and they decided, out of sheer nosiness, to check.

I knew Mill was still in touch with Mo, but there was a definite pact there that meant I didn't get to hear any of the business. And to be honest, Mo wasn't hearing very much, either. As I was about to learn.

Tommy must have seen my colour change and quickly raised his hands in apology. 'She's okay,' he said. 'She's not dead or sick … and, in other circumstances, this would be great news. She's just had a baby. A healthy little girl.'

***

I didn't hear what Tommy said next or for about the next five minutes. I couldn't process, in any rational way, what I was being told. I was completely overwhelmed. It was by turns the saddest and the happiest moment of my life. There was burning shame that I hadn't been there to help Mill but utter joy at the new life in our family. There was the emptiness that my wife and mother weren't there to see and hear this for themselves, but the hope that I might get to see my daughter again. It was like I was immersed in a fog of sudden guilt and massive love. The solicitor's mouth was still moving but, try as I might, I couldn't register a thing, I was so overcome. And I must have started crying, because all of a sudden, Tommy had broken into the drinks cabinet behind me and was handing me a very large brandy, with a shaky hand, and taking an equally large one for himself.

He clinked my glass, and I could see he was starting to fill up himself. '*Comhghairdeas*, Granda,' he said. 'It's going to be great.'

The newsman inside me couldn't help himself and I recovered enough to ask Tommy a bunch of questions.

'When was she born and what was the weight?

'Monday past, 22 November, seven pounds and four ounces.'

'Has she a name?'

'Maeve – Monday was her feast day – but it's after the queen, not the saint, as you'd expect.'

'Beautiful. Auntie Con's daughter was called Maeve, too. And you say the child is healthy?'

'As a seven-pound-four-ounce trout.'

'Will she let me see her?'

'Absolutely – the baby that is.'

The room went silent.

I was already as embarrassed as I was going to be, so I asked my next question. 'Who's the father?'

He shook his head slowly. 'She won't say. It was a brief affair, and she wants nothing more to do with him. She hasn't told him, and she doesn't want him to know.'

The thick-headed so-and-so – she got that from the Madden side. No doubt about it. 'Did she go through all this on her own? Who knew about this? Did nobody think that maybe we could help?'

'She wasn't on her own – your aunt Mary O'Dorrity and her daughter Katie have been looking after her.'

My cousin Katie had been practising as a GP in Monkstown for the past decade. Mary had moved into a granny-flat in her home the previous year, shortly after her husband Kevin's death.

I was just about to flare up when Tommy cut across me. 'Mill wants you and Mo to be Maeve's guardians …'

I was stunned. 'But she's not even talking to me.'

Tommy nodded. He got up, went back to the cabinet, and lifted out the brandy onto the desk between us. There was no point in pretending any more – it might have only been ten o'clock in the morning, but this bottle was heading for the empty bin.

'She thinks Mo knows more than anyone about rearing children. And she's sure that you won't make the same mistakes you did with her.'

'But why us?'

'In short, it's because she doesn't want the child to have the type of life she would give her. She'd either eke out an existence in poverty as a single mother – because, as you know well, she won't touch your money. Or she'd work double shifts to pay a stranger to babysit her. Most importantly, she wants the child to have a family – and you and Mo are it. And unlike a foster family, or an adoptive family, she will be able to see the child anytime she wants. Which, she says, will be pretty much every weekend. She's going to ask Mo to take the baby down to Dublin so she doesn't have to come up to Derry.'

'Does Mo know about any of this?'

'Not a thing. She's my next stop.'

I drained my glass and poured us two more. 'But why doesn't Mill just come home? She doesn't have to live with us, or even work at the *Chronicle*.'

He shook his head like he didn't agree with what he was about to say next.

'She told me to tell you that, with the best will in the world, you don't realise that your daughter isn't one of those stories that you can cut short or tidy up when you don't like her and then write a happy ending onto. That she's her own person, Seán, and she's not coming back.'

In fairness, Tommy knew well the reason for our original fight and couldn't have been more sympathetic. 'Give her time, Seán – my boy still wants to be Vito Corleone when he grows up. And before I forget, he's just been caught with two suitcases full of smuggled cigarettes in the back of his car. Any chance you could keep it out of the paper?'

I laughed. 'Normally I wouldn't, but I've a soft spot for smugglers,' I said. 'It could happen to the mayor.'

CHAPTER 70

1983

Tommy McGinlay was right. Mill did come back. Except, he and I both underestimated the degree of her stubbornness; she still wanted nothing to do with me.

Initially, though, things looked promising and there were even signs of a rapprochement. Mo was clearly working on Mill during their weekend meet-ups – we had, of course, agreed to all her requests – and in early October 1983, Mill sent me a Get Well Soon card, after I'd been released from Castlereagh Holding Centre. I had been detained for forty-eight hours in the aftermath of the IRA prison escape, after someone informed the constabulary that two of the escapees had stayed in the bunker at the manse, before taking a midnight flit through my fields across the border into Donegal.

The story went worldwide, but it was hokum, of course. I had totally clean hands. Unbeknownst to Don Grover, I had just managed to set up a second back channel into the US State Department. Tip had lined us up with a Democratic senator who had three Irish grandparents. And there was no way I was going to jeopardise the security of the new arrangement by drawing any further attention to myself. After the big escape, there had been a query, yes, if I would accept a houseguest for a few days, but when I explained the situation to Paud Devlin, he said they understood and would make other arrangements.

I'm convinced it was Smith who threw the spotlight onto me by making the call to Special Branch to divert attention away from himself. I later learned that the morning after my arrest, he had gone out for his daily jog across the border to Muff, accompanied by two other runners in ill-fitting tracksuits who did not return into Derry with him – or indeed ever again.

Anyhow, after an outcry led by Joe McGinlay, and the bishop, of all people, I was released to an apology from the assistant chief constable – and the card from Mill.

Inside, it read: 'In town on Thursday for a wedding. Will call into the Castle for a bowl of soup at one o'clock if you're about. Will try and grab The Pit.'

251

During the summer holidays when she had interned at the *Chronicle*, the Castle Bar, which was only across the street from our offices, had been our favourite post-production hangout. The Pit was the Castle's dingy little basement snug, much sought-after by those wanting to meet privately – or smoke dope. Mill, I trusted, was still in the former category.

***

I can still vividly remember my first day at school, my wedding day, and the night before I was going off to fight in Spain. I have met with paramilitaries; I have met with popes and presidents; and I have had to tell dear friends that their loved ones are dead. But I don't remember ever being as nervous about anything in my life as I was meeting Mill again. And with cause.

When I went into the Castle, wearing my very newest suit, shiniest shoes and best tie, and saw she was there in The Pit, I nearly broke my neck on the stairs rushing to get to her.

She looked like a film star, right down to her mother's black Audrey Hepburn hair and flashing green eyes. She was wearing a mint-coloured two-piece trouser suit for the wedding and had a velvet red rose pinned to her lapel.

But the guards were up right away. Before I got near her, she put her hand out to shake mine. As if I were her bank manager. 'No hugs,' she said. 'This is business.'

It was like getting hit by a hammer. She must have seen my face drop so she took my arm in a kinder way and bade me sit down.

'I didn't mean to be abrupt,' she said. 'I'm just a bit edgy. How was jail?'

Might as well be honest. 'Better than this,' I said.

And, to be fair to her, she laughed.

There was never any side with her – it was straight to the main course. 'I'm thinking of moving back to Derry.'

'That's great news. When?'

'After Christmas. I've had a job offer. A good one. More money, and I'll be closer to Maeve …'

My poker face must have crumbled again, because she was straight in with another apology. 'No, no. Stop worrying. I still want you and Mo to be her guardians. She needs a family – not a working, single mother. But I'd like to take the gate lodge so I'm near her. Or with her.'

It was perfect. The gate lodge had been empty since Mo had moved back into the manse to help with Maeve the previous year. It would be great to have Little Mill so close.

'No problem, Mill, whatever you need. What's the job, then?'

I could see her take a deep breath. She was really nervous. 'The *Leader* is launching a new free sheet in January. Coming out Thursdays. They've asked me to edit it.'

I was astounded. I had plans to make her a real editor of a real paper and the opposition had stolen her to cobble together a lousy chip-wrapper? 'You're kidding?'

She shook her head. 'EF Cunningham got a hold of my number at the *Irish Press* and made me the offer about three weeks ago.'

I could barely speak. None of us had ever made any secret of the fact that you, Maeve, were Mill's child. And EF knew, like the rest of the town, that Mill was very angry with her old man. But it was a dirty, low thing he did to take her back from Dublin to rub my nose in it.

'It'll be a cross-community paper,' said Mill. 'A genuine one this time. No politics at all. The *Leader* is hoping to tap new advertising markets.'

Of course they were. We had been doing exactly the same thing for two years now, with our free Saturday edition, the *Chronicle Catch-Up*. The *Leader's* new paper would not only target that by coming out two days earlier, but it would also have a serious impact on the ad take of the Thursday *Chronicle*. And while they would never compete editorially with us on a Thursday, they would cannibalise stories from everywhere to fill their pages – making us all look hackneyed. And they would spend every waking moment trying to anticipate our Thursday lead story so they could stick a spoiler on the front to show us up.

And Mill had leapt like an idiot right into the middle of EF's twisted game.

As I looked at her, challenging me, my blood started to rise and I found it hard to keep my voice down. 'Why are you doing this? Do you not know you're going to cut our throats?'

It was like she had been given a mantra to learn. 'The *Chronicle's* become very sectarian in recent years. It's very pro-Church and pro Joe McGinlay. You've got old, Dad, and the paper's got old along with you. Derry needs a vibrant new paper – something young and hopeful, not full of dark politics and dirty deeds. And if I do a good job at the new paper, the *Leader* will be mine for the taking when EF retires.'

I would have gotten onto my knees if it had helped. 'Please listen to me,' I said. 'That man is using you – and he'll discard you the second you're of no further use to him. He is the most devious, evil person I have ever met. You're going nowhere at the *Leader*. Not ever. The paper will pass straight to EF's son David's hands as soon as he's twenty-one. It's the way it's done – it's been run by seven generations of Cunninghams. Do you really think they're going to hand it to the child of a Boston Catholic – and a woman, to boot?'

She looked down at her patent-leather shoes, trying to mask her defiance. Mill had no poker face, either. In that moment, I realised instinctively she didn't care a whit about the job, it was about her showing me once and for all that she didn't need me – and she was letting the rest of the world know it, too.

I flashed her a fierce look and lowered my voice to its iciest level. 'Come back to Derry surely, Amelia,' I said. 'Live in my gate lodge, work for the Cunninghams, take the bread out of my mouth and, all the while, I'll look after your child. And when you're done, why don't you just go across the street and set fire to our offices and be done with it.'

I could see her green eyes go pale with fear. But I wasn't finished. 'You think this is because I wronged you? Well, there comes a point in life, princess, when you have to stop blaming other people for what's happened to you – and take account of the damage you're doing to others. Because, no matter what I ever did to you – and for right or wrong, I always tried to act in your best interests – it is now you, and you alone, who are wrecking this family. You are the one who is controlling all this. Not me.'

But it was too savage, and I could see her eyes start to bulge. Her hands were shaking and her voice was almost a whisper.

'I know, Dad,' she said. 'You're right. It is all my fault. And I'm so, so sorry it has to be this way. I really am. And I still love you dearly. But I have to do this.'

'I love you, too, Mill,' I said. 'But if you do this, you're going to cause damage that could last generations.'

'It's too late,' she said. 'I'm afraid it's done already.'

CHAPTER 71

1987

Don Grover had worked for more than twenty years in intelligence in Ireland. And he had been a very smart guy to begin with. So when my name came up in a Federal investigation in Boston, in relation to an intercepted IRA arms shipment, he didn't stop for traffic lights. He burst into my office, banging the door so hard behind him that splinters flew out of the frame.

I had been expecting this fight, or one like it, for a couple of years now. I was giving Don nothing or next to nothing to report back as long as Reagan was in office. It was pointless even trying to start a discussion, let alone shape policy, given the gung-ho partnership the Brits had struck up with the US under Thatcher. So instead, I negotiated quietly with my senator, who sat on the House Committee for Foreign Affairs, and fed my comments in there.

Unfortunately, the senator was a bit of a Johnny-Kiss-All-The-Girls and wasn't content with what he was getting from me. And like a total mug, and despite all warnings, he had opened up his own direct pipeline to the IRA. Don't get me wrong, he meant well. But back then, the IRA was leaking like a busted toilet and, sure enough, a particularly nasty British security department heard what he was doing, and my honourable friend was flushed out onto the floor.

It was so simply, and beautifully done, too. The senator had holidayed in Connemara three times in the mid-eighties, in a remote hamlet on the coast – many miles from the tourist trail. The spot – it wouldn't have qualified as a village, just half a dozen houses and a pub-slash-store – had a tiny harbour sheltering a little pier from the wild Atlantic. And it was at this pier that an IRA unit from South Mayo was arrested meeting a fishing trawler that contained more weaponry than Iraq. And while Senator Pollyanna couldn't be directly connected to the smuggling, the fact that this was his favourite holiday destination, and that he had known links to Irish republicans, was enough to get him his ass handed back to him by every single British tabloid and a whole bunch in the US as well. The senator, even in those pre-cellphone days, couldn't deny having met with the IRA directly, just in case someone leaked a picture or a tape. The Brits, of course, had arranged with their man inside the operation to direct the IRA boat to its stopping point.

Most of this – though not the Brit involvement – was already public knowledge. But what Don had just found out from the Boston inquiry was that the first time the senator visited Galway, in 1984, it was one Seán Madden, publisher, who had found and booked the holiday cottage on his behalf.

Grover didn't need a map to work out what had gone on and, while he knew well we had no part in the smuggling ring, he also knew he had been played. He was so angry he refused my seat. 'I'm going to ruin your life, you bastard. They're sending me to Finland – to a consulate in the middle of nowhere. Forty-three years old and I'm washed up. But you wait – because I am going to make you pay.'

I let him blow off his steam for a minute so I could better catch my own breath. As you get older, you tend to worry less when people shout and roar at you. At least they're telling you what's on their minds. I fret a lot more when people say nothing – because those are invariably the guys who go off, think hard about things and get all their proofs together. Guys like the Kennedys, who don't get mad – just even. They then send you a solicitor's letter for fifty grand, which, if you're smart, you'll pay immediately, because you know it's only going to cost you another fifty on top to fight it and lose.

But despite his healthy venting, Don, as I've mentioned before, was either a borderline psychopath or a full-on sociopath, so I had to be very careful. He was also more than twenty years younger than me and carried a gun.

'You stopped being of any use here after President Carter left, Don. And you were never going to be anybody's friend again by backing Reagan. You're better off out of here. You actually got about six years more than you should have.'

His preppy face was red with rage. 'You strung me along and opened another route. How do you think that makes me look?'

'I warned you repeatedly, Don. You just didn't hear me. You weren't contributing. You were blocking. And you're not going to take me on, Don. And you know full well why.'

That pulled him up short. 'You've got nothing on me.'

I shook my head. 'Of course I do. I run a newspaper, several of them. I've got something on everyone – right up to the pope. It's how we stay in business.'

'You have nothing.'

'I do, Don. And let me tell you straight up, your employers might forgive the drinking, the cards, and the three children to three different women. They'll probably even forgive the fact that you've been taking money hand over fist from local businesses here to drop their names into industry and tourism briefings. But what they won't forgive is the political data you missed, time and time again. I have a list a mile long of what you could have done, or prevented, if you'd just engaged a little more. Might even have stopped Brighton if you'd had the manners to hear a few people out. Same goes with the connections you could have and should have made. All lost because you followed a party line. And those connections are all now with the senator, no matter how badly burned he is. And yes, I know precisely how much stuff he has, and just how important it is. And yes, it all went through me.'

He leaned over the desk, so close I could smell the sour odour of last night's bourbon on his breath. 'I will expose you, you Judas, and see how clever you are then. I'm going to get your passport pulled for a start. State is furious with you.'

'Do what you want, Don; I'm sixty-five next week. And I could do with a break from all this nonsense. Except, even if you do expose me, nobody here is going to care. An Irish-American publisher working with everybody to try and stop a long war? Who gives a damn about that? The worst they're going to say is that I'm an old fool. And by the way, you can have your passport. With Reagan in power, I'm much safer travelling on the Irish one anyway.'

He had nothing and he knew it. 'The Provos won't like that their pipeline has been blown. They'll blame you.'

'Wouldn't surprise me at all – the Provos blame me every time it rains. I get twenty letters a week from their Comms Department on everything from not enough coverage of their rallies to too much flesh in Madonna's new video.'

I was dishing it back to Don in spades, but the truth is, I felt like a bit of a heel. He had tried hard and taken real risks when the climate was right. But over the years, he had gotten too embedded and too comfortable.

I threw him a bone. 'If you leave my office now, Don, and don't say another word, I'll make a call for you. An important one. We'll sort you out a better posting. Back home. You provided a good service here for a long time, and I appreciate that. We owe you our gratitude. And it's not your fault I double-guessed you. It was political. Seriously. But not another word out of your mouth.'

Don's greatest strength was that he always had the ability to compute his options in microseconds and make the best choice, even if he hated it. He cast me a look of pure, seething hatred, nodded once and left the room silently. I never saw him again.

CHAPTER 72

My sixty-fifth birthday the following week was one of the happiest occasions in my life. I had postponed my intended retirement from the *Chronicle*, as I still wanted to keep my feet wet, so instead, with Mo's backing, I had appointed Gerry Corrigan as overall group editor, to let me concentrate on the Derry paper alone. This was a huge weight off me, as we now had seven satellite newspapers and were trying to start a legitimate radio station. Gerry was as gifted a writer and as laid back a manager as I ever met and was the only nomination for the job, even if his entire concept of fashion started and ended with sweater vests.

Mill's paper, meanwhile, the *Leader Late*, had been causing us serious headaches. She had no budget, no news staff and a remit to avoid all politics, but she had been producing first-class papers week in, week out for more than three years, and the *Late* was now an established institution in its own right. So Gerry's first priority was to try and find a way to strangle the growing child before it garrotted us.

But the day before my birthday, Mill called up to the manse and asked if she could have five minutes with me.

We had been on civil terms since her return; business-like about Maeve, and polite and respectful about family matters – Mary's funeral in late 1986, and the like. But there had been no closeness or kinship – no Sunday dinners or Christmas presents or the like – and to be honest, it was as much from my part as from hers. There's a Derry word 'thran', meaning extremely stubborn – Seamus Heaney was once asked to define it and cited the example of a constipated old neighbour who warned his wife: 'I'll take the syrup-of-figs, but I'll not shite'. And sadly, Mill and I were both as thran as you can get.

As soon as she sat down in my little study, I knew something had changed. The uptight professional had gone, her face was relaxed, at ease and familial. It was as if the clock had gone back to 1980. She took the homemade whiskey I offered her, necked back a healthy mouthful and smiled as open a smile as I'd seen in seven years. 'I'm leaving the *Leader*,' she said.

CHAPTER 73

If I'm to be completely honest, there is nothing I enjoy more in this world than being told I'm right. Whether it's the junior reporter admitting that he didn't actually double-source the story as I warned him, or the assemblyman conceding that he should never have had that last drink with a prostitute, that feeling of sweet vindication never gets old. But in this case, far too much time had passed; there was no victory, only two losers. And the last thing I needed was to be wearing my gloating face. So I horsed back a swift mouthful of Madam Bush's famous barley juice to suppress any involuntary expression of satisfaction.

'You were right,' she said. 'About almost everything. Not about how you did things – you should have talked to me first – but about everything else, you were right.'

I could see from her eyes that Mill was getting ready to laugh at my failing efforts to kill my delight. 'Go on,' she said. 'You're allowed to smile.'

Instead, I just hugged her. 'So what happened?'

'It was never the right fit. But a few days ago, EF let slip that David is going to start as news-ed at the *Leader* after he graduates. He'd told me again and again that he would be moving me up from the *Late* very soon so I could take over whenever he retires. But, as you say, blood trumps talent every time.'

'What's he like? David, I mean.' Never miss a chance to get your eyes on the opposition.

'Young, bright, open-minded – nothing like his father, who, as you warned me, is a twisted, dark mess. Will do a very good job for them if he's given the chance. He's interned with me for the past few summers and is going to be a great reporter. I bear him no ill will at all. He's spent four years at college in London so he can see beyond the parochial view. Might even build a few bridges. Will find it rough going in Orange circles, though, as ... well ... he has no discernible interest in getting married.'

'Like Great-Uncle Irvine?'

'Precisely.'

Irvine Cunningham's one true love had died beside him on a French battlefield. So, shortly after Connie moved back to Derry in 1923, he became her official escort. It was an arrangement that worked beautifully for both of them for more than fifty years.

'Have you told EF that you're leaving yet?'

She grinned. 'I'm not a novice. I want to find out what my offers are first.'

Mill could have had any job she wanted. I would have given her mine – or even taken Gerry's back from him. But she was too fair-minded for that. So I told her what she already knew. 'We're going to have a vacancy for news-ed at the *Chronicle* now Gerry's moving on up. Lot of talent interested in the job, though – I've had calls from some serious hitters from all over the country … Good thing you remembered that quote about blood trumping talent. You might have a chance.'

'What's the money like?'

'Pretty good for a local paper. Plus you get free accommodation, childcare and transport.'

'Opportunities?'

'In five years or so? My job. With all the recent restructuring, I promised Gerry and Mo that I'd stay on until I'm seventy. After that, group editor or chairman. Take your pick. You'll hold the vast bulk of the shares when I kick it – so you'll be in the driving seat anyway.'

'When should I start?'

'Is tomorrow too soon? Or I could get Tommy to knock me up a contract tonight if you'd prefer.'

We both knew that EF would run her out the door as soon as she handed in her notice. He couldn't take the chance that she might learn something – anything – she could take with her.

She nodded. 'I'll come in on Monday. How will the staff take it, when I … I mean, if I come in as news-ed?'

'There'll be no problems, I assure you. The whole town knows how well you've done with that cheap little man's cheap little paper, and they respect the hell out of you for it. Saul Doherty may pout for five minutes. He was next in line. But he's very fair-minded, just like his eldest brother Johnny was, God rest him. So there'll not be an issue. And he knows I'll look after him long-term.'

'Saul? Wouldn't he be a little bit young for news-ed anyway?'

'Not really; he's twenty-six, just a year younger than you. Got a very good degree in English from Trinity. A great reporter, like Johnny was. Does the pub bit, too – three or four nights a week. But, unlike Johnny – or more likely because of him – he doesn't drink.'

'Now, there's a rarity.'

'Yeah, but he's right. It's not like before. Nowadays, there are too many people out there who think if they buy you a drink they own you. Much better to drink water, listen carefully and own them instead.'

She laughed at that and punched my arm. 'You're a bad article, Pops.'

It was so lovely to hear her call me that again. I was on the point of tearing up so took another massive mouthful of whiskey to cover me. I had been 'Seán' since she'd returned from Dublin.

But I had to ask her and there was no better time. 'I don't mean to pry, Mill, but why did it take so long? All of this, I mean. I'm old and stubborn, and can't be turned when my mind's made up – particularly when I'm in the wrong. And I know this was mostly my fault. But you, you were always like your mother. You knew I was a crank and you forgave me anyway. That was our thing. What happened this time?'

She stiffened momentarily, lowered her glass onto the coffee table and nodded sadly. 'I was afraid, Pops, I was afraid that I had let you down, and after that it was that I was afraid I was continuing to let you down. I know it wasn't rational, but for years, there, everything I did was to try to prove you wrong – and prove to myself that I didn't need you or your approval.'

She was lying through her teeth, but she was selling it well. She wasn't quite looking at me but rather at my ear – a trick I'd taught her myself for when you're having difficulty staring someone directly in the eye. Something else was going on here – something big – but she wasn't ready to tell me yet. Which was fine. Every secret has its season. I had her back in my life and, for now, that was all that was important.

⁎

After about another half-hour catching up, Mo rapped on the study door to announce that she'd got us some fish and chips, if we wanted to eat them out on the patio with Maeve. This was less a request and more of a command, as Maeve was still at the age where she loved picnics.

I mumbled something about midges and was about to start protesting that the kitchen was cleaner and warmer when Mill shook her head and took my arm. 'Behave yourself for once and come outside.'

So I did. But outside, there were no chips. Instead, there on the driveway were the eighty or so members of the *Chronicle* staff, from Limavady to Sligo, congregated under a banner, strewn between two cherry trees, which read 'Gotcha'. And after the cheering and singing stopped, I looked behind them, and what I saw made a superb occasion perfect – a sixteen-berth motorboat, with a massive antenna at the back.

I walked down the steps, shook every hand I could, pretending to be mad that they had hoodwinked me. And maybe it wasn't total pretence. I was supposed to be the director of intelligence after all, and they had all conspired to make a complete monkey out of me.

The boat must have cost the guts of £100,000, but I knew immediately that Mo had done a deal to purchase it as a business expense – the aerial gave it away. The *SS Bank On It* wasn't just for fishing and drinking beer on. Radio North West would be broadcasting from Lough Foyle within weeks – slipping quietly from shore to shore, from the Northern jurisdiction to the Southern one, depending on which licensing authority was trying to track us that particular month.

It wasn't that what we were proposing to do was illegal – and, as you're aware, we got our full licence in 1992 – rather that it wasn't fully legal back then. I can't remember the various loopholes Joe used to keep us out of the courts. In real terms, it meant that we were tolerated up to the point that we annoyed someone, then we'd be closed down. Except now we could just hit the high water instead. We had tried various pilot projects already, including one earlier in the year where we set up two separate studios: one in my bunker, the other in Mo's parents' barn over the border. But they were both too static, and a co-ordinated pincer movement would put us right out of business. And besides, they just didn't have the romance of the open seas.

When I climbed on board, I saw that in place of the eight-berth master bedroom, they had already installed a state-of-the-art studio. And there was a little editing cubicle to the rear of this with 'Seán's Room' on the door.

Gerry Corrigan then handed me a rectangular package, which he said was from the senior staff. I opened it to find an ornately-framed certificate at the top of which were written the words 'Royal Pardon'.

'What on earth is this?' I asked him.

'It's for your little office there.'

'Yes. But what is it?'

'Well, you know the way you're always complaining that the cops set you up for that smuggling charge after the war?'

'The one I was fined five hundred pounds for?'

He laughed at me cutting straight to the money. 'The very same. Well, the *Irish News* happened to report about a month ago that a batch of smuggling convictions dating back to the 1950s had been overturned because of collusion between the police and Customs. When the Customs couldn't get the guys they wanted, they worked with the cops to fit them up. Anyhow, Tommy McGinlay rang the Investigation Team and presented evidence on your behalf – that you couldn't have had the *poitín* in your van, as you were supposed to be picking up a consignment of butter and chocolate. And that you'd been framed by the late Constable Mousey Lynch, who, incidentally, is one of the names mentioned all over the place in the dirty 1950s' cases.'

'So I've been exonerated?'

'You have indeed – the charge has been stricken from your record. From this day forth, you are no longer a master criminal.'

I was thrilled, and I just wished Connie had been alive to see it. She'd have busted the certificate over my head, brass frame and all. But there was one thing I wanted to check.

'Did you get my five hundred quid back?'

'No.'

CHAPTER 74

1990

By the end of the Troubles, the various British security services were running so many different factions here that they might as well have been playing an internal chess game with the Six Counties as their board. A few years ago, a visiting agent momentarily dropped his cover as a business investor to tell me that by 1994, there were forty different computer systems monitoring intelligence data on the North. And back in 1990, there wasn't a week would go by that the *Chronicle* wasn't reporting on how one agency or another had either infiltrated, or attempted to infiltrate, civic society here. FRU, Special Branch, MI5, MI6, MRF, 14 Intel, GCHQ – pick a cypher.

It got so that during our pre-production planning sessions we would automatically set aside a page on the mark-up sheets for 'Touting and Scouting' – and some days we needed four. As I told every cub reporter who started with the *Chronicle*, there are two golden rules in journalism: Rule Number One, trust no-one; and Rule Number Two, in case of emergency, refer to Rule Number One.

The guy that arrived at Waterloo Street in early December 1990 was a class apart, however. I knew intuitively that one word from him and all the other tape recorders could be switched off. He was in his early forties, about six-five, overweight, balding and had a shy, hapless smile that seemed to be apologising for his existence. He was decked out like a Savile Row dummy but had left a shirttail poking out at the side of his pants to convince you he was only a yokel dressing up for the occasion. He was perfect – the type of person the average sucker would completely underestimate. For all that, he couldn't hide his natural authority, that of someone who was always the most important man in the room. While he looked nothing like him, he immediately put me in mind of our old friend Julius, who had long since retired to the life of a gentleman don at Oxbridge.

As the new guy took a seat in the little office, he produced what he claimed was a letter of introduction from his employer, which I refused.

'I know who you are,' I told him. 'You're a friend of Smith's, aren't you?'

He nodded.

'So what does Smith call you? I have no interest in whatever name you're going to give me here.'

When the guy spoke it was straight out of Whitehall, though with the faintest hint of a Scottish burr. 'The cheeky bugger calls me Octavius.'

He actually blushed.

I laughed. 'Excellent. The man who followed Julius – the emperor's adopted son. So what has you here?'

His face was quickly serious again. 'It's very simple,' he said. 'With the Iron Lady's departure last month, we might have a chance to make some progress.'

I smiled at that and wondered if he had seen our previous week's photo-spread on the ding-dong-the-witch-is-dead celebrations at Free Derry Corner. Thatcher had never understood that simply labelling a city British and then expecting it to behave as such was about as much use as labelling a loaded pistol a feather duster and expecting it not to blow your head off. She was hated here, not just as a figurehead but also on a personal level for her reckless dismissiveness towards the ten dead hunger strikers. Octavius was right, though: her sacking did open up real possibilities.

'This is all very interesting,' I told him. 'Why here, though? What are you doing in Derry? Why not Belfast?'

He knew I was testing him, so he pretended to think for a second before answering. His answer, as you would expect, was precise and to the point. 'Firstly, it's because most of the main players are here. Or rather those players that we can – and need to – do business with, at least. There's also the infrastructure for talks here dating back to the seventies. And, importantly, Derry is safer and a lot more relaxed than east of the Bann. You can't have the same open-ended conversations in Belfast. There's too much fear there – everyone is too fixed and fixated. There's about a dozen separate communities in Belfast alone, and none of them play well together. Everybody comes in with his own one-line agenda. But in Derry, even the Unionist and Nationalist communities pull together. Possibly it's because you have a common enemy in Belfast, which, you all insist, has been screwing you royally for so long. Or perhaps it's because of the work done by Joe McGinlay and others in promoting peace and partnership. Derry's decision to share the mayoralty between the communities, for example, has confounded the rest of not just Northern Ireland but these islands. Your war is over here – it's time to show the rest of us how you did it.'

He was laying it on thick, way too thick, so I cut him short. 'You're here because you need Paud Devlin, Harry Hurley, Joe McGinlay and Smith,' I said.

He grinned. 'In a nutshell,' he said. 'Very well put. I'll save that one for again.'

I had to ask him the one big question. To establish he was serious. 'Are you going to talk directly to the IRA?'

The two sides hadn't spoken in fifteen years and, from what Smith had told me, there was very little chatter on his back channel either.

'I couldn't comment on that,' he said. 'Way above my paygrade. But anything's possible.'

I was astounded. This was spy-code for 'we've started already'.

I ordered in a couple of cuppas from the bullpen via my fancy new intercom. As I did so, I said a silent prayer they wouldn't send in the Charles and Diana wedding china that Mo had got me as a gag Christmas present. But, of course, they did.

Octavius smiled at his cup then lifted it in a toast. Using perfect Irish, he said: '*Go mbeidh muid uilig beo ag an am seo arís.* May we all be still alive this time next year.'

I made a mental note to warn Paud Devlin not to get too clever during any talks.

'So what do you need me for?' I asked. 'The last thing you want at your private meetings is a newspaper man in the room. We can't help ourselves. Our job is to broadcast the news and serve the public interest. I hope it isn't the American end of things you need help with? Because I have to tell you, I screwed that up pretty badly before.'

He smiled. 'Actually, you didn't. And you know damn well you didn't. You screwed it up so perfectly that there's now a direct channel in place – so perfectly, in fact, that you're not required anymore.'

After Don Grover had departed for a not-too-terrible job in Washington, the State Department had sent another guy to Derry. He was posing as a computer analyst somewhere, installing systems all over the place that he could then monitor, but he was leaving me well alone. However, the real work was now being done directly between Joe McGinlay and the Democrats on Capitol Hill. All of which pleased me greatly – after all, the ultimate goal of a broker is to be redundant.

'You could still be very useful if the Democrats take the White House again next year,' said Octavius. 'They're talking in terms of a special envoy – and they'll need a local, like yourself, to help them read the greens at the start.'

'No problem there,' I said. I just loved the subtlety of his flattery – you're the only man we know that can help the new president, Mr Madden, and your eyes are so pretty.

It was time Octavius got to the main course, so I pointed to the old grandfather clock in the corner – the one that hasn't worked since Connie's time – to hurry him along a bit. 'What else are you looking for?' I asked.

He nodded again. 'Your discretion – or at least as much as you can afford to give us, before you might compromise yourself.'

'I don't follow you,' I said. 'I'm only a simple layman.' This was a lie, of course, but as Connie always said, as long as you don't write it down, it's not a sin.

'There is nothing simple about you, Seán,' Octavius said. 'But I'll explain to you regardless. We're not asking you to ignore the news. If for example one of your readers spots a couple of players who wouldn't normally be seen together, leaving a house together and rings it into you – that's a news story. And you're entitled to report on it. More than entitled – duty-bound, I would say. Likewise, if word eventually breaks legitimately about these putative talks, then naturally you will want to inform your readers about them. But what I would very much like for you to do is to stop flying kites.'

'What sort of kites?'

'We don't need newspapers, particularly those read by the intelligent classes, to be printing stories that are going to distract our players from the work. Your paper, like others, can occasionally allow itself to be used to carry ill-informed gossip, which leads to complications and strife. Like who is splitting from whom over which particular issues. The hardliners are going to step up the war if IRA decommissioning is on the table, says our source in the pub. Or, the Brits are going to expose Joe McGinlay's radical past unless he does their dirty work for them and delivers a four-county settlement – that sort of nonsense. I think you even carried a story last week to the effect that the Northern Ireland Office was going to re-introduce internment.'

I was a little embarrassed about that, but a page-lead had been spiked by the lawyers at the last minute, and the devil was driving. I nodded my apologies. But Octavius wasn't finished.

'As you're aware, according to the broader press at the moment, there are about twenty different sets of talks going on – all urgent and all vital. The Irish are talking to the Belfast priests; Sinn Féin are talking to the SDLP; the UUP are talking to Irish-Americans; Protestant clergymen are talking to former IRA men; and victims are talking to survivors. Everybody claims to be talking to everybody else. But while all of this is very worthy, and I mean this with absolute respect, none of it is urgent and none of it is vital. So I beg you, be very careful not to confuse any of it for what's going on in Derry. What is happening here are the only talks that matter. These are the talks which are being conducted by the British Government and the IRA and which are going to end the war between the British Government and the IRA. So trust me on that – and please don't balls them up.'

He'd obviously been well briefed by Smith. The *Chronicle*, I had to confess, had been caught several times with 'fliers' – stories about talks, splits and fights – which stood little scrutiny under the cold eye of time. These stories had invariably been fed to our hungry and competitive reporters by mischief-making wannabes pursuing their own agenda.

'But in the absence of proper news, we are always liable to make mistakes,' I told Octavius.

He knew well what I was saying to him and smiled again.

'If you manage to help us keep a lid on things, Mr Madden, you will get full access – or as full as we can manage – when the time is right. I would imagine that, while he's not involved in the day-to-day negotiations, Mr McGinlay will be our guarantor when all is agreed. I believe he will also be the public face of the process – and, as you know, his byword is keeping all his politics, and hence his media comment, local. In other words, you will get first go at any story.'

I rolled my eyes. 'Live horse and you'll get hay.'

He looked baffled. 'I, I, I don't follow …'

Typical Englishman, he'd learned the language but never the idiom. 'It's an Irish proverb. It means if you behave yourself and keep your head down, you'll get your reward. But it's only ever used in the ironic sense. As in, that's never going to happen.'

He tried to look offended but couldn't quite pull it off. He knew he couldn't make any promises. So he motored on with his task. 'And the final thing we need from you is for you to stay on in your role as editor until our task is over – it shouldn't be more than a couple of years. We genuinely need the stability – we don't want or need a change of tone.'

He had some neck. 'Listen, Octavius, I've promised my daughter I'll be out of here the second I turn seventy, in about twenty months' time. And if you can wrap up eight hundred years of war in that time, you shouldn't be here at all, you should be out at Lourdes working miracles. I'll go, Octavius, when I decide – not when you tell me.'

He looked hurt. 'What about the other? About the talks.'

I let him off the hook. He needed something to report back – and I, naturally, needed his inside track, too. 'Yes,' I told him, 'the *Chronicle* will steer a careful and responsible path, as it always tries to. But it would help matters enormously if you would give me a direct line for yourself. I can see by the bulge in your coat you are carrying a portable telephone? Or perhaps you've been foolish enough to carry a semi-automatic pistol into my office?'

He laughed. 'Yes,' he said, 'it's a mobile phone. Just like the one you have.'

'Well I'm going to need the number so that, from time to time, I can check my facts with you – if only to make sure that I don't get caught out with any more fliers. And you are going to contact me, let's say, at least once a fortnight to ensure that my editorial speculation is fully and wisely informed – and perhaps guide me about how things, all things in general, that is, could be better progressed. I will never refuse your call and you will never refuse mine. But if you at any stage attempt to use your position to elicit any information, data or gossip from me or any member of my staff, this deal is off, and I will blow the whistle on you, your friends and what you are doing. How does that sound?'

He smiled again. 'It sounds exactly like what I came here for.'

CHAPTER 75

1993

We never found out for sure who was behind the arson attack on the Waterloo Street offices in the autumn of 1993, but we didn't need a roadmap to know it was one of the British outfits.

The *Chronicle*'s relationship with Octavius had been rocky at best since 1992, after we caught him giving a full briefing to a British journalist about the ongoing secret talks in Derry. The reporter, in fairness, had been warned to sit on the story until the time was right – that is, after the *Chronicle* had gone with it. And he was prepared to abide by that. Then his editor sucked down too heavily on the free booze one night at a press dinner in Dublin and thought he would show the so-called Derry oracle, me, how much more he knew than I did. But I am a man who knows better than to drink at these events and said nothing. However, I cottoned on immediately as to exactly who had been talking out of school. I had worked with them for too long.

As you know, this was far too sensitive a story for a London paper to be holding – it needed to be run from Ireland, otherwise it would have felt like the talks were being led or, worse again, imposed from the outside. So when, a short time later, Sinn Féin discovered that one of their junior managers was in the pay of the British, I decided to use it to hit Octavius a good slap on the front page. In October 1992, we exposed the tout and, without giving anything else away, loudly editorialised about British bad faith at this crucial juncture in what we were now calling the 'peace process'.

A month later, after five years of hearings, we were due our final meeting with the authorities in London to agree the new licence for Radio North West. We were assured it was a formality and had a crate of champagne ready to pop on board the *SS Bank On It* as soon as we got the nod. Then, just as I was packing a small case for the flight, Octavius rang me on my mobile to say there had been a 'small glitch'.

'I'm terribly sorry,' he said. 'The radio people have been in touch with the Northern Ireland Office to say that there are some minor inaccuracies in your paperwork – directors' addresses, that sort of thing. Nothing major, I assure you – should only take a few months to fix. Six maximum. But they can't take a chance of approving it as it stands, just in case of challenges to their decision, you understand, at this crucial juncture in the peace process.'

We'd known they were going to strike us back. But this was mean, even by their standards. We shouldn't have been surprised. An old IRA man told me once that, if you can imagine it, if you can dream it, if you can even conceptualise it in any way, then British intelligence have already done it in Ireland.

Our radio station was starting to make a serious impact on the advertising market – indeed, it's still our only media outlet that hasn't been affected by the internet, even today. And back then, full legitimacy was going to allow us to treble our efforts and, we reckoned, our income.

I was incensed. Our plan had been to set up shop in Derry, a few doors up on Waterloo Street. But there was nothing to stop us constituting ourselves in the South and then broadcasting on both sides of the border. So on a whim, I rang our new connection in Dublin, Arnie O'Reilly, and told him that it was about time he started sticking up for his own people against the Saxon foe.

Arnie was a greasy-haired redneck in a sharkskin coat who, if he hadn't been a political operator, would have been selling used cars from somewhere along the side of the Galway to Dublin Road. He was a charlatan, a conman and a guy I would never, ever play cards with. But there's another Irish proverb: 'Aithníonn ciaróg ciaróg eile' – which literally means 'a beetle recognises another beetle'. Though it can also mean 'you can't bullshit a bullshitter'. And in the entire time Arnie was doing business with the British, he was never bested in negotiations.

Arnie was looking for friends in Derry at that time – and an occasional out-of-the-road bed to stay in. And I'd previously mentioned that the bunker might be available if he ever needed it.

'I have to be up Nort' for a couple of nights next week,' he said. 'Okay if I crash wit' you?'

'No problem,' I told him. 'What about our radio station?'

'Leave it wit' me.'

Exactly one week later, while Arnie was staying at the manse, the Irish Government announced it had decided to grant interim licences to four regional radio stations, one in each province – and that Radio North West would provide the service for Ulster. Arnie told me he could possibly have arranged it sooner, but this way I got to buy him dinner in Kealey's world-famous fish restaurant in Greencastle.

The Brits felt they'd made their point and lifted their veto a month later. But we had already committed to Ballybofey by then, and the main offices are still there today.

***

270

While Octavius was a master at playing two sides against the middle, we did not for a second believe he would allow the peace-talks story to break in Britain. So when it did, that October 1993, he was as angry as we were. Well, possibly, not quite. We had been holding our silence for three years and on the final stretch had been gazumped by a Billy-nobody. And, as far as we were concerned, it was all Octavius's fault. He had no business carrying the story outside the tent in the first place.

As you would expect, we struck back through our pages with all our inside track into what had been going on, including biographies of all the players, minutiae about the arrangements, and, to Octavius's great surprise, photographs we had taken surreptitiously of himself and the rest of the British team. And no, it wasn't our proudest hour.

Unfortunately, as can happen, our fit of pique wound up costing Octavius his posting to Ireland and, indeed, what he euphemistically used to call 'his career in the civil service'. He was gone within the week. But by that stage, the provenance of the talks had been established, and the public hysteria of the British establishment having had direct face-to-face contact with terrorists had subsided. Moreover, it had become apparent to all that shuttle mediation was increasingly redundant and that real progress was best made when all the right people were in the same room together, without the need for brokers.

Not that Octavius saw it that way, though. When he rang me to say goodbye, he was icier than I'd ever heard him before. And three nights after his departure, two masked men removed the shutters outside the *Chronicle* offices, using military bolt-cutters, and threw two petrol bombs through the front-office window.

Damage was superficial – glass, paintwork and furniture, nothing structural – and we had a new security system in place by the weekend. As is the way of these things, we had enough suspects to fill Brandywell Stadium and Celtic Park besides. So initially, we took it on the chin.

Then out of the blue, EF Cunningham rang Mill to ask if she'd like to comment on a story he was running the next day in the *Leader*. Security sources – whom they naturally couldn't name – were claiming that a never-before-heard-of loyalist unit had targeted the *Chronicle* because of, quote, 'the newspaper's relentless pursuit of an anti-British agenda'. Asked if the perpetrators may have colluded with the official security services, the source had told the *Leader*: 'I couldn't comment on that. Way above my paygrade. But anything's possible.'

Their source, of course, was Octavius – he had left his signature where he knew I would find it. But rather than being annoyed, I was actually quite pleased that he had taken it all so personally. It was the first time I felt that the British – or certainly any Brit I knew – had such a vested interest in seeing peace in Ireland. Even if he did have to blow up my reception area to make his point.

CHAPTER 76

1994

Despite the fact she ran the show from the day and hour she arrived back in Waterloo Street, Mill never officially became editor of the *Chronicle*. As the peace talks wore on, it became apparent that there were fewer and fewer journalists whom the IRA, the Brits and, most importantly of all, the public could trust. Mill knew that as long as the war went on, she was best placed on the ground – to get the true message of what was going on out to the world. And to that end, she wound up syndicating what was termed 'primary-source copy' to more than fifty regional, national and international newspapers. Had she been remotely interested, she could have made herself a fortune; a host of major media outlets were offering her senior editorial jobs – several in front of the TV camera.

When I turned seventy in 1992, we talked long about her taking the editor's chair as planned. But she asked me if I would let her stay another couple of years as news-ed and reporter-at-large to see the big story through. And I assented, as long as Gerry Corrigan would come in a couple of afternoons a week to let me out for my golf.

The first time Mill fainted was a couple of days after she did a CNN TV interview in March 1994, during which she was asked if there would be an IRA truce that year. Mill answered categorically that there would be a ceasefire and asserted that it would be as close to a permanent end to the conflict as makes no difference.

IRA hardliners in Derry were outraged at the comments. Troublemakers in the right-wing and Unionist papers were forever crowing that there was no difference between an IRA truce and their surrender. Mill was ordered to a meeting of angry republicans, where she robustly defended her analysis. She also went down the throats of a few Johnny-come-latelies trying to establish their muscle in the run-up to a big peace payday.

Mill made the point, accepted by everyone, that given her connections, she was better informed than anybody else in the room – with the possible exception of Harry Hurley, who was actually taking part in the talks. At that stage, Harry stepped in and closed things down – and told her not to worry any more, that it was all a matter of semantics and that he would sort it out.

It was Harry, of course, who had briefed Mill on what to say on TV – and also that she was liable to get it in the neck for paving the ground for him. But they both knew that it was important this prep work was carried out by someone who was respected.

The following morning, however, when she arrived at the *Chronicle* offices, Mill received a parcel in the mail containing a dead rat with its tongue cut out. Which is when she keeled over for the first time.

***

The second time Mill fainted was on the morning of the IRA ceasefire, Wednesday 31 August 1994. The official statement was made at 11.00am, and she had been up all night, preparing stories for a range of different outlets. She and her team had also put together a special edition of the *Chronicle*, which we released onto the streets to coincide with the exact time of the announcement.

As soon as the paper was out the door, I summoned the entire staff to the bullpen for a toast. But just as I handed Mill a glass of 80-year-old Tyrconnell Whiskey, which Connie had left in her will for this very occasion, Mill dropped.

This time I wouldn't let her deter me, and Gerry Corrigan ran her directly to the hospital. He rang me less than an hour later to say the doctors had discovered an arrhythmia in her heart which, given her mother's early death, was very probably genetic.

'They want to operate,' said Gerry, 'though they're calling it a procedure to make it sound less scary. Mill has no interest. She's feeling physically fine and is just blaming the exhaustion. She's spending all her time apologising for the fuss.'

'Thanks, Gerry,' I said. 'I'll come over myself and talk some sense into her. You come back home and mind the shop. There's still a fair bit of work needs done for tomorrow's paper. You'll need to be rounding up all the reaction to today's news. Hire in a freelance or two if you have to.'

He laughed. 'That's exactly what Mill said, though she's threatening to come over and finish the job herself.'

'Handcuff her to the bed there if you have to. And don't leave until I arrive. I'll be there in ten minutes.'

***

Though Mill's death was – is – excruciating, one of my happiest memories is the afternoon I spent with her in Altnagelvin before she passed. Mill had taken a couple of doses of over-the-counter caffeine tablets to keep her sharp the previous night – all within the recommended limit, mind – so they wanted to wait until six that evening before they gave her the anaesthetic. No-one was too worried. The doctors had done the procedure a hundred times before. It was routine.

You, Maeve, came over for an hour yourself, along with Mo, and the four of us laughed and joked about all the money Mill was going to lose now she wouldn't have the Provos to write about anymore. She agreed and said she'd have to get herself a real job, like maybe editor of a newspaper. She'd heard that any donkey with half a brain could do it – and still play golf three days a week.

When you and Mo left, Maeve, Mill took my hand and told me I was the best father she could ever have wanted. And I told her she was the best daughter and the most beautiful one, and that it was a privilege to have her in my life. She was a joy at home and a star at work, and I'd never met the like of her. And I couldn't wait to see what she was going to do with the *Chronicle* in this bright, new era of peace and prosperity.

She said she was so appreciative of how we had all teamed up to take care of her gorgeous and gifted daughter. She even cracked her favourite old joke: 'It takes a village to rear an idiot.' And she said that the child's father had no idea of the value of what he had lost.

I told her how she was the image of her mother, who was simultaneously the kindest and most determined woman I had ever met. And that when she recovered, we would go and meet the extended Harrison family in the US. The pair of us had never actually been to Boston together, so we shook hands that we would make the trip out for Thanksgiving. I would buy her a glass of stout in The Purple Shamrock where I'd once gone drinking with Jack and Tip, and show her the streets in Southie, where I scouted on the booze-runs for Granda Pat.

I don't know why we said and did these things – we normally never talked to one another like that. We were hard-bitten newshounds, after all. Maybe it was because we were both a little scared. Or maybe on another level, we both suspected something. Regardless, I am so glad we did.

As they took her to the theatre, I squeezed her hand, told her I loved her and promised I would be there for her when she woke up in three hours' time. She kissed my hand, told me I was a pest, and that she'd be back in the office soon, and, yes, she loved me, too.

Mill died on the operating table less than fifteen minutes later.

***

There were dozens of obituaries from all over the world, but the one I keep framed on my desk is the little quarter-pager from *Time* magazine: 'Amelia 'Little Mill' Madden, 34, Irish Journalist and Peacemaker.'

I think she would have approved of that.

CHAPTER 77

1994: Autumn

It is unforgivably easy to disgrace someone's reputation once they are dead. I'm not generally a fan of libel laws: they're far too restrictive on all media – particularly here in the North. But I often wonder if some consideration should be given to the genuine hurt caused to bereaved families by reckless reportage. As at present, you can say anything you like about the dead. And sadly, many newspapers will do just that.

The front-page story in the *Leader* the week after Mill's death was a case in point. EF sank to a level so low that his entire living family disowned him, and I have no doubt that each and every one of his ancestors turned in their graves. The headline announced: 'Docs probe if drugs caused hack's death', and it just got worse from there.

'An inside source' – EF's consultant nephew, I suspected – revealed that Mill Madden had been 'using' un-prescribed stimulants and that this may have contributed to her heart attack. The paper also reported that the 'unmarried mother and full-time news-editor' had not spoken to her 'distant' father for seven years.

None of this was a complete lie, of course, but not a word of it was true, either. It was hateful, pure and simple, and it was picked up by every anti-Irish tabloid from here to Fleet Street.

I was long enough in the game to let the red mist clear before acting. My instinctive, visceral reaction was for retribution, and I was seriously considering asking Harry the Hurler for a major favour before he put away his holster for good. But thankfully, my better angels prevailed, largely in the form of Mo warning me not to do anything stupid – if only for poor Maeve's sake. So instead, I attempted to sleep on my wrath for a night, and then for a second night. And when I got up on the third morning, I knew exactly what I had to do.

Gerry Corrigan had assumed both news-ed and editor's duties in Waterloo Street for the duration, so I clued him in – and he said he was happy to help.

The weakest part of any story is an unnamed source, so for three straight days, Gerry detailed two juniors to hound the hospital, the police and the

Leader offices to persuade one of them to give up the mole. We also furnished our reporters with EF's home phone number, his direct line at the office, his mobile number, the numbers of the bars and clubs he drank in and the numbers of every relative and friend of his that we could source.

The leaking of medical information, even of a dead person's, is a hugely serious matter, so I further made it known that I was prepared to use every penny of my savings to take the hospital on in the courts. For as long as it takes – to the House of Lords, if necessary.

Truth be known, I didn't care about the inside man at all. He had only passed on a bit of news as human beings are programmed to do. Yes, I was mad at him, but I was also mad at God – and at myself for not having been a better father. My true unbridled rage, however, was reserved for the man who thought it would be acceptable to rework this news, and turn it on its head, so that he could malign my perfect daughter's perfect name for the entertainment of the wider public.

***

We quite literally drove EF mad. We rang him in the middle of the night, doorstepped him at church and in front of his friends at the Lodge, and made it so no-one could pick up a phone in the *Leader* offices without talking to us. He became a pariah. And, to this day, I make no apologies for that. Then, finally, on the eighth day, the *Leader* ran a three-column front-page apology for its previous week's story. They said that while they would never give up their source, he had disowned the story. He wanted it made known that his remarks were taken totally out of context and that Amelia Madden had died exclusively from natural causes.

Not a single tabloid, all of which had ripped into Mill the previous week, carried the retraction – they didn't have to. It wasn't their mistake, and anyway, she was dead.

In a separate little box on the front page, the *Leader* also announced that its editor, Mr Edward Fletcher Cunningham, had decided to take early retirement on health grounds, effective immediately. What they didn't say, however, was that he had been signed into the Mental Health Unit at Dunavady Hospital by his wife, Mary, and his son, David, the paper's new editor.

***

I am fairly confident that EF was the man behind my shooting at my little office in the *Chronicle* building a fortnight later. Though in saying that, I could never be entirely sure. The various paramilitary factions had been spending that autumn closing their accounts before the Big Peace, and at different stages I had ticked off virtually all of them. Likewise, there were people in all of the so-called legitimate outfits – Irish, British, American, etc – who would love nothing better than to take the man who had the goods on all of them out for a long walk.

But there were a couple of specific clues that led me to EF's door, first among them being that had any of the serious agencies been in charge, I would most likely be dead. This had to have been a renegade action – done by someone with local knowledge – as whoever tried to whack me knew that I came in an hour before the staff, leaving the shutters open downstairs.

Also, David Cunningham had rung me to say that his father had ended his 'temporary confinement'. He warned me that EF was staying in a hostel in Derry, as Mary had no intentions of ever taking him back, but they were in no doubt he was still in need of professional care.

And thirdly, although I never told the police this, the guy who shot me, while disguised with a ski mask, reeked heavily of Glenlivet – EF's favourite scotch.

CHAPTER 78

Bowtie had suggested McCloud should meet him at his offices on Clarendon Street in the heart of the city's Georgian quarter. On the way home the previous evening, they had both agreed that they could do with a full discussion behind closed doors.

After he was buzzed in, the receptionist – a smartly dressed blonde woman of about fifty – immediately left her post to usher McCloud up two flights of stairs to a small, windowless room where Bowtie was waiting. He was back in full-dress uniform, cramped behind a cheap desk, which had just two plastic bucket chairs in front of it. There was no other furniture in the room. No cabinets, no telephone, not even a pen on the table. The Spartan furnishings contrasted starkly with the rest of the plush building.

McCloud knew better than to ask and sat down without comment on the orange seat opposite his host.

'It's completely soundproof,' said McGinlay. 'The walls and door are lead-lined. It's also fireproof. The rest of the building could crash down around us and we'd be as safe as houses in this little iron box. The big front office next door is good – particularly since I got it double-glazed – but if you were determined enough, and had a directional mike or HD camera, like your girl Jeanie has got, you might be able to pick up enough. She'll not get a thing from in here, though.'

He held up his mobile. 'Look – no signal.'

'Good.'

Bowtie eyed him carefully. 'So I take it you finished the tapes?'

'I did … well, whatever you let me see of them at least. They stop at the exact point of the shooting.'

'Yes, anything after that isn't germane – as you, an investigator, know full well.'

'But his impressions might be important?'

'No. They're not. And you don't get the rest.'

278

McCloud nodded. He didn't need to win this point. He was going to take a lot of others.

McGinlay was staring at him. 'So, is the jury back yet?'

'I'm not sure,' said the American. 'I've had a sleepless night trying to put it all together, but I think I might have it now. My second night in a row without a drink, by the way. You're rubbing off on me. It's become clear that if I'm going to remain here any longer, I'm going to need to stay sharp.'

McGinlay smiled. 'Let's hear it, so.'

'We'll start with the easy bit,' said McCloud. 'EF Cunningham shot Seán Madden. I have no doubt about that – nor do any of you. Seán's comment that the gunman had Glenlivet Whisky on his breath was direct and deliberate identification on his part. His attempt to qualify it, by suggesting that there might just possibly have been other people involved, was only to distract us from the reason he had gotten shot in the first place. But I'd bet money that EF wasn't wearing a mask at all – it was more that Seán didn't want to give him up to the police and cause a whole media storm. The "why" bit, though, took me a bit longer – and I still have no proof. But I'm going to watch your face very carefully as I lay out my hypothesis, and I'll know then for sure how close I've got.'

Bowtie instinctively brought his two hands up to cover his mouth, then laughed aloud when he worked out that McCloud had just psyched him. 'You got me,' he said. 'Okay, I'll try to steer you right.'

McCloud sat back in his uncomfortable chair and pulled a little notebook out of the inside pocket of his linen jacket. 'By the time of the shooting,' he said, 'EF Cunningham had hated Seán for forty years – ever since he'd stolen his birthright by buying out the manse. But why would EF wait until 1994? It didn't make sense. My first thought was that he might have wanted to try and hide the shooting under the last-minute bloodletting that was going on before the loyalists called their truce. He could have rung a call into his own office and claimed it for the Ulster Freedom Fighters or whoever – he had the code words. But why wait so long? Why wait until everything was over?'

Bowtie was riveted to the detail while trying to give nothing away. McCloud was getting very close.

'So then,' said McCloud, 'I briefly considered the idea that EF could have been working for Octavius and might have gotten angry that his boss, and himself, had been left out of the big ceasefire hoorah. That they'd been denied their credit. So I checked late last night with my opposite number in Whitehall, and he assured me, categorically, that EF was always considered far too big a "messer" – his word – for them to have anything to do with him.'

McGinlay nodded briefly to assure McCloud he hadn't got anything wrong – thus far at least.

'Then,' said McCloud, 'I checked back through our own lines, just in case Don Grover, or the computer genius who followed him, might have had links with EF and put him up to it. And that was the scariest part, for me at least, because if I'd found anything that linked EF and the Yanks, we would be looking at a full-scale inquiry, possibly at congressional level. And it wouldn't simply be the preserve of a drunk with a notebook and my twelve-year-old helper, Jeanie.'

McGinlay laughed.

'But of course it wasn't the Yanks at all,' said McCloud. 'They wouldn't have gone near EF, either. They laughed at me when I suggested it. And, truth be known, that's all you wanted me to find out. That it wasn't a political shooting – and that neither the Brits nor the Americans were involved. You also knew, by the time I had established all this, that I – as the representative of the US Government – would have seen Seán's tapes, and would have known that it was in our interests never to let them see the light of day. And we wouldn't want the Brits or anyone else seeing them. All of which, of course, I have already recommended. None of us comes out with too much honour from them. And all of this, of course, suits you perfectly.'

McGinlay nodded again. McCloud had done his job well.

But his visitor wasn't done. 'For the record, however, I should now inform you that we have recovered our own copy of the tapes from Seán's study at the manse. Hidden on an old laptop – password One-Two-Three-Four, would you believe? And we now intend to store the same laptop for safekeeping – and, indeed, for protection from yourselves. My teenage hooker broke in while you were all out on your boat on Saturday night. She also took my phone back, by the way, and there's never been so much as a scratch on it. The log showed that there were fifteen hundred separate attempts to break into it. What happened, did you all agree to do five hundred each?'

Bowtie's eyes widened as he worked out that he was not the only big player in the room. He decided to lob in a Hail Mary to give himself time. 'You haven't ruled out IRA involvement yet,' he said.

McCloud shook his head dismissively. 'EF Cunningham was many things – a drunk, a bully, a lousy father and a nasty-minded journalist – but he was not a republican gunman. And we know, for certain fact, that EF was the shooter because, at the risk of repeating myself, Seán told us himself. So I did a little research here, too, and it became apparent the IRA were extremely protective of Seán in the weeks after Mill's death. Mill may have challenged them, but she had also taken risks for them, and they respected the hell out of her for that. Harry Hurley told me that himself when he called into the hotel last night.'

Bowtie sensed that control was starting to slip away from him and winced slightly at the IRA leader's name. 'What else did Harry say?'

'Plenty,' said McCloud. 'The week after Seán's shooting, the IRA picked up EF from outside the Northern Counties Club and took him to Harry's offices for a chat. Actually, "arrested" is the term that Harry used. They were all extremely upset at EF; they saw the shooting as the culmination of a litany of abuse he had inflicted on his city. But the IRA were in a real bind, as they had committed themselves very publicly to a ceasefire. And whacking EF, while discussed at length, was not considered a viable option.'

Bowtie shut his eyes. He knew what had happened next. 'Go on.'

'So, in what Harry insists was a completely unsanctioned move, two of the interrogation team took EF down to his holiday home in Whitecastle, found an old rope and hanged him from a tree in the garden. The rope broke, EF survived, but he was never any use to anyone ever again.'

Bowtie nodded slowly. 'I wasn't there, and I can't confirm it. But that's the version I heard, too. It was horrific, and I can only say that I'm very relieved we never sink to that sort of level any more. Seán, nor anyone else in the family, ever knew about that. As far as they, and the general public, were concerned, it was a suicide bid.'

McCloud folded his hands and looked at Bowtie enquiringly. 'Do you want me to go on?'

Bowtie blew out his cheeks and blinked slowly once for yes. 'Go ahead.'

'Good,' said McCloud, smiling. 'Because we're about to come to the interesting part. You know there's a reason I'm talking to you here today, and not as I normally would to Mo at the bunker?'

He had worked it out. He knew. 'I do,' said Bowtie.

'I don't want to have this conversation outside this room, not ever, and I'm pretty confident you don't, either.'

'I don't. Tell me, what tipped you off?'

'It was Little Mill's relationship with her father that gave it away. I could understand her not speaking to him for a long time – even for a year or two – out of anger. But to stay away for seven years? And yet still want him raising her child? That was bizarre. Unless, of course, she was deeply ashamed and deeply frightened about something else entirely. Or maybe she was being blackmailed. Or both. So I thought about it long and hard, and then some more, and my theory, and it is only a theory, is that EF Cunningham is Maeve Madden's father, and that Mill spent the bulk of her adult life living in terror that he would tell Seán. That's how he persuaded her to work at the *Leader* as well. I could well be wrong on this. But all we need is two DNA samples – they wouldn't even have to know – and we could put it to bed this afternoon.'

There was silence in the little room for a full minute. McCloud didn't mind at all. He could play word games in his head for hours on end while he was waiting out suspects.

Bowtie knew McCloud would sit as long as it took. He took a deep breath, then let it out in a sad sigh. 'My father was Little Mill's lawyer when she had Maeve – and I inherited the whole thing after he died. She met EF in a bar one night when he was down in Dublin at a rugby international – a little over a year after she'd first fallen out with Seán. They spent a few hours drinking and swapping anti-*Chronicle* yarns – he could be quite charming on occasion by all accounts – and she woke up pregnant. It was one of those stupid, life-defining mistakes that we all pray we never make, so we end up inventing our own different ones instead.'

'Why did EF bring her back to Derry – was he planning to do the right thing with Maeve on some level?'

'No. It was, as you correctly reasoned, to torture Seán and to humiliate Mill. EF was so damaged he could never, ever save himself from doing the wrong thing.'

'He let her go back to the *Chronicle* in 1987, though. Why was that?'

'A couple of reasons. First, Mill eventually worked out that she wasn't without power and warned EF that the situation could play out very badly for him, too, if he didn't take a step back – disgrace, divorce etc. But more importantly, it suited him to have the way clear for David. Even if he and his son could never stand the sight of each other.'

McCloud nodded. 'So what happened when Mill died?'

'EF wrote his appalling article in the *Leader* as a final kick at both Seán and Mill, so my father, Tommy Senior, God be good to him, went to Seán two days later and told him the full story. Attorney-client privilege had disappeared with Mill's death. Seán had initially been out for blood when he saw EF's news story, but the Provos and Mo managed to knock some sense into him. And when he heard what my father had to tell him, he resolved to go another route. EF, however, had no such advisors. So when Seán rang him to tell him he was going to expose him, and then hound him to his grave, EF came into the office all guns blazing.'

McCloud nodded. It was all just sad enough and terrible enough to be true. 'The part about Seán using the paper to drive EF mad – is that accurate?'

'Yes, though in fairness, he didn't have very far to go. EF was a breakdown waiting to happen – and Seán knew exactly which buttons to press.'

'Why didn't Seán expose him in the end?'

McGinlay sighed. 'He'd already ended him – or ended his career, his marriage, and his public life at least. The only person Seán would have been hurting if he'd revealed EF was Maeve's father was Maeve – and maybe David.'

'Do they know – either of them?'

'No.'

'Should they? Given it might have connotations for EF's inheritance?'

'No – that belongs to David. He's rescued the *Leader* from the damage his father did to it and deserves anything and everything he can get from it. The *Chronicle* will provide plenty for Maeve.'

'But what about their mutual loathing – do you not think you should be addressing that, given that you know they're brother and sister?

'David has no problems with Maeve at all. He's a grown-up. Your job from now on, McCloud, is going to be to try to talk some sense into Maeve.'

McCloud laughed at how he was suddenly part of the family. And truth is, given all he'd found out, he felt that Maeve needed someone protecting her interests. 'What does Mo know?' he asked.

'Everything. Mo is like myself – the great keeper of secrets. And she's very appreciative of you holding this meeting here, away from the manse, today. Our official line is that EF attacked Seán in a drunken rage after Seán drove him mad. Anything else, as you said yourself, is just utter speculation.'

McCloud smiled again. 'Actually, I said I had no evidence to support my theory but that two DNA tests would resolve it for all time.'

'You couldn't be more correct,' said Bowtie. 'Complete and utter speculation.'

The lawyer stared hard at the American and offered him his hand.

McCloud thought hard for about five seconds and then shook it firmly. 'Complete and utter speculation,' he said.

CHAPTER 79

Maeve was not happy. Not only had McCloud now finished his inquiry, but for whatever reason, he was briefing Tommy Bowtie on the findings, and not Mo, so her morning sessions watching the CCTV feed from the bunker in her pyjamas had come to an abrupt end.

There was also another reason for her annoyance. Bowtie and Mo had met the previous night with David Cunningham to discuss a merger of the *Chronicle* and *Leader* groups. Without her. David had been reluctant to discuss a partnership while his father was still alive, on the grounds that it might kill him, but he had contacted Tommy late on Saturday night to say that EF had slipped into a coma and was unlikely to reawaken.

Maeve was well aware that the best hope long-term for the *Chronicle* was consolidation. Theoretically, they could spend the next five, ten or maybe even twenty years funding their losses from Seán's estate, but the merger could have them balancing the books within a year. The problem for Maeve, though, was that she would have to make nice with David.

Mo was sitting reading the *Irish News* in the sunroom that Seán had built as an extension to the kitchen, finishing her first cup of coffee when Maeve tackled her.

'Why didn't you tell me about the meeting?' she asked.

'With respect, Maeve, it's sometimes simpler when we present things to you as a done deal. If it were left to you, we could still be talking about this in twelve months' time. David shook hands with Tommy and me last night, and it's done. That's all there is to it.'

Maeve reached for a coaster and put down her own cup on the table. She then pulled up a summer seat opposite Mo. 'I should never have published the picture of David in the first place,' she said. 'I was being a smartass. The tough new kid on the block making fun of the trendy teacher. It wasn't fair.'

'No, it wasn't. But he's had a couple of goes back at you since then.'

'Yeah, but he's generally very decent. That was a lovely tribute he wrote to Seán. Even nicer than the one I did.'

Mo felt that her adopted daughter was genuinely mellowing. But she also knew Maeve didn't want bad reports about her getting back to McCloud, either. Not at this stage. 'You can still prevent it,' the older woman said. 'Your shareholding, as inherited from Seán, will be validated within a few weeks. And you've the power to kick us all to the kerb if you want to. I'm going to step down as chairman anyway, Maeve. I'm too old. You need a new leader for the new company.'

Maeve was alarmed. 'You can't leave me now, Mo. Who'll look after the board stuff? I don't have your eye for the financials.'

'Tommy's going to buy himself into the company at one per cent, and both myself and David are happy for him to be the interim chair. I'll stay on the board as vice-chair. What do you think? You'll have sixty-plus per cent of the shares of the conglomerate anyway, so it's your show.'

'What about McCloud? Or do we call him McGillicuddy now?'

'We most certainly do not. He'll receive five per cent of Seán's *Chronicle* shares in a year's time, which will be worth a little more than three-and-a-half per cent of the new company. For all sorts of reasons, I think we have to appoint him to the board. He's better connected than any of us.'

'And is David okay with that?'

'Very much so. They met on Friday night for a chat at the *Leader* offices and got on famously. Apparently, they bonded over how they'd both been kicked around the city by the *Chronicle*.'

Maeve rolled her eyes. 'I went in a bit hard there, didn't I?'

Mo nodded. 'It's your one failing, princess,' she said. 'You can sometimes come across a bit too keen. Talking of which … McCloud's visit to EF tonight has been cancelled. He's got a free block in his diary, if you know anyone who's available. I hear he's going to be at the City Hotel at seven. But only if you know anyone who's interested.'

Maeve tried hard to keep her face a mask, but her shining green eyes gave her away. 'I'll take it under advisement,' she said.

CHAPTER 80

'Okay,' said McCloud, 'time for part two. Why did you get me sent here?'
Bowtie looked shocked.

'You're still in the safe room,' said the American. 'And it's not going outside of here. You asked for me. I checked. Patrick O'Lennon confirmed it when I rang him this morning before I came over. We get up early, as you know. You named me specifically as the agent you wanted to investigate Seán's shooting. Why? It's something to do with a family connection to the McGillicuddys, isn't it?'

The lawyer shifted in his seat. The Yank wasn't supposed to pick up on this – or at least not for a year or two yet. He said nothing.

McCloud waited for a full two minutes before speaking again. 'Okay, then,' he said. 'Just give me a yes or no answer, that's all.'

Bowtie frowned uncertainly. 'Try me.'

'Were Pius McGillicuddy – the IRA man who was sent to America after Johnny Madden's death – and his brother Terence connected to my family in some way? My dead brother was called Terry and my father is John Pius. And McCloud, as Mo let slip, is a contraction of McGillicuddy. In fact, that's what the surviving family in Donegal call themselves now. Though it's spelt slightly differently.'

Bowtie bowed his head and exhaled heavily. 'Yes,' he said. 'Pius McGillicuddy was very probably your grandfather. Seán never felt it was right he should have been exiled for his father's death – he always thought Pius meant well and was trying to save Old Mick's bar from a reprisal attack, and that Johnny's death was a genuine accident. So every time he was in America, Seán made enquiries to try to track him down. To deliver him an amnesty. He once spent a full week in Philly searching for him – that was the last sighting he'd had of him. But it wasn't until the McGillicuddys back home shortened their name that he realised they were probably following your grandfather's lead and he'd wasted his time. And, of course, none of the Donegal family would ever break breath to Sean, so he couldn't check from here. How did you work it out?'

McCloud wasn't for playing that game. 'We'll come back to that in a minute. How did *you* work it out?'

Bowtie held his hands up in apology. 'It wasn't me at all; it was Seán. He spotted you outside the Guildhall when you were here on the last Clinton visit in 2010. He said you were a complete ringer for the McGillicuddys at Lenamore – but better again, you spent your entire time, while you were guarding the president, cracking your damn thumbs. And Connie had always told him that this was Pius's trademark. So he got me to check you out. I'll confess, I thought he was starting to go senile and, to be frank, it wasn't a priority, so it wasn't until Seán got very ill that I tried to track you down. That bit wasn't hard, what with all the computer databases and archives we have online now. And, Holy God, you were exactly who Seán said you were – Alistair, son of John Pius, son of Pius the Philly street-cop. A third-generation thumb-cracker. After we had established that, my good buddy Patrick the ambassador did the rest and got you sent here– he knows nothing about the family connection, by the way. He's convinced we just think you're a hotshot. And we do. Are you mad at us?'

McCloud shook his head in disbelief. 'I'm not mad at all,' he said. 'I'm a little surprised, yes, that you would demand, and then hijack a fallacious attempted murder inquiry, constituted by the United States Government, just to get a look at me. You also stole property belonging to a Federal Agent, libelled him in a newspaper, kidnapped him, withheld evidence from him, threatened to expose him and his staff to danger and ridicule, tried to bribe him with a promotion, and even tried to seduce him with promises of a gorgeous, though possibly psychotic, cyber-stalker. So no, Tommy, I'm not mad at all. I'm just absolutely astonished and baffled at the lengths you go to – and for what?'

Bowtie couldn't contain a smile when it was read out to him like that. 'Step number nine,' he said. 'Wherever possible, make direct restitution to all those you have harmed. And, well, it was too late for your grandfather, and your father has retired, so we thought we'd try and make amends with you.'

McCloud's father had told them little about Granda McCloud – he could barely remember him; he'd died in a car accident back in the early 1950s when John Pius was just four. The family knew nothing of the Irish connection, either. In fact, his father had always told Ally privately that he thought Granda was Scottish but that Granny insisted for the optics that they should all remain Irish.

McCloud started to laugh. 'You seriously think I'm going to let you off with all of this because you quote the AA mantra to me? Like it's some kind of scripture?'

Bowtie looked, held up his hand. 'It was the best I could do in the moment. You weren't supposed to work out the McGillicuddy bit yet. Give me a day or two and I'll give you a proper legal reason why you should forgive us.'

'Not a chance.'

'All right, then. How about a case of Tyrconnell Whiskey Special Reserve? From Seán's own cellar? I'll not tell Jeanie – and maybe get one of the other girls at the hotel to smuggle the bottles in and out for you.'

'You're hoping if you keep me drunk I'll forget all about it?'

'Why not? It worked for me for thirty years of the Troubles.'

They both laughed.

'Not buying,' said McCloud.

'All right,' said Bowtie. 'Last throw of the dice. What about dinner with Maeve instead?'

McCloud paused and bit his lip. 'We'll revisit that in a minute. Don't you want to know how I twigged it?'

'Absolutely,' said McGinlay. There is little better in this world than new information.

'It was because of the thumbs – same as Seán. All I really knew about Granda was that he was called "Thumbs", and that Pop and I had inherited his habit. But until last night, I never knew that Pius McGillicuddy, the exiled IRA man, was a thumb-cracker, too.'

'Last night?' said Bowtie. 'But I'm only after telling you that myself two minutes ago. You couldn't have known before that.'

But he had known. And this was precisely why McCloud had done the lateral-thinking classes. Sometimes crazy notions come into your head and just stick. If you let them. And that is invariably because they're true. The best thing you can ever do in this world is stay out of your own way. He grinned over the table at Bowtie. 'What was McGillicuddy's nickname?'

Tommy thought for a second and got it. '"Old Dog",' he said.

'No,' said McCloud. 'But that's what Connie, and indeed Seán and Mo, called him. And for whatever reason, that rankled. It made no sense whatsoever to me. Why would a guy in his early twenties be called old? So I got Jeanie to hunt back through the *Chronicle*'s archives last night, through all the stuff in the late teens and early twenties and, fair play to her, she found the nugget. A court report from 1919 of two Peadar O'Donnell supporters arrested for distributing anti-British leaflets in Muff. Fined ten shillings each. Charles Hurley, from Derry, probably an uncle of Harry, was the first – and the other was one Pius McGillicuddy from Lenamore, also known as "*Ordóg*" McGillicuddy.'

'Or dog, Old Dog?' said Tommy. 'I don't understand. What's the difference? Surely it was just a typo?'

'Actually it wasn't. The report had also mentioned that McGillicuddy had only spoken to the court in Irish. So I got onto my online dictionary and discovered within seconds that "*Ordóg*" is actually the Gaelic word for thumb. And it's not too hard to surmise how he got that alias. It doesn't prove anything, of course, but if you put it together with Seán's account, it makes a pretty compelling story.'

Bowtie bowed to the Yank. 'I'm genuinely impressed,' he said. 'A couple of DNA tests and we could put it all to bed this evening.'

'No chance,' said McCloud. 'I need plausible deniability. If the Feds find out I've an IRA grandfather, I'll be out of here quicker than a ticking box.'

Bowtie grinned. 'You know that Seán has left provision for five per cent of his estate, consisting of both a cash payment and stocks in the *North West Chronicle*, to go to any surviving heirs of Pius McGillicuddy, late of Lenamore, County Donegal?'

'You're kidding?'

'No. The whole concept of exile genuinely upset him – particularly as he'd gone through it twice himself, albeit voluntarily. He also knew that, despite his best efforts, he might never be able to correct Ireland, but he was damn well going to try and correct his own little part of it.'

McCloud was quiet. It was a huge hornets' nest – and the Feds wouldn't like the attention at all.

McGinlay signalled he wasn't finished. 'But in the event that no heirs be found within a year, Mr Madden decreed that whoever successfully investigates his attempted murder in 1994 should receive the same holding.'

'That's nuts,' said McCloud. 'Who decides what a successful investigation looks like?'

'You're looking at him,' said Bowtie. 'And tag. You're it.'

CHAPTER 81

Later that evening, McCloud had just sat down on a comfortable leather sofa at the back of the spacious City Hotel lobby when he spotted her coming through the sliding doors at the entrance.

She was wearing a white T-shirt, blue jeans, pink canvas sneakers and not a drop of make-up. But every head in the room turned. And for a second it was like time stopped. Without saying a word, she sat down beside him and took his hand. And it felt like the most natural thing in the world. It was what it was. And it was right.

'So?' she said.

'You look familiar,' he said to her. 'Do you come from around here?'

She smiled, but only to let him know she had heard his joke and was ignoring it. 'I want four children,' she said. 'I've been checked out – no heart flutter. So no excuses.'

'I want four children, too,' he said.

She kissed him lightly on the cheek and pointed towards the restaurant. 'You're going to have to buy me dinner first,' she said.

It was, as he would say many times later, the single greatest day of his life. It was the first time he had ever met Maeve Madden in the flesh.

EPILOGUE

1994

The incident itself all happened very quickly. No warning, no words. I just looked up to see a shadow with a pistol and intuitively threw a paperweight at the figure and made a dive under the desk. The first bullet ricocheted off a steel castor on my chair into the grandfather clock in the corner; the second one clipped the back of my thigh. It was at that point I decided I was going to go down swinging, so I grabbed a handful of books off the desk and started flinging them at the gunman, who ran off. I'm pretty certain I caught him on the side of the head with a Collins Dictionary, so there'd be a mark there somewhere.

This being Derry 1994, no-one saw anything – even post-ceasefire. And yes, there was a running joke that the police were looking for a five-year extension to interview all their suspects. When the shock lifted, my wound was surprisingly sore and required four days' treatment in Altnagelvin and another four at the manse. But I was back walking by the end of the second week, and by the third I was back at my desk.

By December, I was fully recovered and back to my real business of mourning Mill. Mo, however, made sure I never went full recluse, and on the day before Christmas Eve, she dragged me up to St Columb's Cathedral for a special End-of-the-War carol service.

Clearly, they were expecting us, and we were ushered to a pew close to the magnificent altar, in beside David Cunningham and his mother, Mary. I was a little nervous about this, as EF had just been committed a second time after attempting to take his own life. Word was that he had suffered irreversible brain damage and would be unable to leave full-time care ever again. And yes, I did feel a little responsible.

We shook hands with the Cunninghams, a little awkwardly, but, as we did, from behind his seat, David produced a slim, three-by-two-foot parcel, which he presented to me.

'We'd like you to have this,' he said.

291

I peeled off the heavy wrapping slowly. And when I saw what was inside, I couldn't speak. It was a framed tribute David had handwritten, with fountain pen on vellum, for his dear friend and mentor 'Little Mill'.

'I wanted to do something personal, Seán,' he said. 'Anything I might put in the *Leader* would only feel tawdry after what happened before. Mill was an angel.'

David's piece was beautiful: it was lyrical, it was lovely, it was wise, and it was warm. He talked about my daughter the role model, a side of her I'd never known: how she had protected him; her patience; her kindness to the bereft; her empathy with the troubled; her loyalty to the truth; her searing sense of justice; how she was a source of light in darkness; and, most of all, her pride in her family – and in me.

But it was the black-and-white photograph, expertly positioned in the centre of the piece that took my breath away. It was a picture I'd never seen before, of Little Mill and myself in our Sunday best, coming out of this very same cathedral sometime in the mid-1960s, me holding her hand. She couldn't have been more than five or six, and she was looking up at me, as if I were her entire world.

'It's from my grandfather Jackson's funeral,' said David. 'I just chanced upon it when I was sorting out some of Gran's old stuff last week and knew immediately where it belonged. It was in a box marked "Family and Friends".'

As the verses of *Adeste Fideles* ascended gently from the cathedral organ, I read and re-read David's letter, then read it again, until my tears were dripping onto the glass frame. And I knew that as long as I had this letter, and these good people around me, I would have Mill with me forever.

And in that moment, I, Seán Madden, also found my peace.

292

Praise for Garbhan Downey's work

'A master stylist . . . Dammit, you can almost taste the steam off the pages.' *Modern Woman*

'Irresistibly funny.' *Irish News*

'Acidic, humorous – he is an expert at the narrative rabbit punch.' *Irish Mail on Sunday*

'Fast-paced, outlandish and funny.' *Sunday Business Post*

'A superb blend of comedy, political dirty tricks, grisly murder and bizarre twists!' *Sunday World*

'Three words – brilliant, brilliant, brilliant!' *County Times*

'It shocks you one minute, has you laughing out loud the next and ultimately is impossible to put down.' *Ulster Tatler*

'Expect a literary smack in the mouth.' *Derry News*

'A rollicking yarn. Read it before Downey goes galloping off in another direction. The Novel of the Year.' Eamonn McCann, *Derry Journal*